PRAISE FOR
THE LAST BATHING BEAUTY

"This novel of first loves and second chances will resonate with fans of historical fiction authors such as Beatriz Williams or Lauren Willig."
—*Library Journal*

"Amy Sue Nathan's story of love and mishap . . . pulls at your heart with its dual narratives of young and seasoned love affairs."
—Historical Novel Society

"*The Last Bathing Beauty* is a pitch-perfect summer read. Full of characters that shine and told with compassion and humor, this is women's fiction at its best."
—Sonja Yoerg, *Washington Post* bestselling author of *True Places*

"Amy Sue Nathan is a true storyteller, and *The Last Bathing Beauty* is her best book. It's an epic tale of family, secrets, loss, marriage, betrayal, friendships, laughter, and regrets."
—Cathy Lamb, author of *Julia's Chocolates* and *All About Evie*

"This book ripped at my heart in the best possible way, and I won't forget it. Told across three generations of smart, determined, compassionate women, *The Last Bathing Beauty* is the loveliest of stories about the sacrifices and triumphs that come from being a daughter, wife, mother, and friend."
—Juliet McDaniel, author of *Mr. & Mrs. American Pie*

"For those who believe in happily ever after, Amy Sue Nathan's *The Last Bathing Beauty* is a real winner. Told with tenderness and humor, readers will love this journey back in time with Boop and the girls."
—Renée Rosen, bestselling author of *Park Avenue Summer*

"Told with empathy and lyrical prose, *The Last Bathing Beauty* is a winning tale of friendship, regret, and second chances with a ring of endearing and spirited women at its heart."
—Heather Webb, *USA Today* bestselling coauthor of *Meet Me in Monaco*

"This story has it all—great characters, sensory-rich settings, and a sweet salute to believing in second chances. The finale will have you cheering."
—Susan Meissner, bestselling author of *The Last Year of the War*

"A moving tale about second chances and the fathomless depths of true love."
—Tina Ann Forkner, author of *Waking Up Joy*

WELL
Behaved
WIVES

ALSO BY AMY SUE NATHAN

The Last Bathing Beauty
The Good Neighbor
Left to Chance
The Glass Wives

WELL *Behaved* WIVES

A NOVEL

AMY SUE NATHAN

LAKE UNION
PUBLISHING

Published by Lake Union Publishing, Seattle

www.apub.com

Amazon, the Amazon logo, and Lake Union Publishing are trademarks of Amazon.com, Inc., or its affiliates.

ISBN-13: 9781542025409
ISBN-10: 1542025400

Cover design by Faceout Studio, Amanda Hudson

Printed in the United States of America

Dedicated to the A-Team:

Mom, Dad, and David,
Priya, Michele, and Gabi

Well-behaved women seldom make history.

—Laurel Thatcher Ulrich

PHILADELPHIA, PENNSYLVANIA

SEPTEMBER 1962

PART 1

ETIQUETTE LESSONS

Chapter 1

Ruth

The heat from the hair dryer helmet burned Ruth's scalp, but the contraption's noise drowned out the beauty parlor chatter around her.

Fair trade, she thought.

Nevertheless, she smiled at her new mother-in-law across the aisle, and Shirley Appelbaum smiled back. Ruth was right where Shirley wanted her—and Ruth knew it. Primped, captive.

Now the woman was eying Ruth's lap.

This? Ruth wondered. *The magazine?* She held it up so Shirley could see the cover.

A frown flitted across her mother-in-law's perfectly lipsticked mouth. Darn, Ruth had forgotten to swipe some on her own lips from the tube Shirley had not so subtly left on the guest bathroom counter. Shirley shook her head. An imperceptible shake, almost like a twitch. She dipped her chin again toward Ruth's chair.

Did Shirley want her to stand? Were they finished? Was Ruth's chair back too far, or not enough, or too upright, or was she committing any of the other apparently egregious breaches of propriety she had seemed prone to since she and Asher had moved in with her in-laws a week ago?

Shirley looked at Ruth's legs, then widened her eyes and grimaced as if she had been pinched—for just a bare second; couldn't have anyone seeing it, of course. Her mother-in-law looked like a particularly intense bug—with freshly polished nails.

Oh! Ruth glanced around the room and crossed her legs to match every other woman under the shop's dryers. She was *sitting* wrong.

According to Shirley's glances and eye rolls during the last week, Ruth did a lot of things wrong. That time Ruth shouted to Asher from downstairs when she'd forgotten something she needed in the attic. ("Oh my," Shirley had whispered in a manufactured titter. "It's not a fish market, dear.") Or when Ruth dared to open the newspaper before her father-in-law had come home, occasioning an ostentatious refolding of every page into its original bundle by Shirley, as Ruth apologized. ("Not to worry, dear—I'll tidy it right up.") She failed to jump up from the table to fetch extra sauce or seconds for Asher. ("He's worked hard all day; it's the least we could do." Shirley said this with an understanding smile as she pushed herself up to wait on her perfectly grown and able son.)

Ruth couldn't fault her mother-in-law's kindness—Shirley was never anything but kind, gracious . . . poised. Proper in all the ways that Ruth apparently fell short. But was Ruth really supposed to be a picture-perfect paragon of demureness and servitude, simply because she now had a ring on her finger? She used to hold a pen in that same hand, writing briefs for her law degree.

Ruth mimicked Shirley by licking her pointer finger and turning the *McCall's* page as if she had been reading. Shirley nodded and tapped her dryer, then flicked her fingers at Ruth. Shirley, whose stylist had already finished with her, patted her hair. It looked perfect in its light-brown beehive, the way it had when she'd walked in, which Ruth gathered was the point. Continuity reigned. Didn't all this sameness grow tiresome?

Shirley flicked again. The other ladies across from Ruth flicked.

Ah! The universal symbol for "turn off your dryer."

Ruth pushed back the oven-like hood, exposing hair on tight rollers. After a brush out and a heavy application of lacquer, her hair would feel like a helmet. Good God, what a lot of effort for something that served no useful purpose. "Yes?"

Shirley smiled—a real one this time. "Oh, my dear, it's just lovely. *You're* lovely."

Ruth was surprised to feel a flowering warmth in her chest. "Thank you, Shirley," she answered, suddenly pleased she'd agreed to her mother-in-law's suggestion that they visit her beauty parlor. Ruth had thought it was yet another of Shirley's attempts to make her fit in better in this exclusive neighborhood of Wynnefield . . . but maybe she really just wanted to spend more time together.

Ruth didn't mind that at all. She couldn't have asked for a better family than her dad and four brothers, but she had to admit that growing up without a mother in a family of rough-and-tumble boys had made her long sometimes for the kind of maternal pride and warmth shining in Shirley's eyes right now. When her mother-in-law reached out a hand, Ruth immediately took it, returning her squeeze.

They'd be okay. Everything was going to work out just fine.

"I know what you need, dear," Shirley said.

"You do?"

Shirley nodded. "Indeed. I talked to Asher and he agrees. There's a . . . well, a get-together of sorts of some of the girls your age in town, and I thought it might be a perfect opportunity for you to make some friends here in Wynnefield and settle in a bit more. Trying to fit into a brand-new city must be as sudden and shocking for you as it was for Leon and me to find out our only son had gotten himself a brand-new bride!"

Oy gevalt. Here we go again. Few conversations had passed since she and Asher had temporarily moved into Shirley and Leon's guest quarters without some mention of Shirley's disapproval and hurt at their secret elopement. And since when did Asher talk to his mother about Ruth behind Ruth's back?

Ruth pushed away the flare of irritation. She'd promised Asher she'd do her very best to get along with his parents—and she wanted to. Really, she did.

She smiled. "Well, that sounds nice. Let me know when they're getting together and maybe I'll drop by."

"Oh no, dear—that's not quite how it's done. Why don't I just get you all signed up for the lessons?"

Ruth raised her daughter-in-law antennae. "Lessons?"

Shirley stood, meticulously squaring the magazine she'd been reading on top of the stack on the table beside her dryer. "Well, think of it more as a refresher course for young housewives . . . putting the final polish on the silver. Nothing you don't already know, of course, but won't it be nice to brush up while getting to know some other housewives your age?"

Ruth didn't know whether her instinctive cringe was from dread at what kind of "polish lessons" her mother-in-law would rope her into, or from being lumped in with the other housewives. This was 1962, the world had changed, and she was going to be a *lawyer*, for goodness' sake—if things went according to plan. "Brush up on what, Shirley?" she asked, forcing her tone to remain neutral.

"Oh, we call them etiquette lessons—silly, isn't it? But really it's just the simple common niceties we can all stand to improve on, don't you think?"

Etiquette lessons. *Oy vey.* Her mother-in-law wanted to send her to charm school.

After a broiled flounder dinner, Ruth cleared away plates of escaped Le Sueur peas and scraped baked potato skins. She was glad to help, to earn her keep even, but the way Asher and his father were expected to just sit there flustered her. Ruth had grown up on New York's Upper West Side in a fourth-floor walk-up, and her father had divided household chores among his five children in a rotation based on their ages, not their sexes. Jacob Cohen was like that. Just. Impartial. Egalitarian.

Unlike the entitled Appelbaum men, who didn't budge.

Were their hands broken? No matter how much she loved Asher, the division of labor seemed unequal. Unbalanced. So unlike the scales of justice.

"Who's ready for dessert?" Shirley asked.

Leon and Asher said, "I am," and chuckled at some obscure family joke.

"Coming up." Shirley brushed crumbs into a small silver dustpan, a tool Ruth had once seen in the hands of a tuxedo-clad waiter during a posh Manhattan restaurant birthday celebration with Dotsie, her best friend. Back then they'd tittered about the fussiness, each girl admittedly partial to the Automat.

The fussiness Ruth feared she was meant to emulate was no longer funny.

Here, the silver implement was part of Shirley's cleanup repertoire. She spot-cleaned the tablecloth with the wet corner of a rag before dipping into the kitchen. Ruth followed.

But for the good of her marriage, and to earn Shirley's favor, Ruth set aside her beliefs for now, hoping to promote *shalom bayit*, peace in the house. She'd known marriage required compromise but hadn't realized only *she* would be compromising.

Things would start to change when she and Asher lived on their own, and when Ruth got a job. When that would be, she didn't know. She and Asher had only agreed on "not long." Or when Asher got established at his father's accounting firm. Of course, Ruth had to pass the bar, which she'd never doubted before. But after a week in Philly, she *was* doubting her and Asher's plan for her to sneakily study. They had wanted to win over the in-laws before telling them Ruth would work.

In the kitchen, Shirley handed Ruth two footed and chilled dessert dishes filled with rice pudding, sprinkled with cinnamon and polka dots of raisins. She carried them to the table on a doily-lined silver tray.

Spoons clinked against the sides of the bowls. Evidently, no one wasted any of Shirley's rice pudding. Ruth had to admit she loved her mother-in-law's cooking. It sure beat scrambled eggs or grilled cheese, or Campbell's soup cooked on a hot plate in the boardinghouse room she'd shared with Dotsie for almost three years.

Once the desserts were done, Asher asked his mother, "Do you mind if we go sit outside?" He glanced at Ruth. Every night since they'd arrived in Wynnefield, Asher had checked with his mother for this particular time alone with his wife, as if he were a teenager asking permission to borrow the car. Shirley always said she didn't mind, as if it were her job to manage the couple's time together. Asher seemed bound to his role of obedient only son. Ruth didn't know what to make of it, but she'd have to figure it out: They were married. Being single wasn't an option for girls wanting a viable future, or for girls like Ruth—never mind that she loved Asher down to her bones and couldn't—wouldn't— picture a life without him.

In New York, Asher had been progressive, their relationship one of opinionated equals—Asher finishing his MBA at NYU and Ruth attending and graduating from Columbia Law, one of seventeen women. In Wynnefield, he had regressed to someone who asked permission to spend time with his wife. What was next? Cutting the crusts off his sandwiches?

Ruth stood and grasped Asher's hand, tugging him toward the front door. "Of course your mother doesn't mind."

They sat outside on patio chairs, their backs to the sidewalk, foreheads slick with leftover summer humidity. Asher fanned himself with the *Evening Bulletin* and handed Ruth the front sections. She opened, folded, and folded again, laying a newspaper square on her skirt. She glanced at the screen door, then the open window.

Creatures of habit, Shirley and Leon would be deep in their after-dinner crossword puzzles. No one was eavesdropping.

Big breath. "How could you tell your mother it was okay for me to attend etiquette lessons? You know I have to study," Ruth whispered. It was their first moment alone since that morning, when Asher had kissed her goodbye in the attic.

"I said *if* you wanted to," Asher said, crossing his arms, his casual tone belied by downcast eyes.

"Why didn't you tell her to ask *me*? She thought I was looking for your permission."

Asher laughed. "Ruth! You have never asked for permission for anything." He sandwiched one of her hands in his. "Nor should you, but—"

"But what?" Ruth pulled away.

"If it's important to my mother, maybe you should go. The bar exam isn't till when? February? You have five months."

"Are you kidding me? You know I have to work twice as hard to have half the opportunities of male lawyers. I can't lose my edge. I talked to some friends at Columbia, and they said prepare to spend forty hours a week for ten weeks. I don't have forty hours in a week. The holidays are coming." She tried not to hyperventilate. "And you promised me a honeymoon in the Poconos when I pass the bar."

Asher nodded.

"I'm not asking for too much. You know getting along with my mother would be good for us both."

Ruth's stomach clenched as she felt her dinner coming back up. She'd understood this in theory, but she hadn't realized getting in good with Shirley would take up so much of her time.

Why couldn't Shirley have asked Ruth if she wanted to go instead of using Asher as ammunition? That would have made it more palatable. She had assumed that Ruth would be seeking Asher's approval for every-thing—the quilt on their bed, Ruth's choice of dungarees for gardening, one extra cup of sugar in the lemonade. Any decision made on Ruth's own had been met by Shirley with "What would Asher think?"

Still, she tried to see the best in Shirley's old-fashioned nature. Ruth had been taught by her father to respect her elders.

"The fact is, it's not about you so much as about how she looks," Asher said. He had a way of helping Ruth see things simply, clearly.

Eloping had etched a chink in Shirley's maternal armor—she thought her son wouldn't have eloped if she were a better mother. Maybe that's why she had mentioned etiquette lessons at the beauty parlor. In front of witnesses. For public compliance, which equaled respect. Respect that had been stripped from the Appelbaums when they were excluded from the wedding. She heard it in Shirley's snide remarks, saw it in the disapproving pursed lips of Shirley's friends.

Ruth would have planned a traditional wedding if she'd known eloping would upend her in-laws' lives. It couldn't have been worse than what likely awaited her with etiquette lessons.

When she was growing up, Ruth had known girls who'd gone to charm school who emerged spouting rules, sticking their noses in the air. She didn't know what they had learned, just that she didn't want any part of it. Her father had never forced her. He had always afforded her the luxury of choice. Piano lessons or flute lessons (neither), roller skates or bicycle (both), charm school or chess (no contest).

Now Ruth was twenty-three, no longer a child, no longer in her father's home. Her choices were her own but affected Asher as well.

That didn't mean Ruth had to forget what she wanted. She wouldn't. The Asher she met and fell in love with in college drank Rheingold with his ZBT brothers and had a wry sense of humor but had always treated her with courtesy. He'd never told her what to do.

"I'll go," Ruth said, staring at the paper in her lap, fighting the tug of war.

"Good." Asher nodded once, less in agreement than in confirmation.

Ruth looked up. She detected a hint of smugness, which set her nerves on edge. "Excuse me?"

Asher shook his head as if released from a trance. "I meant thank you."

"That's what I thought you said." Ruth bent over and gathered a few fallen leaves from the ground. Maybe Asher was the one in need of etiquette lessons. She'd pay good money to see him in white gloves or drinking tea with his pinky raised.

Over the next few days, fall blew right into Philadelphia on a cool September breeze. Knitted sweaters, potted mums, sunset-colored leaves, and bushels of apples appeared throughout the neighborhood. All Ruth's favorites. She even liked hayrides. *Hayride.* She had only ever been on one. The Upper West Side, at least her part of it, below Eightieth, was more concrete than country—a place where buses far outnumbered hay-filled flatbeds.

Ruth stood on the portico of Lillian Diamond's Wynnefield Avenue mansion flanked by marble columns and stone lions, in front of a white double door trimmed in gold.

She shivered with the chill of a new season . . . and unrelenting doubt.

Fall had marked beginnings in Ruth's life again and again and again. Not only did the Jewish New Year occur in the fall—when she and her family and friends would be written in the Book of Life, God willing—but it had been the start of the school year for most of Ruth's life. She loved school, unlike most of the girls she knew; she loved learning for its own sake, not as a way to bide her time until a boy or a husband took precedence.

It made sense then that an opportunity to learn new things and to make new friends would begin in the fall. There! She had talked herself into it.

Ruth stared at her maroon leather loafers and imagined sparkly red pumps on her feet instead, even though they weren't her style. She'd do anything if, like Dorothy in *The Wizard of Oz*, she could click her heels three times and go home. That's where she had fit in simply because she was little Ruthie Cohen. It didn't matter that she had been a lot smart and a little tomboy.

Ruth had always been an instigator—in a good way. She'd started the first Jewish Girl Scout troop in her neighborhood. When their rabbi had said that it was improper—and worse, unnecessary—for girls to be scholars, she and her father started an admittedly somewhat secretive Torah study group. He taught Ruth and two of her high school classmates to be scholars.

Her father had promised her dying mother that Ruth would have the same opportunities as her brothers. He had ensured that. And Ruth's backbone, it seemed, was hereditary from her father. Ruth led a faction of female history majors at Barnard into the meetings of the History Society at Columbia College, which admitted only boys. They petitioned the administrations of both colleges until they'd been permitted, not to join, but to at least participate.

Now as Mrs. Asher Appelbaum she wanted in as well—this time to Wynnefield's inner sanctum. She didn't know yet what that looked like or precisely how to navigate it, but she was smart, a polymath. She could learn.

Confidence tucked into her pocketbook, Ruth looked west, up Wynnefield Avenue. She looked east. She checked behind her. No one strolling up the street or the path. Then she closed her eyes, rocked to the balls of her feet, and tapped her heels together.

One.

Two.

Three.

For a few seconds she allowed herself—maybe forced herself—to believe in an unknown excitement beyond the big, fancy door. To trust the same kind of nervous, uncertain flutter that had drawn Asher to her and permeated their courtship, allowing—no, insisting—that they fall in love and eventually elope. Away from their studies, the couple were prone to impulses opposing their thoughtful, structured daily lives. Their whole relationship had been one of adventures—like last-minute weekends to the Hudson Valley without a map, or trying new food in Chinatown. Ruth was no stranger to life's curveballs. She could do this.

Someone ascended the steps behind her. Ruth opened her eyes.

"I don't mean to interrupt your, um, thoughts—but you gonna ring the bell?" The raspy voice was marked by a Philadelphia accent. Ruth was still growing accustomed to the sounds and the lingo.

Water. Wooder.

Stoop. Step.

Sub. Hoagie.

She turned. A woman had joined her on the porch. Steadying the maroon pocketbook that dangled near her elbow, Ruth held out her hand. "Hello," she said. "I'm Ruth Appelbaum. Are you here for the housewife etiquette lessons?"

"Sure am. Reenie—Irene Pincus. Nice to meet you, Ruthie."

"Just Ruth." Only her brothers called her Ruthie.

"Well, nice to meet you, just Ruth."

Irene's bold-orange lips spread into a wide and genuine smile show-casing straight, large teeth. She didn't have the look Ruth associated with Wynnefield wives, and Ruth liked that about her immediately.

Her mother-in-law's friends, and the neighbors she'd met, were reserved, proper, and subtle with their cosmetics. The lime-green shadow painted across Irene's eyelids drooped and folded at the outer corners and collected in faint crow's-feet, which didn't comply with Ruth's housewife notion and reminded her of a crayon. An exaggerated flip at the ends of Irene's red hair hit the shoulders of her bright-green dress, but the look was more brash than refined and had more indi-viduality than Ruth thought was tolerated. Ruth was more "like a blank slate for makeup and fashion," Shirley had said. "That's a compliment. So many options."

She was quickly becoming fluent in her mother-in-law's language.

Shirley had said the class would be like a small, private finishing school—but how could Ruth finish something she hadn't even started?

"You'll feel better about the lessons once you get used to the idea," Shirley had promised.

Ruth was still waiting.

If her confidence had been Shirley's main concern, why then hadn't her mother-in-law imposed more of her Wynnefield values and suggested Ruth wear something fancier than a plain navy skirt and blouse to the first class? Or hinted that lipstick would be a better choice than Ruth's usual dab of Vaseline? Ruth may have scoffed at—or ignored— the tips, but they would have demonstrated Shirley's support. Her love.

"Let's go in. We won't learn anything standing out here." Irene patted Ruth's shoulder like an old friend would, allowing her hand to linger.

Ready or not, Ruth rang the doorbell.

Chapter 2

LILLIAN

When the doorbell chimed its four notes, Lillian checked her watch.

"Excuse me, ladies." She headed to the front door, with a smile and a slight gesture urging Sunny, her housekeeper, back to the kitchen.

"I'll get it," Lillian said.

It was her job to set these young housewives at ease, to teach them what was expected. Lillian taught by example. That's why she'd chosen her burgundy lightweight worsted wool suit with covered buttons, straight from the pages of the August '62 issue of *Vogue*. Perfect for an early fall day, according to the magazine. Lillian took their word for it. She'd accessorized it with a matching scarf and short strand of pearls—showing the girls how to behave, how to dress.

She'd dressed the foyer as well. A jewel-toned arrangement of dahlias sprang from her favorite Orrefors vase atop the gold-trimmed, ornate marble table. Streams of sunshine, coming through the side-lights, painted colorful reflections on the white wall and floor and stretched as far as the blue-carpeted stairs—adding whimsy to Lillian's formal decor. When Mother Nature grabbed the reins, it relieved a bit of the pressure to be perfect. No one questioned *her*.

Lillian smoothed herself from shoulder to hip and opened the front door. "Hello, ladies."

"Hello," the girls chirped in unison.

These two needed more wardrobe work than the two girls already inside. Lillian assumed the plain girl was Shirley's daughter-in-law. If *she'd* had a proclivity for green eye shadow or dyed ginger hair, Shirley would've mentioned it. Lillian had known the older woman for a decade and was delighted to help the newest Appelbaum fit into Wynnefield society. A little makeup, the right clothes, words, and attitude and—abracadabra!—this girl would be just what Shirley intended to have in a surprise daughter-in-law.

"I'm Lillian Diamond. Come in."

The girls stepped inside.

"I'm Ruth Appelbaum. Thank you for having me." Ruth grasped Lillian's hand, squeezed and released, then walked farther into the foyer. She bent to smell the flowers—though everyone knew dahlias had no scent—and turned to Lillian. "You have a lovely home."

Soft-spoken and polite. Genteel, even. "Why, thank you." What had Shirley been worried about? Ruth might be a plain Jane, but she wasn't a barbarian. "You must be Irene." Lillian turned to the redhead, who attempted a kind of curtsey.

"I'm so thrilled to be here I can't even stand it. I can't believe I'm in this house. I've always admired it from the street but, you know, I never thought I'd be inside."

Was Irene planning to ever take a breath? "And here you are!" Lillian motioned as if she were herding a gaggle of housewives, not two. "Come with me."

They walked under the floral hand-carved archway and down four blue-carpeted stairs to the sunken living room. The decor was intended to impress, so Lillian didn't mind Irene's gawking. Ruth only looked ahead and didn't seem to notice the textured wallpaper in silvery blue that had taken months to arrive, or the ornate custom-made pleated draperies framing the large windows on either side of the fireplace, faced with the same marble as the foyer. Hanging over the fireplace was a painted family portrait—a younger Lillian, her movie-star-handsome husband, Peter, before his hairline had started to recede, and Pamela and Penelope (or Penny, as she liked to be called now), when they were six and eight years old (six years ago, oh my!). They had been happy, then, to dress alike in Lillian's choice of outfits, and their questions could be answered without reading the encyclopedia.

Two matching dark-blue velveteen sofas faced each other, with a glittery gold rectangular coffee table between them. One girl sat on each sofa. The new girls stood alongside Lillian, who reached out her right arm. "May I present Miss Harriet Schwartz and Mrs. Eli Blum—Carrie. Girls, Mrs. Stephen Pincus and Mrs. Asher Appelbaum. Irene and Ruth."

The girls nodded after Lillian sang their names.

"Please, just call me Ruth. Mrs. Appelbaum is my mother-in-law."

A teaching opportunity! "Just remember, ladies, first names are too familiar for most business and social settings unless you're among family or close friends," Lillian said. "You'll be identified by who your husband is."

"I don't mean to speak out of turn, but I like my name. I'd prefer it," Ruth said.

"It's not about preferences," Harriet said. "It's about the rules of etiquette."

"Who sets these rules?" Ruth asked. Her tone was laced with curiosity, not boldness or impertinence.

"Society," Lillian said. Though she wasn't sure she knew.

"I don't mean to be contrary," Ruth said.

Lillian thought that was exactly what Ruth meant to be, while seeming as polite as possible.

"I love that marrying Asher meant becoming an Appelbaum. But I hadn't realized it meant losing my *first* name. My mother gave me that name. She died when I was four," Ruth said. "Influenza."

"May her memory be a blessing," the girls and Lillian muttered in somber unison.

Now Lillian understood why Ruth was there. Shirley didn't want to step on the dead mother's toes, so to speak, by showing Ruth what a mother might have shown her. She had handed the job to Lillian, who knew that was meant to be a compliment, not an imposition. Still, a little forewarning would have been nice.

She recognized something—a lilt perhaps?—in the way Ruth spoke her mind. Yet the girl spoke with great care. Lillian, too, had often spoken her mind to her mother, who always listened intently and pressed Lillian, whom she called Lilly, to study well and follow her dreams. What those dreams had been, Lillian scarcely remembered. By the time she was living with her grandparents she had been expected to be someone's wife. What other reason could there be for allowing her to attend college if not to find a husband?

Sometimes she missed the part of herself who spoke up. That part had been submerged in an unquestioning life with Peter for fifteen years. Quiet compliance was easier than creating the waves that sometimes stirred her imagination.

Another thing she had in common with Ruth—they'd both grown up without a mother.

So that was it. Another reason Shirley had thought Lillian best for the job of teaching Ruth etiquette.

Lillian should have been gratified by the acknowledgment from her mentor, but today she wasn't. How odd that Shirley would exploit Lillian's loss. Or Ruth's.

Lillian tapped a cigarette from a jeweled case, placed it between her lips, flipped open and struck her lighter, puffed and dragged. "Lesson one is gracious greetings." Ruth, Carrie, Irene, and Harriet, sitting next to one another on a sofa, gazed up at her. She exhaled a cloud of smoke and tapped the cigarette on a glass ashtray nearby, allowing the loosened ash to fall into it. Cigarette still in hand, Lillian lifted a notebook from the coffee table, opened it, and balanced it on her left arm as she turned pages with her right hand. "I want you to address one another as if you've just met."

"We *have* just met," Ruth said.

The mild sassiness tickled Lillian, as if a feather had trailed along her foot. Ruth was right. Fresh, perhaps, but correct. The outspokenness should have irked her. If Pam or Penny had backtalked, she would have used it as a teachable moment for undesirable behavior. But somehow this breath of fresh air felt good.

"Talk as if you're mingling in a business setting or a cocktail party," Lillian said. "Where are you from? What do your husbands do? Start with that." There. Back on track.

Carrie, blonde, blue-eyed, and petite, with a Kelly-green silk scarf tied in a bow at her neck, looked to the others and raised her hand.

"You don't need to raise your hand, but go ahead, you start," Lillian said. "Tell the girls about your husband."

"Eli is the new vice-principal at Overbrook High School." Carrie's eyes glowed. "He was chosen over a dozen applicants."

Harriet fluttered her lashes. "My fiancé works for his father. They're lawyers. Scotty will take over one day."

"Stephen owns Pincus Appliance Palace," Irene said. "With three locations."

Lillian and the girls looked at Ruth.

"Oh. My turn; Asher is a CPA. He works for his father." She turned to Harriet. "What kind of law does your fiancé practice?"

"The legal kind? I don't know. Should I? Do you know what kind of accounting they do?"

"Tax accounting."

"It's not wrong to know specifics," Lillian said. "But you don't want to get caught up in business chatter yourself."

Harriet smirked.

"You'll want to know enough to keep your husbands up to speed," Lillian added. Keeping Peter primed on his clients and acquaintances was her specialty. Her husband relied on her to provide details he'd use to woo and impress. She'd once considered his business coups her own, but after fifteen years of marriage, the excitement of Peter's achievements had stopped feeling like hers.

That's what made the etiquette lessons special; they belonged to Lillian. Not that Peter needed them. Even Lillian wished the lessons were more important—not that etiquette was insignificant, not at all. But sometimes, when she allowed herself to dream beyond her life—or even within her life—she recalled short periods of time when she'd pictured herself a teacher, librarian, nurse. Or a meter maid. The woolgathering had never lasted long enough to be anything more. Perhaps if her mother had been around . . .

"Won't anyone want to know what we think?" Ruth asked. "About anything?"

Lillian focused on Ruth, snapping back to the living room. "Once you're friendly with the wives? Sure. Hair. Clothes. Decorating. Children. There will be plenty to talk about."

Ruth shook her head but said nothing. Lillian wanted to tell Ruth she'd adapt, that she'd ignore and eventually forget her recalcitrant self, flourish in happy housewifery and motherhood. But that might be a lie. Lillian might be a lot of things, but she wasn't a liar.

Lillian stubbed out her cigarette. "Just to reiterate, the way I introduced you is appropriate for married women." She looked right at Ruth. "Memorize the first names of the men in your husband's circles, but always address them as Mr. in a business or social setting—and while you may not like it, you'll use your husband's name when introducing yourself." Perhaps acknowledging Ruth's dissent would ease the transition. "You can offer your first name, but it would be rude of anyone to use it unless it was a casual setting. Inviting someone to use your first name sends a message of frivolity in business. I promise you girls, it's not easy."

Ruth reached into her pocketbook and removed a small notepad and pencil and started scribbling away.

"You were already practicing this lesson by meeting me, and one another." Lillian motioned around the room, pleased with her trickery. "Why do you think the way you greet your husband and his colleagues and their wives is important?"

Harriet's hand shot up and she smiled. "Being polite shows you had a good upbringing."

"That isn't a factor here," Lillian said. Harriet was a pretty girl, but there was more to learn. "What do you think, Ruth?"

"Do you want me to be honest?" Ruth asked.

"Not really," Harriet said.

Lillian shook a finger at her before turning to Ruth. "Of course you should be honest. Just remember your manners." That was silly to say—it was clear Ruth was smart and polite, if opinionated. Lillian knew the difference.

"I think when we're nice to other people—no matter who they are—we're showing respect for them, and that reflects on us. People shouldn't have to be a certain way to receive our kindness and respect. Or to have rights."

"We're not talking about rights, Ruth," Harriet said.

"Maybe we should be," Ruth said. "I mean, if we have the influence you say we do"—Ruth looked at Lillian—"we could do some real good."

"Our job is to boost our husbands and keep a home that makes them happy, so they can do their jobs," Harriet scolded, sneering as if Ruth were daft.

"Back to the matter at hand." Lillian turned a few pages in her notebook and spoke without glancing at the page. "Ruth isn't wrong. When you feel good about yourself, you are inherently nice to others, and when you are polite to others, you feel good about yourself. It all makes for a lovely first impression." Lillian consolidated the contents of two ashtrays. "Another thing to remember," she said, "is that your appearance is also a greeting. Don't forget to freshen up before your husband comes home from work. Change your clothes; pick a pretty lipstick. It will make you feel better, and he will see that you are at your best when he walks in the door, not frazzled from a day of shopping or dealing with the children."

"I don't leave the house without lipstick," Harriet said.

Ruth swiped her fingers across shiny lips, which likely had Vaseline on them.

"Look, girls, the High Holidays are only weeks away." Ruth switched the topic in a jolly, if unconvincing, voice. What had changed her tune? "So how about we be the Manners Musketeers until then?"

"What a lovely thing to say, Ruth," Lillian said. Ruth shrugged, as if pushing the effort away as unimportant. Lillian understood Ruth was there at Shirley's behest and was shrugging off nothing.

"I've heard the wives who take these lessons from you sometimes call themselves the Diamond Girls," Harriet said.

"I like the sound of that," Irene said. "Like a club."

They were trying. Even Ruth. No harm in offering the girls a hint to make things easier.

"Do you know what's more important than your name—just as important as being the perfect wife—and will get you out of jams more often than anything else? Something even the husbands don't know?" Lillian asked.

That got their attention. The girls, including Ruth, leaned forward. "What's that?" they asked in unison.

Lillian closed her notebook, then lit another cigarette. She inhaled and blew out a stream of smoke. "Knowing who your friends are."

Chapter 3

RUTH

Ruth stared at Lillian the way some people looked at car wrecks or babies—unable to look away. One moment she was entranced, the next she was appalled. Lillian's almost-black, wavy hair didn't budge—likely set and sprayed to hold for an entire week. Her skin was pale enough to make Ruth wonder if Lillian had taken ill, but with her winged eyeliner, precision brows, and carmine-painted lips, you knew she wasn't simply well, but divine. Ruth couldn't deny it: Lillian personified *striking*.

She'd always considered her own looks ordinary—medium-brown hair and eyes, a medium-sized nose and bust. None of which bothered her like they might have if her appearance impacted her intellect. Even with a best friend like Dotsie back home, Ruth retained a grip on her self-worth. Dotsie's long, auburn hair and "legs for days" never intimidated her. With Dots, she'd never been subjected to that not-quite-up-to-snuff attitude she felt at Lillian's.

Here she had little in common with the other girls, with their homespun values and domestic points of view.

Back in New York, Ruth and Dotsie had been brought together by a common cause—the Midtown Women's Legal Aid Society. Both girls had volunteered, since Barnard, to help women who had experienced mental and physical mistreatment in the workplace or at home. The life experiences of these women were so different from Ruth's, as she had always been treasured. She had been simultaneously intrigued and appalled and compelled to help. The plight of these women drove her the way nothing had before.

But they and all of Ruth's contacts were back in New York.

In Wynnefield, Ruth had to find a sense of purpose like she had in New York—beyond her need for study time.

Lillian walked over and crouched in front of her, then reached out her hand with the grace of a ballerina. Ruth took it like she'd been offered a gift.

"Are you all right?" Lillian asked. "I know it's a lot." She touched Ruth's knee and stood. "You'll do just fine."

Ruth appreciated the kindness and confidence so much that a sob bubbled up in her throat. She gulped it away. She'd been unaware until that moment of her desperate need for a friendly word.

Perhaps Lillian understood how Ruth stood at an impasse—needing to fit into her new life and family, yet reluctant to let go of the old. She had expected that understanding to come from Asher. After all, he had championed her through her years at Barnard and Columbia, knowing she never wanted a traditional life. They'd spent those years discussing the possible trajectory of Ruth's career. She wanted to become a judge. In private, and with affection, Asher had nicknamed Ruth "Your Honor."

Now he was nudging her, slowly but surely, away from her dreams.

Irene shimmied to sit straighter, though Ruth thought it impossible. Lillian smiled and shook Irene's hand, but didn't crouch. "I've seen your picture in the *Jewish Exponent*," Irene said to Lillian. "You're even prettier in person."

"Why, aren't you sweet."

Ruth hadn't thought to compliment Lillian, who had moved to a cream-colored chair next to the fireplace.

Shirley was the reason for Ruth's being in this marble house, with these marble wives. For agreeing to do the classes. Ruth hadn't considered the possibility that she'd benefit from the lessons other than because they would please her mother-in-law. Might these girls really become her friends? And what would happen when they learned she had graduated from law school and wanted a job?

She assessed each of them in turn.

Harriet, prettier than she deserved to be if appearance matched personality, had already met Ruth with disapproving rancor. Each snippet of information Ruth shared seemed to offend Harriet's way of life and add a chip to her shoulder. Ruth's career—any woman's career—would likely set Harriet reeling.

Irene appeared laidback and affable, with an easy smile and a breezy laugh. But she'd chosen to stay home with her children and might be affronted by Ruth's choices—so different from her own.

Through her work with the MWLAS, Ruth had learned most wives were quick to defend their lives—good or bad. The biggest surprise to Ruth was that the women looked normal, even pretty. Hairdos, scarves, long sleeves, concealer, and powder transformed some of these women. Dabs did wonders.

Last was Carrie—reserved, sweet, and modest. She and Ruth didn't share a cause as far as she knew, but they were both new to marriage and to Wynnefield. That might be enough—perhaps they could navigate the whatsits and wherefores of Wynnefield together. Maybe Carrie had already learned what clubs and committees to join and where to shop. Perhaps she had already made friends their age—without babies—or joined a bridge game or book club.

Ruth sensed that Carrie, with her tentative smile and quiet demeanor, was more like her than the others. It would be nice to have a friend while appeasing her mother-in-law—even if that wasn't what she'd planned.

"Your husband is why I'm here," Carrie whispered to Ruth. "They met on the golf course last weekend, and Eli insisted I attend as well. I guess I should thank you."

Ruth raised her eyebrows and lowered them. "Eli must be quite a friendly fellow to get a conversation all the way to what I'm doing. Asher isn't the talkative type as a rule."

"Well, I thought it was nice of him. My husband doesn't usually like me to join clubs. He prefers me all to himself," Carrie said.

"Oh, that's so sweet," said Harriet, who must have been listening in.

Ruth shuddered inside. She and Asher had always planned the time they spent together. They had so many separate activities. Her sorority, AEPhi, his fraternity, the Midtown Women's Legal Aid Society, the Accounting Society—their respective friends, families, and studies. Talking about the time they spent apart was one of Ruth and Asher's favorite activities when they were together.

Carrie blushed. "It *is* sweet, isn't it? How does your fella feel about the lessons?"

"Scotty wants me to be happy. It was *my* idea to be here now," Harriet said. She held out her left hand, ostensibly so the others would ogle her engagement ring. Irene obliged. "I want to start off on the right foot. What about you, Ruth?"

"I just moved here about a week and a half ago from New York," she said, certain she wasn't answering what had been asked. "My mother-in-law suggested I come here."

"Shirley Appelbaum?" Harriet asked.

Ruth smiled because she thought she should.

"You're the one who eloped?" said Harriet. "I heard about you at the beauty parlor."

Ruth itched to point out that Asher had also eloped, but she took the brunt of the blame, as if she'd dragged him down an imaginary aisle by his hair. Is that what they thought?

If so, they didn't know Asher.

Once he set his mind to something, it was impossible to convince him otherwise.

Sure, they'd talked about marriage in passing. And Ruth had assumed she'd marry Asher someday. She hadn't been a girl who day-dreamed about weddings, or honeymoons, or babies, and he knew that.

So, when he proposed with his grandmother's ring, declaring not only his love but the logic behind eloping, she knew he was serious.

"If we marry now, we don't have to be apart. Ever again," Asher had said, clutching her hands as if she might run away. Had he been that unsure of her? "If we were only engaged, you'd have to stay in New York, and I promised my dad I'd be home at the end of the summer."

Ruth's heart had tensed at the thought of any separation. She'd been terrified of losing him. Nothing would have mattered without Asher. If she hadn't known it before, she knew it then. She would do anything for him.

And she had.

"I can't imagine not wanting a real wedding," Harriet said.

"To each her own, girls," Lillian said. "Don't judge."

Ruth blinked. Had Lillian just defended her?

Since Shirley and Lillian were longtime friends, Ruth had expected to be admonished for eloping. Perhaps to save face, Shirley hadn't shared the whole truth about that sunny Sunday in late June that Asher had implored his parents to visit him with the promise of "big news."

After a brunch-worthy spread of bagels and lox, complete with champagne, Asher said, "We got married" as casually as if he had asked them to pass the kugel.

"That's how you thank us?" Shirley had screeched to Asher. "For college, and graduate school, and this apartment, and a job to come home to? You exclude us from your wedding? We're so terrible?" Shirley wiped tears with the backs of her hands and glared at Ruth. "You should have known better."

Should she have?

She hadn't considered any lasting implications of eloping—all she'd wanted was security with Asher.

Leon had wrapped his arm around Shirley and whispered in her ear.

"I will not watch my step!" his mother said, and shifted away from her husband.

"Ma, listen," Asher said. "This was my idea. Don't blame Ruth."

Asher had defended her—which made Ruth want to take the blame. Almost.

"The plan is to work for Dad and for us to live in the attic, right, sweetheart?" Asher continued.

It was? For how long? They hadn't discussed this. They hadn't discussed anything. Wasn't impetuousness the hallmark of eloping? Before she'd said a word to her *in-laws*—the term felt strange—Ruth realized she was nodding.

Shirley sniffed. "You'll love Wynnefield, dear. I just know it."

Ruth hadn't wanted to anger or sadden her new mother-in-law, so she forced a smile, unable to conjure up the right words. This was new—Ruth had always loved and commanded words.

She dragged her reflections back to the present as Lillian waggled her finger. "No gossiping, girls." She stood and walked back through the living room. "Continue getting to know one another. I'll be right back."

Lillian gave the impression she always knew what to say. Ruth envied that.

"I think eloping is kind of romantic," Irene whispered once Lillian had left the room.

Harriet rolled her eyes.

"Thanks, Irene. It was."

Ruth had carried a bunch of corner-store daisies as her bouquet and wore a Dotsie-made daisy-chain crown and a pale-yellow suit. Asher and she had written their own vows, and after the short ceremony they rode through Central Park in a carriage, like romantic tourists.

Irene pushed on Ruth's arm instead of saying "You're welcome." She was an effusive girl, open and unguarded—a strange contrast to her rough edges. "I might not have much romance in my life, but I know it when I hear it. Eloping is romantic—exciting even." She blushed. "I mean, you don't look like you *had* to get married."

"Oh my God, no." Children were not part of Ruth and Asher's immediate plan. They would come later, when Asher rose to partner and Ruth had established her career.

"You didn't get all the goodies like a bridal shower, or registering for china, or wedding gifts, or a—"

"Stop, Harriet," Irene said. "Ruth looks plenty happy to me. Don't make her feel bad. We're all here for the same reason."

To placate their mothers-in-law?

"To become the perfect wife," Harriet said.

Ruth sighed.

"I don't need perfect," Irene said. "But I'd like to teach proper etiquette to my daughters."

"You have children?" Carrie asked.

"Four." Irene grinned. "Two of each." She unlatched her pocketbook and removed a photograph of four children squashed together on a floral, plastic slip–covered sofa. They passed it around, and each one oohed and aahed louder than they had for Harriet's ring. To these girls, the purpose of marriage was babies.

"I'd love a little girl," Harriet said.

"I've heard if you lie upside down with your legs in the air, there's a better chance you get a girl," Irene said.

"That's an old wives' tale," Carrie said.

Harriet crossed her arms, defiant. "How do you know?"

"Because I am—or rather was—a nurse," Carrie said.

"What do you mean, *was*?" Ruth asked.

"Eli didn't think it looked right. Me working."

"Even though you were helping people?" Ruth asked. "How do *you* think it looks?"

Carrie said nothing.

"No husband worth his salt wants his wife to work," Harriet said.

"What if she wants to?" Ruth asked.

Carrie and Irene stared at her.

Harriet cackled and pretended to slap her knee. "Oh, Ruth. You're so funny."

Chapter 4

Lillian

Lillian walked in, heard the last comments from the girls, and held her breath. But the smoke from her inhaled cigarette escaped in a cough and a swirl of gray. She scanned the faces around her.

Harriet was charmingly romantic and traditional yet woefully out of touch. Ruth hadn't meant to be funny; her question struck Lillian as bold and curious. Ruth, new to the community, to marriage, and to the Appelbaum family, exhibited a keen sense of self. Lillian, at least a decade older, envied her—she sometimes struggled with her own identity.

Maybe Shirley also saw her past self in Ruth. Perhaps it was a modicum of envy on Shirley's part that hindered the mother-in-law/daughter-in-law relationship, rather than hurt feelings. What else could it be?

Lillian could tell Ruth was trying to please Shirley because of the efforts she had made by coming to the etiquette class.

Shirley! She'd announced that she planned to pop in on the lesson, which might prove to be too much of a distraction. Lillian stood. "I'll be right back, girls." She'd head off Shirley before she could let herself in the kitchen door and sidetrack the class.

She scampered toward the kitchen. "Sunny," she said, "when Mrs. Appelbaum arrives, ask her opinion on something to keep her in the kitchen. Whatever you do, don't let her into the . . ."

As Lillian passed the pantry, Sunny shook her head and shifted her eyes to the right.

"Don't let me where?" Shirley leaned against the counter.

Lillian's neck prickled. She stopped short. Regrouped. "Shirl, what a surprise!" She kept her voice neutral. "Sunny, did you offer Mrs. Appelbaum a cold beverage?"

"Would you like some ginger ale?" Sunny pulled open the Frigidaire with arthritic hands. "We have a can of Black Cherry Wishniak soda if you'd rather. We also have grapefruit juice. It's Mr. Diamond's favorite. Fresh squeezed, of course." She pointed at the pitcher of juice, closed the Frigidaire, and walked toward the dining room. "Or I could make you a cocktail if you'd like."

Shirley touched Sunny's arm and she stopped. "No, thank you, it's much too early for me. But thank you for asking." Shirley clasped and unclasped the top tortoiseshell button on her maroon cardigan, a shade so close to Lillian's own burgundy suit. This season's latest trend.

Sunny nodded. Smiled. Knew exactly when to back off.

When Sunny began working for her mother after Lillian was born, Sunny's loyalty was to Anna. "Do as your mother says" and "Let your mother be" were among Sunny's favorite sayings. Anna and Sunny had been friends since they were in high school, despite growing up on different sides of the neighborhood. They had bonded in the public library over a shared copy of the latest Nancy Drew novel set aside by the librarian for her favorite patrons. Anna and Sunny adored mysteries.

After Lillian's mother went away, the housekeeper went to work for Lillian's grandparents. Teenage Lillian could always count on Sunny for a diversion to help pull her out of a jam. She helped Lillian hide chicken livers and lima beans in napkins, so she didn't have to eat them.

Their conspiracies evolved and, later on, Sunny helped her disguise high school parties as library outings.

Nowadays, having Sunny in her own house a few days a week reminded Lillian of the good times with her mother and grandmother, even when Lillian got caught in a pickle, like now.

"I came to meet the girls and check on Ruth," Shirley said.

Lillian poured herself half a jelly glass of grapefruit juice. "Everything's fine. Ruth seems lovely."

"Lovely? The girl who ran off with my son is not lovely."

Enough was enough. "She ran right to your attic, Shirl. And she's trying to fit in. Give her a chance." Lillian's words scratched her throat. She had rarely expressed a contrary opinion.

"She didn't give us a chance. I'll never be crowned." Jewish mothers dreamed of a *mezinke tanz*, a Jewish ceremony honoring parents who had married off their last child. The parents would be seated on chairs in the middle of the dance floor while friends and family danced around, kissing them as they passed. Best of all, a specially made crown of flowers was placed in the mother's hair. Every mother wanted—had earned—those flowers.

Lillian should sympathize with Shirley, mourning her moment in the spotlight, but she recalled what she assumed were Shirley's calculated omissions.

"Why didn't you tell me Ruth's mother had passed away? It would have been nice to know. Did you want her here only because we both grew up without mothers?"

"I wanted her here because you're the perfect etiquette teacher."

Lillian flushed. Shirley, normally stingy with compliments, had backed out of her predicament with aplomb. Of course the class was why Shirley had wanted them to meet—and that was fine.

It was the secret that wasn't.

Lillian had been caught unaware and unprepared. How had she looked? How did it make Ruth feel that Shirley hadn't shared this information about Lillian's past? And now Shirley wanted to check up on her?

"If it bothers you that I'm here, Lil, I'll go," Shirley said.

Wide-eyed, Sunny handed Shirley a tinfoil packet, puffed with something edible. "A new apple cake recipe."

Shirley ignored the peace offering and walked through the kitchen, heading for the dining room—not the direction Lillian wanted.

"It would be rude of me not to say hello, Lillian."

Which course to take? Lillian was stuck between her old friend and the new Diamond Girls. "Of course," she said. A short greeting wouldn't interfere with the controlled atmosphere Lillian had so carefully created.

Shirley stopped next to the dining room table and turned to Lillian and whispered, "I didn't think to tell you about Ruth's mother because it's nothing like your situation."

Lillian dreaded reliving her past, but she'd have welcomed the point of connection with Ruth. "How can you say that? Neither of us had mothers."

"You seem to forget one difference," Shirley said. "Your mother is still alive."

Chapter 5

RUTH

From the living room, Ruth could make out her mother-in-law's voice in the kitchen. Ruth shuddered. Shirley was *there*?

Surrounding Ruth, the other girls chatted away, their social demeanors calm and unchanged. They didn't hear the tone and tenor of Shirley's voice, or feel the vibrations of her cadence.

Her thoughts raced to find the perfect way to express the details of their first training to her mother-in-law. No use denying it, Ruth wanted Shirley to feel satisfied, even proud.

"My mother-in-law is here," Ruth whispered. "I'm guessing to check up on me."

The banter stopped.

"How do you know it's her?" Irene asked. "I can barely hear any talking."

Carrie leaned toward the kitchen and shushed the others with a finger to her lips. "I hear something."

Ruth had grown up in an apartment building, listening to sounds and voices through open windows and air shafts. Now, like back then, she had only to close her eyes and blank out all other sounds to transform the vague and muffled voices into clear, full-bodied language. "Trust me," she said. "I can tell."

"So what?" asked Harriet.

"How would you feel if someone checked up on you?" Irene asked.

Harriet shrugged.

"I wouldn't like it," Irene said.

"Maybe she wants to make sure you're okay," Carrie said.

Ruth shook her head. "She wants to make sure I don't embarrass her."

"Embarrass her?" Irene asked. "You've got more class and chutzpah in your little finger . . ."

"I wouldn't go that far," Harriet said.

"I don't understand what there is to check up on." Carrie tapped an index finger on her chin three times.

"Everything, I guess," Ruth said. "To make sure I'm doing and saying the right things."

Irene patted Ruth's back as if to stop her from choking. "Well, we'll see to that."

Lillian and Shirley parked themselves under the living room arch. Was it meant to be a surprise . . . or an ambush?

"This is Mrs. Appelbaum, girls," Lillian said. "Ruth's mother-in-law."

The girls turned toward the announcement.

"Shirley was my etiquette teacher," Lillian said. "She encouraged me to start teaching these lessons about five years ago, and she just popped in to say hello."

Lillian and Shirley drifted into the room. Shirley smoothed her outfit, starting with her maroon sweater set, with its gold leaf-shaped pin fastened beneath her left shoulder, and ending with her tan-and-brown skirt. Hopefully she approved of Ruth choosing the same color for her purse and shoes today—that would mean Ruth had gotten one thing right.

"I'd like to do more than pop in," Shirley said. "But it seems I'm not needed."

"It's not that, Shirl," Lillian said.

"I'm sure Mrs. Appelbaum just wants to prove how well you've started the lessons," Irene said. "And that she can trust you to do a good job."

The unexpected support took Ruth aback, Irene's brio instantly endearing. Did the double meaning skip over Shirley's head—or land on it with a splat?

"Of course I trust Lillian," Shirley said while looking at Ruth. "I only wanted to help."

Splat.

"We've been having a lovely time," Lillian said. "Trust me."

"I do," Shirley said, her face not betraying whether this was true or not.

Ruth was surprised at the cutting tone of Shirley's voice. She had thought it was a voice reserved exclusively for her.

"We've already been practicing our gracious greetings," Carrie said. "Ruth's a natural."

Shirley smiled with thin lips. "Is she?"

Why was that so hard to believe?

"Lucky girl. I guess she had some early lessons," Irene said.

"Thank you, Irene," Ruth said.

Harriet stayed quiet, remaining firmly on the fence.

"Well, then," Shirley said. "I don't want to interrupt."

They'd done it! She was leaving. The mother-in-law spy had been deactivated.

"You're always welcome to pop in," Lillian said.

Though perspiration gathered at her hairline, Ruth walked over to Shirley and kissed her on the cheek. "I'm glad you stopped by," she fibbed. She'd have preferred to navigate this day alone, the way she had when her father had dropped her off at a new school, giving Ruth only a kiss on the forehead, as if anointing her, and a thumbs-up demonstrating his confidence in her success. Although, without Shirley's doubt and intrusion today, Ruth wouldn't have experienced the staunch support of her new friends. Their expression of solidarity had warmed Ruth—and surprised her.

Shirley grabbed Ruth's hands. "I just want you to be happy, dear."

Despite what seemed to be affection, Ruth remained wary. On alert. She hadn't forgotten how Shirley had given her a warning—disguised as advice—on the first afternoon she had arrived in town, while helping Ruth make up a bed for the newlyweds.

"You'll do best to learn our ways," Shirley had said, as if Ruth had moved to Appalachia from New York, instead of to Philadelphia. "It's what Asher will expect."

Ruth tried to appear unfazed as she smoothed the coverlet. "Of course." She'd been with Asher since college—five years. They'd been married since June. Certainly, their *ways* were copacetic.

"We wouldn't want him to be disappointed now, would we?" Shirley had asked.

We?

In that moment, as Shirley straightened the quilt that Ruth had already adjusted, Ruth realized exactly whom she risked disappointing.

She understood that the very survival of Wynnefield's matriarchal society depended on pleasing her mother-in-law. And Ruth's job wasn't to change society, but simply to tolerate it, as had generations before her.

Chapter 6

LILLIAN

Lillian moved gracefully as she led Shirley from the living room back into the kitchen, the clicks of their heels pronounced on the imported tile floor after being muffled by carpet.

"I get the hint; I'm going." Shirley lifted Sunny's carefully wrapped apple cake and nodded to the housekeeper. When Sunny unlatched the back door, its recently oiled hardware added barely a murmur to the conversation.

Lillian hoped her message to Shirley had been received as more than a hint—that it had been as clear as the sky. She could handle the girls on her own. Recently, Lillian had begun to feel as if they needed guiding more than handling, but that notion discomfited her as somehow conspiratorial, so she kept it to herself.

"I want you to know you can count on me," Lillian said as Shirley hesitated in the doorway. "And that you can trust me with anything."

"I do know," Shirley said. "Don't forget to finish the lesson. Or to schedule your outing. We want everyone up to par by the holidays, if possible."

That gave her less than three weeks. "Oh, it's possible, Shirl." The pressure on Lillian's psyche returned. Nothing would interfere with the girls being the best dressed and most charming at Rosh Hashanah services and fall social events. "I'd better get back."

Sunny locked the door after Shirley left. "She's a pip."

Lillian chuckled. "She just wants everything on her terms, her way. It's what she's used to. Like my grandmother."

Sunny lifted her eyebrows and lowered them without saying a word about Lillian's Gran.

When Lillian's mother went away, it was Gran who'd stepped in to raise Lillian, who'd sent her to college, and who'd urged her to marry Peter the summer after her graduation.

Sunny wiped her hands on her apron. "This isn't new, you know. Mrs. Appelbaum has been watching your every move for years."

"She has?"

Sunny nodded. "And she's very generous with her two cents." She clapped a hand over her mouth.

Lillian laughed. "I never noticed until now."

"I shouldn't have to remind you," Sunny whispered, "but this is your house; those are your girls."

Lillian walked into the living room and looked around. Such a disparate group. *I wonder if the girls might do best if they belong to themselves,* she thought. Lillian knew this was a real departure from her usual way of thinking. But her thoughts of independence were confirmed by Ruth and the other girls. At least when they'd finished the course, they'd have one thing in common—social graces.

Lillian lit another cigarette and settled on the sofa across from the girls. She knew her grace looked effortless, as if she sat atop the sofa cushion, instead of sinking into it like the rest of them. The illusion took practice. And strong calf muscles.

"Sorry about the interruption," Lillian said. "In spite of it, we've had a nice start today. I'm glad you all agree things should stay as they are. I'm sorry if it creates any backlash at home, Ruth."

Ruth looked back at Lillian and smiled. "Don't worry about that. I'll be fine."

"Ruth doesn't deserve to be spied on, and neither do you," Irene said.

Goodness gracious! Such a dramatic interpretation of events. Still, Lillian had wanted the girls to be friends, and lickety-split, they were. The speed was remarkable.

All they'd needed was a common cause.

Chapter 7

RUTH

Ruth turned off the car engine and peered out the windshield at the supermarket in front of her. Busy housewives bustled back and forth, entering the wide doors, coming out with their purchases, some with toddlers in tow. Everyone doing their best to be the perfect family. To fit in with everyone else.

She walked inside the store, eyed the merchandise, and double-checked the grocery list Shirley had given her.

> *McIntosh apples 3 lbs. No bruises.*
> *Golden Delicious 3 lbs.*
> *Sunkist navel oranges 5 lbs. No dents.*
> *Pink grapefruit 4. Not the yellow.*
> *Chiquita bananas 4–6. No brown spots.*

Ruth bristled at having everything spelled out for her as if she needed direction, but she was still glad to be trusted with this task. Shirley wouldn't have asked her a couple of days ago.

She was even happier to notice the back of Carrie, with her telltale blonde hair and green scarf. Connecting with Carrie and others earlier that day had been a tonic for her loneliness, a surprising highlight for Ruth since her arrival in Philadelphia.

"Fancy meeting you here," Ruth said as she pushed her cart next to Carrie's.

Carrie smiled and motioned for Ruth to join her. They strolled to the apple bins and compared Golden Delicious green to McIntosh red. They heartily agreed the former worked better for cooking, the latter for noshing. They laughed about it.

Carrie leaned in. "Kind of absurd that your mother-in-law was there today. I think you handled it really well."

"Are you kidding? I was totally *farmisht*."

"You couldn't tell." Carrie chuckled. "You looked cool as a cucumber."

Ruth felt warmth and connection radiating from Carrie, and she welcomed it—plus, Shirley would appreciate her making friends. Wouldn't that show her mother-in-law that Ruth was committed to creating a good life in Wynnefield?

"Do you want to have coffee tomorrow?" Ruth asked as she examined the apples for bruises.

"That sounds nice, but I'm usually busy in the mornings."

Ruth was surprised at how disappointed this made her feel. "Just one cup. I can come to you, if that's easier. Lillian said we should become friends, didn't she? Friends have coffee."

"Can't argue with that." Carrie pulled a pencil and paper scrap out of her pocketbook. "Here's my address. Eli leaves around eight, so let's say eight thirty, just to be safe."

"Eight thirty it is." She felt as elated as she had the time she discovered a handwritten invitation to join AEPhi, the Jewish sorority at Barnard, slipped under her dormitory door.

Ruth entered through the Appelbaums' basement, and as she carried the grocery bags upstairs, she heard Shirley's voice in a one-sided conversation. Her mother-in-law was on the phone.

Ruth pressed her back against the butler pantry, with its wall of cabinets, and clutched the Penn Fruit bag tightly so the produce didn't fall and become bruised.

Snooping did not become Ruth. Still, it wasn't her fault she could hear Shirley, so Ruth wasn't eavesdropping. Not technically.

"Don't you worry," Shirley was saying. "I'll call you when it's over."

Worry about what? Hair appointments? When what was over? A bridge game?

Ruth caught herself. It wasn't right to prejudge, yet Ruth had distilled Shirley's life into just two categories. Home and social, and the required preparations for each. Shirley had mastered the housewife culture and seemed suited for it, as did Lillian and Harriet.

Ruth came from hardworking, passionate women. Though she'd never met her grandmothers, her great-aunt extolled that they'd been proud suffragettes. Ruth didn't remember her mother, but heard that she'd worked as a talented seamstress, specializing in elaborate dresses such as wedding gowns and theatrical costumes. The Singer her mother had used remained a fixture in their home, a reminder to her of Bess's work ethic and expertise.

Once she heard Shirley hang up, Ruth shook off the past and stepped into Shirley's sight line. "I'm back."

"Thank you, Ruth. The boys will be home in an hour. Why don't you set down the bag and go freshen up."

This wasn't a suggestion—more like an order—yet Shirley had barely glanced her way. Ruth deposited the bag on the counter. She wanted Shirley to examine the bounty, to see that Ruth could at least be trusted to shop correctly.

No thanks were forthcoming. Shirley unloaded the fruit into the Frigidaire so mindlessly, she might even have dented a precious Sunkist orange in the process.

Ruth combed and sprayed her hair and changed from her navy skirt and white blouse to her belted white cotton shirtwaist with printed apples across the full hem and buttoned cuffs. She dabbed a little rouge on her cheeks and applied lipstick. She spritzed perfume from the atomizer that had been left on her bureau. A floral scent of roses trailed after her.

She felt ready for the evening. *Almost.*

Instead of returning downstairs, she grabbed a bar exam study guide she'd stowed under the bed and cozied up on the padded window seat. Just a page or two.

The next time Ruth glanced at the clock, thirty minutes had passed. How would she explain her absence? Ruth popped off the window seat and tossed her book onto the bed. She ran down the steps, her skirt floating up and then back into place as she slowed near the landing.

Whenever she and Asher got their own home, it would be a place where she could not only run down the stairs, but could read quietly whenever she wanted to. A place to host dinner parties and impromptu picnics on the floor. Where all of that would be allowed, even welcomed. It would be a merging of the two of them, the best of their families rolled into one.

But it was too soon to press for that. They'd barely moved in and hadn't yet talked of leaving, only of saving enough money to make it possible.

Another reason to find work as a lawyer.

Maybe she and Asher could share an office. That way they could leave the bedroom for bedroom activities. She smiled at the thought.

But first, tonight's dinner.

Ruth had taken too long. A white tablecloth was already draped over the dining room table, and the pot roast aroma had filled the first floor, leaving just a hint of Shirley's trademark citrusy Jean Naté beneath.

She took a breath and stepped toward the kitchen. *Just jump in.* "Shall I set the table for four?" she asked.

Shirley stood at the stove; her lipstick had been reapplied to a crisp and clear apple red. "Thank you, yes. You look lovely, Ruth."

Ruth felt her cheeks flush and she tugged at her belt, basking in the compliment as she went for the dishes. She'd learned how to set a proper table long before arriving in Philadelphia. Her father was a printer, not a caveman, but prior to Ruth's first dinner with her in-laws in their home, she'd allowed her mother-in-law to show her a place setting as if this were something new.

Whom did it hurt?

In succession, she carried four dinner plates to the table, four bread plates, four salad plates, four water glasses, and all the useful, as well as pointless, silverware. She walked by her mother-in-law to retrieve the napkins from the pantry and the relish tray from the refrigerator.

"I'm sorry it took me so long to freshen up," Ruth said.

"It's okay. You'll get the hang of it," Shirley said. She pointed to the cabinet with her manicured nails. "The napkins on the left side of the cupboard have been ironed."

By the time the table was set and the water glasses filled, Asher and his father should be home. One of the benefits of Asher joining his father's firm, Appelbaum Accounting, was that he would always be home for dinner. "Except February through April," Shirley said. Ruth would be a tax widow.

"All done." Ruth walked into the kitchen and tied on an apron. Shirley, who was stirring something at the stove, looked up briefly and smiled but said nothing, magnifying the silence between them.

When Ruth cooked dinner in her and Asher's own kitchen, she was going to hum, maybe even sing. She broke through the quiet by clearing her throat.

Her mother-in-law turned to face her. "You looked like you were having a good time at Lillian Diamond's."

"Yes, and I saw Carrie at Penn Fruit. I'm going over to her place for coffee tomorrow."

Shirley's eyebrow raised and she seemed genuinely pleased. "Good for you. We'll defrost something for you to take." She didn't wait for an answer but returned to stirring the pot, letting steam waft into the air.

Ruth stepped back from the rising cloud of vapor that threatened to flatten her hair and melt her makeup. Her mother-in-law dumped a colander full of string beans into the boiling water. Then she turned back to Ruth and smiled. "That's a lovely shade of lipstick."

"Thank you. Do you want me to watch the string beans?" Ruth held up a giant spoon, indicating she could wear lipstick and stir string beans at the same time. The only thing she couldn't—wouldn't—do was call Shirley *Mom*. Ruth had only one mother, Bess Cohen.

Asher had explained to Shirley that, since Ruth's mother had died when she was four years old, asking Ruth to call her *Mom* was an insensitive request. Her mother-in-law's only acknowledgment of this perceived slight came via flinches and grimaces when Ruth called her Shirley in public.

The string beans danced in the rolling boil. Shirley puttered around the square kitchen. Ruth could sense her stealing glances her way. Was she not string-bean trustworthy?

Ruth pictured the book she had dropped on her bed. She wished the words and theories wound right down the steps and into her brain. She wished needing to study didn't mean she had to take time away from setting the table. Otherwise, how would she find those four hundred hours?

Push it out of your head.

Ruth shut off the burner when the string beans turned a bit more gray than green. Her shoulders pricked from an imaginary breeze. She didn't have to look to know what caused it; she could feel Shirley's eyes on her.

The front door squeaked open, then clicked closed. Thank goodness. Asher would help her.

Shirley removed her apron and crouched down to peek at dinner—and her reflection probably—in the window of the Hotpoint. She ran her fingers over her cheeks, perhaps appraising the smoothness of her skin. When Shirley stepped away, Ruth patted her hair and was glad she had applied lipstick. In that moment, the swipe of color on her lips made her feel . . . what? . . . *wifely*. Despite everything, the thought of Asher—happy to see her, and finding her pretty—set her heart aflutter.

She hadn't expected this, yet it felt great. Freshening up would now be part of Ruth's plan.

"We must have taken a wrong turn, son," Leon said. "Our wives have been replaced by movie stars."

Silly, loving compliments were Leon's shtick and made Ruth and Asher chuckle. Still, Shirley flushed as she swatted at him. It was almost endearing.

"Smells good, Shirl," Leon said, sniffing the air.

Though he was as warm as she was cool, there was no kiss or furtive glance between them. Ruth wondered if maybe that's how it was after thirty years of marriage. She only had her uncles and aunts to go by. Her family was demonstrative—ferociously hugging and planting loving kisses on cheeks and atop heads for anything from hello to a major milestone, like her college graduation.

Public affection didn't come naturally to any of the Appelbaums. The first time she'd kissed Asher on the cheek as they walked through Morningside Park, he blushed to purple and all but wiped it off, glancing around for gawkers, of which there were none. Ruth laughed and enjoyed mocking him as she chased him for another kiss. Asher let himself be caught, but only once he was sure there were no onlookers.

Ruth had failed to warn him about the effusiveness of her father and brothers. Upon their meeting a month later, each of the Cohen men wrapped Asher in a bear hug, which she was certain was as much about proving their strength as showing affection.

Asher, she was just as certain, still had nightmares from the encounter.

Over the years they'd been together—even before they'd married—Asher had relaxed a bit, loosened his tie on occasion, laughed louder and harder. He'd even pecked Ruth on the cheek in public.

Today he kissed Ruth full on the lips. This always made his mother raise her eyebrows.

"Welcome home," Ruth said. She longed to wrap her arms around his neck and whisper about her day. Hear about his in return. She wanted to sweep his hair from his forehead and plant a kiss hard and loud enough to leave a Pink Peony lip stain. But that brief kiss was already too much for this household.

"Hello, wife," Asher said with a smile. With her thumb, Ruth wiped away the smudge of lipstick on his lips—an intimate act she couldn't resist—though she wished she could have kissed it away. Ruth didn't need Lillian Diamond's etiquette class to tell her that would be taking her greeting too far.

Asher broke from Ruth and kissed his mother's cheek. Ruth could tell by Shirley's pursed lips that kissing her second had been a faux pas.

In the beginning of their stay in Wynnefield, Asher kissed his mother hello first, opened her car door first, inquired as to her well-being first. Ruth might not have known a lot about being married, or being an Appelbaum, but she did know his behavior was askew.

"Perhaps you'd like her to tuck you in," Ruth had said later.

Asher got the hint.

Once they were all seated at the dinner table, napkins in laps, relish tray passed, salads consumed, Shirley inhaled as if making space inside. "Tell the boys about your day, Ruth." Shirley passed the bowl of mashed potatoes to Leon. "Ruth went to Lillian Diamond's."

"For the etiquette lesson, that's right," Asher said. "How did it go?" His eyes implored Ruth to be gentle.

"It was fine," she said.

"Fine? There is nothing bad about bettering yourself." Shirley set the dish of pot roast back on the table with a thud. "Mark my words, Asher, the first time you entertain clients you'll be thanking your lucky stars for Lillian Diamond and her etiquette lessons."

"I guess," Asher said. "What did you think, Ru?"

Could they handle the truth? Ha.

"It was marvelous, wasn't it?" Shirley said.

"It was fine." Ruth's face grew hot.

Asher glanced at her. "Ma, let her be."

"What?" Shirley asked.

"Take it easy, Shirl," Leon said. "I expect it's hard to be the new girl."

"It doesn't have to be hard," Shirley said.

"I'll get used to it," Ruth said, not certain she believed that.

"Of course you will."

Ruth wasn't sure Shirley believed it either.

"Maybe etiquette classes aren't right for Ruth," Asher said, and she gave him a grateful look.

"You listen to me, Asher," Shirley said. "Just because you're the son of Appelbaum Accounting doesn't mean you don't need to worry about your image with your associates and your clients—you need to worry more. Leon?"

He didn't hesitate. "She's right. Those lessons are important. Ruth will be the one to get you through all the social functions during the gentile holidays and help you keep the names straight at Har Zion. Those are skills a person has to learn. Take it from one who knows."

Asher reached his arm around Ruth and squeezed her shoulder. Was he reassuring her or turning down her volume? Ruth couldn't read Asher's signals. That in itself unsettled her and wiped away what had been her growing appetite.

"Enough of that. Now tell us your actual impressions, Ruth," Shirley said. "'Fine' is a flimsy answer." She lifted a modest forkful of roast into her mouth.

Ruth thought she'd experienced intense scrutiny in law school. Those professors were sparrows next to hawklike Shirley Appelbaum.

"Everyone was very nice, but I expected there to be more students—there's only four of us." Ruth turned to Asher. "I'm having coffee at Carrie Blum's tomorrow. She said you met her husband on the golf course. Eli?"

"Eli Blum? Right. Nice guy. Seemed concerned his wife had trouble making friends."

That seemed odd. Carrie had been so easy to like.

Ruth looked at Shirley. "The girls were fascinated that you were the one who used to teach the classes. So was I. I felt foolish, because they thought I knew."

"Why would they think you knew?" Shirley said.

"Maybe they think you are my mother-in-law and so would have told me." Ruth stepped on Asher's foot under the table, hoping he would say something. "I would like to have known."

"This isn't about me."

"Oh, that's right," Asher said. "You did teach etiquette."

Leon nodded in assent.

"I didn't really discuss it with the children," Shirley said. "They were busy enough."

How busy could they be? Ruth and her brothers always listened to their dad's workday tales.

"Why did you stop teaching the lessons?" Ruth asked.

"Lillian's a natural."

Shirley didn't look up—or answer the question.

Ruth would get the answer another way. "Do you miss it?" she asked.

"I keep busy," Shirley said.

That wasn't what Ruth wanted to know. She was trying to understand Shirley. They were family now.

Asher looked toward the ceiling. "We had some of the girls stay here, right?" he asked.

"I can't believe you remember," Shirley said.

"What was that first girl's name? Cousin Louise!" Asher said. "God, I haven't thought of her in years. It's all coming back to me."

"Who's Cousin Louise?" Ruth asked.

"Dad and I painted the attic before she arrived so she could stay there. Whatever happened to her?"

"Nothing happened to her, son. She moved on," Leon snapped.

Ruth was startled by the reaction. What was the big deal?

"A lot of girls from out of town wanted etiquette lessons back then, and some of the wives had the girls stay with them. Louise took to you kids the moment she met you, and she fit right in." Shirley sounded genuinely fond of the girl.

"Wasn't she related to us? Cousin Louise?" Asher said.

"So she wasn't from Wynnefield?" Another surprise to Ruth.

"No and no," Shirley said. "She was the niece of a friend of a neighbor, I think from the suburbs."

"So we had a stranger staying here?" Asher sounded surprised.

"She wasn't a stranger—I just told you." Shirley seemed agitated by the quizzing.

"It's not important, Ash," Ruth said, smoothing things for her mother-in-law. "It was hospitable of your parents to let her live here."

"Yes, it was," Asher said.

"It was a favor, a long time ago," Shirley said. "Now that's your room."

The random knickknacks on the bureau. The perfume. The writing paper in the desk. Ruth had assumed they'd been placed in the room for her comfort. Maybe they'd been for Louise, whoever she was.

"Hey, it's a long time since I had my first piece of meat. I'll have another helping, Shirl." Leon always knew how to lighten a room.

Shirley shook her head at him with a sly, almost imperceptible glance, probably not meant to be intercepted, and passed the pot roast.

At bedtime, Ruth stood in front of the dresser and lifted her hairbrush from the silver mirrored tray. These beautiful discards she now used as her own had been used by some mysterious Cousin Louise. Of course, Shirley would have had them scrubbed and sanitized between guests, but it struck Ruth as odd that Shirley was so vague about where Cousin Louise had come from and why they called her *cousin* when she was not related to them.

Shirley wasn't vague about anything.

"We should have told them we were getting married," Ruth blurted. She had been holding it in all evening. "Your mother still holds that against me."

"I told her it was my idea," Asher said.

"But I'm the one who has to live up to her expectations—she thinks you're perfect."

Asher snuck up behind her, wrapped his arms around her middle, and kissed the back of her neck. "You'll see—going to these etiquette lessons will make all the difference in how she treats you. If she thinks you're helping my career along, she'll be happy. Just give it time."

Ruth whirled out of Asher's arms, away from the distraction of his kisses, and climbed into bed. She was irritated with her husband, which rarely happened. She hated keeping secrets. Not being able to tell the truth about her aspirations. Despite having somewhat enjoyed meeting the women at today's etiquette lesson, Ruth wanted Asher's support for *her* success.

"I want to start studying for the bar without hiding what I'm doing so I don't run out of time." She opened the book on her lap and flipped to a section on constitutional law.

"Please be patient. The more my mother likes you, the easier it will be. It's happening, Ru. Just be patient. Please." Asher took the book from her hand, set it on her nightstand, and kissed her cheek.

Her first impulse was to grab the book back, but he was so cute: the way he stood beside the bed, smiled at her, then kissed her nose, her lips. She was grateful she'd found this man. Grateful for how much she loved him.

She gave herself a mental shake. Cute or not, she had to be sure he saw her point. A good lawyer wins her arguments, and there was no time like the present to practice.

"Just because I want to be a lawyer doesn't mean I love you less. In fact, it means I love you more. I want to be the best version of myself, so you have the best me."

During her sophomore year at Barnard, Ruth had met Judge Jessica Polk, a Barnard alumna who addressed Ruth's class on social responsibility. "Compassion is worthless unless accompanied by a commitment to justice," the judge had said.

Ruth hadn't thought about justice before that day. Ever since, she'd thought of little else.

She'd snagged a summer job working for the judge, where she typed and filed. Ruth eagerly listened to and absorbed the judge's advocacy for poor women, children, and female workers. She had never realized that women lawyers might be more relatable than men in this situation. Two years—and two additional summer jobs—later, Judge Polk endorsed Ruth's application to Columbia Law.

Ruth understood the correlation between working hard and getting what she wanted.

But now Asher was kissing her—and she wanted that too. Very much.

"Ruth Appelbaum, I love every bit of you. The part that's going to pass the bar. The part that's going to become a lawyer." He snuggled beside her in bed. "Right now, we're newlyweds. Don't we have time for that too?"

Asher had a point. A little while ago she'd wondered about his parents, about their lack of affection, about whether couples stayed amorous over time. Here they were, the only moment in their lives when they'd be newlyweds. Did she want to sacrifice that?

No. What Ruth wanted included Asher *and* meaningful work *and* a peaceful home. She pulled up the blanket and nuzzled her husband.

Asher was right. This was the time to be newlyweds. She had to trust he'd support her career when she needed him to. Somehow, Ruth would get it all.

Chapter 8

RUTH

At twenty-five after eight in the morning, Ruth walked up the path of Carrie's brick house, called a *twin* in Philadelphia, though her brothers had called duplexes like these *double trouble* in New York. She carried a tinfoil-wrapped bundle carefully—Shirley's swirl *kamish* bread, another Philly term to get used to. Back home, they called it *mandel* bread. Ruth had to admit she did enjoy her mother-in-law's recipe, as the texture was softer than biscotti, perfect for dunking but wouldn't break your teeth. And who didn't love the taste of almonds?

Carrie waved from her side of the long, covered patio, where she sat on a chair, waiting. Steam rose from two cups on the small table beside her. Efficient. Prepared.

Ruth presented the small packet to Carrie.

"Thank you." Carrie's pink polished nails were as shiny as the silver corner she lifted. She peeked inside and sniffed. "Yum."

"I didn't bake them." In that moment, Ruth wished she had.

"I didn't grow the coffee beans." Carrie shooed away Ruth's unease and they laughed. Cream, sugar, napkins, and spoons were set on the table as well. "How do you like your coffee?"

"Thanks for this," Ruth said. "I take both." She fixed her coffee and sipped.

Carrie crossed her leg and held her cup at her knee, a casual yet elegant posture. "Thank you for suggesting this. I'm sorry I hesitated yesterday. I don't have many girlfriends."

"You're new here, like me. I'm sure you will in time. This is a good start, don't you think?" Ruth was hopeful. She wanted a friend—a confidante. Not a best friend, necessarily. Dotsie could never be replaced, and that would be asking a lot of any new relationship, but Carrie could be an *in addition to*, like a second-best friend. After meeting yesterday, and after just a few minutes sitting side by side this morning, Ruth felt secure and comfortable, like she and Carrie had developed a kinship almost at first sight.

"How do you like Wynnefield?" Ruth stirred her coffee with a piece of kamish bread and bit the softened cookie in half, enjoying the extra sweetness it gave to the meeting.

"It's nice," Carrie said. "This part of town is a little fancier than I'm used to, but Eli wanted one of the bigger twins. He thought it looked better with his position."

"What do *you* think?" Ruth asked.

Carrie seemed surprised by the question. "I'm sure it's lovely, I didn't mean to suggest otherwise." Again, she shooed away any concerns with a flick of her wrist.

"Do you miss Atlantic City?" Ruth asked.

"Not really. Well, I miss my parents. And my sister. And my nieces. And the ocean and the boardwalk, even the sand." Carrie broke into a wide grin followed by a droopy frown. "I guess I miss it more than I realized. But talking about it would hurt Eli's feelings."

"How so?"

"Eli wants our life to be enough for me. If I talk about home, he thinks I'm not happy here."

"And are you? Unhappy, I mean." Ruth quickly added, "Sometimes I miss New York. That doesn't mean I don't like it here. I even missed my privacy when we first got married."

Maybe that wasn't entirely true, but Carrie's silence prompted the fib.

"Oh my God, me too," Carrie said. "So what do you miss about New York?"

How much should she divulge?

"I miss school," Ruth said. "I miss the opportunities."

"You're smart, I can tell," Carrie said. "The way you spoke at Lillian's yesterday. You'll do great here. You'll make your own opportunities."

Ruth was used to hearing she was smart. She hoped the rest was true. "You're smart too—you went to nursing school."

"Any girl with a little sense and a roll of bandages can be a nurse."

Ruth was startled by the self-effacing comment. "You don't believe that!"

Carrie sank into the chair as if it were too big for her. "No, not really," she said.

"You mustn't say things like that; it's unfair to you. Becoming a nurse is a wonderful accomplishment. Don't let anyone tell you otherwise."

"It's easier that way." Something in Carrie's voice hinted at sadness. "You wouldn't understand."

Carrie suddenly looked older—worn, even—which troubled Ruth.

"Maybe I would. You can trust me."

Carrie shrugged.

Ruth would have to take the first step. "What if I tell you a secret first?" When Carrie raised an eyebrow, Ruth continued. "I went to law school. Actually, graduated at the top of my class."

"What?" Carrie was frowning. "And Asher knows?"

Ruth chuckled. As if she could have kept law school a secret. "Of *course* he knows. When we met, I was already planning to go to law school. But my in-laws don't know I'm going to take the bar exam and look for a job."

When Carrie nodded, Ruth knew she had a trusted ally.

"Do you think Asher will allow it?"

Allow it? Permission had never been part of their relationship. "Of course. Asher's all for it."

Carrie seemed to ponder something. "No offense," she said. "Who hires lady lawyers?"

"I guess I'll find out."

The girls shared an easy laugh.

"Please don't say anything," Ruth said. Though she trusted Carrie, theirs was a friendship in its infancy. She felt the air pressure release from the balloon that was inside her. "We can't let his parents find out before we tell them ourselves. That would be a disaster that may never be forgiven."

Carrie drew an imaginary X on her chest. "Cross my heart and hope to die."

Chapter 9

LILLIAN

Alone in the living room the day after the lessons, Lillian stepped into a warm ray of midafternoon sun. Normally she'd welcome its glow, but she wasn't feeling quite right. Her fingers were icy. She closed her eyes against the glare, and colorful sparkles danced on the inside of her eyelids like personal fireworks. Her heart pattered and she struggled to catch her breath, once, twice, three times.

She opened her eyes and reached into the end table drawer for a cigarette, certain to calm her nerves. Sunny was in the kitchen preparing dinner, so Lillian had a few moments to pull herself together. She might as well use them. She grabbed her lighter.

This smoking habit had snuck up on her about ten years ago, when it started seeming less of a choice and more of a necessity. What bothered Lillian more than the cigarettes was the fact she used them when she was flustered or anxious. Like now.

Was this how it had started for her mother?

No. Shortness of breath and occasional unease were not the same as a nervous breakdown. She was no longer going to push her feelings aside. This new resolve made her anxious.

Besides, she was worrying for nothing. The first etiquette lesson had gone well, even if she had to ask Shirley to go home. It wasn't so much that Lillian had wanted Shirley to leave, as that Lillian had wanted to handle the etiquette class on her own.

Well, maybe that was the same thing.

No wonder Lillian had been flustered. She'd been selfish and insulted her teacher, guide, and friend. Shirley didn't deserve to be pushed aside. Over the years Shirley had helped Lillian. It would have made her happy had Lillian included her.

Then there were Ruth's novel ideas complicating things. According to Ruth, it wasn't Lillian's job to make anyone happy but Lillian.

What an absurd concept.

Lillian had no idea what would bring her happiness.

She clicked her jaw and exhaled smoke rings, a brash, private talent usually reserved for teenagers congregating on street corners or diner waitresses on break. Ruth's words floated inside the last circle. "We could do some real good." It was the only time Lillian had heard her old thoughts aloud, out of someone else's mouth. She couldn't shake them.

"I'm going out front," Lillian yelled to Sunny.

On the patio, Lillian lit another cigarette, inhaled, and filled her lungs. With the cigarette dangling, and the ashes growing, she raced against the precarious embers and picked up a few golden leaves that had floated to the front path. Keeping busy was the best distraction from troubling thoughts.

Sunny pushed open the front door, carrying a glass of iced tea. After two decades, Lillian still checked behind Sunny, half hoping her mother would be trailing behind her friend, carrying sugar cubes and a long spoon, even though Lillian had stopped using sugar after high school. The other half of her was relieved it was only Sunny with saccharin tablets. No mother.

Sunny was short and round. Anna had been tall and slim. But when Lillian allowed herself to think of her mother, she did so most easily in the wake of Sunny's expressions, her laugh, her walk. This proximity to her mother's oldest friend afforded Lillian closeness to her memories—and distance from guilt.

Would Lillian have been happier or more content if she'd visited her mother more than twice a year since she was eleven? She wouldn't venture a guess, but she was certain life would have been different if her mother hadn't been committed to Byberry.

Sunny set the iced tea on the wrought-iron patio table decorated with scrolls and flowers that always reminded Lillian of her childhood birthday cakes. Sunny wiped the condensation on the glass with her hand and dried her hand on the corner of her apron. "Send the girls in when they get home—I made cookies," she said.

"They could do with half a grapefruit."

Sunny disagreed. "On the first day of school, they deserve to be happy."

Happy? Why did that word keep coming up today? Lillian had assumed her daughters *were* happy, but truthfully, she'd never thought to ask.

The gate creaked open and Pammie and Penny sauntered through, shoulder to shoulder, giggling. This connection was what Lillian had wanted for her daughters ever since Penny was born. Lillian had woken up after the delivery to the words she'd hoped for: "It's a girl." Sometimes, though, Lillian felt like an outsider in her own family, which she reasoned was absurd. She was their mother, not a third sibling. Still, an absence of understanding between them saddened her.

"What's so funny?" Lillian asked.

Her daughters quieted and turned, almost in unison. As Pammie stood straighter, her medium-brown hair splayed onto Penny's shoulder, almost replacing Penny's darker locks. At these moments, the two years between her girls dissolved. They looked so much alike, so much like Peter, with easily tanned skin, long noses, and wide, light-brown eyes with long, dark lashes. Passersby often mistook them for twins.

"What's wrong?" Penny asked.

"Who died?" Pammie snapped.

Penny elbowed her big sister in the ribs.

"Ouch!" Pammie rubbed her side. "What? The last time Mother met us outside after school, Great-Aunt Minnie had died."

Lillian hadn't realized her behavior patterns were so predictable. "No one died. I just wanted to talk to you."

"Are we in trouble?"

"Speak for yourself," Penny said. "I haven't done anything." Here's where the sisterly camaraderie ended. Pammie rolled her eyes.

Lillian chose to ignore the bait. They were good girls, even if Pammie sometimes snuck off to see her boyfriend instead of studying at the library. If that girl studied as much as she claimed, she'd earn higher grades—maybe be class valedictorian.

"No one's in trouble," Lillian said. "I just want to ask you a question. Sit down."

Pammie and Penny set their books on the table, pulled out chairs, and sat. They avoided eye contact with Lillian, and it hurt that her daughters felt discomfort at the notion of talking to their mother. Lillian forced three little coughs. "I want to know if you're happy."

"Happy with what?" Penny asked.

"Your lives, I guess." Lillian wasn't sure. She'd never been asked about her overall happiness and wasn't certain she'd ever contemplated it. But recently she'd noticed an apprehension in her days; she didn't know what she was waiting for, just that it felt more akin to waiting for a punishment than a present.

Perhaps that vague anxiety she'd felt had been unhappiness. She'd only ever been asked if she'd been happy with a specific dress, or pair of shoes, or the outcome of a dinner party. She wanted more for her daughters.

"Are you happy with your plans for the future?" She should include Peter in this discussion. "Daddy and I wouldn't want you to have any regrets." Probably. Lillian figured Peter had never considered this. He likely assumed his daughters would be content to marry well. What if they wouldn't?

"I have a cool boyfriend, and I'm sure Donald is going to propose after graduation," Pammie said. She did look pleased with this, yet her sister looked stricken.

Lillian remained silent, though it took some effort. The child was fourteen!

"Did you and Daddy change your minds about sending me to teachers college?" Penny asked.

"No, of course not," Lillian said. Penny had wanted to be a teacher since her first day in kindergarten. Peter didn't view this job as an impediment to marriage, but as a placeholder.

"Then I'm happy," Penny said.

Lillian looked at her older daughter. "Pammie, would you like to go to college?"

"Why?"

"To be educated, silly," Penny said.

"You don't need to be educated to be a housewife, smarty-pants," Pammie said.

Lillian cringed. Apparently Pammie viewed Lillian's own bachelor's degree in history as a waste. It's true—the girls had never seen her use that education, and she rarely even mentioned it.

"You can meet smart boys in college," Penny said.

Sunny stepped outside, grasping two Coke bottles and carrying a plate of cookies. She set it all on the table and pulled a bottle opener from her apron pocket.

"I don't know who you're talking about, but I'd say smart boys are good," Sunny said.

Pammie and Penny bit into their cookies, chewed with their mouths closed, and nodded. "We're talking about college boys," Penny said after she'd swallowed.

Sunny smiled as if she'd been in on the conversation all along. "My husband went to college. I always thought it made him sophisticated." She swept at her shoulders as if she'd somehow been accumulating dust. "There's a lot more to being smart than what you learn in class." Sunny opened the Cokes and handed one to each girl. "The people you meet, the discussions. It can make someone—anyone—much more interesting. That's what I think it did for Harold."

In gratitude, to show solidarity, Lillian grabbed a cookie. She didn't really care if Pammie went to college, but she was driven, in that moment, to make her daughter understand that she *could* go to college. Lillian's daughters—and even the Diamond Girls—should be sharp when it came to their own needs.

That's what had prompted Lillian's stress this afternoon. Once Ruth had brought up the idea of self-awareness, it had embedded itself in her. Maybe that was what bothered Shirley too.

"Ask Sunny," Pammie said.

"Ask me what?"

"Mother asked us if we were happy," Penny said.

Lillian's limbs prickled, feeling suddenly covered in frost to the point of frozen. She'd never have asked Sunny if she were happy. A lifetime of connection, years of employment, and Lillian had no idea what Sunny's answer might be.

Was happiness that far outside of Lillian's perception?

"That was considerate of her, don't you think?" Sunny asked.

Pammie shrugged. "Are you happy?"

Lillian wished she could whisk her words into the bin along with the invisible dust from Sunny's shoulders. Yet, at the same time, she needed to hear the answer. Lillian also wanted to know whether her mother had been happy until her father died. And yet at age thirty-five, she was somehow reluctant to find out. To ask the questions.

Sunny sat on the step and inhaled a big gulp of air, as if resigned to her fate or ready to deliver a monologue. "Well, let me see, I had a husband I loved, and now my son is a teacher. I own my house, and I do good work that I enjoy. I'm glad to wake up every day. I guess I'd say I'm happy."

Not a bad list. Lillian finally understood. Happiness differed for each person. There was no universal measurement. Darn. If happiness was something she wanted, she'd have to figure out what it meant. To her.

"You're happy even though you cook and clean for your job?" Pammie said.

Lillian gasped at her child's impudence. "Pammie, apologize."

With a wave of her hands, Sunny shooed away Lillian's embarrassment. "It's not what you do, but why you do it," she said to Pammie. "I work for your parents for the same reason I worked for your grandparents. Your grandma Anna was one of my dearest friends. I promised her I'd watch over your mother. And I have."

Their penchant for fiction had tethered them through high school, even though Sunny's family had moved to a duplex on the far side of Fairmount Park.

The wrong side, according to Anna's mother.

The girls drifted apart when Anna married Percy and moved to Overbrook Park. But years later, when Sunny showed up on Anna's doorstep as a young widow in need of a job, Anna hired her on the spot, their bond unbroken. A friendship restored.

"But our grandmother doesn't know you're here," Penny said. The girls only knew that their grandmother lived in a hospital.

"*I* know I'm here," Sunny said. "That's what's important. Anna still matters to me."

Lillian shuddered at the revelation that this job was meaningful to Sunny not because of her, but because of her mother. Lillian didn't know if Sunny needed the money—certainly the wages weren't enough to live on, even in Parkside—or if she was tethered to a long-ago promise.

The housekeeper gathered up the empty Coke bottles. "Your grandmother loved being a housewife and mother. It takes a special person to put everyone else first, to plan meals and activities, to stick to a budget, to be a nurse and a teacher for a grown man, and to raise children."

"You hear that?" Pammie was almost shouting at Lillian. "I'm like you and I'm like my grandmother."

God forbid. A crashing wave of emotions—from grateful to embarrassed, from devastated to elated—ran from the tips of Lillian's toes to the pit lodged in her throat, like she was watching an episode of *The Edge of Night.*

"I want you to be like yourself, Pammie." This was Lillian's most maternal thought ever, and it came out sounding a bit stern.

"Mother, don't be silly. Who else could I be? I'm happy that I'm going to have a wonderful husband. You and Daddy said you would buy me and my future husband a house as a wedding gift. What on earth do I not have to be happy about? I know you went to college, but Donald's not going, so why would I want to?"

For the first time, Lillian regarded Pammie as if she were a bird in a gilded cage who'd never been shown she had the ability to fly. Yet Penny had learned on her own, no credit to Lillian.

She had not equipped either of her daughters with the tools to gauge their own happiness, or even their own capacity for happiness. No wonder Lillian couldn't assess her own.

"Yoo-hoo. Anyone there?" a woman's voice called from beyond the hedges.

Sunny descended the path to greet the visitor. Duke, a black-and-white springer spaniel, pulled five-year-old Susie Gold into the front yard. The dog went right to Pammie, who tousled the furry neighbor and scratched behind his ears. Mrs. Gold followed close behind her daughter. "I'm sorry," she said, "Duke has a mind of his own and no manners."

"That's okay," Pammie said. "He knows I love him, don't you, boy?" She nuzzled the dog.

"We were hoping you'd say that. Mr. Gold and Susie and I have a bar mitzvah in Wilmington in two weeks, and we'll be gone all day. We were wondering if you might like to dog-sit. You'd have to walk and feed him, but otherwise . . ."

"Yes!" Pammie looked at Lillian, the teen's eyes wide with joy and anticipation. "I mean, may I?"

Pammie had always loved animals, but Peter had said no to any pets, except for the occasional carnival goldfish won with the accurate toss of a ping-pong ball. Armed with only water from the spigot and fish food flakes, Pammie had kept her last fish alive for three months. She'd spent hours reading about goldfish, staring through the bowl.

Peter had said she was obsessed. Thinking about it now, Lillian would reclassify that as happy. Yes, happiness was an individual thing.

Though a goldfish wasn't a dog, maybe this was a nudge. Pammie could work in a pet store or for a vet. She could study animal husbandry. Funny word. Lillian was steps ahead and decided to play devil's advocate. "Taking care of a dog is different from playing with one," she said to disguise her enthusiasm.

"It really would be a big help," Mrs. Gold said. "I hate the idea of a kennel, but we'll have to leave early in the morning, and we won't be home until after dinner. How about if we do a trial run?"

Pammie nodded, with no attempt to hide her excitement. "When?"

Mrs. Gold glanced at her watch. "Tonight? Penny can come too—keep Susie out of our hair."

Lillian's daughters pleaded with clasped hands. Could she really say no to them?

"And they can stay for dinner if that's okay. To learn Duke's routine."

"Are you sure?" Lillian asked, to be polite. She and Peter would have an evening to themselves.

Susie smiled and nodded. "We're sure."

Duke barked as if adding his vote, and they all laughed.

Mrs. Gold grabbed Duke's leash, and Susie followed as they walked off across the lawn, waving at Sunny on the steps before she disappeared inside the front door. The girls changed into play clothes, which is how Lillian still thought of their casual after-school and weekend wear, even though Pammie and Penny had been too old to play for quite a while.

Lillian longed momentarily for the days of baby dolls, matching smocked dresses, and patent leather Mary Janes. She had taught her daughters about being a housewife because they'd watched her dote on Peter, watched how she single-mindedly focused on him and ignored herself.

It was time to rethink her daughters' roles before it was too late.

Perhaps it was time to rethink her own and the example she set.

Lillian kissed the girls on their heads. "Mind your manners, but have fun."

"What will you and Daddy do without us?" Penny asked.

Lillian pecked her younger daughter's cheek for good measure. "We'll think of something."

Once the girls had walked past the hedges, Lillian turned to Sunny. "Why don't you go home early? I'll finish up dinner."

Sunny's mouth dropped open in faux protest while her hands began slipping on her sweater, buttoning it from the bottom up. "First a dog, now dinner. What has gotten into you?"

Lillian knew exactly what had gotten into her, and there'd be more of it before the night was up.

Chapter 10

LILLIAN

Lillian stood alone in her kitchen and pulled the red ties of her apron around in front of her and tied them in a large, symmetrical bow. She smoothed the fabric, her hand sliding over the blue rickrack trim and momentarily reaching into the empty patch pocket. The apron was a ploy, of course, as much as her Halloween hobo costume had been at age nine, complete with charcoal beard and a bindle fashioned from one of her father's work shirts.

Lillian never cooked a morsel.

She peeked at the supper Sunny had prepared, as she had throughout her marriage.

These days, Sunny cleaned the Diamonds' house twice a week and cooked on the third day, filling the Frigidaire with delicious family-style meals Lillian couldn't have replicated if she'd tried—meatballs, meat loaf, brisket, pot roast, roast chicken. Baked chicken, chicken fricassee, chicken pot pie, cutlets, noodle soup.

And all the side dishes.

So long as supper was on the table, Peter didn't care who had prepared it.

He never questioned Lillian's happiness either, which could make tonight a challenge.

In college, there was work to be done by the motivated. Lillian, intent on making the world a better place, had stuffed envelopes until midnight for a local councilman, instead of attending parties. Her only complaint was the occasional paper cut, and she was content, knowing she was making a difference.

The exhilaration that accompanied her contribution had prompted her to volunteer for the National Foundation for Infantile Paralysis when a friend asked her to. How exciting to work alongside the activist and fellow Philadelphian Miriam Moore, who was researching a polio vaccine. Lillian had agreed that as a healthy young lady, it was her duty to help.

Then, that junior-year summer, she'd seen Peter Diamond again on the Margate City beach. In his own way, Peter had adored Lillian since the moment they'd met on the same beach when she was fourteen, Pammie's age. He had been a skinny fifteen-year-old and his family lived in their oceanfront house every summer, not a walk-up rental two blocks from the beach, like Lillian's family.

She was living with her grandparents back then, and she'd wanted nothing more than to be plucked out of Overbrook Park, to be married, and to have a husband provide a life for her. That was all her grandparents wanted for her.

Peter excelled as a provider even then—when his teenage care consisted of buying ice cream from a vendor and giving her carefully chosen seashells, instead of this five-bedroom house with an iron gate.

When she saw him again, he had grown from a scrawny boy into a handsome senior at Penn. Thoughts of Peter replaced thoughts of polio and politics. Dreams of a lush life with a handsome husband eclipsed those of a meaningful life.

Not that she was a bad person now, Lillian rationalized. She'd just been diverted from her ideals. Anyway, they'd found a vaccine, and she'd made sure her girls had gotten it. In a small way, Lillian had contributed. Now her efforts were focused closer to home.

The closest she'd gotten to doing anything useful in years was stuffing envelopes for birthday party invitations. And teaching young wives to be better wives.

It didn't have to stay that way. Did she have the chutzpah to tell Peter she was yearning for something more? That she might have found it in her musings this afternoon? Not in giving etiquette lessons, but in turning the Diamond Girls' efforts to something more worthwhile? Perhaps she could rekindle her own ideals in them.

What magnitude of work could the Diamond Girls do if Lillian taught them social responsibility along with manners? Yes, this was a noble thing to do. They could come up with a common purpose that would put their talents to real use.

Besides, who was stopping her?

The savory aroma of pot roast filled the kitchen. Cooking had always eluded Lillian, likely because her grandmother had coddled her by keeping her out of the kitchen. Her grandparents' aim was to ensure that she would marry a man rich enough to hire a cook. Yet Lillian excelled at identifying ingredients and spices by nose and taste. As Lillian closed her eyes and Sunny's chicken soup burned her tongue, she could name every ingredient that flavored the fowl: sweet onions, earthy carrot, spicy garlic, herbaceous parsley and dill, and a squeeze of lemon—her grandmother's secret ingredient, now Sunny's too.

Lillian hadn't known it at the time, but this parlor trick—identifying the ingredients without the knowledge of how to cook the dish— would become a metaphor for her life. To sample instead of to savor. To decorate rather than create.

She shone when it came to reheating and presenting meals, displaying them beautifully atop lettuce leaves and lavishly garnished with gherkins, radish roses, carrot swirls, and olives speared with ruffled toothpicks. No one noticed that Lillian's meals had been cooked by someone else.

The young wives she'd hosted would doubtless be home preparing their own creative and romantic dinners, fawning over husbands, paying themselves no mind. They were lovely girls, and they would soon have perfect manners. Lillian thought about her daughters and realized with a shock that those were not the lives she wanted her daughters to emulate.

No. And she still had time to change things for them.

Lillian envied the Diamond Girls in a way. They brimmed with hope, love, naïveté. Reality had yet to set in. Even the older one, Irene, had a fresh and capricious essence uncommon in the other twenty-eight-year-olds Lillian knew. Irene would be the eager beaver of the group. There was always one who pulled more than their weight. Though with four children—four!—there likely wouldn't be many elegant dinners in that house.

Carrie was the quiet one. Fresh-faced. The sweet peacekeeper. A bit of a loner with much to learn. Lillian always had to watch the quiet ones. Those were the girls most likely to surprise her with their under-the-breath swearing or inappropriate familiarity with the racy section of Saks Fifth Avenue's lingerie department.

Friendship was the secret bonus of these lessons—and truly the best part, though Lillian never advertised that. Husbands wouldn't authorize their wives' participation if they didn't see a visible benefit to the family. At least, Peter wouldn't have. But if friendships were a side effect of learning how to be a better wife, so much the better.

She considered Ruth. The girl was unsettling, somehow. Her college education still so fresh.

Her own college friends had fallen away when Lillian married Peter. Her grandparents were delighted. After all, they'd agreed to her going to college primarily so that she would get an M.R.S.—a Mrs. in front of her name. That hadn't been Lillian's goal initially—she'd wanted to get away from home, to mix with other young people and study. She had hoped to find some kind of vocation.

That vocation had morphed into her becoming an ideal wife, one whose suburban friends would watch a toddler while she napped, or while she organized and alphabetized bookshelves and spice racks. They would offer honest criticism about the shape of her behind in a particular outfit too, if she asked, though she had never needed to worry about that. She kept herself trim for Peter.

She had thought, when she became engaged, that being a wife and, later, mother would be enough to make her happy.

She understood the value of female camaraderie but, with the exception of Shirley's friendship, Lillian considered herself a collector of acquaintances.

Lillian had never been trained to perform kitchen chores and found them tiresome—one of the many ways she differed from the mother she remembered. So she cut the radish roses and carrot swirls she'd seen in the *Ladies' Home Journal* with care as she considered Harriet—apparently the most natural housewife Lillian had met. Ready to devote her time and energy to her future home life and husband's career before she even said "I do." Harriet would learn soon enough that being a perfect wife wasn't as easy as it looked.

Maybe Lillian should tell her to get out while she could.

She slapped a hand over her open mouth as if she'd spoken aloud. What an awful thing to even contemplate! Misgivings were so unappetizing. Even if they were true.

If only someone had told her that housewifery and motherhood could be not only dull, but stressful. So much time and effort devoted to beauty and the social mandates. Not even charge accounts around town and Sunny doing the cleaning and cooking could make up for the nagging feeling that something was missing.

Lillian sure didn't cover that in her lessons.

To the neighbors, to family, even to wives who should have known better, life fit Lillian like a beautiful dress all the girls envied—but it itched to high heaven underneath.

No one fathomed, not even Peter, that for several years, on nights prior to hosting his family or colleagues, Lillian writhed in sweat, lying awake, sometimes unable to catch her breath. The pressure of helping Peter remember his manners, his meetings, his clients' names. Always choosing the right ties and pocket squares for him, in addition to her own wardrobe of flattering, appropriate dresses and separates, required the endurance of an Olympian. It was fun at first. Soon, though, a chore.

She was obliged to learn about current events and politics in case Peter hadn't brushed up—which she'd thought initially would be an interesting challenge. It turned out to be pointless because no one talked to her about those topics. Nor did they discuss these subjects in her presence. News and politics were not appropriate subjects for a woman.

Yet Peter was impressive as he repeated the topics and names he'd co-opted from Lillian. These victories were now void of joy. And that void was growing.

As a student—even as a newlywed—she had believed she could do anything. She opened the oven and basted the roast. See? She'd learned to cook a little, but that was no remedy for boredom. So why not talk to Peter about her dissatisfaction—her need for an interest beyond the home and family? Take the leap?

Lillian would work Peter with a strategy he'd never see coming. The girls were gone. She'd surprise him with midweek romance. No man could resist that.

She set the dining room table for two, displaying her mastery over china, crystal, silver, and taper candles. She placed them atop a crisp ivory linen tablecloth and folded the matching napkins into swans for a bit of whimsy.

Lillian took one last look and straightened the tablecloth. She'd set their places catty-corner from one another—Peter's at the head of the table and hers to his left, instead of at opposite ends of the table as was customary.

She sighed. There was a good chance Peter wouldn't notice any of it. Not the dress, the meal, the intimate place settings, or the upcoming greeting. And the opportunity to broach the subject she needed to talk about would disappear.

An elegant weeknight display for just the two of them was an experiment. Heck, an experiment was exciting, wasn't it? She and Peter followed a rigid schedule, and this kind of dinner wasn't on it.

Lillian believed that shining within the confines of routine made her reliable, and that's what people wanted and expected. But perhaps that only made her boring. Still, changes in the family's practice were not hers to make. Were they?

She could talk to Peter—he was a kind man, if a bit predictable. Wasn't that what she loved about him? Sound. Reliable. Like her. Or was that boring too? Surely not!

She banished negative thoughts. Peter was a fine husband. A good man, if unimaginative. She wasn't frightened of him, but of her own potential disappointment. What if she expressed her desire for change and Peter didn't heed it?

He ran a company he loved. His perfect wife was at his beck and call. If he was pleased by tonight's romantic surprise, she would address her other thoughts. They would discuss her admittedly vague ideas for finding a worthwhile project, and he could help her sort through them. Clarifying her thoughts was almost impossible on her own. They just kept spinning around her head.

She smoothed the tablecloth one last time.

If only Ruth hadn't riled her so, showing Lillian that she should have tried to do more, volunteer more, contribute more to the world at large—all within the status quo—without forgoing any of Peter's expectations.

Well-behaved wives didn't make a mess out of an already tidy life.

Then again, perhaps well-behaved was overrated.

Her thoughts roiled in her head until a momentary thrill buzzed through her—the manifestation of this imagined agency, this pretend control—only to give way to doubts again.

The popular idea that behind every successful man was a strong woman implied that the woman was pulling some strings. But her jurisdiction over Peter was never certain, like that time Lillian had deliberately withheld the name of his client's wife, when of course she knew it. He'd looked at her, his eyebrows raised, and she'd shrugged. She'd wanted him to pull the name out of his own hat instead of hers, or at least to acknowledge at some point how much he needed her.

Peter had simply turned around, flashed his bright smile, and told the woman she looked taller, younger, thinner, and smarter than the last time they'd met. Lillian knew darn well he hadn't a clue what her name was. Later, Lillian's tiny rebellion had dissolved into guilt—she had let him down, and in doing so, had let herself down. Meanwhile, Peter gave every appearance of remaining completely at ease and oblivious to her mutiny.

She shouldn't have done it. She loved Peter. She didn't want to give him less; she wanted to give herself more. Like Ruth had said.

The front door closed with a bang. Lillian whisked off the apron. Hausfrau was not the look she was going for. It wasn't a mistake, though, to wear her royal blue shirtwaist with its tight matching belt and coordinating kitten heels. Peter had always loved her in blue.

In her imagination, Lillian leafed through her notebook of happy housewife, husband, and home tips. Then she checked her reflection in the mirror hung over the server and smoothed her hair. She undid one button and adjusted the collar and neckline to reveal a peek of cleavage, no more. But certainly no less. It mattered how she looked when her husband walked through the door. Isn't that what she taught in her lessons? How was a man supposed to care if his wife didn't?

She'd dressed up for many occasions and gotten merely a nod. She tried to release her anticipation and focus instead on how good she had it in prestigious Wynnefield, on this street, as mistress of this house. She pressed her lips together and headed for the foyer.

Why did her thoughts continue to center on what was missing instead of what she possessed?

It wasn't Peter's fault that she felt shortchanged. He bestowed on her a generous personal allowance, in addition to household funds. And she had to admit, she liked that. Lillian paid Sunny's bus fare out of her own money and often added an extra dollar or two to her pay envelope every Friday. Her mother would have approved. Lillian tipped generously, treated her friends in restaurants, purchased thoughtful gifts. She socked away the rest for a rainy day that might never come.

Lillian smiled wide and sucked in her stomach as she stepped into the foyer. *No Peter.*

He'd had time to hang up his trench coat and fold his suit jacket over the banister. He must surely have noticed the dining room table. Anyone who stood in the circular entryway was treated to a glimpse of the traditional walnut table flanked by ten chairs, all set under a Baccarat crystal six-arm chandelier that had belonged to Peter's parents.

Before getting to know the Diamonds, Lillian had assumed most Jews emigrated in the early 1900s, as her father had as a baby, but Peter's family had been in Philadelphia since the 1870s. They had made their fortune in textiles.

Lillian stepped toward voices coming from the den, the room she'd redecorated recently with a modern flair and palette of greens and golds.

Peter had already flipped on the television.

"I thought I heard you," she said. Gracious greetings. *Do as you teach.* "Welcome home. Did you have a nice day?"

Peter turned from the evening news and smiled. His eyes crinkled closed. They made a striking couple, he with sandy hair and brown eyes, naturally tanned skin, and a physique envied by men and adored by women. Lillian's coloring provided a perfect foil for his. Dark hair, blue eyes, pale skin. They were balanced, symmetrical, appealing.

"It was fine," Peter said. "Where are the girls?"

I know you like me in blue. Thank you for noticing.

"The girls are watching Susie Gold and their dog for a few hours."

"On a school night?"

"Practice for a dog-sitting job—I couldn't say no. The girls adore Susie and the dog."

"Lillian, I don't want a dog."

She ignored this. Now was not the time for that conversation. "I made pot roast. I thought we'd eat in the dining room tonight."

His face softened. "It smells good, Lil. I'll be in in a minute."

"I'll get it on the table." She felt brightened by his flicker of enthusiasm.

Peter looked at her, eyebrows raised. "Did you say pot roast?"

So he *was* listening—at least to the menu.

"There are only four girls in my class this time."

"Well, that should be easy then."

"I wouldn't say it was easy, Peter. We're planning to finish all the lessons before the High Holidays."

"They're learning to host parties and wear the right clothes and use the right forks, aren't they? It can't be that difficult."

"What's that supposed to mean?" Lillian seethed. "You make it sound like that's all we wives do. We manage households and our husbands' careers, raise children, prepare meals, arrange the social calendar."

But wasn't he right? Wasn't that exactly what the etiquette classes taught them?

"It's not supposed to mean anything. Don't get testy."

"Right."

Peter saw her as a housewife, mother, and etiquette teacher because that was all she'd let him see. How could she show more when she wasn't sure of anything else?

"Lil, why don't you fix me a plate and bring it to me in here. I want to watch the news." Peter seemed suddenly drawn.

"But . . ."

"But what?" Peter smiled—he did that when he wanted to smooth things over. Perhaps he wasn't in the mood for discussions. Perhaps he didn't want to ruffle his wife's feathers. "I'll be careful. I won't drop a morsel on your new sofa."

"But I set the table."

Peter scrunched up his nose and stared at Lillian as if she were speaking a foreign language. Pointless to argue.

"It'll just take a minute." She gritted her teeth so that he didn't discern her growing agitation. Peter never recognized the effort she expended daily to keep him at ease.

"Oh, and one more thing," he said.

"Yes?" Lillian softened and sweetened her tone.

"Today's the first day of school. The girls should be here, not out. I want to have family dinners on weeknights, like always. In the kitchen. The dining room is for company."

Lillian's insides tumbled off a cliff. Her effort had been for naught. Her eyes burned as she choked back tears.

"Call and tell the girls not to dawdle when the Golds get home," Peter said. "And to make sure they wash off the dog stink."

Once Lillian had set up Peter's TV tray, adjusted the volume on the television, refilled his tonic water, and delivered his food plate, she returned to the kitchen and stared at the pots and pans crowding the sink. Had he even noticed that she wasn't eating with him? No matter, she'd lost her appetite for pot roast—and for Peter. Maybe the work of scouring pots would rinse her mind. No, she'd either wash the pots later or soak them overnight and scrub them before Sunny arrived at ten tomorrow.

Peter thought Sunny arrived at nine every Monday, Thursday, and Friday.

Lillian found the secret especially sweet in the moment. Every week, she had three stolen morning hours alone, before Sunny arrived, and many hours to herself on other days. She would have liked more. She always wanted what she didn't have.

Lillian threw on the beige cardigan hanging off the back of a kitchen chair, grabbed her pocketbook, and walked out the side door, closing it with a timid click.

The weather was chillier than she'd anticipated, but Lillian had to get out of there. Needed one cigarette to calm her. She willed her discontent away like puffs of smoke.

Peter's indifference more than saddened Lillian. It also frustrated and angered her. Two unattractive emotions, her grandmother had often said.

She ground out her cigarette with one foot and shimmied like she was doing the twist. The truth was as ugly as the crushed, lipstick-stained Marlboro butt.

Discontent choked her far more than any smoke could. Lillian did nothing meaningful. Nothing that reached beyond Wynnefield or reflected her own interests. She had so much and did so little. Sure, Peter donated to charities and Lillian organized the Purim Carnival each year, but what had happened to the girl who stuffed envelopes, who stayed up all night chatting about a better world? What had she done to create one since then?

She had once wanted to be a teacher, then a librarian—both ways to help educate the next generation. Perfect for women with degrees. You could even keep working if you were married. Not if you became pregnant, of course. She didn't remember releasing those dreams. They had been replaced by fulfilling the expectations of marriage and family.

What was wrong with her? She must be a horrible person. Selfish, self-involved, ungrateful. Except she wasn't.

So she must be misguided, off course. Was it too late to find her way?

Women were happy with much less than Lillian had. She knew that. She opened her mouth, but instead of words of self-consolation, an understanding struck her.

Doing all the right things for a husband and family didn't guarantee happiness.

Lillian wished someone had warned her.

As manners maven of Wynnefield, and as someone known to be a distinguished housewife, simply because she was married to a Diamond, Lillian had kept the door on her inappropriate thoughts bolted. Now they swelled and exploded as if ignited by dynamite.

She should tell her students. She should tell her daughters.

Here was her new raison d'être—she must use her God-given voice. If she could do it without blowing up her life.

A few hours later, her daughters were home and in bed, though Lillian knew Penny would read by flashlight until she conked out.

She poured herself a gin and tonic at the rolling glass bar cart Peter had purchased to add a little pizzazz when hosting parties. So unnecessary. Their house screamed opulence—wasn't that pizzazz with extra pizzazz?

The cocktail warmed her inside and out.

She had a good life. Did she really have to rock the boat now?

Maybe she had overreacted to the failed attempt at time alone with Peter. She'd spent years waiting for the perfect feelings to arrive, and now it might be too late to do anything about it.

Perhaps she could tell Peter she wanted to get a job at the synagogue or a library (not retail, for heaven's sake). Not for the money, but to keep busy. She wouldn't change *her family*, just her habits.

She could explain that the right job, when she found it, would add meaning to her days. That she'd be contributing something to society, even if in a small way. The girls weren't babies anymore, and she could use her wages for gifts, lunches out. They were affluent. People knew she didn't *need* to work, so no one would question why she wanted to work. Peter would let her work because he loved her.

A man's inattention was not the world's worst offense.

Peter stepped into the living room and stood next to Lillian. He fixed himself another Tom Collins—his weeknight choice—as she sipped her drink and stared straight ahead, daring herself to be honest with her husband.

"I have that meeting tomorrow," he said. "I have to get everyone on board with this new plan for imported fabric."

Peter leaned over a little too far—from drink, perhaps—and Lillian slyly propped him up, kept him from falling. There was something satisfying about being a pillar. "George Sullivan will be there, right?"

"He'd better be. He's the holdout."

Lillian took a step away from him. "Peter—you need to cut him some slack. His mother died in May, so if he is there tomorrow, say something nice and go easy on him. By the way, Jay Martin's son just went off to Princeton, so remember to congratulate him. Are you catering lunch?"

Peter said nothing. This was like pulling teeth.

"If you are, remind Wendy that he's allergic to shellfish and that Barry Jones has an intolerance for dairy. Eat so they eat. You know they spend more on a full stomach. We'll have a light dinner—I'll get cold cuts from Manny's. I'll see what Sunny has prepared and I'll adjust the menu." Lillian could alter meals; that wasn't cooking. "Oh, and don't make their drinks too strong, so they can sign the contract."

Peter ran his hand through his hair, betraying his nervousness.

What was he worried about? They'd done this dozens of times before. Lillian prepped Peter on personal details and reminders before a meeting, a dinner, a party. He had never asked her to do it—it was just what she did.

What would happen if she stopped?

Lillian imagined the neighborhood's social hierarchy melting like a sandcastle at high tide. That would leave her with a shapeless mess—or the job of rebuilding.

The next morning, with a good night's sleep behind her, Lillian tried to embrace the status quo. Life always looked brighter in the light of day. She eyed Peter in his custom-tailored blue suit, smoothed his collar, and kissed his cheek, being careful not to leave a lipstick smear.

"For luck."

He smiled, planted a kiss on her forehead, and departed. Peter's affection was as inconsistent as his golf swing. If only it received half as much time and attention.

With Peter gone and the girls already in school, Lillian was all alone. Face it, she mused, she was alone even when Peter was there. She poured a quiet cup of coffee and drank it black, staring out the kitchen window, across the driveway, into the morning gray of her neighbor's kitchen. She didn't know Faye well, only that she was in her early fifties, was married to a cardiologist, and puttered around her kitchen wearing a robe each morning, whereas Lillian dressed before heading downstairs every day.

Faye's robe did not reveal whether she wore flannel or lace beneath, just as the faraway cup she raised to her lips did not reveal its contents. Coffee with cream, milk, sugar, saccharin? Tea with lemon? Honey? Wine? Something more potent?

Unintentionally, her mysterious neighbor revealed a truth about Lillian. Lillian knew only part of her own story as well.

She'd married a nice Jewish boy, moved to the best neighborhood, and lived in one of the nicest homes. She had the most modern appliances, a maid three days a week, two healthy, beautiful daughters, and at last count, a secret stash of almost seven hundred dollars, which she didn't need, in a Maxwell House tin hidden in the back of her closet. Her life was everything she'd ever wanted. More, even.

Why was it, then, that Lillian felt like she was suffocating?

Chapter 11

RUTH

Before dawn, Ruth sat up in bed, but Asher didn't budge, not even a bit. She gazed at his sweet, sleeping face. A soft whistle came from his nose, and his dark, loose curls fell on his forehead. When his eyelids fluttered, Ruth decided his lashes were longer and darker than any gentleman's had a right to be. She found these noises and unconscious movements endearing—alluring even. She kissed his forehead like a mother might kiss a sleeping baby—the way she'd seen her manly brothers kiss their sons, besotted.

Love in all its iterations sparked behaviors and decisions some would call erratic, out of character, foolish. Ruth had moved away from her home, her family, and her friends because she wanted this love—this marriage. Maybe she'd have to wait a little while before she could be honest with everyone about her career, but that would happen soon.

Careful not to wake her husband, Ruth slipped out of bed and tucked the covers around him. She dipped her hand into the nightstand drawer where she stored the study guide. Just because she was waiting to share her plans with her in-laws didn't mean she couldn't prepare. After all, she had 399 more hours to go. At least. Flashlight in hand, Ruth snuggled onto the window seat and flipped through the study guide.

When the sun rose, so did Asher. He propped himself up on one elbow and beamed at her. That gaze sent pleasurable shivers up her spine. Ruth was overwhelmed, overcome. She never wanted to disappoint him—she couldn't imagine a day when she'd tire of his admiration. He crooked his finger and Ruth hurried back to bed.

She could wait just a little longer to chisel down her 399 hours.

Later that morning, Ruth sat outside on the front steps. The sun was shining through high, white clouds, and crisp air swirled around her as she balanced a sealed Tupperware container on her knees. She looked up to the sky, closed her eyes, and let the sun spread its warmth over her. In a few minutes, her new friends would be here to pick her up.

She plucked a leaf that had escaped the lawn cleanup from the boxwood. She tucked it into her pocketbook and vowed to press it inside one of her thickest novels, a memento from her first autumn as a married woman.

She fiddled with the Tupperware container on her lap, which Shirley had carefully packed herself after Ruth told her that Irene had invited the girls on a picnic this morning. "Irene said not to bring anything."

"Of course she did. That's what she's supposed to say."

Shirley pulled an in-case-of-emergency tinfoil-wrapped apple cake from the freezer and set it on the counter to thaw. An hour later, she sliced up half of it and set the pieces into the milky white rectangle that now sat on Ruth's lap, rescuing her from housewife humiliation.

When a dark-green sedan drove up the street and idled in front, Ruth leaned forward and waved. Irene waved back from the driver's seat. As Ruth stood, her stomach flipped with nerves. The unexpected emotion gave her pause. Did she care whether these women liked and accepted her? Yes, yes, she did. Until now, she hadn't looked for approval from anyone. The realization that she wanted it threw her.

A child's hand waved from the backseat window of the car. That hand was attached to Irene's youngest—Harry or Hedy, something with an H and Y, or was it a T? Ruth should have paid better attention, like she normally did.

The short brown curls she could see from her vantage point on the steps gave no clue as to whether they belonged to a boy or girl. Her gut didn't tell her, or even hint. Ruth didn't mind children, but she was partial to adults. She trusted a maternal instinct would surface when she needed one.

She hoped so. She didn't have a mother, but weren't these things a given? Didn't every woman want a child of her own?

Whoever that little person was, bouncing in the back seat, he or she was joining the picnic. Perhaps Ruth, Harriet, and Carrie were the interlopers. However it happened, she had been delighted to be included in the outing—it proved she was trying. She'd maximize this chance to get to know the Diamond Girls plus one.

Ruth slid into the front seat of the sedan and closed the door with a thud. She drummed the Tupperware lid. "Apple cake. Enough for us all, courtesy of my mother-in-law."

"Carrie's not joining us, so we'll have more than enough. I figured you'd bring something."

Shirley had been right. Irene had expected Ruth to bring something, and Ruth herself hadn't known. She had so much to learn. That's what she disliked about beginnings—they could be awkward as heck. She would have to jump in and get over that part quickly. Ruth turned around and waved. The toddler waved back.

"Well, hello there. I'm Ruth."

"Say hello, Heidi." Irene peered into the rearview mirror. The child said nothing. "Sit back, darling, here we go."

Ruth whirled to the front as the car moved forward. *Heidi.* "Thanks for thinking of this," Ruth said. "And for making it happen."

Irene chuckled. "Stephen knows I can't be cooped up in the house all week, so sometimes his brother picks him up on the way to work and then I have the car. That way he knows I'll also go to the supermarket and run all the errands. I was out at Penn Fruit as soon as the other kids were off to school."

Ruth's in-laws had given Asher a car for college graduation, but since he went to work with his dad every day, he left his car at home for his mother to drive. Growing up in New York, with its excellent mass transit, Ruth rarely needed to drive and, while she could, she never was that comfortable with it. Walking or riding buses was easy in Wynnefield, but she really should drive more often to get comfortable with operating the car, and to improve her skills.

She made a mental note. Though it still wouldn't have occurred to her to ask the girls to a picnic.

"It's thoughtful of him to leave you the car."

"Not really." Irene's tone was more matter-of-fact than malicious. "Then I don't make him babysit on Saturday and I can run errands all by myself."

"Oh." How different were their lives! Ruth had so much to get used to. What would the rules be for a working woman lawyer when she and Asher had kids? Would she be able to relate to these women and their household errands then?

Irene stopped the car in front of a large stone duplex and beeped the horn. "Today was selfish of me. I like to get the baby out in the fresh air in the fall, and I thought it would be a good way for us all to chat in a more casual setting. You know, no big house and fancy-pants rules."

Harriet emerged from the front door.

"Although I think *she* likes those," Irene said.

Harriet bopped down the steps, toward the car, and right into the back seat. "Hi, girls, and hello to you, little lady," she chirped, addressing Heidi, who bounced in reply. Ruth hadn't elicited that kind of reaction.

"So, what did you ladies bring?" Harriet said. "I brought the fall fruit salad from *Ladies' Home Journal*. Are we picking up Carrie next?"

Irene shook her head. "Said something about a pot roast in the oven and that there will be other chances to get together and have some fun."

Pot roast? Ruth had had coffee with Carrie yesterday and she hadn't mentioned she wouldn't be coming on the picnic. Ruth felt a modicum of disappointment. Maybe they weren't as close as she'd assumed.

Minutes after they arrived at the park, Irene covered the picnic table with a red-and-white gingham cloth and set out a stack of egg-salad sandwiches on rye, wrapped in waxed paper. Pickles, coleslaw, a can of chips, chocolate chip cookies, Harriet's fruit salad, Ruth's apple cake, and a thermos accompanied them. Irene draped towels on the attached benches, placed silverware into one empty coffee can and matching gingham napkins in another, then unwrapped red flowers—marigolds, maybe? Ruth was not a flower expert. Harriet arranged the blooms in a small mason jar. Anyone who passed by would have thought the girls were throwing a party, not a picnic. A week ago, she would have found this silly; today she found it charming.

When Ruth was a child, her father had joined her for tea parties as readily as chess matches. Would he have considered his time with Ruth to be babysitting if her mother had lived? She had no idea how involved her father had been as a parent while her mother had been alive. Had he regarded his time with her brothers as a chore? Ruth couldn't fathom it. All she knew was that her father tended to all the siblings' needs. She missed the idea of a mother more than she missed a mother she didn't remember. But watching Irene with Heidi, Ruth wondered what picnics would have been like with her mother and what kind of a picnic she would have with her own children one day.

Heidi ran to the sandbox after two bites of her sandwich.

"She's so sweet," Harriet said.

"She is by far my easiest baby," Irene said. "No colic. Slept through the night at four weeks, potty-trained by her first birthday. And to think she was an oops." Irene blushed. "Eat," she said, pushing a sandwich toward Ruth, seemingly embarrassed by what she'd called her child.

Ruth bit into the sandwich straight away, afraid Irene would fly it like an airplane into the hangar if she didn't do it on her own. "Delicious."

Harriet touched Irene's arm, not willing to let that "oops" faux pas go. "You should say *surprise*."

"Except nothing's a surprise with your fourth. My body said, 'Here we go again, Reen.'"

They all chuckled.

"You're so funny," Ruth said.

"In high school, I was voted most likely to become a comedienne."

Another kindred spirit with career aspirations? Ruth felt a jolt of hope that she wasn't the only one. "Is that what you wanted to be?"

"What do you mean?" Harriet asked before Irene could answer.

Ruth ignored her. "After high school, what were your dreams? Your plans? Did you want to be a comedienne?"

Irene's laugh was hearty, as if the notion were outlandish, but it had a sweet undertone that wouldn't offend Ruth. "Oh no, I wanted *this*. To marry Stephen, have babies, plan picnics."

Barnard offered a top-notch, girls-only college education, yet even there, Ruth had met girls in high pursuit of the so-called M.R.S. degree, conferred upon those women who graduated not with a job, but with immediate prospects of becoming a wife. Her freshman roommate had snagged a Columbia junior and dropped out over Christmas break. Ruth had met Asher in college, but she would have never married him before graduating. She was different.

"You're very good at all this. So much attention to every detail," Ruth said, and she meant it. "But was there anything else you wanted to do?" How could this be enough for Irene? For anyone?

"Do you mean four kids and a husband isn't enough?" Harriet's words were clipped, her tone accusatory, as if Ruth had been caught crushing dreams instead of encouraging them.

"I was just wondering; I didn't mean anything by it. Some girls do want jobs or careers, you know."

Harriet crossed her arms. "I've met girls like you—all the independent women nonsense. Why would I want to take care of myself if there is someone who will take care of me? That's not for me. I quit Wanamaker's the day after we got engaged. Scotty wouldn't have it any other way."

"Then why did you go to college?" Ruth asked.

"To find the best husband," Harriet said.

"I wouldn't have time for a job, let alone a career," Irene said, smoothing things over. "When the kids are in bed and the housework is done, I do the books for the stores."

"You do the bookkeeping? For all your stores?" Ruth asked.

Irene nodded. "I've always been good with numbers."

Exasperation caused Ruth to stand. "Irene, that's a job."

"No, I'm just helping my family. What Stephen does all day with the stores is work. He's earning money to provide for us, and he's landing corporate business now. It's stressful to schmooze and sell appliances all day, knowing you have a wife and four kids depending on you."

"He wouldn't have the life he has without you," Ruth said. Why didn't the girls see themselves as integral parts of the lives they lived? They had no one to teach them. Again Ruth was grateful for her upbringing.

"Of course not. Men can't have babies." Harriet's tone partly suggested that Ruth was her intellectual inferior. It also suggested that Ruth was as annoying as a buzzing fly that needed to be swatted.

Ruth didn't want to ruin the festive day by pushing too far. She sat down and rested her head in her hands. Everything went back to husbands and babies for these girls.

Irene seemed to notice Ruth's discomfort. "What about you, Ruth?" she asked.

Ruth looked up, at first silenced by caution, then drawn by the lure of turning things over, giving them a surprise. She glanced at Irene, then at Harriet, then back to Irene. No. She wasn't quite ready to divulge anything, so she simply shrugged. Best not to make more waves right now.

"You're all talk, Ruth," Harriet said. "You pretend to be so different from us. You're the same."

"Nothing wrong with that," Irene said.

Except Ruth wasn't the same. She didn't believe she was better, but her ambitions set her apart. "Okay. I'll tell you, but you can't say a word."

"I promise," Irene said.

Harriet snorted. "Sure. What's the big secret? How important can it be?"

Ruth had to defend herself. "I'm a lawyer," she snapped. "I graduated from Columbia Law School in New York. I was one of seventeen girls with two hundred forty men."

Irene's mouth hung open. Even Harriet had been stunned silent.

"I still have to pass the bar exam. I have to find four hundred hours to study." She couldn't believe she had to explain it all. At Columbia they got her. They were even proud of her.

"And then?" Harriet asked.

"She has a law degree. That's quite an accomplishment," Irene said.

"Your husband let you do this?"

"It's not a matter of anyone letting you, is it, Ruth?" Irene asked with a smile. "We all want different things, Harriet."

"I'm guessing you've always wanted to be a wife and mother," Ruth said.

Harriet nodded.

"I've wanted to be a lawyer since sophomore year." But she wasn't one, was she? She had to pass the bar. She couldn't give up. She wouldn't give up.

Harriet shrugged as if she couldn't be bothered to understand.

"I think you'd be good at whatever you set your mind to," Irene said, watching Heidi.

The compliment might have been maternalistic, as if a pat answer for one of her children. Still, Ruth held on to the kind words and tucked them inside. Then she gathered the napkins, stored the silverware, and stacked the empty bowls, as if her actions would help to pad Irene's kindness and keep it safe.

"My cousin married a mean drunk who hit her and threatened her," Irene said. "Nobody helped her. I bet she could've used a lady lawyer."

Harriet widened her eyes. "That doesn't happen in Wynnefield."

"Is your cousin okay?" Ruth asked, as she pictured the women she knew in New York. She hoped Irene's cousin hadn't experienced the same fate, but she didn't ask for details. Maybe after she passed the bar, she would investigate more.

"Her brothers ran him off, threatened to knock him off if he ever came back. No one's seen hide nor hair of him in sixteen years. Personally, I think he's at the bottom of the Schuylkill River."

"You're not serious," Harriet said.

"I'll never tell," Irene said, a gleam in her eye.

"What if it wasn't true?" Harriet sneered.

"Why would someone lie?" Ruth asked.

"You tell me—apparently you're the expert," Harriet said.

Ruth turned away. It had been risky revealing her graduate degree in front of Harriet, but she had tired of life's charades since coming to Wynnefield. "Not an expert. Just educated in that field." She wouldn't mention the work she'd done for the MWLAS, and the abused women she'd met there. Better to downplay things for now. She had shocked the girls enough for one day. She didn't feel like making any more excuses for her life.

She and Harriet loaded the picnic supplies into the car while Irene walked to the sand pit and scooped up Heidi.

How much could Ruth trust these women? Maybe she should have kept her mouth shut about law school and the bar exam. What if Harriet blurted out about the bar exam to Shirley the next time they were all at Lillian's? Ruth wanted to be the one to tell Shirley. She didn't want to make a choice between Asher and her career. Getting a law degree was a lot more complicated for a dutiful wife than a standard bachelor's that your husband could mention in social circles as one of your many accomplishments. If Shirley found out, she'd want to know more. She would be concerned about Ruth's plan of taking the bar. After all, no one took the bar if they didn't plan to practice law. What a can of worms that would open if her in-laws heard about it before she and Asher told them! The elopement was hurtful enough. She didn't want Shirley to feel left out of another big decision in her life.

"Harriet," Ruth said in a sweet, but not patronizing, tone. "I know you don't agree with me about law school, but my in-laws don't know about my graduate degree yet, so please don't say anything. My mother-in-law is so old-fashioned."

"So much for not needing permission."

Ruth bristled. Harriet had a point, but her situation was only temporary. To keep the peace in the family.

Like a good lawyer, Ruth would not allow herself to be goaded into verbal sparring by the likes of Harriet. "We're just waiting a little longer to tell them. Until I settle in."

"Whatever you say. I don't stick my nose in where it doesn't belong."

Ruth banked on that being the truth.

Chapter 12

LILLIAN

Monday morning, after Lillian had given Peter two reminders and one complaint, he left her the car and called a taxi to drive him to the office.

She backed the car out of the driveway. Etiquette lesson two had always been her favorite and, even with bobbing doubts, she didn't want to be late. Today they would be shopping at Saks, and she'd be helping the girls choose new outfits to fit their bodies and this lifestyle, helping them see themselves as sophisticated, even grown up.

That had seemed like a worthy cause in the past. Yet Lillian had started to redefine "worthy cause." Her focus had changed from how the girls looked or behaved, to how they *felt*.

So what if she was conflicted about her life? Today wasn't about her. There was nothing wrong with teaching the girls how to look better. Then she recognized the judgment that thought implied and cringed.

Well, if she was honest, her assessment might be judgmental, but it was the truth. The girls could look more refined, maybe except for Harriet, who seemed to have a knack for current fashion and trends.

Lillian didn't blame the girls for their shortcomings—not the way she blamed herself for her own—and wasn't that what mattered?

She stubbed her cigarette in the ashtray, eased the Lincoln onto City Line Avenue, and left her doubts on the road behind her as the car turned onto Fifty-Fourth Street.

Lillian pulled into a parking spot. She checked her face in the rearview mirror and reached into her purse for her compact. She dabbed powder on her nose and chin to ward off any shine. After snapping the compact shut and tossing it back into her purse, she was ready. Threading her arm through the bag's leather handles, she stepped out onto the asphalt. The routine comforted her as much as a bowl of chicken noodle soup.

She strode toward the revolving door, head high, adrenaline coursing and buzzing through her, adding a rhythmic bounce to her step. She felt solidly in her element. The stores Lillian frequented—Saks, Gimbels, Lord & Taylor—the places she was seen without Peter, were where she floated with an effortless, even autonomous, grace.

Lillian flushed with shame at the thought, deepening the color of her cheeks.

Because without Peter's charge account, she couldn't buy dresses, coats, cosmetics, or the latest fragrance. She gazed at the ground; the stones embedded in it sparkled, cheering her slightly. Surprising—the places she could find beauty if she just looked.

Did it irk her that her social status and shopping privilege—while generous—were reliant on Peter's permission and the money he provided? Or was she grateful?

She couldn't deny it. Both were true. Lillian was unaccustomed to being wishy-washy. It didn't feel good, and she strode toward the shopping experience to keep on solid ground.

Ten minutes later, Ruth, Irene, Harriet, and Carrie were gathered beside Lillian, surrounded by the cloud of new perfumes and the crystal atomizers of the fragrance department. The rich, sweet scent of jasmine assaulted Lillian, sending her into the past. Every night before Lillian's father had walked in the door from work, her mother had patted her neck and wrists with Dorothy Gray Jasmin Bouquet eau de cologne while sitting at her vanity table.

"It's his favorite," her mother had said between dabs. As a girl, Lillian had giggled and swooned at the idea of her mother's romantic gesture. Did her father ever acknowledge it? Comment on the scent? She didn't remember.

As an adult, Lillian fixated on the choice of that perfume. Had it also been her mother's favorite fragrance? The question vexed her.

"Is Shirley coming?" Harriet asked Ruth. Lillian knew the answer.

"Not today," Ruth said. "On Mondays she plays mah-jongg."

And, of course, the meat loaf. Lillian knew Shirley also made meat loaf on Mondays. Her friend and mentor was a creature of habit, set in her ways. Inflexible. Maybe it was a good thing this shopping day was on Monday. She didn't need Shirley to check up on either her or Ruth.

Lillian turned to the counter girls. "Thank you, ladies. We'll be sure to stop back."

She smiled and waved, always polite to anyone who assisted her, whether at the San Marco with Peter on a Saturday night for surf and turf, or at Gimbels when she wanted a *yontif* dress for the holidays. And at Woolworth's when she needed a new pencil.

Lillian might have been a stickler for propriety, but not at the cost of kindness. She'd learned that from her mother, who'd worked in the layette department of Gimbels. The precious employee discount enabled Anna Feldman to afford the store's holiday clothes for her daughter. Ill-behaved and snooty customers often insulted her mother and sullied her pleasant disposition. On more than one occasion, Lillian had heard her mother cry in the bathroom at home. Little Lilly couldn't imagine any other cause, so she blamed the cruel, rude characters in her mother's Gimbels stories.

Still, department stores brought primarily happy thoughts of her mother. Her father, a broad, brawny navy yard mechanic who used coarse language, had wanted her mother to quit the job. Anna was a realist who knew better—they couldn't afford it.

She never complained about working, but Lillian had sensed the subject was a springboard for the arguments between her parents. She and Peter had no such touchy topics because Lillian always behaved as was expected and kept dissenting opinions to herself.

As a child, her parents had argued and fought. That likely meant Anna had spoken up and her husband didn't like what she'd said. Gran had said Anna liked to stir the pot. It was more of an accusation than a statement.

Maybe a little pot-stirring was harmless. *Wasn't it?* Lillian flinched, not sure she believed it. Look what had happened to her mother. Her mother had gone away.

The Diamond Girls—Lillian quite liked the epithet—fell into line behind her. They trailed through furs, leather goods, and children's wear, their heels and soles clicking in time with hers, like a trail of tap dancers.

Lillian held open the door to the women's dressing room, ushering the girls into its soft lighting and sense of privacy. "Take a seat and we'll get started." She motioned to the gold, fabric-covered slipper chairs set in a semicircle around the fitting platform flanked by a three-way mirror. Lillian stood next to the platform.

"Since today is our second lesson, I'd like to hear how you incorporated the gracious greetings of lesson one into your lives. Then we'll move on to why we're all here."

Irene raised her hand.

"We took your advice. The girls and I had a picnic." Irene smiled widely.

The comment surprised Lillian. She didn't recall advising a picnic, but it showed initiative.

"To get to know one another better," Ruth said, as if sensing her confusion.

Lillian nodded. "Lovely."

Ruth took this as her cue to add, "I applied lipstick before Asher came home."

Harriet rolled her eyes.

"Good for you, Ruth." A little lipstick never hurt. A girl should always look good, no matter what.

Seemingly pleased by Lillian's compliment, Ruth demonstrated a skill from lesson one—conversation. "We missed you, Carrie."

Irene nodded.

"You missed quite the gabfest," Harriet said.

"You missed quite the spread," said Ruth.

"Friday is laundry day."

The girls looked at each other.

"I thought it was pot roast day," Irene said.

"It's probably both," Harriet said.

"I did my laundry while the pot roast was in the oven. Eli likes efficiency."

"What do you like?" Ruth asked.

An awkward silence filled the space between the girls as they waited. Lillian waited for Carrie's answer too.

Nothing. Lillian understood the background of that uncomfortable nothing.

Housewives were often "of one mind" with their husbands. She had always been that way with Peter. Housewives like Ruth—who had their own answers even after saying *I do*—were exceptions, not the rule.

Prickles of envy skittered across Lillian's heart. She wished she'd had the forethought and chutzpah to tell Peter what she really wanted at the beginning of their marriage.

"I'd like to hear more about the picnic, Irene," Lillian said, not really caring about the event. She wanted to shift Ruth's attention from Carrie, who had taken to fidgeting in her seat. This was shopping day.

"We went to Fairmount Park with my little Heidi," Irene said. "I made egg salad sandwiches. I add olives, you know. Gives it a little zip."

"It was delicious," Ruth said.

"Sounds perfect," Carrie said, calmer now that the attention had been deflected away from her.

Irene beamed a bright smile, a natural hostess. Compliments did wonders.

Before Lillian had to listen to the entire picnic menu, and perhaps the dullness of all the accompanying recipes, God spared them by sending the salesgirl through the door. Lillian immediately recognized Maryanne, with her ginger beehive and button cloisonné earrings. A matching pendant settled at the base of her throat. In a black dress—Lillian thought the color a tad morose for daytime—Maryanne slinked like a cat to her side. At least Maryanne didn't have to wear a smock like the other salesgirls, so Lillian sucked back any opinions about her color choice.

Maryanne Deering must have been at least six feet tall—taller than Peter—with willowy limbs. What accounted for her gracefulness had probably made her a lanky girl. She was too tall to appeal to most men. Her eyes were small, but bright green and symmetrical, bordering an unremarkable nose. She was neither pretty nor homely. She wore a thin gold band on her left ring finger, which could have been a ruse to ward off unwanted advances, though her being married wouldn't necessarily dissuade a scoundrel. Lillian didn't know if Maryanne had to work, if she wanted to work, or where she lived. All Lillian knew was that the salesgirl had assembled some of Lillian's favorite outfits. The woman had talent.

She suddenly looked at Maryanne anew. Lillian had readily undressed to her girdle and brassiere in front of Maryanne on previous shopping expeditions, but she had never thought to ask the woman about herself. Was she the same type of aloof customer who had upset her mother? Lillian's chest tightened with guilt.

"Hello, ladies, I'm Maryanne. I'm here to help, acquire additional sizes, zip zippers, coordinate accessories, and assist our seamstress if there are alterations. Then I'll call you at home when your selections are ready for pickup, or I can arrange delivery. As I get to know each of you this morning, I may pull other selections from the floor. Just to give you options."

"We have a surprise for you girls." Lillian clapped her hands to reinforce Maryanne's words. "Maryanne and I have chosen outfits for you in advance, according to the measurements you provided." Lillian could let the girls peruse Saks on their own, or perhaps in pairs. But she had Maryanne to consider. This would ensure that Maryanne received her commission, which Lillian assumed she needed the way her mother had.

Indecipherable chatter broke out between Irene and Harriet. Lillian distributed a personalized fashion collage that she had created for each girl. "These give suggestions for styles and the color palette that will suit you. You can use them for reference when choosing outfits for your body shape and complexion."

It didn't hurt to look one's best, did it? Perhaps the point was for the girls to please themselves first, their husbands second. Feeling good had always contributed to looking good, but Lillian had never given her own opinion as much clout as Peter's.

"I've been helping housewives build their wardrobes for fifteen years," Maryanne said. "I worked at John Wanamaker's until 1958, and I've been here since. I know this inventory like the back of my hand."

"She does, girls. You can trust Maryanne completely." Lillian held Maryanne in high esteem, not only for her taste, but for her knowledge and honesty. Lillian hadn't realized until then that women had likely regarded her mother in the same way.

Even Ruth was pointing at the collages, whispering, and nodding.

"I assume you obtained your husband's permission to put your choice on his account, or that you have a check already signed," Lillian said. She had her secret coffee can, but it was filled with Peter's cash. She'd have to earn money, open a bank account, and write checks to have any real power. But she'd need Peter's permission to do her own banking—so where was the autonomy?

"I'm window-shopping," Carrie said. "I hope that's okay. I like Eli to choose my clothes."

"He does a good job," Irene said.

"Don't fix what isn't broken," Harriet said. "I'm sure if my fiancé doesn't approve, I'll return it, even though I have my father's check today."

Ruth scoffed. Lillian gave her a hard look. That's the way things were. Men—husbands—controlled the money.

"Whatever arrangements or understandings you have are fine," Lillian said. "I'm here to make things easier for you, not harder."

"We thought we'd have a little fun," Maryanne said. "There are three suggested ensembles already in the dressing rooms for each of you. We're going to play a little game."

"To help you learn to choose appropriately for different occasions," Lillian said, "we'd like you to select the right outfit for meeting your friends for lunch at Wanamaker's in Center City. Not that there's anything wrong with a picnic. We just weren't thinking of a park when we chose the clothes."

"A park is more realistic for me," Irene said, a nod to her four kids.

"Well, yes. I imagine it might be." Lillian had always made time for lunch. Weekend babysitters had been a sacred part of their lives. Peter had insisted, though it seemed like a luxury. "Just play along for today. Or imagine their father agrees to babysit."

Irene cackled. "That's a hoot."

Ruth opened her mouth, then shut it as if she'd changed her mind, then opened it again. "My father raised me and my brothers. I don't think he ever called it babysitting."

Lillian had never thought to call it anything else.

"That's different," Harriet said. "If you'd had a mother, things would have been different."

Lillian knew Harriet meant that for Ruth. But it also hit Lillian hard. Either way it wasn't very nice.

Ruth crossed her arms and drew her shoulders up to her ears.

"Harriet!" Carrie said. "Shush!"

"That's neither here nor there," Lillian said. "The matter at hand is the clothes, not anyone's family configuration." Somehow what should have been a fun day had gotten derailed. She was determined to get it back on track. "Find your dressing rooms, girls."

"Take your time," Maryanne said, lightening the mood. "Ask one another's opinions and talk it over. Remember, two heads are better than one."

"We chose the outfits with the latest styles in mind," Lillian said. Boldness coursed through her as she remembered her younger self, bopping around a dressing room, unaware of the social ramification of her choices.

Those were the days. Oblivious. And yet they'd given her a freedom that had drained away over the passing years.

"If there is an item or outfit not to your taste, speak up. Maryanne will find an alternative. You won't hurt our feelings." There. Lillian was offering them choices.

She wished someone had said that to her when she was in her twenties; instead, she mimicked others and adopted a popular style. Now the girls she taught adopted *her* style. She had always felt flattered, as if they'd been presented with options and they'd chosen her.

"I'm all for independent thought," Ruth said. "But I don't know fashion at all."

In this moment, the leader wanted to follow. Lillian found that intriguing.

"You can trust our choices and still listen to your intuition. It's important to look good but also to feel good in your clothes. That's how you'll find your own style." This wisdom emerged from deep inside Lillian, erupted from a corner she hadn't known existed. She wanted to jot down her own words so she didn't forget them.

The girls scattered into the dressing rooms marked with their names. Maryanne straightened the chairs and moved the empty clothes racks into position. One for discarded items. One for purchases headed to the cashier and her commission.

Chapter 13

Ruth

Ruth pushed through the dressing room door that bore a clean, white paper with her name on its front. Once inside, she came nose to clothes with the outfits Lillian and Maryanne had chosen for her. Ruth stood there in awe, then swept her hand across the fabrics. So many different textures. Nubby. Scratchy. Slinky. Soft.

It had been a while since she'd enjoyed similar outings in New York with Dotsie. Those were always special because she was with her best friend. Now here Ruth was, with her new friends Carrie and Irene in the very next rooms. Of course, Harriet was there too. She was tolerable. Ruth knew she should be studying, but, darn it, she was having fun. She was afraid she was losing sight of her goal of trying to study.

Ruth didn't know what to make of Lillian, upper crust and coiffed, yet not quite a snob. "I chose clothes for you," Lillian had said. "But wear what you want."

Was it some sort of test? A trick, perhaps?

Maybe Lillian didn't truly know. Wouldn't that be something. Ha. Ruth had gone and lost her mind among the mannequins. Women like Lillian and Shirley—even Harriet to some extent—stood steadfast, certain of everything.

Well, Ruth might not be certain of everything, but she was crystal clear on one point. Despite the promised transformative properties, these clothes wouldn't magically appear on her body. She would need to choose.

Wearing only her slip, stockings, and brassiere, Ruth rifled through the clothes, serenaded by the clicking hooks of the hangers as they slid along the rack. While she might not have a sophisticated fashion sense, choosing appropriate clothing had elements of a grade school exercise. Common sense, not fashion sense, was in order here.

The too-small skirt and sweater had been placed among the selection as a trap, or rather a decoy, for sure. At first glance, they looked suitable, but on closer inspection, that low-cut neckline wasn't right for lunch with the girls.

Another trap was that black dress. Ruth wouldn't be fooled. Even she understood that black was for formal functions and funerals. She paused for a moment, wistful. If only she could benefit from the women's combined expertise and find an outfit appropriate for eventual law firm interviews. She stopped herself from contemplating that further. Today wasn't about the job Ruth wanted; it was about the life she desired.

She ran her hand along fabric-covered buttons. She turned over the tag on a gray dress that Dotsie, who favored green, would have dubbed "drab with a pleated skirt." She checked the label.

Arnel acetate

$9.97

The whopping price tag made her decide this was the perfect frock. She should choose expensive clothes for a make-believe lunch at a fancy restaurant.

When Ruth and Asher had first arrived in Philadelphia, two naive weeks ago, the fancy lunch had been real, not imagined. Ruth couldn't believe that, after the wedding blowup in New York, Shirley would treat her to a day out. A very special day.

The reality was, Ruth learned, that though the outing highlighted Independence Hall, the Liberty Bell, Betsy Ross's house—even shopping at Wanamaker's—it had been designed to assess Ruth.

Even lunch at the Grand Crystal Tea Room. Their visit to the largest, most elegant restaurant in Philadelphia (oysters!), and one of the fanciest places Ruth had ever been, had been finely calculated. After the wedding outburst, Shirley claimed this treat was her attempt to personally share her city with her son's wife.

Ruth appreciated the effort, thanking Shirley a dozen times. She imagined daughters attended fancy lunches like this with their mothers, something she'd never experienced, and it touched her. Made her feel a tad more like other girls. Girls who grew up with mothers.

Amidst the gratitude and richness of the day, Ruth had utterly failed to notice fashion. It never occurred to her that clothing could matter so much.

Unlike her mother-in-law, who was impressed, but not overwhelmed, by the restaurant, Ruth had been awestruck by the crystal chandeliers and yellow velvet chairs. She soaked up every detail, fixating on Shirley in order to mimic her nuanced affect and movements. The way Shirley folded her hands and flipped her hair. How Shirley ordered her meal, sipped her tea, placed her flatware.

While Ruth had hoped Shirley would love her because Asher did—the way her father had with her brothers' wives—she would take no chances. For Asher's sake Ruth hoped to develop a mother-daughter relationship, but she realized Shirley just wanted to mold her into a perfect housewife. She carefully stockpiled tidbits of information about the things that mattered to her mother-in-law—Shirley's friends' names, her favorite games, magazines, shops, food—all to be used to woo the woman, just in case loving Ruth didn't come naturally to her.

Now she stood in her underwear in Saks with a secret and a husband who seemed to have forgotten his promise.

What looked best? She didn't know.

Ruth clutched her own blue button-down blouse to her chest and pushed through the saloon-style louvered doors. She was surprised neither Lillian nor Maryanne were around to help her choose. No matter. She would ask Carrie, her new friend.

Her brassiere, garter, and stockings were on display as she tiptoed across the common area to Carrie's dressing room and pressed her cheek to the door.

"Psst, Carrie, can you help me? It's Ruth." This is what girlfriends did, wasn't it? They helped each other with outfits.

"I'll come over in a minute."

Not the response she'd hoped for. Ruth was surprised to realize she was dying to see what clothes hung in Carrie's dressing room. She wondered if they would be much different from her own. Who was she—now wanting to study different outfits—and what had she done with Ruth, the studious one? She returned to her dressing room, hung her blouse on a hanger, and pawed through the clothes. Corduroy slacks with a matching jacket? Hmmm. Appropriate for apple-picking, not a tearoom. The next choice: a skirt and shirt set—alphabet print in Dacron polyester and pima cotton. Too whimsical.

Ruth slipped the gray dress over her head, buttoned up the double-breasted bodice, and smoothed the tiny, tight pleats before fastening the belt.

"Knock, knock."

"Come in."

Carrie walked through the door in a peach-colored dress. Peach? No, more the color of a pumpkin. With its wide neckline and collar, and two rows of matching buttons, the dress emphasized Carrie's bust and hips, as well as her complexion's warm glow. Very flattering. But even Ruth knew that red scarf Carrie had tied around her neck didn't go.

Carrie leafed through the dresses before turning to Ruth and giving her decision. "I think you found the right one. You look stunning."

Stunning. That word had never described Ruth. Especially in a gray dress. "It's not a bit dull?"

"Dull? No, it's the color of a mourning dove's wings. It's lovely. And it brings out the gray in your eyes."

Really? Ruth removed a compact from her pocketbook, opened it, and looked in. She widened her eyes. No gray. Her eyes were light brown.

"Trust me. You might not notice it, but you have specks of gray in your irises. I noticed the first time I met you. It's very rare. I can't be the first person who's mentioned it."

Carrie was sweet but full of poppycock.

"You are."

"Be that as it may, brown eyes are a sign of empathy, and gray eyes are a sign of wisdom. A powerful combination that just so happens to match the dress."

Ruth looked at her feet, the dress, the wall, anywhere but straight at the source of such a compliment. She was accustomed to receiving accolades for her brain, not her looks.

"What would you call that color?" Ruth pointed to Carrie's dress.

"Pumpkin, I guess."

"Right." Ruth slid back into her shoes and looked away from Carrie. "You don't need the scarf. It's lovely, don't get me wrong—but they're going to ask you to take it off." Ruth rubbed the end of the scarf between her fingers. Carrie stepped backward, making the scarf slip out of Ruth's hand.

"I have a scar I like to cover."

Ruth nodded. So that was it. Now all of Carrie's scarves made sense. They were more than a fashion trend. "Let's ask Maryanne for one that goes better with that dress."

"I don't want to be a bother."

"You could never be. Come on."

Carrie's dressing room doors rattled shut as Ruth walked out of the dressing area toward Lillian and Maryanne. Carrie must be too embarrassed to make a fuss. Ruth would handle this for her friend.

Before Ruth could bring it up, though, she caught a glimpse of herself in the mirror. Such a new image. She stepped on the platform to get a closer look and shifted at her waist. The skirt floated, the pleats fanning out like a ballerina's dress before falling back into place.

Maryanne sidled up to Ruth. With firm but gentle hands Maryanne tugged at the shoulder seams, waist, cuff, and hem. Assessing. "It doesn't need much."

No, it didn't. Ruth glanced at herself again and allowed a smile. She looked pretty.

"Good choice," Lillian said. "I knew it would bring out the gray in your eyes."

Did everyone notice the gray but Ruth?

Maryanne unlatched a glass box. "Try this." She pinned a sparkly circle brooch over Ruth's heart, making her immediately uncomfortable.

"Are those diamonds, because—"

"No one is suggesting you buy yourself jewelry," Lillian said.

What a relief! Maryanne stepped away from Ruth, eyed her carefully, then moved in and repositioned the brooch. "This is only to show you how one small accessory can change your look."

It did make a striking difference. Maybe her mother-in-law had a pin Ruth could borrow. Of course, it needn't contain jewels. "Oh, I almost forgot! Carrie would like a scarf to go with the pumpkin dress."

"That boat neckline doesn't call for a scarf," Maryanne said.

Maybe, but that wasn't the problem, and it wasn't Ruth's place to tell them about Carrie's scar. Ruth pursed her lips and looked at Lillian. "Carrie would like a scarf."

Lillian nodded, making Ruth smile. She had fulfilled her promise to honor any dissent from the girls.

"I'll join you in accessories, Maryanne."

Ruth sat on a chair with her back to the mirror.

Lillian turned to her. "Be back in a jiffy."

Ruth waved. "Okey dokey." The expression caught on her tongue as the ladies left the dressing room. It was something Ruth might have said in law school . . . but she wasn't in law school now. She wasn't even in New York.

Ruth Appelbaum was having fun.

Chapter 14

LILLIAN

Lillian and Maryanne left the girls pondering their potential new outfits in Saks's dressing rooms and went in search of the perfect scarf for Carrie.

"You know she doesn't need it. It will spoil the overall look," said Maryanne, as they backtracked through children's wear, shoes, and fine jewelry to the fashion accessories department.

"I agree—but I think we should let them make a few mistakes and learn that way."

Maryanne raised her eyebrows. "You're in charge," she said.

The petite blonde accessories clerk stepped aside, and Maryanne slipped behind the counter as smoothly as if she'd donned custom-made shoes. Maryanne seemed to breathe more slowly, her tight smile relaxed, as she returned to her element.

It had not occurred to Lillian that the job of helping the girls find clothes might be arduous. Was that how Maryanne felt when helping Lillian? Did Maryanne sigh with relief when Lillian left the store? The last thing she wanted was to be like one of her mom's fussy customers.

She stared, trying to read Maryanne's temperament, to extract her thoughts, but the clerk whizzed around, and all Lillian saw was the back of her head. Lillian had never meant to cause angst, but truth be told, she had never gone out of her way to set Maryanne at ease.

Lillian leaned across the counter. "Can I help?" she asked.

Maryanne opened her eyes wide and shook her head, without stopping what she was doing. She pulled out boxes of folded scarves, opened them, and fanned the selections like playing cards. She plucked a few from each box and laid them side by side on the counter.

Lillian never tired of seeing silk, that beautiful fabric produced by lowly moths, then nurtured and cajoled into becoming a delicate adornment for humans. Soft. Sensuous. A symbol of luxury and culture. She could relate to its path. "They're all lovely," she said.

"They are." Maryanne pursed her lips and twisted her mouth to the side.

"What's wrong?"

"Mrs. Diamond, forgive me for overstepping, but in all the years we've been doing this, I've never known you to yield so quickly. You know as well as I do Mrs. Blum doesn't need a scarf—we chose that dress for the neckline."

They had. Lillian stretched her back, deciding how best to put this. "How long have we known each other, Maryanne?"

"Four years. You were one of my first customers."

"And I trusted you, even though you were new."

"I had a decade of fashion experience."

"And Carrie Blum has two decades of experience in her own body, so if she wants to wear a scarf, we bring her a scarf. She's not intending to buy today, so her faux pas won't reflect on you." Lillian hadn't meant to sound snooty, but face it, that had become her norm. Maryanne was right to be surprised, even disapproving. In the past, whatever she and Lillian agreed on, went. And they were always in sync. Now her grandmother would have said Lillian had gotten too big for her britches. As if Lillian would ever wear britches.

"Mrs. Diamond, that's not what I meant."

"Of course it is." Lillian softened her voice to a whisper, hoping it evoked friendliness. "I know your clientele comes from word of mouth.

And from wives admiring styles you've put together. And you don't need to worry. People appreciate the chance to make choices of their own, don't you think? I think it's time the Diamond Girls were responsible for their own choices. I'm not dragging this group anywhere; I'm simply giving them a path to follow. If they so choose." She sounded radical and right, her tone soft yet solid. *Unwavering.*

Lillian tapped her fingers on the counter and awaited Maryanne's reaction. Maryanne had been the unwitting sounding board for Lillian's newly unearthed point of view, and Lillian could tell that she was curating her response. She could tell because she'd spent years suppressing her own thoughts and watching her words around Peter. Her vigilance around her husband exhausted her.

Maryanne always had to watch her words in front of her clients, Lillian realized. As she was doing now. That wasn't what Lillian had intended. Maryanne looked away, smoothing and straightening the scarves.

"What do you think? You don't have to hold back with me. You can say whatever you want," Lillian said.

"I imagine you have enough to do with looking after Mr. Diamond and your daughters and these girls. You don't need to hear from me."

"You're wrong." The universal assumption that a husband and children were all that mattered to a housewife was flawed. Eager to hear Maryanne's thoughts, she leaned back against the counter. "Your opinion matters to me. What do you think of the girls having their own style? Do you think it might backfire?"

"Not if they follow your lead," Maryanne said. "They could do a lot worse. And isn't the purpose to guide them?"

Lillian wasn't sure. The rules of her life—of society, of women and duty—were getting muddied. She had a job to do: to prepare these girls for the future. Yet the future of young women was beginning to seem like a Liberty Bell starting to crack. "Am I guiding the girls if I dictate what's right and wrong instead of providing the information and letting them decide?"

"I think it depends how rigid you want to be. In the past, you've held on tight to your rules. Colors, styles, necklines, hemlines. I've always admired you for that."

"Do you have children, Maryanne?"

She looked up, wide-eyed, as if Lillian had just shined a flashlight in them. "I have two teenage girls."

It was only then that Lillian noticed the faint worry lines on Maryanne's face. The crow's-feet around her eyes. "Well, I admire you for working and raising your girls. I have two of my own, so I know that can't be easy."

Maryanne smiled. "It's not, but it's a decision Bill—that's my husband—and I made. The extra money will pay for college or whatever they decide to do after high school. Bill makes enough to support us, but we decided we wanted more than to 'get by.'"

Lillian flushed with uneasiness. All this time, she'd never shown an interest in this shopgirl. Saleswoman, she corrected herself mentally. She had seen her as no more than a clerk. "Your girls must be proud of you, and grateful."

Maryanne chuckled. "Teenagers aren't known for their gratitude. I think mostly they're glad I'm not home after school to bother them."

"I know what you mean. Even when they're at home, they seem to be in a world of their own."

Maryanne smiled sympathetically. "One day they'll understand how I wished I could have been there. Don't get me wrong, I love my job, but ideally—"

"You'd like to be home?"

"I'd like to be home."

The grass was always greener, as they said. To Lillian, a job that let her contribute financially to the household—and have access to her own money, her own will—seemed wonderful.

She could only admire Maryanne's determination to provide her daughters with an education. Lillian had always been able to take it for granted that Peter's salary was more than enough for anything she and the girls needed or wanted, including college. And they *had* to go to college. Not to get an M.R.S. either.

Lillian draped two silk scarves over her arm as Maryanne emerged from behind the counter. "You made lovely choices for the girls today, but I'm not surprised."

"That's kind of you to say, Mrs. Diamond."

"I'd like it if you called me Lillian."

"Are you certain?"

"I am."

Maryanne gave her a shy smile. "Thank you—Lillian."

They sauntered back through the store, but Lillian abruptly paused in front of a rack of children's wear and turned to Maryanne. "Can I ask you a question?" Lillian didn't wait for an answer. "What do you like best about your job? Assuming you really do like it."

"Nice clients like you."

"I was not fishing for a compliment; I'd like to know."

Maryanne shifted her gaze from side to side as if looking for spies or a trap. "I like doing something that I'm skilled at. But more important, I like that because I work, my girls can go to college if they want. With the extra money, we've been able to afford tutors when the girls needed them, and that's how we'll pay tuition. My job is bigger than its tasks. It can create my daughters' future."

Lillian looked at Maryanne with new respect. Her answer was candid, honest, even inspiring. This woman was working with a purpose, and getting her daughters married wasn't her goal.

"Is it only about your daughters? What about you, Maryanne? Do you enjoy your job?"

Lillian knew the question was forward, but she really wanted to know. Was it a bad thing if Maryanne had been motivated by her children and not personal growth? Now that she was questioning her priorities, Lillian wanted to discover what brought meaning to her own life.

Even taking the time to consider that seemed a luxury. Yet it didn't feel entirely comfortable. It felt like an unwanted gift wrapped in a bow of misgivings.

"I've never thought about that before." Maryanne scrunched her face, perhaps shuffling her additional responses. "Well, I like having something interesting to talk about when I go home every day. No shortage of stories. Nothing inappropriate or private, of course."

Lillian chuckled. "No explanation needed. My mother worked at Gimbels. She came home with the best stories." The middle-class excess her mother had described had been hard for Lillian to even imagine then. Nightgowns, buntings, blankets, bloomers, diaper covers, bibs, bonnets, and more, all chosen by customers before the birth and delivered after. Like items brought about by some magic in a fairy tale—not like the reality in their lives, the lives of average, working people.

Years later, Lillian's layette shopping experience had surpassed anything her mother had described—she'd bought one or more of everything in blue and then in pink. Oh, how she had missed her mother that day. Missed being able to share her own fairy-tale life. Somehow, talking with Maryanne made Lillian think about her mother and remember the good things. Was it just the lack of pretense? The easy conversation? How had she never recognized the parallels before?

Lillian and Maryanne smiled at a kinship neither of them had imagined. Maryanne reached over and straightened the toddler clothes on the rack beside them. Little blue sailor suits with matching wool caps.

"I bet your mother is happy for you," Maryanne said. "Being on the other side of the counter, so to speak."

The question ruffled Lillian's mood. Her mother? Happy for Lillian? Happy about anything? The mother she remembered, the twinkle-eyed Anna Feldman who used to hand her a small wax-paper sack containing chocolate-covered pretzel bits (milk and dark), was long gone. The sack had been full of pieces too broken for the candy-counter girl to display or sell. She blinked back a tear.

"Perfection is overrated," her mother had said. Did she still remember that as she spent her days staring mindlessly out of the hospital window?

Lillian wished she could recall the truth of her mother's smile. Whether it was genuine or not. Back then, Lillian had seen only a yummy snack inside the bag, not a metaphor for life. What else about her mother had young Lillian missed?

Chapter 15

RUTH

Ruth snapped to attention as Lillian and Maryanne stepped into the common area of the dressing room. They each smiled, and Lillian held out the selection of scarves. Spoiled for choice. A few moments later, Ruth walked into Carrie's dressing room carrying Lillian's top recommendations, grateful to offer their mentor's good taste. Ruth was independent, not foolhardy.

"I like this one," Carrie said, lifting the solid silk square, a few shades lighter than her dress, more of a cantaloupe color than pumpkin, but still part of the food group. "I'll be out in a minute."

"Oh. Okay."

Ruth shuffled backward, pushed through the louvered doors, and, as they fluttered closed behind her, stopped to gaze at the cream-colored rectangle covered in hand-painted, deep red-orange poppies that was still draped over her arm.

The scarf, a soft, luxurious piece of art, reminded Ruth of *The Wizard of Oz*. Inspired beauty. Carrie should try it on as well. Life was all about having options. Without knocking, Ruth stepped back into the dressing room, and stared.

A purple and black circle the size of a quarter, maybe larger, marked the left side of Carrie's neck.

Ruth gasped before she could catch herself. "That's not a scar, Carrie. That's a *bruise*."

A scar represented the past. A bruise was current.

Carrie slapped her hand over her bruise and growled. "I know what it is."

Things like this didn't happen to girls like Carrie.

"What's going on in there?" Irene asked from another room.

"Just pinched myself with the zipper," Carrie yelled so the other girls could hear.

"Ouch! Be careful," Irene said.

"See you all in a minute," Harriet said. "Carrie, are you okay?"

"Yes, I'm fine, thank you."

"Here, let me do it," Ruth said.

Carrie lowered her hand and looked away as Ruth stepped closer. As if handling butterfly wings, Ruth wrapped the cream and floral scarf around Carrie's neck.

"I'm such a klutz." Carrie turned her head to the left. "Bumped right into an open kitchen cabinet door. I swallowed a few aspirin and held an ice pack on it earlier. It's more embarrassing than painful. You won't say anything, will you? I didn't tell anyone about your law school, or the bar exam, or your wanting a job—not even Eli."

"Of course I won't say anything." Ruth arranged the scarf and tied it into a loose bow draped over Carrie's right clavicle. "But you have to promise to be more careful." A protective instinct tugged on Ruth's heart; invisible yet experienced as strongly as if it were made of reinforced steel.

They walked out to the common area, meeting the other girls at the three-way mirror so they could admire each other's choices.

There was nothing she could do in this moment, so Ruth allowed herself to have fun, twirling and giggling like a teenager with the others in their new outfits.

Surrounded by the other girls, she found the day overwhelmingly festive.

The rest of the morning at Saks was filled with fittings for those who were buying. Hats. Gloves. Shoes. Girdles.

After the girls settled on their purchases—Ruth chose the gray dress, Irene went with an asparagus-colored twin set, and Harriet decided on a coffee-with-cream pillbox hat—they gathered back in their chairs wearing their original outfits. Shopping bags and garment carriers lined the wall behind them.

"What did you learn today, girls?" Lillian asked.

"Buy your girdle one size too small," Harriet said, making everyone laugh whether she intended to or not.

"I was thinking more what you learned about yourselves," Lillian said.

From Saks? This wasn't an esteemed university, or even a second-rate college. Ruth hadn't considered she'd learn anything about herself at a department store.

And yet, she had. She'd learned that the compliments she'd received while wearing the gray dress had instilled confidence for her upcoming job search—and she was dying to say so. She wondered if she could transfer the confidence the girls were giving her about her looks to everything else she was trying to accomplish—especially passing the bar exam.

"I tried outfits I never would have chosen myself, and I liked them," Irene said. "I learned to take chances. With wardrobe, that is."

"That's a great lesson," Lillian said. "Ruth?"

Chapter 16

RUTH

The minute Ruth walked in the front door, proudly carrying her new clothes in their festively wrapped bags, she was greeted by a toddler. Asher's niece Judy ran to her and wrapped her pudgy little arms around her calf. Ruth was surprised not only by the unexpected guests, but by the delightful rush that ran through her at Judy's welcome.

Even Shirley chuckled at her granddaughter's enthusiasm, though Abigail quickly removed the little mischief-maker so Ruth's packages didn't get soiled.

"Looks like someone had a successful day," Abigail said, eyeing the bags. "Can we see?"

Abigail had been friendly to Ruth all along, welcoming her into the family, not holding the elopement against her. Welcoming this sisterly gesture, Ruth unwrapped the gray dress, holding it up for Shirley and Abigail.

Shirley took a step back, assessing the color. "It picks up the gray in your eyes."

She seemed pleased with Ruth's choice. As if she might be a stylish Appelbaum woman yet.

"Pretty dress," Abigail said. "Lipstick?"

Tucked in the Saks bag was a shiny new tube, which Ruth produced and opened, displaying a creamy, deep pink shade that set off the dress and her brunette hair.

The women nodded their approval as baby Judy said, "Yipstick!" and threw her arms around Ruth's leg again.

What was happening? Ruth had grown up secure in a male household, without mother or sisters, and this new family still felt strange. Yet there was a level of comfort seeping into her, being around these women, these females who were now her kin. At least in name. The same feeling she got with her new friends.

Ruth picked up Judy. The child felt wiggly and tender and made Ruth's heart swell. She hadn't experienced that with Irene's Heidi. Was it different with a child in your own family?

She nuzzled her nose against Judy's, and the child giggled.

The women were still admiring Ruth's dress when the door opened. Leon and Asher sauntered in and greeted the family. When Asher tried to take his niece, she wouldn't let go of Auntie Ruth. Even Shirley raised an eyebrow at that one.

It felt good, Ruth had to admit, to be a part of this clan. Even if she had her own ideas of how she fit into the scheme of things.

After dinner, when the guests were gone and the kitchen cleaned, Ruth went to their bedroom, slid her pumps off, and removed her nylon stockings.

Asher ambled into the room. He shut the door and peeled off his shirt.

"Is that a frown? It must be that you missed your husband, because it looks to me like you had a pretty nice day."

She had new outfits hanging in the closet and sample cologne spritzes lingering on her décolleté.

Today, she had thought less about the bar exam and potential interviews than she had in weeks. A sense of disloyalty and disappointment in herself crept in.

As if caring about her clothes held the same weight as fighting for laws that helped protect abused women and children.

"What's wrong?" Asher asked.

"Nothing."

Today she had behaved like a housewife, concerned only with the world that swirled around her in that dressing room. That had to stop. She needed to pass the bar and use the legal system to fight for the rights of women and children.

The day of fun distractions had ended.

Ruth pulled out her review book, slammed the drawer, and leaned back.

"Why are you grumpy?" Asher asked. "You don't usually slam drawers."

"I'm just thinking about everything that's going on."

Asher wrapped his arms around her. "I thought you had a good time shopping. And I thought we had a nice visit with my sister and Judy." He wasn't wrong. "You're so good with the baby. She really likes you."

Asher's hug suddenly felt like a vise.

Ruth wiggled away. "What is that supposed to mean?"

"It's not supposed to mean anything. I thought you would be glad baby Judy likes you."

"I am." Ruth looked at her hands. "But you know I don't want to have a baby now."

Asher flinched. "Where did that come from? We agreed we don't want a baby yet. All I said was you're good with her, which you are."

Ruth laid her head on her husband's broad shoulder. "I'm sorry. I do like the baby." She turned away, afraid if she looked at Asher, she'd spill what was really bothering her. She bent her head. "I had so much fun today that I forgot I'm not just a housewife like the other girls."

He laughed. "You've never been like other girls." He hugged her again, and this time it felt warm and supportive.

"This is harder than I thought it would be," she whispered.

"Marriage?"

"Life." Ruth gazed at this burly, kind man to whom she was bound by law and love. "I want to be a good housewife; I do. But I'll just wither and die if I have to read another issue of *McCall's*. Why can't I read the newspaper *and* make dinner?"

"I just want you to like this. All of this," Asher said.

Ruth grasped Asher's hands and stared at him. "I love being your wife. And I do want to be a good one. I also want to contribute to society, and I don't mean by hosting a buffet for the Sisterhood of Wives. I want us to have children one day—and I want to make sure, if it's a girl, that she has opportunities. Not just because she has an amazing father who will permit it, but because that's what's right and there are laws to protect her. I want to make sure everyone's daughter, and mother, and sister has opportunities and is protected no matter what. And their children too."

Asher seemed to hold his breath for a very long time, trying to make sense of this strange mood his wife was in after having such a happy day.

It bothered Ruth that she had to explain herself again.

When he exhaled, he looked slightly sadder. "I'd be lying if I didn't say that sometimes I wished I was enough for you. But then you wouldn't be the girl I fell in love with. The girl at the head of her class, studying with a group of Barnard girls on the grass in the quad, spouting some historic fact, waving her arms. You were something else then, and you're something else now." He kissed her again. "My something else."

Ruth felt relieved. She hadn't misjudged him. "I hate secrets. Hate lying."

"You mean to my parents?" Asher scratched his chin. "Maybe it's not so much a lie as a surprise."

Asher was clever, but Ruth couldn't be comforted by semantics. He knew she wasn't convinced. "Look, I know you don't want a life like my mother's—stuck in her simple ways."

Ruth whirled out of Asher's arms. "I don't think it's simple at all, Ash. Your mother raised three children. Managed her marriage so your father always looked good. Planned her own activities, a social life with your dad, and events as a family. Even with a cleaning lady, she ran this household. Taught etiquette lessons. Allowed people to live with your family. Not to mention being involved with the Sisterhood, mah-jongg, bridge, and, I'm sure, the PTA." She paused to take a breath. "You're underestimating her. I'm sure she's always done ten things at once. I don't think having a daughter-in-law who's a lawyer will rattle her. She might even be proud."

Ruth thought saying it aloud might allay her fears. It did not.

He stared at her, concern written on his face. "That you work? No. I know my mother."

Ruth planted her feet. "I want to start studying for the bar without hiding."

Asher scratched his head like he suddenly didn't know this woman at all. "The more she likes you, the easier it will be. It's happening, Ru. Just be patient. Please. This is hard for me too, you know. I don't want to disappoint you. But I need my mother to be on board."

"We've been here two weeks; we've been married for seventy-eight days. The longer we wait, the harder it will be. She'll feel betrayed."

"I think if we wait, there's a better chance they'll accept it."

"Ash, I'm taking the bar and getting a job. I want your parents to be happy for me or I wouldn't have gone along with this. But I don't need their approval. I didn't go to law school to be a housewife spending all my time with women who have easy lives. I want to do the good I know I can. This is not a surprise to you, Ash."

She hadn't meant to be so confrontational. She bristled at pushing against him, but didn't have a choice.

"I know." Asher nodded.

When he buried his head on her shoulder, she chose to believe him.

"Can we wait until after the holidays?" he asked. "If an opportunity to tell them hasn't presented itself, we'll create one."

Rosh Hashanah was only two and a half weeks away. A reasonable request.

Possibly. Or was that Asher's way of putting things off? Of not having to confront his mother? Of postponing having Ruth speak her truth? Was Harriet right that Ruth needed their permission to live her life?

Maybe. But no matter what else she believed, Ruth understood that compromise was the cornerstone of a solid marriage. Asher would step up and defend his working wife when the time came. Harriet and everyone else would see. Ruth needed to believe that. She wasn't ready to give up on her dreams or her marriage to Asher.

"You promise? No matter what?" Ruth asked. "After the holidays?"

"I promise."

Chapter 17

LILLIAN

Lillian hummed, which was unlike her. Maybe she wanted to be a Lillian who hummed. She was seen as accomplished and well turned out, not playful or fun. But here she was, sidestepping around the kitchen to the beat in her head, purring. The light heart of a girl with nary a care. Which she was not. She was an accomplished etiquette teacher.

Today at Saks had been fun, as she'd hoped. She taught the girls how to look their best and showed them they needn't be overbearing to get what they wanted. And her time with Maryanne had evoked Lillian's mother in a way that wouldn't have happened if Lillian hadn't decided to do things differently.

There was a comfort about the memories of her mother when she was around Maryanne.

Even though Anna was institutionalized, they had once had happy times. Had shared broken pretzels.

She too might be a broken pretzel—and that was okay. Anna had shown her that perfection was overrated. The pieces were just as sweet, just as crunchy.

Pammie came into the kitchen. Penny, as always, was on her heels. "Can you teach me how to make breakfast?"

Lillian laughed. "Don't you want dinner first?"

Pammie gave an exaggerated sigh to indicate teenage exasperation at a parental joke.

"For Donald," Pammie said. "So I know how to make him breakfast when we get married. He likes pancakes with lots of syrup."

Lillian stepped back from the fowl and rinsed her hands. "You're fourteen. There is no way you need to be thinking about making breakfast for an imaginary husband. I'm sure whatever you make for the man you marry will be fine. In the meantime, what about *you*? What's *your* favorite breakfast?"

"Mother! My favorite breakfast will be the one that comes when I wake up as Donald's wife."

Lillian felt her heart beating a little faster and took in a breath. At least she'd been a junior in college before marriage had really occurred to her. But fourteen? She couldn't, wouldn't, let Pammie waste her life like that.

Lillian sighed. "I just meant I was interested in *you*, Pammie. Penny too. I want to know what you'd like to have in that same breakfast with Donald. So both of you are happy."

"I'll take pancakes, please," Penny said. It pleased Lillian that Penny could be so willing to assert her own preferences at her young age. Maybe she wasn't such a bad mother.

"Why can you teach all those other girls to be wives and not me?" Pammie stomped her foot.

"Pammie!" Lillian looked square in her daughter's face. "I'll be happy to show you how to make breakfast, but you need to watch your tone."

Lillian wiped her hands on the dish towel and tossed it on the counter. When she turned to crack eggs into a bowl for the breading, she realized Peter was standing in the doorway. She hadn't heard the front door open.

"What's going on?" he asked. "Dinner's not ready?"

Lillian glanced at the clock. She *was* behind in her timing to get the food ready and set the table. Not by much. But enough to have missed meeting her husband at the door.

"Just a little behind schedule. I can make you a cocktail." Lillian knew she looked flustered, an unusual state for her to share with the world. When she glanced at Penny, the girl had a sheepish look, yet Pammie hadn't released any of her steam. She needed to set them a better example.

"How did things go at work today?" Lillian asked. "Did you win that client away from Fine Fabrics Mills?"

Peter ignored the question. "What's this about her tone?"

"We were talking shopping, that's all. I took my etiquette class to Saks today."

Pammie huffed. "That's not fair. I'm the one that needs a new coat, Daddy."

"Your coat is fine," Lillian said. "No one here needs a new coat."

Would Maryanne's daughters expect new coats, knowing how hard their mother worked? Lillian had never asked for anything—her grandparents had provided the necessities without spoiling her. She had always had what she needed, and occasionally what she wanted. She'd never stopped to think whether providing every little thing for her daughters might be turning them into young women who expected everything and gave nothing.

"Your mother knows these things," Peter said.

Pammie slumped with disappointment.

"May I be excused?" Penny asked. "I have math homework."

"Me too." Pammie's voice betrayed her resignation. "Except it's vocabulary."

Peter pointed to the dirty dishes on the counter. "Put those dishes in the sink for your mother, and then yes, you may be excused." He had taken her side in front of the girls again, but Lillian could tell he wasn't happy with the late meal and the dramatic encounter. The girls scooted upstairs, and Peter padded to the den. She heard the click of the television and the newscaster's voice.

The middle of the night brought a special silence, Lillian thought, as she watched Peter sleep soundly beside her in bed. She wondered if her tossing and turning would wake him. A well-behaved wife made sure her husband was rested in the morning, yet her turmoil wouldn't allow her to relax.

Peter had rescued her like a knight in a shining Chevrolet. Rescued her from hovering grandparents in an Overbrook Park row house. From being the girl whose station in life would be defined by a crazy mother, making her less than a solid choice for marriage. He'd known about her mother and married Lillian anyway. The man was a mensch, when it came right down to it. But she had always felt that she owed him unalloyed loyalty because of that.

Without marriage, how would she have been seen by society? As a spinster. She could never have afforded the type of affluence and privilege she enjoyed now, even with a career. She would never have had her daughters.

As she watched Peter sleep, she was grateful he'd seen her as a Diamond in the rough. And, while he had rescued her, she had rescued him right back by becoming the perfect housewife, someone who impressed clients and colleagues. Who contributed to his success.

But her nagging thoughts wouldn't let her sleep. She tiptoed downstairs. There was no harm in jotting down some of her ideas, was there?

Lillian padded to the dining room and pulled out her blue notebook. She set it on the table and flipped to the back, where she'd stashed blank paper and pencils. Maybe it wasn't time yet to approach Peter—or anyone—with her new ideas on how to expand the etiquette classes, how to broaden women's sense of self, but she could prepare. She could shape her ideas for when the time was right. After all, did she need his permission to head in a new direction with the classes? These women needed to know more than just how to be well-behaved.

Lillian wrote furiously. She started with her misconceptions about pregnancy and motherhood. Next, her ideas on the realities of marriage and men gushed out like clean water from a hydrant.

She stopped to read her words and a sigh coated her insides. Though the picture she painted was a dreary one, laden with loss and systemic apathy, the more she emptied her heart, the more it filled with hope. By sharing where she'd been complacent with herself, she could help her girls go right. Her daughters included. Their lives could be meaningful and informed. They would understand that they had choices.

She scribbled away, optimistic and inspired, lost in her new endeavor. When she registered the footsteps descending the stairs, she gasped. She gathered her papers and tucked them out of sight, then closed the notebook, feeling more like the cat that ate the canary than a housewife, awake too late.

"Lillian, it's after midnight. What are you doing?" Peter stood at the edge of the room, where the foyer's marble floor met the dining room carpet. Blue pajamas. No slippers, no robe. Lillian warmed at the thought he missed her, or worried about her.

"Just working on additions to the etiquette lessons for the girls."

"In the middle of the night?"

"Inspiration struck. I didn't realize what time it was."

He shook his head, clearly nonplussed. "Fine, just come to bed."

Lillian stored her notebook in the buffet. "I've got some new ideas. It may take me some extra time to get this ready. A few weeks, probably."

"As long as it doesn't interfere with anything we need, you can keep yourself busy however you like."

However I like? Lillian smoldered. "It's not a matter of *keeping* busy, Peter. I'm plenty busy."

"What then, Lil? I'm tired."

The middle of the night was as good a time as any to be honest. "I'm not very happy with myself." She was careful not to place the blame on him.

"What?"

At first Lillian mistook his grimace as concern, then realized it might be disappointment. She should have kept her thoughts inside, but it was too late. "I don't know. I just need more."

Peter waved his arms in the air and spun in a circle, his sleepiness replaced by confusion. "More? Are you telling me this isn't enough for you? What more could you possibly want? Tell me, Lillian. A new car? A pool? Don't tell me this is about a dog."

This had nothing to do with possessions—not appliances, trinkets, jewels, clothes, or cars.

"This is about your mother, isn't it?"

The suggestion stunned her. It was unlike Peter to bring up her mother. He'd always been supportive in the past. Never threw her family history in her face like other men might.

"No. Not exactly. It's about women." Lillian had no idea that describing her feelings outside of her own head would be so difficult. Her words sounded so outlandish that they came across like a foreign language, even to her.

Peter sighed. "If you're this unhappy, maybe you should see a psychiatrist, Lil. Ben Parker's wife goes to one. Jerry Stern's too. Gave them pills to feel normal. The fellas say they work."

"What are you saying? That I'm . . ." Lillian felt liquid pooling in her eyes and she thrust her arm forward and pointed at him. "You take that back!"

"Then don't be hysterical!"

"Peter! You promised you'd never use that word!" Tears streamed down Lillian's face. He knew that word grieved Lillian as much today as it had when she was eleven, when her father had died. When her mother had gone to the hospital.

Peter raked his hand through his hair. "Damn it. I didn't mean it, Lil. But really? This isn't enough?"

Lillian didn't want to hurt Peter; she did love this man. It wasn't his fault she was—what was she besides lucky? Privileged? Blessed?

And discontented. The word *unhappy* stuck in her throat and tangled up her thoughts.

There must be something wrong with her—a woman with a life like hers had nothing to be unhappy about. Still, the ideas bounced around like pinballs in her brain.

"I'm just tired. Forget it." *And confused,* she thought. *Disillusioned.* But it wasn't because of Peter. He'd been a good husband, a good man, and she had blindsided him. In the middle of the night.

Peter reached for her hand. "I think you spend too much time and energy on those housewife lessons."

"Maybe so," she said as they walked upstairs. She noticed how solid her fingers felt when wrapped in his. She wasn't ready to let them go.

Chapter 18

LILLIAN

Dreary weather was no excuse for a dreary disposition. She must not be moody about what she would teach the girls today. Lesson three should be clear-cut and precise. The financial futures of these girls and their families depended on their knowing how to contribute to their husbands' successes.

Lillian set aside Thursday's gray sky and drizzle and forced herself to smile as she set out one crystal dish with butterscotch hard candies and another with spearmint leaves. She rearranged the throw pillows on the sofa and swept her index finger along the mantel to check for nonexistent dust. She straightened the framed photos and aligned the coffee-table books. Fastidiousness was a compliment to her guests and a way to teach tidiness by example.

Deep breath.

She placed her hands on her hips and surveyed the room and then herself. She preferred her print dress with the covered buttons. The wide border, replete with purple plums, green leaves, and golden accents, reminded Lillian of her mother's china serving dish when it was filled with plum chicken during the High Holidays. She loved it when memories made her happy instead of sad. Her smile no longer fake, she drew open the curtains in defiance of the overcast sky.

Shirley walked into the living room without even saying hello, unwrapped a butterscotch with the familiar cellophane crinkle, and popped the candy into her mouth. Lillian heard it click against her teeth.

"Thanks for coming a little early," Lillian said. She felt bad for being resentful earlier. Should she tell Shirley that she'd been thinking about changing what they taught the girls? Shirley had started these classes—they were based on her teaching. Changing the focus of them might offend her mentor.

"I didn't want to be late."

Lillian couldn't imagine keeping her own unhappiness a secret from Shirley—now that she'd admitted it to herself. She had known Shirley for so long; should she reveal her desire for change? Would her longtime friend help her navigate these unheard-of problems or hinder her in making changes?

Lillian watched her remove a spearmint leaf from the bowl before floating into the wing chair she preferred.

She took in another deep breath.

The doorbell rang, preventing her from saying anything. Of all the times for the girls to come early. Lillian opened the front door, and the threat of rain brought a sultry cloud of moisture to the room. Ruth, Carrie, Irene, and Harriet entered in a cluster. The girls sat on the sofas in the order they'd become accustomed to, each wearing a dress in fall colors—olive, gold, rust, brown—in fabrics of gabardine, corduroy, and pima cotton.

Ruth's waves bounced as if freshly set, which meant she hadn't used hair spray. A small rebellion against conformity, no doubt. Lillian noted the medium coral shade of her lipstick. She scanned the others. Carrie wore short white gloves, Harriet a pillbox hat, and Irene had toned down her eye shadow. Lillian appreciated when the girls worked her fashion advice into their routines.

Yet no one looked like a Lillian copycat. Good.

In years past, any mimicry would have filled her with a sense of accomplishment. Now she reviled the idea of separating these young housewives from what made them unique.

Shirley sat facing the girls, but Lillian felt the weight of her stare.

"Girls," Lillian said. She glanced at Shirley—maybe for approval, maybe for permission. "Lesson three is about interacting with your husband's boss and colleagues. Some people think smart girls are a detriment to their husbands. I don't. However, a man is judged by the choices he makes, and marrying well is among them. So—in social situations—don't speak unless spoken to." Why did Lillian say that? She didn't even know if she believed that anymore.

"So, is it okay for us ever to be smart?" Ruth looked directly at her mother-in-law, and Lillian wondered if they'd had any weighty conversations between them. If Lillian hadn't known better, she'd have suspected Ruth's glance was a challenge.

Lillian cleared her throat. She needed to be careful she didn't step into raw territory for her friend. "It's not about *being* smart. It's about being perceived as *too* smart. The fact is, men are in charge, so we have to work within their system. Use our intelligence to further their careers." Lillian wished she outwardly agreed with Ruth, but she still kind of believed in the system. That's the way it was, even if she was starting not to like it.

"You want me to pretend I'm not smart? That's absurd." Ruth seemed to have forgotten that her mother-in-law was in the room. "I'm not going to hide like there's something wrong with being intelligent. Being as competent as a man."

Shirley drew an audible breath, but Lillian ignored her. She could smooth this over without Shirley's help.

"That's not what we're implying. I'm suggesting you use your memory, your ability to notice details and patterns, to fill your husband in on things that advance his career—and your way of life. It's a social rule of thumb to make things easier for everyone."

"Not everyone. Just the men."

Oh, Ruth. Any man would condemn Ruth for being opinionated—an epithet never applied to their own gender.

Another reason to arm girls with as much information as possible. Her daughters would *be* these girls in a few years, and already her own Pammie had a similar way of making a point that put people's backs up.

When it came right down to it, she admired Ruth's moxie. And she worried on Ruth's behalf. She certainly wasn't making it easy on herself in Asher's family. The next time Lillian looked in the mirror, she was sure she would see gray hairs sprouting atop her head and lines carved above her brows.

But Lillian had promised to prepare these girls before the High Holy Days, and she had no time for imaginary aging. "I'm here to help you girls, and you're here to help your husbands. Remember—always think before you speak, and when you're called on to converse, think about what is appropriate for the social situation." She glanced over at Shirley, who was nodding in agreement while she kept her eyes pinned on Ruth. "For example, Ruth, imagine you're at a cocktail party with your husband, who goes to refresh your drinks. You smile at two nearby colleagues of your husband, who then ask what you think about the latest news." Lillian tried to hide her cringe. She'd been waiting for that question her whole life and had never been asked. "What do you say?"

"I might bring up the topic of NASA's latest space probe disaster. I think," Ruth said.

"I'd turn it around and ask what *they* thought about the news," Harriet said.

"Never a bad idea." Shirley made her point of view perfectly clear.

"Face it, girls, no one asks housewives for anything other than recipes," Irene said.

"Asher married me *because* of my brain, not in spite of it." Ruth cocked her head defiantly in Shirley's direction. "He expects me to contribute to a conversation."

Ruth's hackles were up—Shirley's too, by the look of her.

"Contribute, yes. Hijack it, no." Shirley's eyes were like gimlets now, and Lillian was glad she wasn't on the receiving end of that stare.

The other girls were commenting quietly in the background. Lillian mustn't let the lesson get away from her, couldn't let Shirley or these girls down. She spoke over their ongoing prattle. "Ladies, this is about social behavior that reflects on your husband. We live in a man's world—and will for the foreseeable future."

She almost choked on the words.

No matter how Lillian would like to change her life, the social stratification would always remain. She did love Peter, her daughters, their way of life. She understood that his success was, in large part, because of her social skills. But what if she—

Ruth interrupted her thoughts. "What if we want more?"

A momentary silence fell over the assembled women. Lillian had no idea how to answer. Not with Shirley in the room. She found herself struggling with the truth.

Shirley piped up as if she knew exactly what Lillian had been wrestling with. "These rituals are the cornerstone of our community. What Lillian is saying is that you use your smarts to your family's advantage. Help your husband get ahead. Buy that glamorous home, that shiny car. Send your children to the best schools. You don't have to brag about your role in it. In fact, you shouldn't."

"So it's okay to be smart as long as no one else figures it out? I'd go crazy." Ruth was throwing caution to the wind now. She looked incredulous, and her mouth barely closed after the words came out.

Crazy. That word again. Lillian's skin crawled at the memories from her childhood when they took her mother away.

Shirley emitted a tinkling laugh, like the sound of ice crackling in a glass of vodka.

Lillian hated conflict in her home, and the sound added to her nervousness, but she felt compelled to support Ruth's urge for freedom

from these suffocating social constraints. "Of course, anyone would."
Not everyone. Just Ruth. And maybe Lillian too.

"Don't get me wrong," Shirley said. "I believe in what we do here.
These rituals you're learning are what maintain our way of life. But
there's more to life than children and husbands and good manners."

Lillian couldn't believe her ears. Apparently neither could the girls,
who sat up straight. Ruth didn't take her eyes off her mother-in-law.

"Housewives are uniquely positioned to see what's going on in the
world—and to do something about it. That's why I have my hobbies.
But we're not talking about me."

Oh. Hobbies. Not what Lillian had in mind.

"Hobbies won't change the world." Ruth's tone was dismissive. She
was publicly chastising her mother-in-law.

Lillian held her breath as she waited for Shirley to retaliate.

Shirley merely smiled a long-suffering smile, as if to say, "You see
what I have to put up with?"

This lesson had gotten away from Lillian, and she had to corral it
again. "Most men—and women—want housewives to focus inside the
home. But I don't believe you have to choose. You can be a good wife
and mother and have more in your life. Just find one small way to start."

"Why do we have to keep it small?"

Lillian composed herself and opened her mouth, but Shirley
chimed in first. "These etiquette lessons are one small way to begin.
Your shopping trips. Lunches with your friends. Keeping the peace in
your family. *Staying happily married.*" She looked pointedly at Ruth.

"We all understand that our social system is ingrained. We must be
careful how we make changes. Don't push too far at once. If a change
is too drastic, the whole set of dominoes will come crashing down."

"And people will think we're responsible," Carrie said.

"*And* think you're hysterical," Shirley said. She was looking at
Lillian now.

Hysterical. She'd chosen the word deliberately, no doubt. Lillian tightened her hands so no one could see them tremble.

"I heard they have pills for that," Harriet said, breaking the tension. "And I heard they work."

All the women, except Ruth and Lillian, chuckled.

"With four kids, I could use those on most days." Irene laughed. Even Ruth managed a small smile.

"I . . . I think . . . you . . . understand what . . . needs to be done. All right then." Lillian forced a smile. "We've had enough for today." She hoped she didn't look as pale as she felt. The lesson hadn't gone as Lillian planned. Shirley's presence had derailed it completely.

Chapter 19

RUTH

A measly drizzle was falling as the girls walked out of Lillian's house, chatting about their third lesson and the benefits of supporting their husbands.

Before Ruth could get out the door, Shirley put a hand on her arm and asked her a question about Asher's schedule for the evening. Ruth was relieved that Shirley didn't confront her about the public disagreement. The other girls—all of them had brought umbrellas—skittered down the front path toward the street.

After satisfying Shirley about Asher's plans, Ruth crossed the portico and walked into the gray afternoon, leaving Shirley inside. Her friends had gone, so she lifted her face to the sky, searching for fresh air to replace the stifling atmosphere she'd just left.

Water hung in the air, misting her face like the lightest spray on a hose. As the rousing wind stirred things up, the drizzle left a film of cool condensation on her skin and clothes that grew from the soaking droplets. Ruth rounded the hedge to the sidewalk and found her friends waiting there, smiling under an assortment of umbrellas.

It was a pleasant surprise. Ruth had felt like the Lone Ranger in that meeting. The only dissenting voice. The solo mission. Yet here were her friends, wanting her as part of the group, even if it was simply to walk home together.

"Thanks for waiting," Ruth said. "Let's go." She pointed to the corner, and they all hurried in that direction. Then, as if by some mind-reading trick, or as if Lillian's voice were in their heads, the girls slowed to a respectable walk.

Irene and Harriet in front, smoking; Ruth and Carrie behind.

They strode in step. Left, right, left, right. Laughter and banter.

Ruth eavesdropped on the details of Heidi's friends and Harriet's engagement party. She listened to Carrie's pot roast secrets. Ruth mentioned plans for apple-picking, additional fall shopping, and a couples' night she would like to host once she had a home of her own. They gabbed over and around one another, but somehow Ruth heard it all. She let go of her disappointment about hearing what women *should* do and enjoyed what she and her friends were doing in the moment. She wanted to keep these women in her life. Things would change when she was working, but for the time being, this was fun, and it would please Shirley.

What would happen to their group when the etiquette lessons ended? Would this bond be enough to maintain friendships when she worked as a lawyer? When Harriet got married? With Irene juggling four children and Carrie planning for one? After she passed the bar, surely Ruth would make lawyer friends, but they would likely be men. It was refreshing to have girlfriends—women friends.

Irene glanced at her watch. "You girls can dawdle; I've got to pick up the pace so my mother isn't alone with all four kids. The older ones will be getting out of school soon."

"I promised my mother I'd come right home, too," Harriet said, though Ruth couldn't imagine why. Harriet had no children and was only engaged. She must be planning a big wedding. Ruth had seen enough of her New York friends submerged under the list of things that needed to be taken care of, to be thankful that her own ceremony had been small. Harriet and Irene waved and scampered away.

"I have to get home, too," Carrie said. "Eli likes supper on the table at six." Ruth had heard this before. Eli left at eight in the morning. Eli ate dinner at six. Carrie had told her several times. Perhaps it was an occupational hazard for vice-principals. Having to stick to a tight schedule with so many students to take into account. The drizzle stopped and Carrie turned to Ruth.

"Let's catch up to the other girls," Carrie said. "Harriet walks right by my house."

It occurred to Ruth that Carrie might be avoiding a private conversation with her. Was it something Ruth had said? Had she come on too strong about women's intelligence in the lesson? After all, Carrie was smart. She'd been a nurse.

Ruth was hungry for more female conversation at the moment. Shirley was her only other source, and that was usually awkward, to say the least. In a year, things would change. Today she wanted to meander home, even in the rain, admiring the shiny, wet colored leaves and the pots of mums on the steps and patios. The pumpkins waiting to become jack-o'-lanterns. She wanted to revel in the cool air. She wanted to do that with Carrie. Tomorrow she had to get back to her studies.

She yearned for anything but polite conversation about being polite.

She wanted to talk to her friend.

As Carrie sped up, Ruth waved. "Slow down, it's slippery out here."

Carrie was already a step ahead, so Ruth reached out to slow her, get her attention, but as Ruth skimmed Carrie's gloved hand, she yanked it away.

"Don't grab at me." Carrie hissed, caressing her left wrist like it was painful.

"I'm so sorry. Did I hurt you?" Ruth asked.

"No, no. I'm sorry. I just don't like being touched."

"Let me take a look. Promise I won't touch you. You might need medical attention."

Carrie pulled her sleeve down even further. "You're crazy!"

"Listen, I'm your friend. I think you need help."

"You think I slit my wrists?"

Ruth stared at her. What had prompted that random remark? Why would she say that for no logical reason? *Had* she slit them?

"You're safe with me." Ruth reached a hand toward Carrie and, as Carrie batted her hand away, Ruth's fingers grazed her wrist again.

"Ow. Cut it out." Carrie winced.

Ruth held up her hands like a crossing guard holding up a stop sign, though a crossing guard probably didn't have a prickling chill creeping up her neck. She shrugged her shoulders to squelch it, to no avail. The buzzing jumped to her arms as if to empower them.

Trust your instincts.

Ruth had to make a move. If she was wrong, she could apologize.

She grabbed Carrie's hand, rolled down the glove, and gently pushed Carrie's cuff up past her wrist to look. The skin was mottled purple and green with yellow edges.

Ruth worried that she was coming on too strong. A lawyer should ease up, consider all the evidence. That type of mark could come from multiple sources. Had Carrie worn a cheap metal bracelet that had dyed her skin?

"I banged it on the edge of the counter," Carrie said, looking away.

Ruth pitched her voice lower, trying to express concern without judgment. "Is that true?"

"Why would I lie?" Her voice held an air of indignation.

Ruth shrugged, but there was an unseeing look in Carrie's eyes.

Carrie lifted her chin, her expression defiant. "I'm accident-prone. That isn't a crime."

Accidents happened. And attacks happened. Ruth had seen so many victims of violence—they still haunted her. Tender young children with black eyes, broken ribs, missing teeth. Women who had been punched so hard their bones had shattered when they bounced against cement or metal. Ruth had worked with girls who had despicable boyfriends and husbands, and she helped them extract themselves when she could.

But those women weren't like Ruth and Carrie. They were the disenfranchised, the poor, the laborers, the tenement residents. Not the wives of vice-principals. Of educated people.

Ruth had sat on Eli's patio, imbibed his coffee, listened to his wife relate tales of his job. Eli had golfed with Asher.

Ruth leaned closer to Carrie. "I can help you."

"I don't need any help. I need to make dinner." Carrie walked faster, but Ruth kept up, determined to not let this go. "It was an accident, I swear. He just doesn't know his own strength. Drop it, Ruth. It won't happen again."

Ruth's stomach clenched as if she had been punched. Carrie had admitted it.

"He apologized, Ruth. Forget what you saw." Carrie shook her head. "I can't believe I'm even telling you this. He bought me flowers and he's going to manage his temper, he promised. No matter what I do, okay?"

Heartbroken for her friend, Ruth wanted to wrap her arms around her.

She didn't dare. Carrie didn't like to be touched, of course not.

Not all markings showed. Many women had hidden trauma. Beaten verbally and emotionally, they had also been brutalized.

Most of those women had been beaten by their husbands or boyfriends. Black eyes, broken ribs, bruised backs. Carrie's mark had been mild in comparison. Still.

A few had unfairly lost jobs or housing because of it. A few had been unjustly arrested, as if they weren't the victims. Ruth had scoured New York laws that would protect them. There were very few.

"There is nothing you've done or could do that makes this okay. You know that, right?"

Carrie's eyes flashed. "Did you not hear me? He said he'll stop. You need to mind your own business."

Ruth had seen this before—women protecting their men, even their bad men.

She plowed on. "What do you mean, 'he said he'll stop'? How long has this been going on?"

Carrie turned on Fifty-Second Street. "You've got it all wrong. He *will* stop. It's under control."

How had Ruth not seen this right away? Here she had thought she was gaining new friends, and she hadn't been one herself. Of all of them, Ruth was the one who had experience with victims of abuse. How did she not know this was happening to Carrie? She'd been at her house. She'd seen the bruise on her neck. Ruth had told Carrie her deepest secret, and she didn't know about Carrie's.

Was this type of abuse among respected, educated people simply a lone, isolated case, or were there more women like Carrie, suffering in silence? A dirty little secret that was never discussed in polite society. If it could happen to Carrie, it could happen to anyone.

Carrie's voice softened. "Trust me. Everything is fine, Ruth. Or it will be."

"How can you be so sure?"

"Because I'm expecting." Carrie stopped walking and touched her belly. She looked longingly at her abdomen for a moment, as if she were receiving a gift that would anoint her with special powers, a golden touch that would right the world and keep her safe.

Ruth fought a feeling of nausea. She wanted to scream. A baby was the last thing Carrie needed. Experience told her that this was a setback for her friend, because it stopped a woman from taking action to get help. She swallowed, and camouflaged her fear with a smile.

"Eli has been frustrated since we got married because I wasn't getting pregnant fast, but now, that's not a problem."

"You're going to have the baby with a man who hurts you?"

"He's my husband, and the baby's father, so of course I am."

A sad truth washed over Ruth. She'd seen it before. Babies and children meant to save a relationship, only to end up being used as hostages, creating more broken bones, more bruises.

Ruth's bluntness overtook her. "A baby isn't magic, Carrie. It won't make everything okay."

"Don't be ridiculous, Ruth. A baby changes everything." Carrie rolled her eyes. "You don't understand marriage yet. You're a newlywed. You'll understand when you get more time in."

Ruth would never see abuse as normal. And if she knew one thing about herself, it was that she was not a bystander. "Come home with me. Let us help you."

"Ruth, mind your own business. I mean it." Carrie's voice held more than a hint of exasperation.

"You're my friend. You are my business."

"Then be happy for me. I'm going to be a mother. It's the answer to my prayers."

A veil of sadness dropped over Ruth. "I hope you're right."

"Of course I'm right. I will finally give Eli what he has wanted all along, so he'll have no reason to—well, he'll be happy. We'll be happy. He is going to be a wonderful father." Carrie looked into Ruth's eyes. "Please don't mention the baby to anyone. I haven't told Eli yet, and I want to tell him first. And don't discuss my private life with anyone else either."

Ruth promised nothing. But she nodded, mostly because she was stunned to see a girl like Carrie behave this way.

Carrie shifted in place, a frown confirming her uneasiness. "You're blaming my husband for something that's not his fault. You have no way to know this, but I'm not easy to live with. I'm quite fussy."

"Being fussy doesn't merit physical punishment. And what's going to happen when the baby starts fussing?"

"Stop with the nagging! Eli is a good man. Would I have married him if he wasn't?"

Ruth tamped down her anxiety. Carrie was a smart girl; she'd made it through nursing school on her own. Eli was a respected educator. Having a temper wasn't a crime. Surely Carrie would leave him if she or the baby were in danger. Ruth didn't want to lose this friendship, or hurt her friend any more than she'd already been hurt. There was nothing she could do. "I just want you to be safe."

Carrie smiled. "We will be. Now do I have your word this stays between us? I can't be around you if you won't respect my privacy. Ruth?"

Ruth said nothing. She wasn't prepared to promise that. If she stayed silent, she wouldn't have to lie to Carrie.

Carrie quickened her pace again. "So, I know where I stand." She sounded furious. "In that case, I'll have to ask you not to call the house or come by."

Flabbergasted, Ruth stopped. "You're kidding me! Carrie!"

Carrie kept on walking, swinging her arms.

"I only want you to be safe," Ruth whisper-yelled.

Carrie stopped in midstride and swiveled around. "How many more times do I have to tell you? You need to butt out. I'm fine." She continued on her way, as if she didn't want her words to catch up to her. "Perfectly fine," she called over her shoulder.

Ruth scurried up behind her. "You're not fine."

"No, not with friends like you." Carrie crossed the street and made her way through a group of little boys. When they dispersed, she raised her voice. "Go home, Ruth. Maybe if you focused more on being a good wife than wanting a career, you'd be busy and wouldn't feel the need to attack my marriage."

Ruth was stunned into silence. Carrie had shifted the blame away from Eli and onto Ruth. It occurred to her that Carrie had never told anyone about these attacks, that no one knew. That Carrie was afraid. She felt even worse for her friend. "I didn't. I would never . . ."

Carrie cackled like the Wicked Witch of the West.

Ruth had to give it one last try. "Let me help you with this—*issue.*"

"Don't you get it, Ruth? You *are* the issue."

Carrie turned the corner and was gone.

Ruth plodded toward home, her feet dragging as if they had weights tied to them. Ruminating on this wouldn't help, but she couldn't let it go. She could never let things go. A good trait in a lawyer—not such a good one in a wife, or daughter-in-law, or friend.

Her legal training told her she was obliged to keep a client's confidence. But Carrie wasn't her client. Ruth knew she was clueless when it came to social relationships in a place like Wynnefield. She wished Lillian would cover the subject of discretion when a friend was suffering. It would be far more meaningful than learning how to balance a teacup on one's knee or fold one's napkin on their lap. She suspected that etiquette rules didn't apply here.

Maybe if Ruth went to Lillian in private, she might advise her. She was their teacher and guide.

Another consideration was that keeping Carrie's secret might put her friend in danger. Losing her friendship might be a small price to pay to keep Carrie and the baby safe.

If Ruth were home in New York, she would have gone to her father and then to Dotsie, but they couldn't help her with Carrie in Wynnefield. She didn't have time to waste.

PART 2

LIFE LESSONS

Chapter 20

LILLIAN

Lillian sat at the dining room table, her blue notebook open in front of her, pencil in hand. She jolted when she heard three loud knocks on the front door. She glanced down at her hand. That pencil had been still against an empty page. Not a word written.

She checked her golden wristwatch, with its well-placed diamonds. How long had she been in this trance? A while now. Since the girls and Shirley had left. She had intended to make notes about their session, yet she felt so distracted, she couldn't find the words.

Three more insistent knocks. What impatience and impertinence!

There were stomps coming up the basement steps. Sunny could hear the thumping all the way down there too. "Here I come," Sunny said, as if the visitor could hear her from the floor below.

"Don't rush," Lillian called. "I'll get it."

She flipped her notebook to a new blank page, jotted the word *doorbells*, set down her pencil, and stood. Even though the etiquette lessons didn't feel as important to her anymore, she still needed to get them done, to plan them, to make them worthwhile.

Then she stopped and wrote the word *tap*. There was a better way to command attention, even without a doorbell. These tips were important points for civilized behavior.

Knock. Knock. Knock.

Lillian made a few tsks under her breath as she headed to the door and the awful racket.

Peeking through the sidelight, she saw the source of her annoyance. She groaned at this rude interruption, then whirled around to ensure there was no witness within earshot. She held the polished brass doorknob, inhaled, exhaled, smiled, and pulled open the door. Wide and polite. The proper thing to do. She might be conflicted, but she wasn't a barbarian.

She had to remind herself that Ruth was still a student.

"Hi, Ruth . . . You seem to be unable to find the doorbell. What can I do for you?"

"Oh, sorry. I'm too upset. I know I was here a few hours ago, but I need to talk to you. It's important."

"Come in." Lillian kept her smile graceful as Ruth stepped inside.

Hearty and spicy dinner aromas mingled with the smell of bleach, and both followed Sunny out of the kitchen door and into the dining room. Lillian motioned for Ruth to sit.

"Would you like some coffee or tea, Mrs. Appelbaum?" If Sunny had been perturbed by the loud door pounding, she gave no sign of it.

"Tea would be lovely, thank you," Ruth replied at the same time that Lillian said, "That's not necessary."

Lillian tapped her index finger to her lips as if to take back the words, or to soften them. Of all people, she shouldn't be contesting an offer of hospitality. Worse, Ruth—this girl who had such confidence, such fight—looked like she'd just lost a war.

"Cream and sugar?" Sunny asked.

"Please," Ruth said, and Sunny slipped out of the room.

"I'm sorry to bother you." Ruth tapped her fingers on the table in a rapid patter. "I didn't know where else to go."

"Calm down and tell me what's going on." Lillian didn't consider herself particularly intuitive, but the Ruth in front of her was about as subtle as a dump truck unloading its freight.

"It's Carrie," Ruth whispered just loud enough for Lillian to hear. "I should have spoken up earlier, as soon as I saw, but I didn't even—I mean—I never. I said I wouldn't tell, but now, how can I not?" Ruth's words shot out hard and fast like BBs.

"Slow down, Ruth, I can't follow you."

Ruth inhaled. "Carrie has bruises on her."

Lillian blinked. "What do you mean?"

"I mean that I touched Carrie's hand, she flinched, and I got this weird feeling—an instinct, I guess—and I pushed up her sleeve and her wrist was bruised."

Why had Ruth come to her with this scuttlebutt? "That doesn't mean anything except that Carrie's probably a klutz and was embarrassed."

"Are you serious? She pulled her arm away. She didn't want me to see her wrist." Ruth's voice rose.

"Not everyone likes to be touched, Ruth. I expect it made her uncomfortable."

Ruth dismissed Lillian's response. "You don't understand. She was afraid of what I might see."

Her mother's long sleeves flashed into Lillian's mind for some reason. She ignored it. "What did Carrie say about the bruise?"

"That he didn't mean to do it."

"He?"

"Her husband, Eli."

"See? It was an accident."

Sunny returned with the tea. She smiled at Ruth as she slid the china cup and saucer across the polished table. As she swiveled to leave, she raised one eyebrow at Lillian.

"You didn't see the mark on her wrist. Or the other one." Ruth lowered her voice to a breathy breeze, the way adults during Lillian's childhood had whispered *cancer*.

"Other one?"

"That's why she insisted on a scarf on Monday. There was a bruise on her neck. She said she walked into a cabinet door. She said it was an accident."

"I'm sure it's exactly what Carrie said it was." It had to be. Nice suburban people didn't do such things.

"Does Carrie seem like a klutz to you?"

Lillian had to shut this down. It would be terrible for Carrie and Eli if this rumor tainted their reputation. Highly unfair. After all, Eli was a vice-principal. And it wouldn't look good for Lillian's classes—or their community—if something like this got around, whether or not it was true, which Lillian doubted very much. Ruth was young, a newlywed, not from here. Those New York types could be excitable.

But Lillian liked Ruth. "Husbands and wives fight. Some more than others. Carrie probably took an accidental spill when it happened."

"So it's okay if he hurt her?"

"It's none of our business." What people did in their own homes was no one else's business. Her grandmother had taught her that. She'd shut down any questions Lillian had tried to ask about what had happened to her parents. Eventually, she'd learned not to ask.

She still felt that way. Lillian surely didn't want anyone poking around her and Peter's marriage.

"Carrie was here today, and she was fine. She wasn't upset. She didn't ask for help. Where did she go after our class?"

Ruth's shoulders slumped as she appeared to study the wood grain in the dining table, dragging a finger along the walnut. "She went home to make a brisket."

"She went home to make dinner for her husband." Lillian stood. "Which is what you should do, Ruth. And what I should get back to." She looked toward the kitchen, then started for the front door. "If Carrie and her husband *are* going through a rough patch, the best thing you can do, *if* she asks, is help her figure out how to fix it. And I'd say brisket is a good start."

Ruth walked through the door and turned back to Lillian. "How can you be so calm? Aren't you worried?"

"About whether our dinner will overcook? Yes. About Carrie? No. And you shouldn't be either."

"How can you be so sure?"

"Because things like that don't happen here."

Ruth stepped onto the portico and Lillian shut the door.

After she left, Lillian turned around to find Sunny standing in the foyer with her hands on her hips, her head cocked to the side. She shook her head, picked up the teacup, and disappeared into the kitchen.

Lillian gathered her notebook and pencils from the dining room and straightened the chairs. There. No evidence the room had been used for anything other than *for show*, or the occasional appropriate gathering.

Peter would be home soon. Ruth sitting there, fidgeting like a child, insinuating herself into Carrie's marriage, was the last thing Lillian wanted to explain, or lie about. She had to compose herself more after this unexpected visit. Ruth's incredulous stare, her worried and shaky voice seemed to remain in the room. The remnants crawled over Lillian's skin.

It was none of their business, yet there they had been, whispering about other people's lives. Even if Carrie and her husband were having some newlywed strife, that's all it was, nothing more. Ruth had no proof of anything. She was Shirley's daughter-in-law, but that was no reason that Lillian should believe Ruth over Carrie.

Tink.

Clank.

Thud.

Lillian could hear Sunny setting the kitchen table, reminding her of the time. She should call the girls away from their homework, but frankly, she liked the quiet before Peter came home and dinner began. Sunny needed to catch the bus, and Lillian had kept her longer than usual today. Lillian poked her head into the kitchen.

"You can leave, Sunny," she said, jerking her head to the side as if Sunny wouldn't know where to find the door. She had already untied her apron and pulled it around to her front.

"Do you want to talk about it?" Sunny wrung the apron as if it had been washed and she'd been charged with removing all the water.

Lillian held out her hand and motioned for Sunny to hand her the apron. Lillian hung it on the back of the kitchen door that led to the garage. "Do I want to talk about what?"

"The Appelbaum girl."

"I don't know what you heard . . ."

"I heard enough." Sunny walked around Lillian and to the coat closet. She slipped a bulky, dark-green sweater off a hanger. Though Lillian had never asked, the garment had been expertly handmade, by the looks of the stitching. Sunny pushed in one arm, then the other.

"I don't want to be involved in any gossip. Gossip can destroy families," Lillian said. Some things were better left unsaid. "And you shouldn't either."

Sunny buttoned her sweater and headed to the front door. "It didn't sound like gossip to me."

"Well, that's all it was." Lillian clucked her tongue as if adding auditory punctuation.

"If you change your mind . . ."

It was comforting to have Sunny in her life. If she had to grow up without a mother, at least she had her mother's best friend. But this wasn't something she could talk over with the help.

"Have a nice night." Lillian wished she could travel back in time twenty minutes and ignore the knocks on her door—or better yet, that Ruth hadn't stopped by. "That sort of thing doesn't happen here," she added.

Maybe. But something made Lillian's stomach churn, though she tried to ignore it. It couldn't be true—she'd have known. This was a good neighborhood.

"It happens everywhere," Sunny said. She opened the door and turned back, her full pink lips set in a line, with no forthcoming smile. She stepped onto the portico, looked at Lillian, and raised her eyebrows. "Don't forget to warm the rolls."

Lillian puttered in the kitchen as if there was something to do besides set full serving plates onto the table. She couldn't shake Ruth's visit. Jewish men were supposed to be good husbands, but Lillian knew all men had their downsides. Carrie, a newlywed, would settle into the rhythm of being Mrs. Blum, the wife of a vice-principal. He worked with children, for God's sake, and had been vetted by the school board, the PTA, and the superintendent.

As Lillian arranged slices of Sunny's meat loaf into flower petals around a mound of mashed potatoes she'd whipped up herself and topped with chives, she said a silent prayer of gratitude for the abundance she sometimes took for granted.

An abundance she needed to hold on to. Not just for her and Peter, but for future generations of their family. Her grandchildren. Great-grandchildren.

Pamela and Penny knew nothing but this lifestyle. Would they marry well enough to have someone else cook their meals? Should Lillian concern herself with the potential of their future husbands? How would Lillian handle it if one of her daughters pursued a real career? Wanting to be a teacher didn't really count.

Or chose to remain single—or received no proposals? God forbid.

In a moment of doubt, the idea of her daughters' future flustered Lillian. The notion of independence should thrill her, yet she perspired from fear that her daughters would be ostracized from something beyond their control.

She knew what that feeling was—the feeling that she was somehow tainted because her mother had been taken away. Whispered about when she wasn't around. The feeling that misfortune had struck her family through no fault of hers.

Lillian was certain that her mother hadn't had the time to consider any part of her daughter's future, before she'd been unable to do so.

Because of that, Lillian was driven to become what her mother had not been able to become—a housewife who dedicated herself to her husband, and a mother who raised children to adulthood. These were lofty goals—at least, Lillian had thought so at the time.

Perhaps the lack of her mother's example was an example itself. Maybe Pammie and Penny would want to assert themselves in ways Lillian had not. Would they have whatever opportunities they wanted? Would they be dependent on marrying well?

What about Carrie? What *was* the truth? Ruth wasn't a liar—perhaps misinformed somehow. Perhaps Carrie—

Stop this nonsense, Lillian told herself. *You have no business worrying about the rumor concerning Carrie when Peter will be home soon.* With the cold dinner rolls evenly arranged on a baking sheet on the counter, Lillian went to the bottom of the steps that led to the second floor and listened for any activity upstairs. She heard silent stretches interspersed with low-volume chatter and the occasional giggle that floated downstairs as the girls slogged through their homework.

They wouldn't run down the steps until called, wary they would be asked to help. They had been spoiled by Lillian's need to give them an easier childhood than hers had been. Maybe she should change that now. It was time to prepare them for any social curveballs life might send their way. Pammie was right. It wasn't fair that Lillian spent so much time training other girls.

It was hard to not spoil her children. And they so enjoyed each other's company. Someday Lillian and Peter would be gone. Encouraging her daughters to be close to each other was important for their future too.

An only child with a working mother and workingman for a father, Lillian had spent hours alone most days and reveled in the time she spent with her parents, especially delighting in stolen days at the beach or a full week together for summer vacation.

She waited all year for that special week—to have her parents to herself. Her daughters only vied for her attention on shopping excursions. Lillian sighed. Maybe easier didn't equal better. Pammie and Penny had one another. No matter how much Lillian had disliked the body changes and discomforts of pregnancy, she would never be sorry she had given each of them a sister.

She wished she had more relatives her age. After her father died, and her mother was taken away to the mental asylum, Lillian's grandparents hadn't maintained her relationships with her cousins. Her grandparents would never explain why Lillian was suddenly estranged from the cousins she loved. The cousins she'd played dolls with, played hopscotch with, and jumped rope with. As an adult, she realized it was because she had been tainted by her mother's breakdown.

How she'd wanted a sibling! A sister would have been a lifelong companion, someone who would have had the same experience of losing her parents and growing up as the overprotected child of her grandparents' dead only son.

Their expectations of Lillian had been high—different, but no worse, than Peter's.

She'd always assumed it was because they didn't want Lillian to relate to the unhealthy side of the family. They wanted her to focus on her father's side—the wholesome, untainted side. Wanted Lillian to improve her station in life.

She wished she'd quizzed her grandparents more about it while they were alive. No matter. She would do better with her own girls—had done better with her own girls.

She and Peter wanted their daughters to marry well. Marry someone who could afford a cook, a housekeeper, a gardener. Someone who could pay for their clothes at Saks instead of making them with an old Singer.

It couldn't hurt if she gave her girls a bit more training. She had no idea what else they might want to be. How their fortunes would change as they went through life. Starting tomorrow, she would make sure her daughters learned some life skills.

Lillian slipped the dinner rolls into the oven, set the timer, then hurried into the rec room. She slipped off her shoes, bounced onto the sofa, and tucked her stockinged feet sideways. Ahhh. She had a few minutes to relax, and she was going to savor each one of them.

She couldn't stop thinking of her daughters' futures. Of her future. Of the future of women.

She reached over for the small notepad Peter had left on the side table and scribbled.

> *What am I?*
> Housewife and mother
> Teacher
> Friend
> *Do I excel at some of it?*
> Yes.
> *Is my dissatisfaction hereditary?*

The last question had popped into her mind before she even knew it was there.

Is it hereditary? Is that what made my mother . . . ? She would not even think the word.

Lillian tore off the paper and grabbed a stack of photo albums from the bookshelf. The blue one with the black pages that sheltered her childhood vacation photos—she made sure to grab that one too.

She needed to look her father and mother square in the eyes, imagine what they might say about their daughter's life, imagine what she would want them to say—and how they would sound.

She could easily hear her mother's voice in her head, always calm—as was her demeanor. Anna meant business but was kind. Lillian's father sounded as if his voice rolled over gravel in his throat.

She wanted to remember them at the beach. They'd been happiest at the beach, hadn't they?

Lillian set the photo albums on the floor and, since her dress was thankfully A-line, she sat cross-legged and pulled the older album into her lap. She tucked the torn list inside. If she threw away the paper, Peter or the girls might notice it.

Today she landed on a page with a square black-and-white photo of her family on the beach in Margate City—the same beach where she and Peter had met years later. The location had been painted in what she remembered as bold blue letters onto the lifeguard stand in the background. She must have been seven or eight then. In the photograph, she was digging in the sand, squinting at the camera. She peeled the photo out of its black, sticky corners. It was thicker than an ordinary photograph, more like cardboard than paper, and Lillian realized two images had stuck together, likely decades ago. She peeled the photos apart with relative ease, and only a minor tear.

A new photo. One she'd never seen.

The second image revealed Lillian with her father and mother, standing on the beach in front of a wooden lifeboat. Her father had a cigar in his mouth and his arm around her shoulder. Lillian's mother, modest and unseasonably dressed in a light-colored skirt and long-sleeved blouse, smiled tightly, glancing to the side, as if caught unaware or embarrassed.

Lillian flipped it over. In her mother's neat, loopy cursive it read: *Me, Percy, Lilly 1938 Margate City.*

Lillian looked at her family again, longing to be that little girl whose world had not yet imploded. The two-inch-square photo filed among Lillian's cache was no more than black and white and shades of gray—so that if she didn't know her father's swim trunks were navy blue from her own memory, she could have imagined them green or black or something garish like purple.

But they weren't, and when Lillian looked at the photo, she saw blue.

A photograph was like that. She could look at it and know what had happened before, during, and after the moment the shutter snapped.

With no one to confirm or deny her memories, Lillian processed them as fact—a happy childhood that had ended too soon. Early memories were replaced with a new, painful reality. *Her life after all the dominoes fell.*

Lillian's swimming suit in the photo, as well as her mother's skirt and blouse, was painted by imagination. Yellow with red rickrack for her suit and a sky-blue skirt and white blouse with embroidered blue daisylike flowers for her mother. Lillian rubbed her fingers together and swore she could feel the texture of the embroidery. She closed her eyes, inhaled through her nose, and smelled the sweet cigar mixed with pungent ocean air.

How different her life would have been if she'd been raised by her mother instead of her grandparents. They were set in the ways of the past and wanted Lillian to be too. How much more would she know about the world if her mother had coached her through her teenage years? Revealed the ins and outs of being a woman?

"Lil?" Peter said. "Lillian?"

She looked up. *Peter.* When had he come home? She hadn't heard the door or footsteps. Then the girls walked into the den. When had they come downstairs? She tucked the photo into her waistband and stood.

She felt a bit woozy. Was it from the beach memories? From the tension of the etiquette lesson? The rumors about Carrie or Ruth's discomfort?

She couldn't put a finger on why she felt so shaken. Why something profoundly wrong—or maybe not *wrong*, but different—was throwing off her day. Snaking through her insides like a bad piece of food.

She had to put herself in the present. Let go of the rest of her day. There was her family, in front of her, staring at the woman who had always been their rock. Who was looking at old photos instead of preparing their meal.

She heard the ding of the timer from the kitchen. It was time to take out the dinner rolls.

Chapter 21

RUTH

Ruth had to admit that bedtime with Asher was her favorite time of day. She had washed up and donned her satin nightgown, and when she looked over at her husband, he was smiling at her and patting the bed beside him.

"Are you going to tell me what's wrong?"

She was lucky to have this man, who noticed how she was feeling and cared about her. Thank God he was nothing like Eli. She'd grown up being valued by the men in her family, and she would pass that tradition on to any daughters she had because Asher would be their father. She slipped into bed beside him, her satin gown folding sensuously around her legs.

"I found out something troubling today. About a friend." A momentary doubt struck her. Would Asher believe her? She wasn't entirely sure how much she could say, plus Asher had golfed with Eli. They shared the same social circles.

This Philadelphia world was new to her, and she was still learning the ropes. Things could get out of hand quickly if she wasn't careful. What had they said in today's etiquette lesson? That all the dominoes might fall.

"One of the other wives from the etiquette lesson?"

She thought about telling him who, but was still reluctant to betray Carrie's confidence, even to Asher. Not yet. "Yes. And I told Lillian about it, but she didn't believe me."

"Why?"

"Because she said I didn't have proof. And that it was none of our business what happens between a husband and wife."

Asher seemed to chew on that. "Hm. Lillian has a point."

Ruth looked at her husband askance. "But what if that friend needs help?"

"What if you only think she does?"

Was he right? He must have caught the look in her eyes, because he smoothed the covers over her. Gentle. Caring.

"Look, Ruth. People's reputations are important. So is their privacy. Just like our privacy is important to us. Things we keep between our family and no one else. Lillian knows how things work. She was probably trying to save you from making a mistake that could hurt you. Hurt us. Hurt our family and our reputation. Indiscretion isn't taken lightly around here."

Who was this man she married who had forgotten all the work she did in New York? Who didn't believe her? It wasn't the Asher she remembered. "But I think my friend needs me."

"What did she say?"

Ruth closed her eyes and took a deep breath. "She said it was none of my business."

Asher chuckled. He was making fun of Ruth.

Her face heated.

He pulled her closer. "That's what I love about you. Your big heart. Your passion to help others."

She was wrong. He wasn't making fun of her. So she tried to bask in his compliment. But was he suggesting she put aside her worry about Carrie?

He didn't get it. Didn't understand. *Thank God.*

In the morning, shadows woke Ruth. Fall sunlight felt its way through bare branches to create movement that danced across the pink walls and flowing curtains. Nature showed off sometimes, even in a neighborhood that consisted of as much stone and concrete as grass and trees. She had so much studying to do. How did she let herself get so distracted?

Ruth reveled in the view from her bedroom window, which overlooked a tree-lined street instead of a New York neighbor's fire escape.

Escape.

That's what Carrie needed to do. Maybe Ruth could talk her into taking a little vacation. Getting away from Eli could help clarify things for her—help her see things for what they were.

Asher had already left for the day. Ruth swept her foot to the left, feeling the cool sheets instead of his thick, hairy calf, confirming that she was alone. She reveled in her solitude for a moment, claiming the bed as hers.

She loved her husband, loved sharing this bed and benefiting from the warmth of his bulky body, but time to herself had always been elusive. First living with her father and brothers, then with other girls at Barnard and after that Columbia, now with Asher and his parents.

Ruth didn't want to live alone, but she craved—she missed—having something that belonged just to her, like the bar exam. Ruth sprang from bed. What was she doing lying around? She had to prepare for her friends. She would worry about study time later.

She needed to go to the bakery, set the table, find blocks and toys for little Heidi, brew the coffee, and, of course, dress in something simple and hostess-like. *Simple and hostess-like.* If only she owned an outfit like that. She made a mental note to shop for one.

She had her fingers crossed that today would go well. She'd invited all the girls for coffee before her argument with Carrie, and now she wasn't sure if Carrie would show up. They'd ended yesterday on a negative note, to say the least.

Carrie's and Lillian's faces tumbled into Ruth's thoughts and twisted her heart into a jumble of sadness and disappointment. If Carrie didn't show, what was she going to say to Irene and Harriet about her absence? She couldn't tell them that Carrie didn't want Ruth in her life.

Carrie might spread rumors about her to cover up her own problem.

She might make Ruth out to be the villain the way Lillian suggested she was. Carrie could easily paint her as a gossip who spoke out of turn about things she knew nothing about. And Lillian might corroborate this.

Ruth knew the truth, but she seemed to have made a mess.

Lillian Diamond had turned away from the situation like one of those graceful and beautiful pink flamingoes Ruth had seen at the zoo. Dozens of people had lined the fence to watch the birds, who were blind to all the activity around them. Maybe they didn't know any better.

Dressed in a green floral A-line and her brown run-to-the-store shoes, Ruth donned her wristwatch and a pair of earrings, then left the attic.

The cool air pressed her into a soft gallop down the steps. Chill swooshed around her legs, the thin nylon stockings covering them providing little protection against the cold. If Leon was anything like her frugal father, it would be closer to Chanukah than Rosh Hashanah before the radiators hissed with heat.

As she moved from the second-floor landing to the staircase and down to the foyer, a gentle sweetness tickled Ruth's nose. Shirley must be baking, which wasn't unusual. She served dessert after dinner every night. That was in addition to always having ice cream and Oreos around—two of Asher's favorites, tastes he'd acquired when he lived on campus. His mother always had plenty of homemade goodies available too. Rice pudding, apple cake, cherry turnovers, cinnamon curls, chocolate chip cookies.

Ruth grew up loving bakeries. With one at the bottom of their building on Seventy-Eighth Street, bakeries and the smell of baking were a part of home. She didn't need to learn to bake; the Ostermans baked for her. She wouldn't mind treating Asher to nostalgic and delicious desserts when they had their own home. Ruth hoped baking was something she would be good at—something she could ask Shirley to teach her.

Something they could bond over.

Ruth stepped into the kitchen and the aroma and stared at the sight that accosted her. Today's baking had been for her benefit. Shirley had arranged perfect pastries on a platter, which sat in the middle of the kitchen table.

So much for taking charge of having coffee with her friends.

Ruth's smile might have looked genuine, but it had the intention of hiding her disappointment.

"Good morning," she said. "Something smells wonderful." She had to admit, everything looked and smelled mouthwatering.

"Asher told me your friends are coming for coffee, so I made kamish bread."

"You didn't have to do that." Ruth would have preferred to eat Liss's cinnamon buns. Soft. Flaky. Loaded with cinnamon and butter and drizzled with a creamy, white sugar topping. "I asked Asher to tell you I'd get up and go to Liss's."

"I thought homemade would look better. Be better."

Better for whom?

"Oh, okay." But it wasn't. After her dreadful day yesterday, Ruth had wanted at least one thing to go as she'd planned today, and the only thing she had control over was the darn cinnamon buns.

Ruth remained determined to help Carrie. She looked forward to having guests in her home this morning. If she ever needed allies, it was now. Could these girls, all domestic and homespun, step up and be who she needed them to be? Ruth didn't consider it betraying a confidence when her friend was in danger.

The mission ahead darkened her thoughts. Maybe she should tell her mother-in-law. Feel things out in advance. Get guidance.

But would Shirley react as Lillian had? As Asher had?

It was risky. Besides, if there was one thing Shirley Appelbaum didn't need to know about, it was Ruth's troubles. She had nearly two weeks to go before Rosh Hashanah. Before they would break the news of the bar exam, and of her career choice to be a working attorney. She needed her mother-in-law to think highly of her by the time she and Asher told her.

"I didn't mean to overstep," Shirley said. "I know you don't bake."

Of course Shirley knew she didn't bake. Another of Ruth's shortcomings in housewifery.

"What time are the girls coming?"

"Ten."

"So late?"

Ruth nodded. Yesterday, on the walk home, when she invited the girls over, she hadn't thought to ask if there was a specific time that was considered appropriate. She should have suspected there were rules about coffee too. She'd gone to Carrie's at eight thirty, but she'd assumed that was because Eli had just left for work.

"You can brew the coffee closer to ten. I showed you how, right?"

Ruth nodded, both humbled and annoyed. She had made instant coffee for her father since she was strong enough to pour a kettle over the Sanka. He always drank it black. She chuckled inside at the notion of her father using tiny silver tongs to dispense saccharin tablets, and it brightened her thoughts. A little.

"You can use the dishes and linens in the butler's pantry," her mother-in-law said.

"I thought we could sit in the kitchen, if that's okay."

"Of course. There are small round tablecloths folded on the second shelf."

"The girls wouldn't mind plain and simple." Or bakery goods. "But this is better," Ruth said, trying to cut Shirley some slack as she gently lifted a piece of kamish bread. She'd grown up calling it *mandel brot*, next to her Italian friends, who called it biscotti, but when in Wynnefield, do as the Appelbaums do, and say.

"Of course they wouldn't have minded, but that's not the point. The point is to always do your best. This is about you. Didn't you tell me one of the girls made you a picnic lunch? Irene, wasn't it? Isn't she the one with a lot of children?"

Ruth gulped. "Yes, she did. It was lovely. And delicious." Irene had four children and a husband, *and* she did the books.

Ruth thought that when Shirley looked at her, she probably saw a slacker. Maybe she was right. Ruth should have realized the need to exert a similar effort. Her effort was focused on passing the bar. Shirley wouldn't think Ruth was a slacker when she knew Ruth was studying for four hundred hours.

But in the world of Wynnefield housewives, Shirley had saved the day again.

"Oh, I almost forgot," Shirley said. "Carrie phoned her regrets this morning. Said you'd know why she couldn't come."

Ruth cringed. She hoped Carrie was okay. Was this the beginning of the end of her new friendships? Was she destined to be alone in this new life? To earn scorn not only from Lillian, but from Shirley too? Perhaps even from Asher—since he warned her not to pursue things that might be rumors?

"Something wrong?"

Ruth snapped the piece of kamish bread in half. "No, no. I was just thinking how delicious your kamish bread is. I'd . . . I'd love it if you'd show me how to make it." Kamish bread was a perfect distraction from everything else going on.

Shirley stepped back and eyed her daughter-in-law with a smile. Her mother-in-law seemed to like that request.

At least one itty bitty thing was going right today.

A short time later, Ruth, Irene, and Harriet gathered around the kitchen table with coffee and cigarettes, sipping their fresh-brewed Maxwell

House. Harriet had oohed and aahed over the table linens and saccharin case. She flicked her ashes into the green ashtray that matched the appliances.

Ruth had never taken up smoking, no matter how glamorous it looked, no matter that it seemed chic once she was in college and the girls didn't smoke in secret. She didn't like the smell, let alone the taste.

Dotsie had said that a cigarette added sophistication. Harriet likely concurred. Though Ruth disagreed, she liked having these women share their habit around her. She even welcomed the choking smoke and stinky smell right now. It reminded her of Dotsie, of true friendship. It gave her comfort, a hope that she might have more of it. Stinky smoke would be a small price to pay for being part of this group. There was a tug-of-war between Ruth's desire for a career and her desire to be one of the girls. Who knew she would face such a problem?

Harriet glanced at her watch and stubbed out her Lucky Strike, a masculine cigarette for such a girlie girl. "Carrie's really late—should we give her a call?"

Ruth felt a little sheepish. "She sent her regrets. She can't make it."

Harriet usually took things at face value. Did she have to choose today to wrinkle her brow in a question? She stared at Ruth, expected her to speak.

"She was busy," Ruth said.

"Since yesterday? She loved the idea on the walk home. I hope nothing's wrong."

Ruth looked at their faces as they waited for more. What if she made things worse for Carrie or her own family? She was trying to solve a problem, not create one.

These women might not have known each other for long, but they had become friends. Peers to Carrie. Maybe Ruth was underestimating them. What did she know about *their* instincts? Their intuition?

She wanted to trust these girls, even Harriet. They were caring people, weren't they? They might see Ruth's side. Maybe even pipe up with other facts or observations, other things they'd noticed about Carrie. Facts that could support Ruth's argument that Carrie was in real danger. They might be able to help Ruth get Carrie some assistance before anything drastic happened.

Before Carrie ended up like the women Ruth had seen at Legal Aid. Running for their lives.

Yes. These girls right here were Ruth's friends—Carrie's friends—and could be allies. Ruth tested the water. "Things weren't going so well at home, I think."

"You're worrying me," Irene said, her cigarette bobbing with each word.

So they did suspect. Irene was a mother. Of course she would be the first to notice something wrong. Ruth waved them closer.

Irene leaned her elbow on the table, nearer to Ruth, ready for what was next.

Harriet raised an eyebrow as if saying, "Out with it!"

Ruth planned her words carefully. Opened her mouth.

Shirley walked into the room carrying Heidi. "Someone needs the bathroom!"

All three women popped their heads up. Stared.

"Oh, I'm sorry, Mrs. Appelbaum," Irene said, reaching under the table for her bag of baby supplies.

"I'll take her," Shirley said, putting her hand out to take the bag. "If that's okay."

The baby nodded and the girls laughed.

"Oh my God, Ruth, your mother-in-law is a dream," Irene said.

Shirley turned and headed upstairs, mumbling to Heidi on her hip.

When the sound of footsteps receded, Ruth inhaled. There was no way to ease into this discussion. "Carrie had bruises on her arm yesterday. And at Saks, I saw one on her neck."

Harriet shrugged. "So?"

"Well, she's not clumsy," Ruth said, knowing she would have to divulge more. Would have to dive into muddy waters. Calling her dad or Dotsie wouldn't help. They weren't in Wynnefield. She needed help here, now. In the span of one deep breath Ruth would betray Carrie again, but this would be critical to helping her. Helping Carrie's baby. "Eli roughs her up."

"What are you trying to say?" Irene scrunched up her nose.

Ruth huffed. It shouldn't be so difficult to understand, but then again, wasn't it a challenge for Ruth to comprehend too? Didn't she discount it at first? "I mean her husband hurts her. I assume he squeezes hard enough to make a mark."

"He does not," Harriet said.

"And if he does, it's none of our business," Irene said. "Maybe you didn't see what you think you saw."

Ruth couldn't tell by Irene's tone if she was accusing her of lying or if she thought Ruth didn't have enough proof yet.

"What did Carrie say?" Irene pressed.

"She admitted it. Well, she didn't deny it."

"What didn't she deny?" Harriet asked. "You're using what she didn't say to make claims against Carrie's own husband? A vice-principal? That's a pretty sketchy way to be convinced of something so awful."

"What would you say if I accused your fiancé of leaving bruises on your neck and your wrist? You'd deny it, wouldn't you?" Ruth could feel the heat rising in her chest.

"I'd tell you that you were crazy, he'd never do that, and how dare you say so. And to mind your own business."

"Exactly. First Carrie said it was an accident. Then she said he was sorry and wouldn't do it again. *Again!*"

Harriet rolled her eyes. "That kind of thing doesn't happen here."

That's the assumption Ruth had made, and it had been echoed by Lillian.

They were wrong. Ruth knew it.

175

"She was with us yesterday," Irene said, sounding noticeably irritated. "She was fine. Couples fight. Some get physical. It's between them, and I'm sure it's not dangerous."

"You're overreacting." Harriet lit another cigarette.

"I'm not," Ruth said. She wanted to pound on the table, make *somebody* listen to her. Instead, she lowered her voice to a whisper. "I think she's in danger. She thinks everything will be okay when she tells him she's expecting." Ruth felt bad for betraying Carrie's confidence, but she was in danger. Ruth had to speak up.

Irene gasped. "A baby!"

"Ruth!" Harriet said. "Carrie wouldn't sleep with him if he hurt her."

"I don't think she would have a choice; she'd be afraid to say no."

"Leave it alone, Ruth. Be happy for them," Irene said. "Let them adjust to the news. I'm sure they're fine."

"Irene's right," Harriet said. "And it's not like he'd hurt his own child."

Irene checked her watch. "My, look at the time."

The girls stubbed out their cigarettes and gathered their belongings, sunglasses, and pocketbooks. Ruth understood it was a ruse, but she didn't know if she was more angry, hurt, or disappointed. One thing she knew—she couldn't feel more alone.

"That's it?" Ruth asked. "You're leaving?"

"We can't butt into someone's marriage," Irene said.

"He hurt her." Ruth didn't know what other words to use to make them understand. She wished Dotsie was there. Or one of her college friends from New York. Or someone from Legal Aid. They would listen to her. They would see the need to protect Carrie.

"Says you," Harriet said. "Marriages are private. I think you're overstepping."

"Me too. It's none of our business," Irene said. "And if it was true, which I doubt, there's nothing you can do."

Ruth suddenly felt like she didn't know anything about anything anymore. Was she overstepping? Overconfident in her knowledge? Was everyone else right and Ruth wrong?

Shirley came downstairs, cuddling Heidi, and the girls cooed at the child. Shirley noticed the women had their bags and were ready to go. "Leaving so soon?"

Harriet must have seen the chance to get in Shirley's graces with her knowledge of social parameters. "We started at ten. A bit later than usual."

Ruth was ready for them to leave.

Later that day, when Shirley had gone out, Ruth called to check on Carrie. No one answered the telephone. Well, at least Ruth had the house to herself, with no more social obligations until dinnertime. That was a blessing. She would capitalize on the break to study. She couldn't waste a minute. She ran upstairs, plopped on the window seat, and opened her study guide.

Several pages in, Ruth looked up. Her whole future was at stake, yet she was unable to concentrate. Today was another disaster. Yesterday she'd alienated Carrie and Lillian. Today it was Harriet and Irene. Still, she couldn't let go of her worry about Carrie. She had to help her friend, but how?

When Ruth walked up the cement toward Carrie's house, she remembered how much she had liked their conversation on the covered patio. How quickly they had gotten comfortable in their relationship. As Ruth rang the doorbell, she hoped that Carrie would remember that too. Ding-dong.

She hoped that Carrie had had time to cool off from their argument yesterday. That she'd give Ruth another chance to be her friend.

Ding-dong.

Ruth heard movement inside. Soft footsteps. Yet no one answered the door. If Carrie had household help, someone would open it, would let Carrie know she stopped by.

The door never opened.

Ruth's gut told her Carrie was home. Alone. That she had somehow peeked out and seen who it was. Ruth thought about ringing one more time and decided against it. She turned and went down the walk.

When she got home she found herself still alone. Shirley was at her Sisterhood meeting, or maybe it was mah-jongg day. Ruth wasn't sure of anything anymore.

She went right to the kitchen and pulled out flour, sugar, milk, and eggs. She took out the KitchenAid stand mixer. She would bake a cake for her husband. She couldn't focus on her books right now. At least it would look like she was trying to be domestic, for now. Prove to herself—and her in-laws—that she could fit in. She could be a good wife *and* a lawyer. She was competent. But could she be a competent friend?

As she worked furiously, the kitchen filled with the scent of yummy batter. Warm wafts of sugar floated around her. Yes, baking was definitely a mood enhancer.

An hour later, when the kitchen timer went off, Ruth delighted in the pleasant scent as she opened the oven door.

Her face sagged, just like the middle of the cake.

She tested it gently with toothpicks. The inside was only half-baked. The rim was like a brown brick. There was no salvaging this mess.

She dumped it in the garbage and watched the heavy mass sink to the bottom; its gooey middle hit the wall of the bin as it went, smearing uncooked batter along its path.

Ruth plopped down at the kitchen table, buried her face in her hands, and cried.

Chapter 22

LILLIAN

"Constance, Susan, and Peppermint," Lillian said, flipping the switch off the percolator. The Saturday morning coffee had finished brewing a half hour ago, when she had set a breakfast of hash and eggs, toast, and coffee in front of Peter. She lifted his now-dirty dishes from the table setting in front of him and placed them in the sink with unnecessary firmness.

"What are you talking about?" Peter rose, mouth agape, pushing his bottom jaw to the right. This expression of his annoyed her. He would not twist his face like that if he knew it demoted him from a Jewish Jack Kennedy to Barney Fife. The plaid golf knickers didn't help.

"Philip Tanner's wife, daughter, and blue-ribbon golden retriever," Lillian said. "And don't mention Russia if you don't want to rile him."

Peter nodded. He'd be seeing Philip Tanner soon.

That would have to do. He could work with those facts. She had lost the motivation to look for more. She was tired of propping him up all the time.

"Got it." Peter saluted like a Boy Scout and grinned, also quite like a Boy Scout—resolute, yet coy. "Wish me luck." He kissed her forehead.

"Luck," Lillian said.

Peter walked out the kitchen door to his last golf-game-plus-business-meeting of the season. Earlier, he'd promised to sink a hole in one for his company, and then he'd laughed. His own best audience, Peter had been trying to sink that particular "hole in one" for Diamond Textiles since July. It would be a big account, a generous addition to the family's income. Constance, Susan, and Peppermint. Lillian was doing her part.

You're welcome.

Lillian set a large cup on a saucer, lifted the coffeepot, then filled her cup to the rim. Saturday morning coffee on her own was indeed "good to the last drop."

There was a time, maybe ten years earlier, maybe less, when a Saturday *without* Peter at home—playing with the girls or ignoring them to wash the car or read the paper—would send Lillian into nostalgic riffs, reminiscences, and longing for more time together. Not today. Not after fifteen years of marriage.

Today she sipped her coffee as steam rose from the cup, reveling in these quiet moments to herself and wondering if she should go to a psychiatrist to have her head examined. She ought to tolerate Peter's time away, not look forward to it—what was wrong with her?

Reality had upended her youthful imaginings, and the disparity between them flashed in Lillian's mind like déjà vu. That was it.

Oh, come on, she chided herself. She loved Peter and still found him attractive (and judging by some of the men around the neighborhood, with their balding heads and double chins, that likely wasn't true for all wives). She relied on Peter for their beautiful house, full icebox, and comfortable life, and to provide for their girls. Her husband delivered without complaint. But.

Was Peter the one responsible for hemming in Lillian's ideas for a more fulfilling life? Hardly. Why, he hadn't a clue what those ideas were. He knew she was up in the middle of the night, and he worried about her mental health. Was that genuine concern or just concern about how things would look to the outside world if she were to become unstable, like her mother?

Tap, tap, tap. Her fingernails worked against the wood of the table as if they were trying to give her a Morse code message. What was really troubling her?

Ruth's visit crept into her thoughts. Something still bothered her about that. Ruth had accused Carrie's husband, a respected vice-principal, of terrible things. But surely this wasn't her problem. Lillian would keep Ruth's problems to herself.

But she'd promised herself she would stop avoiding difficult truths, so that younger housewives might feel they could challenge the status quo too. So that her children would have choices as they grew up.

What was stopping her from keeping that promise now?

Peter and Lillian had dinner out, just the two of them. It had surprised Lillian when Peter had requested that she book this specific restaurant yesterday. It was undoubtedly romantic. There were candles at the table, and a piano player who was skilled at ballads, but didn't play so loudly it kept them from enjoying each other's company. Lillian chalked Peter's good mood up to the fact that he had finally scored that hole in one with Philip Tanner. Maybe he did appreciate her help.

So she was allowing herself to enjoy tonight more than she thought she would.

Perhaps she spent too much time focusing on what was wrong with her life—and not enough on what was right. Like the way Peter was smiling at her from across the table. The cute way he cut little bits of his steak and swirled them in the sauce like he was rounding up fall leaves.

They arrived home before eleven. Lillian checked on the girls, awake but in bed. By the time she slipped into their bedroom, Peter was already under the covers. She eyed him reading his book and had to admit, she did find him sexy.

Lillian flipped the door hook into the latch. Peter looked up from his novel, then returned to it.

She meandered around the bedroom. Earrings, necklace, and rings each returned to their own compartments in the oversize mahogany jewelry box. It was a bridal shower gift from Peter's grandparents. That, and the traditional and old-fashioned cedar hope chest. Both were monogrammed.

She set her shoes in the box in the closet and then placed the box back on top of the shelf along with her clutch. When Lillian picked up her hairbrush, she noticed the photo of her parents that she'd discovered in the album and propped it up on her vanity.

She took one more look at the family, caught at that happy moment on the beach. She had memorized the details, but the image itself captivated her. The tilt of her mother's head, the smile on her father's face. The way they each rested a hand on her shoulder. Lillian could have stared at their faces all night, but she turned away when she felt Peter's eyes on her.

On the bed, he was waiting for a signal. *The* signal.

The bedroom etiquette lesson flashed in Lillian's mind. The subtle and not-so-subtle things she would suggest to the girls. Keeping a husband happy in the bedroom could offer a little leverage, she'd say.

Peter expected romance tonight but would not demand it. He wasn't always tuned in or attentive, but he was always a gentleman. She was grateful for that—it showed he respected her.

She stood at the foot of the bed, the soft, semisheer nightdress and robe draped over her arm.

In a grand, unmistakable gesture, Lillian laid the robe on the folded-down bedspread. She carried only the negligee toward the bathroom and did not lock the door.

Once back in the bedroom, she left the lights on and welcomed Peter to her side of the bed.

The next morning, Lillian brewed coffee and defrosted some of Sunny's kamish bread. Peter sauntered into the kitchen and kissed her on the lips. The girls were still asleep, so she kissed him back and lingered. They had been friends all these years. Peter had been a true friend, moving her mother into a better institution, never complaining about paying for her care. Never throwing Lillian's family history of mental illness in her face. Not even the other night, when he mentioned the psychiatrist. He only seemed genuinely concerned for her welfare.

"I thought I'd rake the leaves first thing," Peter said when they broke from the kiss. They had hired a gardener, but this chore was one Peter had always liked to handle himself. He seemed to derive a mysterious pleasure from working on the fall cleanup.

Lillian added cream and two sugars to his cup. "I'd like to visit my mother?" She posed it as a question, which was not how she meant it.

Peter blew into his cup to cool the coffee. "When?"

"Today."

He sipped and stared at Lillian, a look of concern in his eyes. "Why today, Lil?"

She didn't expect her own answer. "Peter, I miss my mother."

"You've never said that before."

Surely she had. She tried to remember, but nothing came to mind. So Peter was right. Lillian gulped, ashamed of her omission. But she did miss her mother now—and she wanted to ask her about the past. Whether it was because of the beach photo, or Maryanne, or her restlessness, Lillian didn't know.

"I didn't realize I missed her. I found a new photo from when we were all together; it had been stuck behind another in the album. Happy times at the beach. I thought she might want to see it. She doesn't have much to look forward to. It might bring back good memories."

"Is this about the other night? I didn't mean to upset you."

At least he realized that he'd crossed a line in suggesting that Lillian needed a psychiatrist.

"No. No, it's just that I haven't seen her in a while. After all, she is my mother."

So that afternoon, Lillian and Peter pulled into the long, curved driveway alongside a hedge of deep-blue hydrangeas with bright-green foliage—a smart choice, as those leaves faded later in the season. As the road turned, the lawn, bushes, and trees came into view, and the main building of Friends Hospital splayed out before them. It was as wide as a city block and as grand as a picture-perfect French chateau, with its pale-yellow stucco and inset stones around the windows. The structure didn't look much like a mental hospital, but after all, wasn't that the point?

They might have been anywhere.

They could pretend they were anywhere.

It had been impossible to pretend she was anywhere but a mental institution when Lillian's mother had been a patient at Byberry, the state-run asylum housed in fifty buildings on ninety acres just ten miles away. Anna Feldman had been committed to that hospital by her in-laws right after Lillian's father had died—or that's how it had seemed to an eleven-year-old. She hadn't known it was a hospital for people with mental problems. She'd expected her mother to come home, but she never did. There was no point in crying about it, her grandmother said.

She hadn't asked or dug around for more information. Her mother's diagnosis had been a nervous breakdown, hysteria, and later, presenility. Lillian had been so young when it all happened. She had been grateful to her grandparents for keeping her mother safe.

That's how Lillian saw it, even though none of the treatments had worked. They wouldn't describe the treatments, saying she was too young to understand. Every time she heard her grandparents whispering about another treatment, she would eavesdrop, praying that this time her mother would be cured and come home.

It was to no avail, and Lillian learned to stop hoping. Stopped expecting any treatment to improve her mother's—and her—life.

Anna Feldman had never recovered or improved. Her mother would never come home.

Lillian was, essentially, an orphan.

Then and still.

When Lillian was eighteen, she and Peter became engaged. He was young to already be running Diamond Textiles alongside his father. Only once she was engaged had she agreed and arranged, behind her grandparents' back, for Peter to meet her mother. He had insisted.

One sunny Sunday, Lillian and Peter walked hand in hand into a long, dark building—Building N6, it was called—and down a hallway that reeked of urine and bleach. Lillian held a handkerchief over her nose in an attempt to mask the smell, but the nausea she felt required an effort of will to keep at bay. Peter only wrinkled his nose and kept striding down the corridor.

They walked past a dozen closed doors, hearing screams, cries, and moments of uncanny silence, before they reached her mother's over-crowded dormitory.

Her mother had been positioned in a chair by the window. Displayed, in a way, with her arms and legs placed in what looked like uncomfortable and unnatural angles—posed for visitors. The first time she visited as a child, Lillian had known that the arrangement of her mother's arms and legs wasn't true. The mother she remembered had been soft and warm. This mother's spindly arms had been crossed on her bony lap as if to contain her movement.

Her mother hadn't recognized Lillian since age twelve, though Anna babbled about a Lilly she thought was someone else. Lillian had been crushed. She assumed it was a temporary situation, brought on by whatever medicines or treatments her mother was given.

It had to be. A mother didn't forget her only child.

After Peter's first visit, Lillian had led him back to his car, listening with relief as the main doors clanged shut behind them. She managed to hold her feelings in check until they reached the parking lot. She was used to ignoring her heartache. And she wanted to see Peter's reaction to her mother before she said anything else. Would this change his love for her?

Peter had been silent during the walk back to the car, and Lillian couldn't tell what he was thinking until they reached his car, and she heard a gag and retching sound. When she looked his way, Peter was bent over, and vomit spewed from his mouth.

Vomit. She didn't have to ask what his reaction meant. She had been foolish to think he would still marry her after he met her mother, after he saw who she came from. They rode home in silence. She felt numb, but Lillian was no stranger to dominoes falling. Here they went again.

But things hadn't turned out the way she'd thought they would.

Not only did Peter still plan to marry Lillian, but a week later he arranged to have Anna Feldman transferred to Friends Hospital, a Quaker institution, and the first private psychiatric facility in the country. One of its finest.

In those days, she looked at him and saw generosity of spirit. Was he still the same Peter?

Even before they were married, and when her grandparents were still alive, Peter paid the bill. He hadn't complained or mentioned it in the past sixteen years. And twice a year they visited Anna together. The visits didn't last long, and Lillian was sure Peter would rather rake leaves, but he came without complaint, like he did today.

He'd brought Lillian this time because she'd asked. He was the same Peter. Older, wiser, but the same man, devoted to his family. To doing what it took to keep everything upright.

He hadn't objected or rolled his eyes, the way some people might have done.

Now here they were, driving the winding road toward Lillian's unfortunate past—the one they usually pretended didn't exist. Neither of them brought her mother up in conversation, and Lillian was grateful for that.

She sighed, then camouflaged her bubbling emotions with a cough. Peter's quiet cooperation was proof he loved her, no matter what else transpired—or didn't—between them. He had her back in this, which is why she did what she did. Her service to Peter's life and career—and even her love—was laced with gratitude. How selfish she must be to view her life as less than enough when he had done so much.

When he kept her dominoes standing.

After Peter shifted into park, she reached out and squeezed his hand. She had been too critical of their life, of him, and of herself. "Thank you for doing this," Lillian said. She glanced through the windshield. Her mother's residence hall, dressed in ivy like a college dormitory, peeked out from between oak trees.

"No problem. Shall we go?"

A few minutes later, she and Peter were walking side by side down the same sun-soaked hallway they had first been through sixteen years earlier when they moved her in.

This place always smelled like lemons.

As Lillian pushed through the door to the courtyard, Peter gently laid his hand on her shoulder. "Don't expect too much," he said. It wasn't a mandate so much as a cautionary note. He was right. She mustn't hope for anything. Her mother hadn't recognized her in person last time, and she might not recognize her in an old photo either.

In spite of Peter's comment, Lillian simmered with hope, an uncommon sensation, especially here. She couldn't believe she'd never shown her mother pictures of herself before. She'd brought photos of her own wedding, the girls, and her house, but she'd never thought to show her mother a photo of herself and Lillian's father. No one had suggested this might be a way to jog Anna's memory—to help her emerge from wherever she existed inside her mind. Lillian patted her pocketbook.

She wanted some things to change; perhaps one of the changes could be her relationship with her mother—or at least Lillian's understanding of what had happened to her mother that had resulted in this lifetime of illness. Anna had been a saleswoman, with a job she loved. Maybe this photo would help her talk about her life—her work—before she got sick. Shed some light on Lillian's own desire to have satisfying work.

The nurse, easily identified in a white uniform, stockings, and cap, walked up to Lillian and Peter. "You're here to see Anna?" she asked.

Lillian nodded and realized Peter had stayed back a pace or two. "Yes, I'm her daughter."

"You're in luck. She's having a good day," the nurse said.

Lillian didn't know what that meant and was afraid to ask. It had been years since she'd seen the mom she remembered—the fun mom on the beach, the kind mom who kissed her good night. That mother seemed to have disappeared completely.

The nurse pointed to a bench in the garden where Anna sat in the sunlight like usual, gazing out in front of her. Lillian paused, and Peter gave her a gentle shove but stayed back. She walked slowly over and found a seat next to her mother, leaving space between them. She didn't want to risk getting too close to this frail woman, causing one, or both, of them to buckle or break.

"Hello, Anna," Lillian said. Her mother turned her head toward the daughter she didn't recognize and smiled politely. Prickles covered Lillian's throat as she saw the sunken blue eyes that she knew matched the color of her own.

She tried to think of a happy memory of her mother, but almost never could. This person was her mother, familiar, yet not, and that hurt Lillian.

"Did you bring me dessert?" Anna asked, without greeting.

Lillian should have brought something sweet. The faint glimmer of Lillian and her mother sitting at their kitchen table on Seventy-Sixth Street, dunking chocolate cookies into milk, flickered past her eyes. "Next time," she said. She fumbled with the pocketbook on her lap. "But I do have something you might like."

Anna frowned. "I don't like raisins."

"I know." Neither did Lillian or the girls.

Confusion replaced irritation on Anna's face. "You do? I thought you were new here."

A band tugged tight around Lillian's heart, and her throat felt thick. She made herself swallow. "No, I've been coming here for a long time."

"Huh," Anna said. "I don't remember you."

"That's okay," Lillian said. "I remember you."

Anna smiled like a little girl caught unaware.

Peter stood a few yards away, watching and talking to the nurse. His arms were crossed out of concern, not consternation, Lillian was sure of it. The staff would tell him anything he wanted to know. He'd become Anna's legal custodian when he began paying the hospital fees.

The photo of the little family on Margate City beach was right where Lillian had tucked it in her wallet. Smiling, she held it out so Anna could see it, but her mother only grimaced. The nurse stepped toward Anna, but Peter touched the woman's arm and shook his head, then nodded at Lillian.

"Who are those people?" Anna asked, staring fixedly at the picture. "Is that a photograph of your family?" She held her hand out.

Lillian glanced at it again. That's exactly what it was. She held her breath and handed the picture to Anna.

"How did you get this?" Anna asked, and for the first time she seemed oddly engaged. Not necessarily happy, though.

Simple answers worked best, Lillian decided. Nothing too involved. "I had it in my pocketbook."

Anna pointed at Lillian in the photo. "This little girl is Lilly. This is my daughter." Pressure pulsed in Lillian's throat. Her mother had recognized her. She wasn't forgotten. She felt the tears welling up inside her and pulled out a handkerchief. "If you blow your nose when you're crying, it will stop the tears," her mother used to say when Lillian was little. It still worked.

Her mother asked, "Do you know Lilly?"

Lillian managed to keep her voice soft and steady. "I do."

Anna turned her body toward Lillian. "Is she safe?"

The voice was almost pleading, and Lillian saw true concern in her mother's eyes for the first time. She found it hard to speak.

"She is."

The decision to talk about herself in third person seemed natural. Her mother recognized ten-year-old Lilly, even if she thought the thirty-five-year-old in front of her was a stranger. How come she'd never recognized the younger Lillian when she visited, yet suddenly knew her from a photo?

"Are you sure?" Anna wrung her hands and tapped the photo, her finger right on Lillian's father. "Because he's a bad man." Anna thrust the photo back at Lillian as if it were on fire.

She must not recognize her husband. She had adored Lillian's father.

"No, this wasn't a bad man. He was Lilly's father, a good man."

"Did you bring me dessert?" Anna asked abruptly.

Lillian tucked away the photo. "Next time. Do you want to tell me about Lilly?"

Anna gave a misty smile as she gazed at the last rose blooming on a bush nearby. "She's my firecracker."

Firecracker. Lillian had entirely forgotten that her mother had called her that. She choked back a pit in her throat and wiped one runaway tear.

"But they won't bring her to see me." Anna was talking in the present tense, as if Lillian were still ten years old.

"Who won't bring her?" Lillian asked. This was more than Anna had expressed in two decades. And all in response to that one photograph. It seemed like a peek at her family of the past had spurred Anna's mind into action.

"Percy's parents love Lilly, but they don't want her to know. They don't want anyone to know." Anna stared off as if in a trance. "My husband died," she mumbled. "I was glad."

Lillian froze in place, cold as a snowman inside and out. Clearly her mother was muddled and didn't know what she was saying. Her parents had fought sometimes, which was scary, but he was a good man, a good provider. He'd prided himself on that.

She'd had enough. With a muttered "I have to go now," Lillian sprang from the bench and hurried to Peter. She grabbed his hand, grateful for his steadfastness and for the life to which she could return. "Let's go."

She took a last look back and saw the nurse put her hand on Anna's arm in a gesture of consolation or to calm her—Lillian couldn't tell.

Lillian was the one who needed comfort and peace of mind. Any clarity about the time in her life when she was happy, about her childhood, wouldn't be found here. Or with her mother. Her mother couldn't remember either. Or wouldn't.

Lillian stared at the photo of her family while she and Peter walked back to the car. Her mother had seen something different, something untrue, in that picture. "You should have heard her," Lillian said. "She sounded sane one minute and crazy the next. She recognized me, but she thought my father was some bad man. But I know she loved my father. She fell apart when he died. And she never recovered."

"It's no wonder, then, that she doesn't remember that time." His eyes were kind, kinder than she had any right to expect under the circumstances. Most people wouldn't even mention a relative who was locked up for life—it was as bad as having a parent in jail. She felt a surge of gratitude for him again.

"You're right."

Peter steered Lillian around a planter—just in time for her to miss bumping into it. "Watch where you're going. Maybe the photo wasn't a good idea." He held on to her arm protectively.

Lillian stopped walking. "But she knew it was me on the beach."

"No, she knew it was her daughter on the beach. She didn't know that photo was over twenty years old. She's not in her right mind."

"But what if she is? Sometimes, I mean. She knows she likes sweets and hates raisins, and she never mixes that up. She said Lilly was her 'firecracker,' and that's what she called me. Why would she say my father was a bad man? Why would she think I wasn't safe? And that she was glad he died? That was the worst part. What if she had said that to my grandparents?"

She could tell Peter was turning her words over in his head. Finally, he said, "That sounds like paranoia, doesn't it? Reason enough to have someone put away. She obviously wasn't in her right mind back then."

"I guess. But how do we know that, when it comes right down to it?"

"Listen, you have no proof other than her accusations from today. She's never said anything before about this?"

Lillian shook her head, then she pivoted and marched up the brick road to the main building. She'd never questioned what she had been told. Her mother had gone crazy. What if Anna had lost her mind *because* of her treatments, not despite? She'd heard of such cases.

But—what if Anna's recollections were correct? She'd recognized Lilly, after all.

"Lillian!" Peter yelled. She stopped and turned around, ready to argue for her right to answers to questions that were decades past due. But he was stretching his hand toward her. "You deserve to know. Let's get some answers."

Dr. Paul was not a man accustomed to impromptu appointments. He walked—almost stumbled—into his office, where Lillian and Peter sat waiting, as if crossing the finish line of a race.

"Thank you for seeing us on such short notice," Lillian said.

"My secretary said you wanted to see the admitting records of Anna Feldman." He looked at Peter, but Lillian cleared her throat and Dr. Paul turned to her.

"I'm her daughter. I was a teenager when she came here." Lillian should have asked about her mother's history a decade ago.

"I understand, and I'm sorry. And since Mr. Diamond is her custodian, I need his permission to discuss this with you."

"*His* permission? I'm her daughter." Lillian's volume had risen more than usual.

"Of *course* you have my permission," Peter said, stopping any rising tide.

"Very well," Dr. Paul said. "I was not working here in '46, and unfortunately, the records from Byberry State Hospital are incomplete. All I can say is that it's fortunate for her that you got her out of there."

Lillian leaned forward. "Why was she admitted?"

The doctor checked the file in front of him. "She was admitted here with a diagnosis of presenility."

"No." Lillian was becoming impatient. "Why was she admitted to Byberry?"

Dr. Paul leafed through the stack of papers. "It says here 'grief madness.'" His eyebrows rose. "My word, we don't use that terminology today. Wait, there's a photo."

"Of my mother? Let me see it."

"I don't think—"

She looked him squarely in the eye. "I am not a child, Dr. Paul."

Avoiding her gaze, he handed the picture to Peter, who looked at it and frowned. "We don't know that this is Anna."

Irritated by his condescension, and even more curious now, Lillian reached for the photo, but Peter held it back, hesitant to let her see. She cocked her head at him.

Silently, Peter handed Lillian the photograph.

Not a face. A close-up of someone's forearm. In the center of the picture, near the bend in the arm, a round pale scar. It looked to be the size of a quarter.

The photograph had been clipped inside her mother's file, but there was nothing to identify the owner of that arm, or that scar. Lillian fought to recall her mother's bare arm and realized that she hadn't seen it for years. Anna always wore long sleeves.

She looked at the back of the photograph. The blue writing was smudged but legible.

Patient said she had been burned with a cigar.

Nausea roiled Lillian's insides. That burn mark was horrible, cruel, but this couldn't be her mother. Lillian would have known if her mother had been hurt that way—if she'd had a scar.

He's a bad man.

Anna's words of less than an hour ago echoed in her mind. After seeing the twenty-four-year-old photo of her family, she'd recognized Lilly. Had she recognized Lilly's father too? That picture had been taken on the beach in the middle of summer. For the first time, it occurred to Lillian how odd it was that her mother was wearing long sleeves on a hot beach day.

"He smoked cigars," Lillian whispered.

"Who?" Peter asked.

Lillian bolted from her chair, dropping the photo on the floor. "I have to see her again."

She ran from the room and ran down the same hallway she and Peter had walked earlier. Then, she had been filled with trepidation. Now energy pulsed through her, and her stride lengthened. Had her mother told anyone about her troubles? Worse, had she been involuntarily committed to hide the truth? Was her mother mentally ill or had she become ill *after* they'd locked her away?

Peter caught up to her. "The doctor says she may not remember anything."

"She doesn't have to remember."

Lillian scanned the garden, but there was no sign of her mother.

"Are you looking for Anna? She's in her room. She can't be late for weaving," a silver-haired woman in a wheelchair said, as she crocheted something in lavender wool.

Lillian was pretty sure her mother didn't weave anything, especially from the look of her withered limbs.

Without a word, she swirled around and ran back inside, past Peter, to her mother's room.

Knock, knock.

"Mom—I mean Anna—may I come in?"

No answer.

Lillian turned the doorknob and pushed open the door. Her mother lay on the bed, her eyes closed.

"Anna, are you awake?" Lillian whispered as she walked nearer the bed. The room, sparse but clean, reflected no past and no personality. It occurred to Lillian that it was wrong for her mother to live in such a sterile environment. The next time she came, Lillian would hang yellow gingham café curtains. Gingham was cheerful. Her mother's favorite color was yellow. She would fill the room with yellow.

Lillian sat on the edge of the bed. Peter stood in the doorway but said nothing. Lillian lifted her mother's arm and pushed up the sleeve of her blouse and ran the pads of her fingers up and down Anna's forearm. Scars faded, but if one had existed, Lillian believed she'd feel it.

Nothing.

Relieved, Lillian took a breath. How could she ever have believed something like this would happen to her own mother? Or that it could have been caused by the father she adored?

"They're both gone," Anna said, her eyes still closed.

"What's gone?" Lillian asked. Or was it who?

Anna opened her eyes and looked at Lillian.

Lillian thought she saw a flash of recognition in Anna's eyes, but whatever it was, it quickly dissolved.

"My scar and my Lilly," Anna said.

Lillian shook her head, trembled, as if the ground below her was cracking. "Your scar?"

"Let's go," Peter said. "That's enough."

"No, it's not," Lillian said, catching her breath. "What scar?"

Anna touched the other arm and Lillian knew she had checked the wrong one. Even though the external scars had faded, the internal one stayed deep and ragged.

"Who did that to you? Was it someone at the other hospital?" Horror stories about Byberry and other asylums had flooded the news in the 1940s. But something inside Lillian told her that her mother had arrived at Byberry with the scar.

Anna didn't answer, then she said, "We can't eat in our rooms, so if you brought me dessert, we'll have to go to the lounge."

"I'll bring dessert next time. I . . . I just came . . . to make sure you knew that Lilly is safe."

"Oh, I'm so glad." Anna sighed and stared into the room, away from Lillian. "If you see her, will you give her a message?"

"Of course." Lillian patted Anna's hand and leaned closer. At last she'd hear a personal message from her mother, even if Anna didn't realize it. A message just for her.

Anna closed her eyes again. Lillian hoped she hadn't fallen asleep. The silence went on too long, and Lillian shook Anna's arm. "What do you want me to tell her? To tell your Lilly?"

Anna opened her eyes again. "Tell Lilly to always be a firecracker. My Lilly always loved Independence Day."

She had. Allowed to stay up late to watch the fireworks, she and her mother used to stand side by side, staring up at the sky. While her father lit the touch paper on the fireworks with his glowing cigar.

After forty-five minutes with Dr. Paul, and after reviewing a dozen medical articles and quoting a myriad of research findings, Lillian's heart finally stopped racing. He'd explained that patients with early onset dementia, like Anna, could dip into some long-term memories—like a young daughter—and forget others—like physical pain and the passage of time.

Her mother was content and well cared for at Friends. At least that was a blessing that Lillian could hold on to. A blessing that was due to Peter, that would never have happened if she hadn't married him.

Dr. Paul addressed Peter, as if he were Anna's offspring, not Lillian. "We chose not to dwell on the—" He hesitated. "Marital problems that might have precipitated her condition. If Anna was hurt by her husband, it's better for her that the memory be vague, that the pain be blurred."

Lillian nodded, pretending that the doctor had actually spoken to her instead of her husband. If her mother's erratic memory meant that her memories of Lillian—and her father—were vague and blurred, so be it. It was a small price to pay for her mother's peace of mind. Especially after all these years.

"Is there anything we can do for her?" Peter asked.

Dr. Paul looked at Lillian. It was the first time he'd addressed her voluntarily. "Even if she doesn't remember you, she enjoys your visits, you know."

Lillian suddenly felt ashamed that she'd become only a bystander in her mother's life.

The doctor was still talking. "The fact that she has lost her memories doesn't mean you can't enjoy yours. You can honor your mother no matter her condition."

"How so?" Lillian asked, knowing Dr. Paul was now managing *her* mental well-being and wanting to milk his professional opinion.

"By doing what she would have wanted you to do."

Anna wanted little Lilly to be a firecracker. Surely she was too old to be jumping up and down with enthusiasm, making noise, forcing people to get out of her way. That's what firecrackers did. Lillian wondered what being a firecracker would mean for a wife and mother. Was she living up to Anna's expectations?

"You're a mother, Lillian. What do all mothers want for their daughters?"

A husband, children, security, she would have said, not so long ago. Yes, but no. The real answer became clear and settled into Lillian like a familiar song. What did any parent want for their child?

"She would want me to be happy."

Chapter 23

LILLIAN

It had been years since Lillian had been to Sunny's house, and she felt intrusive arriving on the woman's doorstep unannounced, uninvited. Doing so went against every rule of etiquette. Yet when Sunny answered her knock and saw Lillian's face, she simply said, "Hello," opened the door wider, and invited Lillian to step into her living room.

Normally Lillian would have looked around, taking in the surroundings for information she could use later, to buy Sunny a gift or inquire after something like the slipcovers on the sofa or the chintz curtains. But she was still shaken from the visit at Friends Hospital.

Peter had let her talk on the way home, merely nodding from time to time, for which she was grateful. When they had arrived home, he started raking the leaves. Nothing would deter him from finishing what he'd started. Although Lillian felt exhausted by the day's events, she told him she had a few errands to run and needed the car. The first place she went was to her mother's best friend. The closest thing Lillian had to a mother herself.

"Your mother used to get that look when she didn't want to say what was eating her, but she needed to say what was eating her."

Lillian chuckled. Sunny knew them both so well. She depended on that reliable memory of Sunny's to help her rebuild her own. That's why she'd come.

Sunny indicated the sofa and, when Lillian sat, Sunny slid down next to her. "This is about that girl from the other day, isn't it?"

Lillian shook her head.

"All right then. I can see it's going to take my cherry pie to get it out of you." Sunny rose and headed toward the kitchen.

"Sunny, wait. It's not that girl. It's . . . it's about my mother. I just went to see her."

"I haven't seen her for a while. She didn't know me last time I went. Must have been a month or two ago. Is she okay?"

"Maybe. I'm not sure. I don't think so."

Anxiety was visible in the tension on Sunny's face. "That's not good. So how can I help you?"

"When I saw her today, she recognized me in an old photo I had with me. It's the first time she's done that. She still doesn't know who I am now."

"That's good, though, right? A beginning, maybe?"

"Perhaps." Lillian fell silent for a moment before asking, "My father. Was he a good man?"

Sunny looked directly at her, startled. "What makes you ask that?"

Lillian stared back at her. Sunny should have answered yes immediately.

"Did he . . . did he ever hurt my mother?"

Sunny looked down at her hands. She cleared her throat. "I worried this day would come."

Tears ran into Lillian's eyes, but she reached out to Sunny, encouraging her to continue.

"I showed my mother his photo. She said he was a bad man. She seemed happy that he was gone, that I—or rather little Lilly—was safe. It seems she has a burn mark, and I'm worried that he may have . . . may have . . ." She couldn't continue. Lillian felt a cold prickle of sweat on the back of her neck. She didn't want to hear the answer, but there was no escaping it now.

Tears welled in Sunny's eyes. "I never knew for sure. I only suspected. When she started wearing long sleeves and dark stockings in summer. When she wore collars that covered her neck. Wore lots of makeup and pushed her hair over one side of her forehead. What went on behind closed doors between couples . . . people didn't talk about it then. It was considered nobody's business."

Lillian took Sunny's hand and held on, wishing it was Anna's. An echo of what she'd said to Ruth about Carrie flashed into her mind. "They don't talk about it now. Poor Mom. She must have felt so lonely and afraid."

"I should have asked. Made her tell me. Not helping your mother— my best friend, who took me in when I needed work—is the greatest regret of my life." Sunny did not meet Lillian's eyes. Her head bent as if in prayer.

Not helping. That's what caused regret. Lillian would have wanted to stop her father if she'd known then, but what could she have done? No one ever talked about bad things, unless they were happening to someone else. And that was only to gossip, not to help. She wasn't ready to think about the fact that the vacation she remembered didn't exist, not for Anna anyway. Lillian said, "You did the best you could back then. She was so young. You were both so young."

"I'm sorry I didn't ask Anna. Didn't help her—and you—escape. That's what a real friend would do. It's why I visit your mother in the hospital. I just wish I could make it up to her somehow—I should have tried harder to rescue her. After all, I knew, deep inside, that he hurt her."

Lillian could barely breathe. Sunny was the only person who'd been part of her mother's anguished life, and she was bearing witness at last.

"Please . . . please forgive me." Sunny's voice broke as she said the words.

"It's not for me to forgive you. It's not your fault. She never told you. If only she had. Maybe you could have helped her."

As she stroked Sunny's hand and let her cry, Lillian thought of Ruth telling her about Carrie, and how she'd been unwilling to listen or to help. She'd immediately blamed Ruth for the problem, rather than Eli. All to maintain the status quo.

Lillian felt sick to her stomach as a realization struck her, and she grabbed the arm of the sofa to steady herself. Her life had been uprooted in a single day when her father died and her mother was institutionalized. And today Lillian, who had been robbed of a mother because of abuse, was herself perpetuating the problem by ignoring Ruth and Carrie.

All her mother wanted was for Lillian to be safe and happy—what every parent wants for their child. Perhaps she'd thought that remaining silent would protect Lillian from her father's anger. But it was the silence, the fear of addressing the issue, that had ended in Lillian having neither parent—and in her mother living this shell of a life. Lillian wondered who she would have become if she had known. Would she have grown to be the woman she was or become scarred for life?

"You okay, Lilly? I know this must have been a shock for you."

"I'm fine." Lillian wasn't fine at all. "But this has made me realize there's something I have to do." Now that she understood the damage secrets could do, she would be the friend that her mother had needed—to Carrie. Today's clarity made it essential.

Etiquette be damned. Lillian was too shaken by this understanding of her history, and the way she was allowing it to repeat itself with Carrie, to even say goodbye to Sunny. She wobbled to her feet and staggered out the door, letting it slam ungracefully behind her.

Chapter 24

RUTH

Ruth had always assumed that women like Lillian were impervious to everything that caused problems for other people. Dirt. Rude people. Even germs. So she was surprised when Lillian called Shirley at the last minute and asked her to teach the day's lesson because she was ill. Ruth was dying to ask Shirley what sort of germs could take down someone as strong and stoic as Lillian, but she knew that was none of her business.

She had been told she'd poked her nose where it didn't belong too many times already over the past few days. Had alienated her friends and Lillian. Even Asher was losing patience.

She felt more alone, more incompetent, than she'd ever dreamed possible.

Ruth was relieved that Lillian was ill and was grateful that Shirley had agreed to host lesson four, on elegant entertaining, at their house. After the brush-off Ruth had received from Carrie, Irene, and Harriet, she felt that being in her own home, with Asher's family, would at least give her a modicum of equanimity that she wouldn't have had at Lillian's. After all, Lillian had told her in no uncertain terms to mind her own business and had ushered her out the door.

Ruth had no idea how the others were going to treat her today, after she'd betrayed Carrie's trust and dished on Carrie's abuse. She wasn't in a hurry to find out either.

Shirley was carrying bowls of macaroni salad and coleslaw to the dining room. She had gone to a lot of trouble on the Diamond Girls' behalf. The dining room table was laden with rice pudding, lemon squares, and rows of cookies coated in chocolate and dipped in rainbow jimmies. Mini challah rolls stuffed with tuna salad and egg salad had been stacked in a spiral. Ruth doubted it would be as tasty as Irene's egg salad. She wasn't sure she would identify any of this as elegant entertaining, but she believed it appropriate for an informal luncheon, and it was plentiful. No guest would leave hungry. That thought seemed inconsequential, given what was going on. But she knew Shirley cared about that.

Ruth offered to help, and they arranged the food to look more attractive. Moving a dessert tray a little this way or that. Adding a cornichon or radish garnish here and there. This feeling of working in tandem with another woman besides Dotsie or her college friends—being in sync with a woman of Shirley's generation—was new to Ruth.

She had aunts, but this was somehow different, and Ruth wondered if this was how daughters felt when they did things with their mothers.

Any minute now, the other girls would be arriving. She had no idea what to expect today—if they even showed up.

As for Carrie, she still hadn't answered any of Ruth's phone calls. Ruth couldn't help but worry about her. And she worried that she was letting Asher down too, since she was sabotaging their happy new life by ruining the friendships she'd only just made.

Ruth was letting everyone down.

She hadn't been able to help Carrie. She hadn't been able to fit in here with Asher's life and with his family. She'd found it increasingly difficult to focus on her studies for the bar exam. She'd heard some people didn't pass it on the first try. At the rate her life was going, she might be one of them. And that, more than anything, would ruin her plans.

Ruth shifted the flower vase on the dining room table over a few inches to the right, balancing out the shapes and sizes. When she looked up, she noticed Shirley smiling at her. Even that didn't lift Ruth's spirits.

"Ruth Appelbaum, you've got housewife in you after all."

Was that really a compliment? "Thank you. I enjoy helping you. Learning how to do things your way."

At least for today, she had someone in her corner.

Harriet was the first to arrive, arms laden with a large Tupperware bowl. Ruth removed the lid and set Harriet's Jell-O mold on the table among the other salads.

"This looks wonderful." Harriet's words were intended only for Shirley. She hadn't met Ruth's eyes directly, and her demeanor toward Ruth—after the Carrie incident—was noticeably cool.

Shirley puttered around the table, shifting plates and bowls an inch to the left or right, and then back again. "It's not fancy-schmancy like it would be at Lillian's, but I didn't have a lot of notice, so it will have to do."

After Irene arrived with another Jell-O mold and chocolate chip cookies, they all gathered in the living room, decorated in soft fabrics and shades of green. The girls milled about until Shirley sat on the Barcalounger and pushed herself to recline. The wooden arms, slats, and legs reminded Ruth of her father's favorite chair, where she'd spent many happy hours on his lap listening to stories about her mother or seeking shelter from her brothers' roughhousing. She grabbed on to this unexpected memory of joy. She might need every one she could get before the day was through.

The girls arranged themselves along the sofa, leaving space for Carrie. *Ruth, empty spot, Irene, Harriet.* It didn't escape Ruth's notice that the other girls left the space around Ruth, like she might be carrying something contagious.

It was five past and Carrie still wasn't here.

Ruth's stomach churned with angst. Worry bubbled up. Carrie was always prompt. She hoped her friend was late because she was mad at Ruth and not because she was in serious trouble.

Her stomach was doing jumping jacks now. If Carrie was avoiding them all because of Ruth, she might have made everything worse. Her friend might have no one to go to if . . . She shuddered. Stopped herself from completing that thought.

"We'll just wait for Carrie before we get started." Shirley righted the chair. "We'll go through our lesson in the dining room. I hope you girls are hungry; the food's not just for show."

"What would we have been doing if we were at Lillian's house?" Harriet asked.

Irene smacked Harriet's knee. "Mrs. Appelbaum, she didn't mean anything by it."

"No, I didn't, but you have to admit the surroundings are different here," Harriet said, glancing at Ruth.

Shirley seemed surprised by Harriet's candor, but didn't seem to know exactly what she meant.

Ruth did know and, while it flustered her, she took offense on her mother-in-law's behalf. It was one thing to be mad at Ruth, but it was entirely unfair to take it out on Shirley. "Harriet, that's not nice," Ruth said.

Shirley was aware enough to know the air in the room needed calming, and she raised her arm as if to forestall any argument that might erupt. "Lillian and I do approach things differently, but I can assure you it's the same lesson." She smiled. "I suppose I can begin by telling you what I remind myself every day—it's not only my job, but my privilege to make someone feel comfortable in my home. Elegance is just another way of saying *refined*. Elegant doesn't have to mean fancy."

The doorbell rang. "Ah. There's Carrie," Shirley said.

Ruth slouched a bit; anxiety had tightened her muscles and straightened her posture—and exhausted her. Shirley walked to the front door alone, and the girls could hear the door open and Shirley greeting her guest.

But when she returned to the room, it was Lillian, not Carrie, who was by her side.

Lillian, who appeared fresh and well, not ill at all.

"Look what the cat dragged in," Shirley said.

Wasn't this considered extremely rude, coming unannounced?

Ruth stood. "Where's Carrie?" She noticed all the eyes on her and realized she'd spoken out of turn.

"Hello to you too, Ruth," Lillian said.

"You're feeling better?" Irene asked.

"I am. I had a hectic day yesterday, and thought I needed a lie-in, but once Peter and my daughters left, I realized it was the last thing I needed. Especially knowing Shirley made lunch."

"We're staying here, then?" Harriet asked.

"We are. It would be rude to leave, don't you agree?" Lillian raised her chin as if she wasn't going to let another lesson get away from her like lesson three had.

"I suppose." Harriet looked at her hands, somewhat humbled by Lillian's subtle admonishment.

"I know this is different from what we'd originally planned, but there's no shame in needing a break," Lillian said. "I had a busy weekend, but you girls are good medicine. Entertaining can be very therapeutic. It surrounds you with pleasant people." She took a moment to smile at each of them.

Ruth couldn't tell if she was more surprised or relieved that Lillian was being gracious to her. All her friends had told her to mind her own business; Harriet and even Irene were standoffish today. Lillian wasn't. Ruth decided that probably had more to do with elegant entertaining and etiquette than Lillian's real feelings toward her. She remembered the discomfort of being ushered out of Lillian's house all too well.

Shirley looked at her watch. "Should we get started?"

Ruth squirmed. The seat beside her was still empty. "I'm sorry, I know manners and lunch are important to all of you, it's just that Carrie's not usually late." Her voice sounded shaky, and she hoped the others didn't notice.

Irene raised an eyebrow and Harriet gave a little huff. They clearly had their own ideas about why Carrie hadn't shown up. Or they didn't care.

"I'm sure she'll be here any minute," Shirley said. "Why don't we wait in the dining room?"

They left their seats in the living room and converged around the dining room table. As the girls fumbled with notepads and pencils, the doorbell rang again.

The sound jarred Ruth, yet no one else seemed to take it as anything more than what was expected. Ruth was worried about Carrie; the others were nonchalant. Had they heard anything Ruth said? Didn't the suspicions linger in their thoughts?

"See?" Harriet said, looking pointedly at Ruth.

She was so relieved, she didn't take offense at Harriet's haughty attitude.

If Ruth's suspicions were correct, Eli wouldn't stop what he did to his wife, and Carrie would need friends more than ever. She had no family or other friends in this town. Ruth spun around, anxious to answer the door herself.

"Lil, would you get the door?" Shirley asked.

Ruth's shoulders tensed as Lillian nodded and walked away. Shirley babbled on about table arrangements, invitations, and seating charts, and the girls scribbled furiously in their notebooks. Ruth barely heard any of it, her attention focused on Carrie's entry to the room.

A moment later, when Lillian returned, she returned alone.

Ruth's breath choked in her throat. No Carrie. Where was she?

Lillian headed straight for Ruth and, tugging on her arm, whispered in her ear. "Can I see you for a moment?"

Ruth was perturbed. *What now?*

Lillian raised her hand and spoke in an audible voice to the others. "Carry on, ladies, we'll be right back."

"Everything okay?" Shirley asked.

"Yes."

Satisfied, Shirley pointed to the food and began to describe each dish to the assembled guests. Lillian tapped Ruth's shoulder. "Come."

Once they were in the hall, Ruth asked, "What's going on?"

"Follow me."

They walked back into the silent living room, where a strange woman was sitting at the edge of the recliner. Way overdressed for the time of year, she wore a long coat, sunglasses, and a scarf around her head. The woman wore no lipstick, or even makeup, and her lip looked puffy . . .

Oh God. Ruth felt sick to her stomach.

It was Carrie.

Slowly the woman removed her sunglasses, exposing a black eye. Carrie looked away as she pulled the scarf from her head, and Ruth tried not to gasp audibly. Her friend's features had been pummeled into unnatural colors that were grotesque for a human. Her cheek showed signs of dried blood, and the split lip was making it hard for her to smile, though she was trying.

"Oh, Carrie!" Ruth hoped her face didn't show how horrified she was. She didn't want Carrie to feel even worse. It was one thing to see battered women—strangers Ruth didn't know—when they showed up at Legal Aid. It was entirely different to see such brutality inflicted on someone she knew. Someone who was her friend.

Someone she'd tried—and failed—to help. She felt angry but determined not to repeat the mistake.

"I'm sorry, Ruth. I . . . I didn't know where else to go."

Ruth hurried to Carrie's side. "You have nothing to apologize for. You did the right thing. All that matters is that you're here, and safe." She stroked Carrie's hair, then looked up at Lillian. She wanted to scream "I told you so" or "This wouldn't have happened if you'd listened to me." Instead, she whispered, "We need to call the police."

Carrie gasped. "No police."

"Carrie, please."

Carrie shook her head and winced. Ruth could only imagine how much it must hurt to move. But, she realized, Carrie was right.

Ruth wasn't sure about the laws in Pennsylvania, wasn't sure what recourse there was for an abused woman. The police were notoriously reluctant to get between a husband and wife, and she'd seen the results of that inaction too many times to risk it now. Ruth had no idea where the local Legal Aid groups were or who could help Carrie in this situation.

If only Dotsie lived here. She was a social worker. She'd know who to call. Shirley had a phone book and the yellow pages, but Ruth doubted they had a category for spousal abuse.

She looked at Lillian again. "What do we do?"

For once, Lillian was absolutely still. She appeared to be in some sort of shock. This was a vastly different Lillian from the one who, only days ago, was so sure of herself, sure of what she knew about families and privacy and how to behave. A different Lillian from the one who had dismissed Ruth so casually and told her to go home and cook beef.

The silence was broken by the sound of footsteps and the rustle of skirts as Shirley, Harriet, and Irene walked into the living room. "What's the holdup?" Shirley asked. "The food's getting—"

"Oh my God!" Irene yelled, and ran to Carrie.

Irene lifted Carrie's hand to her cheek. "I'm so sorry." Carrie turned her head and tried to hide. "Who did this to you?"

The question surprised Ruth until she realized Irene wasn't sup- posed to know about the beatings. Gratitude filled Ruth.

Carrie didn't need any more pain than she already had. Didn't need to know her friends had talked about her behind her back. That they hadn't believed her. Irene might wear overly green eye shadow, but poorly applied makeup was not a gauge of a person's worth. What mattered was Irene's kind, compassionate heart.

Her eyes downcast, Carrie whispered, "Eli."

"Eli? Your husband?" Shirley sounded bewildered.

"Ruth knew. Tried to warn me." It was hard to make out all of Carrie's words, because speech was clearly painful.

"Ruth?" Shirley looked almost angry at the news. "I wish you had told me."

Ruth *had* tried to tell people about Carrie, and she had been met with nothing but denial and accusations about her own behavior. Why would Shirley expect her to share anything in those circumstances?

Perhaps she was expected to keep her mother-in-law informed of all the latest rumors—that's what Lillian had called them. Was that how females in a family worked? Shirley didn't seem the type of woman who would want to know about anything unpleasant. Ruth had assumed—since everyone else told her to mind her own business—that Shirley would rebuff her too. Perhaps be even more cross with Ruth, since Shirley expected her daughter-in-law to know better than to tarnish anyone's reputation. In particular, she should know how to make the Appelbaums look good to the outside world.

Shirley pulled a green velvet wing chair nearer to the recliner and took hold of Carrie's hand.

"I didn't think you'd believe me," Ruth said.

Shirley rolled her eyes. "Baloney."

Shirley was full of surprises. But what really mattered now was that Carrie was here and safe, that Ruth would be able to help her.

Shirley rubbed her fingers lightly against the back of Carrie's hand. Irene took Carrie's other hand; the rest sat around them in silence. Ruth struggled to know what to do next.

Carrie stared at the floor, then pulled her hands free from Irene and Shirley and wrung them in her lap. She wore no gloves, but her long sleeves covered her arms and wrists as if they were hiding secrets too. "I didn't walk into a cabinet or counter. And I didn't fall. Well, I did fall, but it wasn't an accident."

"You made yourself fall?" Harriet asked.

"Don't be stupid," Ruth hissed.

Harriet huffed.

Carrie looked up with a weak smile. "I'm having a baby; the doctor confirmed it."

Ruth patted Carrie's back. There was no question what Carrie needed to do, but Carrie seemed unsure.

Shirley laid her hand on Carrie's shoulder. Ruth expected her to say that was wonderful or *mazel tov* or to give some motherly advice. Shirley remained pensive.

Carrie opened her mouth to speak and sobs gushed out. Words popped out between gasps, but they had no cohesion. "Special." "Bottle." "Waiting."

"Shh," Shirley said. "We have all the time in the world."

Shirley's soft response surprised Ruth. Where was her mother-in-law with all the opinions, all the answers?

The others remained silent as Carrie pulled a handkerchief from her pocketbook and dabbed her unbruised eye. "I wanted it to be a special night. When I broke the news about the baby. I made New York strip, brought out a bottle of champagne. This is what we'd been waiting for." Carrie attempted a smile in a forgotten moment of hope, before her eyes filled again.

"When I told Eli, he was so happy. He hugged me, twirled me around the room. He said he was proud of me. He was my lovable Eli." Carrie looked back at the floor. "Then he said he wanted to move to Bala Cynwyd. That it was a better place to raise kids than Wynnefield."

Irene shifted in her seat and Lillian blew out a breath. Between them, six children were being raised here.

"I said I didn't want to move. That was it."

"What's the problem? It's literally across City Line Avenue," Harriet said.

Ruth really wasn't sure how long she'd last without punching Harriet, or at least wrestling her to the ground like her brothers might. Even in a situation like this, the woman point-blank refused to understand what was at stake.

"I don't have a car and I don't know anyone there. I've finally made friends." Carrie looked at each of them. "I don't want to move. And that's what I told him."

"That's your right," Ruth said, and glared at Harriet.

"He accused me of awful things. Asked me if the baby was his, said he wouldn't raise the milkman's son. Called me an ungrateful bitch. Then he slapped me, and I stumbled backward and fell over a kitchen chair."

The women grimaced in unison. Carrie gingerly lifted her blouse, revealing black-and-blue ribs, as if needing to provide proof. "Honestly, if it was just me, I wouldn't care."

This was the saddest thing Ruth had ever heard. Carrie was willing to take a beating to stay married to this man. As if her own safety and happiness didn't count.

"But the baby . . . ," Carrie said.

"Are you bleeding?" Shirley asked.

Ruth blinked, not sure what to make of Shirley's question. Was she concerned about medical problems, or was she gauging whether anyone would believe Carrie without the sign of blood?

"Any pains in your stomach?" Shirley persisted.

"No."

Harriet gave an exaggerated sigh. "You know, he has to live in the city to work at the high school, right? Maybe—"

Harriet's willful ignorance was too infuriating to bear. Ruth snapped, "Maybe what?"

Harriet ignored her and dug in. "C'mon. If he's so bad, why did you stay? And why did you sleep with him?"

"How dare you question Carrie's—" Ruth's face felt hot and was likely redder than her lipstick.

"Stop, both of you," Irene said. "We can't know what this is like."

The women fell silent. Irene was right.

"I love him," Carrie said. "He was fixated on moving away—he wouldn't let it go. Said he didn't care what his school contract said—that he'd get out of any restriction."

"Entitled bastard," Shirley whispered.

A tiny gasp left Ruth's lips before she realized it. Her mother-in-law. The etiquette-stand-by-your-husband queen.

"What else happened?" Irene asked.

"What makes you think anything else happened?" Harriet said.

Irene shrugged. "Something must explain a onetime outburst like that."

Ruth tried to decide what to say. Irene knew there had been previous attacks. But if Ruth spoke up, and the other girls didn't show any surprise, Carrie would know they'd talked about her, that Ruth had betrayed her trust. There was no sense in piling more pain on this drastically wounded woman, so Ruth remained silent. These girls didn't understand because they hadn't seen what Ruth saw in New York. She wanted to defend Carrie, but that was not important. What was important was to help Carrie get out.

Lillian's face had faded from peach to gray. "One time is one too many." Her words were coughed out, scratchy, after a too-long silence.

At last, someone was making sense.

"You're right. So we have to call the police," Irene said.

"I said no!" Carrie said. "That would jeopardize his job."

"Until he hits you again. I think the police is the only way to go. At the least, it will keep Eli on his toes. Let him know he's being watched."

Shirley's scoff was full of contempt. "The system won't help her. They'll take his word over hers."

Ruth had no idea that Shirley would know about the law. She looked at her mother-in-law anew.

"He's allowed to do this?" Lillian asked, her eyes wide.

"Absolutely," Shirley said.

Lillian put her hands on her hips as if she were challenging this new side of Shirley. "And how do you know?"

"It's not so much allowed as tolerated," Ruth said. "He'd have to kill her to get in any real trouble."

Carrie gasped.

Lillian slapped her hand over her mouth, muffling a yelp.

Ruth's heart pounded, her indignation rising with each thump. They couldn't let this happen to Carrie and the baby.

Carrie, pale beneath her bruises, stared at Ruth.

Silent sobs clogged Ruth's throat. If only she could make Carrie leave Eli. But she couldn't. It was all up to Carrie.

No one spoke. The passing of the occasional car, the chirping of a bird, all sounds seemed to be louder than normal in this room of anticipation. This room of fear.

Fancy food, pretty clothes, ample money, and higher education didn't matter—and etiquette could go to hell. There was a beaten woman in their living room. Were even these privileged women powerless to help?

Shirley left the room and headed for the kitchen.

Where did Shirley go, just when they all needed her?

Guilt swallowed Ruth. She'd have known the Pennsylvania laws and precedents if she had finished studying for the bar exam—or she'd have access to them through professors, and librarians, and fellow students. She'd have the same kind of connections and insights she'd left in New York. The particulars she'd lost amidst the picnics and lunches and shopping trips.

They sat in silence as Shirley returned with a bag of frozen peas and gently placed it over Carrie's bruises. After five minutes according to the wall clock—what seemed like five hours according to Ruth's internal clock—Carrie finally spoke. "You have no idea how hard this is."

Shirley gently rearranged the frozen peas over another spot, so Carrie's skin didn't get too cold in any one place. "I do. I know it's hard," Shirley said, training her eyes on Carrie.

Ruth was surprised and touched by Shirley's compassion, by her attempt to show camaraderie in order to help this poor girl she barely knew.

"How could you possibly know? No one knows how hard it is." Carrie's voice was a whisper, but that whisper was tinged with anger.

"Because it happened to me," Shirley said.

Chapter 25

LILLIAN

The room fell silent. The faces around Lillian showed disbelief, confusion, irritation, and shock. And, in her own case, hopefully nothing at all. Lillian deliberately arranged her expression into something as blank as a whitewashed wall, though beneath her coral silk blouse her heart was pounding.

Lillian was sure she'd misheard, or at least misunderstood. Shirley was her best friend. She'd been here in Shirley's living room countless times over the years. Things like that didn't happen to people like them; they weren't beaten by their husbands, weren't abused. Not here.

Lillian's parents were a different story. Her father was a laborer, her mother a seamstress. These things could happen in their neighborhood.

But Carrie? And Shirley? Shirley was the woman who'd taught Lillian how to be the perfect housewife and hostess, how to teach etiquette lessons, for goodness' sake.

Lillian looked around Shirley's living room. Carrie, Irene, and Harriet were looking at Shirley—and no wonder. Ruth's face had drained of blood, and her eyes held a dazed expression. For once she said nothing.

Lillian's heart sank. Not *Leon*. That sweet man adored his wife; anyone could see that. He could never have beaten her up—not even in some distant past. Yet she'd never known Shirley to lie. Omit the truth maybe, spin a few euphemisms, but not out-and-out lie.

It was Shirley who broke the silence. "I was engaged to someone else before I married Leon."

Lillian heard a collective sigh and realized she hadn't exhaled in quite a long time. She hadn't been the only one holding her breath.

"My first fiancé beat me—badly."

Lillian saw something in Shirley's eyes that made her want to comfort her. "Shirley . . . I'm so sorry. I had no idea. You never said."

She suddenly wondered if Shirley had assumed no one would believe her—just as Lillian hadn't believed Ruth about Carrie.

Her mother's scar. The cigar. Keeping her husband's abuse locked away to protect herself, her family. So as not to encounter any of the shame or blame associated with it. After all, people in the neighborhood she grew up in used to say that the wives probably deserved it. That marriage was private. That it wasn't their place to interfere.

Shirley nodded at Lillian before she went on. "No, I never said. I was ashamed of it. It was rough. He broke my arm, and my ribs. I had a concussion. Besides, he was always sorry afterward."

Sorry? When he'd broken her bones? No wonder Shirley was so tough.

Ruth gasped and reached out for her mother-in-law's arm. Lillian was glad that Ruth hadn't hesitated to support Shirley. The girl hadn't hesitated when it came to Carrie, either—and Lillian had done nothing to help. Worse, she'd practically kicked her out the door.

Irene was visibly upset by Shirley's story. Even Harriet looked shaken. As for Carrie—her tears were flowing unchecked now. Little rivulets streamed down her face.

"In the emergency room, he told them I fell off my bike," Shirley said. "I don't think they believed him, but no one did anything. Not the police, not my parents. God forbid I break the engagement. My mother asked me what I'd done to deserve it, and my father acted like the bike charade was true."

Lillian was grateful that all eyes were on Shirley as she felt a wave of rage rising within her. It must surely be visible on her face. Her grandparents must have known that their own son hurt Anna. Tortured her. And they'd done nothing. Except had her committed—so the rest of the world wouldn't learn the truth about their son and his family. Her grandparents hadn't rescued her. They were the reason she'd needed rescuing in the first place. They'd stolen her childhood. She clenched her fists and looked around for a cigarette. There was no rule of etiquette that could deal with this situation.

Shirley continued in a calm, controlled voice. "My fiancé was highly educated, from a good family. He lived on his own—he was studying law. Leon lived in the apartment next to his and was finishing his studies in accounting. The police never questioned Leon about what he might have seen or heard. But he knew something bad was going on, and he came to see me in the hospital. They decided to keep me in for a few days, maybe as a way of protecting me. But I didn't even want to see Leon because I looked so terrible."

Lillian squeezed and released Shirley's arm.

The other girls nodded, urging Shirley to go on.

"He told me he'd suspected what was really going on. Said he was sorry for not intervening somehow. There was nothing he could have done, anyway, and I told him so. I'll never forget the look in his eyes when he told me I never had to lay eyes on that guy again."

Irene wanted details. "Did he have a plan?"

"I guess so. I never asked. I was desperate and naive, so I just had to trust him. I wanted him to make my fiancé go away."

Ruth gulped. "What happened?"

"Leon went to a lawyer who said there were no laws that covered my case. I was only a fiancée. Not that a wife would fare much better."

Lillian couldn't stop the groan that escaped her lips. Even if her mother had reached out for help, there probably was none to be had. Not from family. Not from friends. Not from doctors. And definitely not from the law.

"He went to the wrong lawyer," Ruth said. She looked over at Carrie. "It's different now."

"Others said that since I hadn't called the police, hadn't pressed charges, it was a 'he said, she said' situation."

Shirley, who had always seemed so in control, suddenly showed a level of sadness that had never surfaced in Lillian's presence. Only now did Lillian appreciate the toll this was taking on her friend. She was sorry Shirley had not told her before, but likely Lillian would not have known what to do. Would she even have believed her?

"Even though he'd hurt you enough to put you in the hospital?" Ruth asked.

Shirley nodded. "Leon was my only advocate. He went to the police. But when they told him to 'watch your step,' Leon figured they were paid off."

Harriet said, "Well, see, it turned out okay. It brought you to the right husband. God works in mysterious ways."

"Stop it, Harriet," Lillian said, and covered her mouth with her hand, distressed at her lack of manners, but also proud of speaking up for her friend.

Even the other women seemed shocked by her callousness. Except for Ruth, who scowled.

Shirley glanced at Harriet and raised an eyebrow, then addressed the rest of them. "Leon promised I was safe, and I don't know why, but I believed him. I had to. No one had ever taken my side before. Not like that."

Lillian, unsteady all of a sudden, propped herself against a chair. Had her own mother had *anyone* to go to? Anyone at all on her side? She must have felt so lonely, so hopeless. And, once she had been sent away, she didn't even have her daughter for love or comfort. Lillian couldn't change the past, but she could, and would, change the future—for Carrie, hopefully, and for her daughters, who should know about these things too.

"So what happened to the fiancé?" Irene asked.

"I don't know," Shirley said. "I never saw him again. Thank God."

"Oh wow." Irene leaned in as if getting closer would provide answers. "Do you think Leon had him knocked off?"

The unexpectedness of the question, and its sincerity, made them smile.

Shirley chuckled. "I think he ran away. They found his car abandoned in Fairmount Park."

Lillian whispered, "This can happen anywhere, to anyone."

"I have to admire your courage in telling us about it," Ruth said, putting an arm around her mother-in-law's shoulder. Shirley leaned into her daughter-in-law for a second, and then sat up straight again.

"I had no choice. Carrie needed to know that she's not alone."

Carrie looked up from her lap and right into Shirley's eyes. "You got safe," she whispered. "You got out before you had children that could be harmed."

Shirley turned and pointed to Ruth, Lillian, Harriet, and Irene. "I've told you this for Carrie's sake. Each of you has to honor that by trusting me. And Carrie has to be able to trust all of us. I know what to do to help Carrie, but my solution relies on secrecy. You cannot tell anyone what happens here, ever." She looked at each of the women in turn.

"I'll do whatever you say," Irene said, and crossed her heart.

"Of course." Lillian nodded and wrapped her arms around her middle to keep the others from knowing how deeply Shirley's story had affected her. How closely it paralleled Anna's life.

"Me too. No question," Ruth said. "Just tell us what to do."

Of course Ruth was in. Lillian suddenly felt relief that she had a way to make amends for having let Ruth down, for having let Carrie down. Courage. That was part of being a well-bred woman too.

"You're not going to hurt Eli, are you?" Carrie asked.

"His pride, probably, but no, he won't be hurt physically—the way he hurt you." Shirley spoke with determination and without any sympathy for the man.

"What if it was a onetime thing?" Harriet asked, as if still trying to find excuses for Eli.

Lillian shushed Harriet again.

Shirley frowned. Ruth wasn't the only one losing patience with that girl. "You need to understand something, Harriet. The only way it's a onetime thing is if somebody dies," Shirley said.

Lillian shivered. Maybe her mother had been lucky. A terrible thought.

"I imagine this has been going on for quite some time," Shirley said to Carrie.

Carrie nodded, though her head moved no more than an inch. She looked back at the floor.

Lillian covered her face with her hands. How long had this gone on with her parents before her father died? She remembered all the times her mother had sent her to her room, and she'd hear the fighting begin. Her father shouting, her mother pleading. How had she not remembered that until now? She squeezed her eyes shut. She mustn't cry, not yet. As a child Lillian had never imagined what was going on. She could barely imagine it as an adult.

Ruth rested a hand on Lillian's shaking shoulder. "Don't worry. We'll make sure Carrie will be fine."

Lillian knew Ruth thought she was shaken solely over Carrie's situation. Lillian didn't correct her.

"How can you be sure?" she asked, thinking of the many years her mother spent institutionalized.

"She has us to help her now," Ruth said.

"She does," Shirley said. "But there's one more thing. We can only help Carrie if she wants to be helped." She paused and directed her question at the exhausted woman opposite her. "Carrie, honey, you have to answer me honestly," Shirley said. "Do you want us to help you get away from Eli?"

Carrie's eyes widened. "Get away? Leave? I don't want to leave."

The women in the room showed confusion—maybe at the question, maybe at the answer.

Lillian didn't understand either. Would Anna have been safer if she had taken Lillian and left before Percy died?

Shirley's voice held a soothing tone. "We understand."

Although clearly most of them, like Lillian, didn't.

Shirley went on. "Of course you don't want to. If we're lucky, it can be temporary, but for now, we need to remove you and the baby from danger. It's the only way," Shirley said.

"Isn't there some other way to make him stop?" Irene asked.

Only if somebody dies. Those words rang over and over in Lillian's head. Somebody. Not necessarily the wife—is that what she'd meant? It couldn't be.

Carrie looked at Shirley with pleading eyes. "There has to be. Isn't there?"

"I wish I could tell you that there was." Shirley sighed.

Carrie slumped back in the chair, wincing as her battered ribs hit the cushions. "I guess you're right. I do need your help. For my baby."

"Then you have to trust me and do what I say." Shirley waved her hand around the room. "I mean all of you." The roomful of women stared at Shirley, waiting for more.

"You cannot tell anyone—and I mean anyone—what we're about to do," Shirley said. She'd said it already, but Lillian was pretty sure that this was meant for the younger generation. Shirley knew she could trust her old friend.

"Not even Asher?" Ruth asked. "Your own son?"

This younger generation, Lillian thought. *Could they really keep a secret?* Straightforward women like Ruth would have a hard time justifying lying to their husbands—or anyone, really—yet someone's life was at stake. Men like Eli—like her own father—probably didn't stop unless they were forced to.

Shirley nodded at Ruth. "Even Asher. He's a good man, but he is a man. And he plays golf with Eli, doesn't he? So no. Not even him." Then Shirley looked directly at each one of them. "You must all promise not to talk about what goes on here for the next few days. Call it a special project if you have to explain why you're busy. And if you must lie—then yes, lie. This is a matter of life or death. Carrie is your friend. If you can't keep a secret, please, in the name of all that is holy, leave now. But do not tell anyone what you know—or Carrie's safety, and the safety of her baby, will be in jeopardy."

"Don't you think you're blowing this out of proportion?" Harriet asked.

Had she learned nothing from this conversation?

"No, she's not blowing it out of proportion," Lillian said. "Carrie needs our empathy and understanding. That's part of being a fine woman too."

Harriet shrugged this off. She scooped her pocketbook handle onto her arm. "I can't do this. I won't say anything, but as for the rest, it's not my business. And I won't lie to Scotty. I won't tell him unless he asks me, but—" She began to walk toward the front door, then turned back. "I'm sorry, Carrie. I'll call you." She closed the door behind her.

No one tried to stop her.

"Let her go. She isn't helping anyway," said Ruth, turning back to Carrie.

"Ruth's right. Let her go," Shirley said to the rest of them. "We need all the energy we can muster without Harriet's objections, because this only gets harder."

Lillian surveyed the others with a sense of pride. By allowing her to leave, they sent Harriet a message louder than any protest. Their friendship would not tolerate Harriet's behavior.

Carrie rested her forehead on Shirley's shoulder and said, "She's fibbing. She wouldn't tell Scotty."

"How can you be sure?" Shirley asked, her brow wrinkled.

Ruth answered for Carrie. "She'd never let on there was an imperfect marriage in our midst."

The five women squeezed chairs around a Formica kitchen table that was only sized for four. The sandwiches, salads, and desserts meant for the etiquette class crowded the kitchen counter, where they'd moved everything. The mingling aromas teased Lillian into a sensation that felt like nausea.

So much for etiquette. They were planning to break all those rules now. The disassembled buffet marked the urgency of the situation. Normally Lillian would have balked at the mess in Shirley's kitchen, but fastidiousness had no place here.

"You should eat something," Shirley said to the group. "You'll need energy if we're going to get this done."

The girls picked at the food on their plates as if searching gingerly for their appetites in the macaroni—ashamed to be wasteful, yet too anxious to eat. "Make sure you eat at home, at least," Shirley told them. "You need to act normally to allay suspicion."

Shirley told them she would be sure to stop at the butcher's for lamb chops later. That was normal. It made Lillian chuckle at her friend. She knew how Shirley's mind worked. No matter life's upheavals, Shirley's brain would still plan menus. She admired her determination.

"Our 'special project' will change your lessons, Lillian. Are you okay with that?" Shirley asked.

Ha. Given all that had transpired here, the lessons were no longer a priority to Lillian. "I am, if you are," Lillian said to the girls.

They nodded.

"I don't want anyone to miss out because of me," Carrie said. "The girls have been looking forward to the etiquette lessons, and I'm sure Lillian has worked hard to prepare."

"That's the last thing you need to worry about. Nothing is as hard as what you've been through," Lillian said.

"Lillian's right. You're more important than etiquette lessons," Ruth said. "Besides, it's only you, me, and Irene now, and we're with you."

Irene nodded. "Absolutely."

"But—" Carrie said.

"Your safety is more important than anything else," Irene said.

Over the next half hour, Shirley had Lillian, Ruth, and Irene scribble notes to be sure everyone was clear on the details. Carrie would have to leave Philadelphia and go somewhere Eli couldn't find her. No one questioned the verbalized plan, but the occasional raised eyebrow revealed a skepticism that it might succeed.

"Trust among us is the key ingredient," Shirley reiterated as she detailed all the supplies Carrie would need, including luggage. Shirts, skirts, dresses, shoes, hosiery, undergarments, hair care and skin care supplies, cosmetics. She wasn't to look like a fugitive, but a regular traveler, Shirley explained.

Lillian would never doubt Shirley again. Shirley obviously knew what she was talking about. Lillian's lessons had been all about blending in, but she hadn't expected they could be about saving a life. The less attention Carrie attracted—the more she fit into her new surroundings—the better. Blending in was critical to her safety.

They would need accommodation for Carrie. Shirley suggested calling friends and family outside the Philly area, preferably with children, an extra bedroom, and the willingness to feed one more person.

Lillian had no family other than Peter's, and she would never call them. So she probably couldn't help there. But she could certainly provide the suitcase and clothing Carrie would need.

Shirley dug in her pocketbook and removed a tattered sheet of paper. "This is the plan we used for helping other women in similar situations in the past. Copy this down and read it if you can't memorize it. It will help us get Carrie started, and it's the action plan that will get her to safety."

The specifics of the action plan were not to be spoken of outside this house, for Carrie's sake.

Lillian recognized the importance of that. Her own mother had been whisked away before she could escape or defend herself. How different Anna's life might have been if she had found help before things got really bad. If she could have escaped before Lillian's grandparents silenced her by putting her in an institution for the rest of her life.

"You're amazing," Lillian said. "I had no idea."

"It's the right thing to do." Shirley shrugged off the compliment. "We'll do this on the eve of Rosh Hashanah. People will be too preoccupied with the holiday to pay any attention."

At first it struck Lillian as odd that they would choose the holy days to make their move, but, as she thought about it, she realized there was no sacrilege here. The God they believed in would want Carrie to get away. To be free from harm.

"Someone will drive Carrie to the Greyhound station in either Easton or Scranton. Only the driver and I will know who took her and where. Carrie will leave Philadelphia and board a bus to her first destination when Eli is at services."

Irene spoke up. "I don't get it."

"You know that during the evening *minyan*, the men gather for prayers. Eli will attend, won't he?" She directed this at Carrie.

"He usually does." Carrie looked even more anxious, if that were possible.

"The fact that we women aren't counted in a minyan will work to our advantage. Eli will be expecting Carrie to be in the kitchen preparing the holiday meal."

Except Carrie wouldn't be there.

Carrie's clothes and belongings would remain at their house, suggesting she was somewhere nearby, when in reality, she would have collected the provisions for her new life from Shirley's house, where they would be stored until then. By the time Eli realized she was gone, she truly would be.

In time, they would have to hope that Eli would grant Carrie a *get*—a Jewish decree divorce—arranged through a liberal rabbi in Omaha. The choice of town was meant to throw Eli off the trail. Wherever Carrie landed, it would not be Omaha. Lillian reasoned that return addresses could be dangerous too and marveled at how well conceived Shirley's plan was.

"That pretty much covers it," Shirley said, and the rest of them set down their pencils.

Without a word, Lillian pushed away from the table and stood. She was ready to make up for not being able to help her mother.

"I'll be right back," she said, and scurried out the back door.

It took her less than ten minutes to rush home, get what she needed, and return to Shirley's house. When she burst through the back door the other women looked at her, bewilderment plain in their faces.

"What are you staring at?" Lillian tapped her head and then tugged on her hem. "Is my slip showing?"

Shirley nodded at the Maxwell House can Lillian held in one arm. "Did you think we were out of coffee?"

Lillian shook the coffee can, which made a rattling sound of metal on metal. "Seven hundred and twelve dollars and change."

Shirley shook her head as if she must have misheard. "Did you say—?"

"Yes. Seven hundred and twelve dollars and seventy-five cents, to be precise. Whatever you have in mind, money will help, right?" Money always helped. She set the can on the table.

"Where did you get it?" Irene asked.

Shirley raised an eyebrow. "It seems our Lillian is thrifty—and generous." She laid a hand atop the can. "Are you sure?"

Carrie, who'd been staring at the coffee can, shifted her gaze to Lillian. "I can't let you do that," she said.

Lillian touched her heart. "Look, it's my money, and I can decide what to do with it."

"What'll happen when Peter realizes it's missing?" Ruth asked.

"Impossible." Lillian smiled and set her hands on her hips in a Superman stance. "He doesn't know it exists." She sat on an empty chair, ready to do her part, whatever that was. "Now what did I miss?"

Chapter 26

RUTH

After Lillian surprised them all with a coffee can full of money, the women decided to move into the living room.

"Carrie looks exhausted. She's had a difficult day so far, and you remember what it's like in early pregnancy. The smell of all that food might not be the easiest thing to deal with right now. I know it made me feel queasy for the first three months." Irene looked at Carrie as she said this. "It gets better as you go along," she reassured her friend.

Ruth knew that, in a few years, that most likely would be her journey too, after she passed the bar exam and went to work. She helped Carrie put her feet up on the sofa while the rest of them perched on chairs.

Lillian got right down to business, repeating, "So, what did I miss?"

"Shirley was just about to explain how she's done this before. Hidden girls from their dangerous husbands, I assume," Ruth said. She couldn't believe she was saying this about her mother-in-law.

"Or fiancés. Or boyfriends," Shirley said.

"I've known you for more than ten years, and I never suspected. You never said . . ." Lillian trailed off.

"It wasn't necessary for you to know. I'm only telling you today because Carrie needs our help. The fact is, I'm a member of a local group called the Secret Esther Society," Shirley said.

Her mother-in-law! A member of a secret society. Ruth looked at Shirley anew—fascinated and impressed.

Shirley had kept many secrets. She suddenly felt that she didn't know her mother-in-law at all. Maybe she'd be more sympathetic to Ruth's desire for a career than Ruth had thought.

Not thought. Assumed.

"We hide women who are in danger from the men in their lives—and as a group, we hide in plain sight until we're needed. We have no official meetings. We communicate by letter or in person, in small groups like this. If we make telephone calls, like we'll have to, we don't share personal information; we use a code name."

"I get it. Esther," Ruth said. "Like in the Megillah."

Shirley nodded.

"Clever," Irene said.

"Being clever has nothing to do with it. The organization was started out of necessity. I wasn't the only one in an abusive relationship."

"I'm sorry. I didn't mean anything by it. It was a compliment to the clever choice of name. And the meaning it would have to Jewish women."

Ruth wanted Shirley to know she admired her, but now was not the time.

"How long has this been going on?" Lillian asked.

"The violence? Since the beginning of time, I imagine," Shirley said, her voice taking on a weary note.

Could it be that they actually had something important in common? Wanting to care for women in situations like Carrie's?

"So how did this rescue operation happen?" Ruth held up her page of notes. "How did the society get started?"

"About twenty years ago, a friend came to me, concerned about her niece in California. Her husband beat her up, and my friend wanted to send her someplace to recover. Somewhere the man wouldn't be able to find her."

"And after what had happened to you, you couldn't say no," she said.

Shirley cocked her head. "I didn't want to say no. I wanted to help these girls change their lives. After a while, word got around, and we started arranging to hide any girl who reached out."

"That's incredible. And no one outside the organization knows it even exists?" Ruth asked.

"It's the only way it can work. So we're sworn to secrecy."

"That's why I've never heard of it," Ruth said. She wished there'd been something like that when she lived in New York. She'd known girls there who could've used a safe hiding place.

"Good. You're not supposed to have heard of us," Shirley said.

So, to the outside world, Shirley adhered to the perfect social system, yet a select few knew that she had a system of her own.

Ruth realized that she had misunderstood Shirley for all these days. Her mother-in-law might understand Ruth wanting more for her life.

"It sounds risky for everyone," Carrie said dubiously. "Even with code names."

Ruth hoped she wasn't changing her mind.

"It's less risky than leaving you in that house," Shirley said. "And if it goes according to plan . . ."

"We save you and the baby," Ruth said.

"So what's next?" Irene asked.

"A safe place for Carrie to go?" Ruth asked.

"Yes." Shirley nodded. "Ruth, you and I will make phone calls tomorrow when Leon and Asher go to the office. Lillian, I assume you can do the same when Peter leaves. You and Irene, stop by with your lists of telephone numbers in the morning. We'll call anyone you haven't been able to reach and mark a map with the locations we're able to secure. Remember, only call people you can trust to be empathetic and discreet. Even better, ask them to refer you to someone else so it's harder to connect the dots. It's not easy to find helpers at this level, but Carrie has the hardest job—and that is to pretend things are okay."

Shirley leaned down to whisper something in Carrie's ear.

Carrie blushed. "Shirley says I can act affectionate if I feel safe enough."

"You're not serious!" Lillian said.

"Anything to throw him off track," Shirley said.

"What if something happens in the meantime? Before Carrie's out of there?" Ruth asked. She hated to bring up doubts at this point and didn't want to frighten Carrie any more than necessary, but she knew the violence wasn't likely to stop. They needed to be prepared, especially Carrie.

"I think she'll be safe for a few days because he'll want the bruises to fade before Rosh Hashanah services, where someone might notice."

"Ruth thought we ought to have called the police. Are you saying we shouldn't?" Lillian said.

Shirley answered promptly. She'd obviously thought about this before. "We should leave the law out of this. We will not get any solutions from *them*. They're all men, for one thing, and they stick together. It's up to *us* to help women in trouble."

It struck Ruth how much Shirley's history was like that of the women she'd tried to help at Legal Aid. And that Ruth's own beloved husband could have been a child living in a violent home if Shirley had married that man. She felt a new sadness over this. Shirley had tried the legal system after she'd been injured, and it had failed her.

Another reason Ruth had to become an attorney. This system had to be changed.

"Up to all of us." Shirley shuffled her notes into a tidy stack as if accentuating her point. Then she unrolled a map of the United States that had been lying unnoticed on top of some books in the bookcase. "As we go, we'll mark an X where we can confirm possible shelter for Carrie. We'll keep a detailed list, and my people will use that information to set up her itinerary."

Shirley tapped her pencil on her chin. Ruth noticed she did this when she needed to think.

"We need to add a few more things to the plan. First, we must collect baby supplies." She pointed. "Add those to your lists."

"No need. I've got it covered," Irene said. "I saved everything."

"And we'll have to tell the host families so they're aware of Carrie's situation. Don't forget maternity clothes, as well as larger hose, shoes, and foundations."

"So if we get everything together and find these families—and Carrie can persevere for a few more days—you believe she'll be safe?" Ruth asked.

"I do."

"Have you ever hidden any of these girls in Wynnefield?" Irene asked.

"As a matter of fact, yes, I have," Shirley said.

"Where did they stay?" Lillian asked.

"You know I can't tell you that."

An hour later, after all the details, instructions, and information, Ruth and Shirley walked Carrie home. The fact that the women walked in relative silence struck Ruth as very different from their usual cheerful chatter on the street. Yet she understood the risks of anyone overhearing their plans. If the women said anything at all, it was only to comment on the weather, shopping, the upcoming holidays—anything that passersby wouldn't notice as unusual.

Ruth hoped Carrie would have the courage to go through with it, and that nothing would go wrong. But she didn't dare ask now that they were outdoors. There could be no slips in secrecy. Carrie's life depended on it.

When the three women reached the front door of the Blums' twin home, Ruth mused about how anyone who viewed it from the street might be deceived by its welcoming and tidy exterior.

"Promise you'll come over to our house tomorrow at ten," Ruth said, as Carrie pushed inside. "If you don't show up, I'll come over to check on you."

"I'll be there," Carrie said.

"And till then?" Shirley asked.

"I'll do everything you said," Carrie whispered.

"Good girl," Shirley said. "Bye, Carrie. See you soon," she added, extra loud, in case anyone was listening.

Ruth patted Carrie's arm before her friend closed the door and the dead lock clicked, a foreign sound in a neighborhood of open doors.

Ruth's throat seized. Eli might be inside. That same man who thought nothing of beating women. Her throat loosened with the embarrassing realization that she and Shirley were safe. That Eli was not a threat to *them*. She scurried down the walkway and didn't speak until she knew they were out of earshot of anyone in the house. "How can we leave her here?"

"I know it's hard, but we don't have a choice. We're not ready. If Carrie just walked out, Eli would follow her. We have to act as if everything's normal—for her sake."

Ruth and Shirley retraced their steps toward the Appelbaums' house. The rustling leaves and temperate breeze made for good walking weather. Ruth wished they had farther to go. There was so much she wanted to ask her mother-in-law.

"We can start on dinner. We need to work on the brisket." Shirley pushed open the front door and walked in.

Ruth followed her. She wanted to talk more, not be mired in cooking.

"Perhaps you'd like to help me." Shirley glanced at Ruth.

A rush of warmth flooded through Ruth. She knew Shirley never let anyone help her with her famous brisket.

Emboldened, she continued. "I think I know where some of . . . some of the girls stayed."

"I figured you would."

"In our attic?"

"Yes."

"Cousin Louise?" Ruth asked. "She was your friend's niece?"

Her mother-in-law looked at her, brow furrowed, then relaxed. "You know I can't say."

"Well then—how many girls have you hidden?"

"Between all of us? Quite a few."

"Quite a few, ten, or quite a few, fifty?"

Shirley reached into the refrigerator for the beef, then straightened up and looked at her. "Ruth Appelbaum, is this a cross-examination?"

Ruth felt a small adrenaline rush at the legal jargon. Rosh Hashanah would be here soon enough, and Ruth would have some explaining to do.

She had assumed her in-laws would react a certain way, but today she had learned there was more to them than she'd suspected. They had been burned by the legal system when it came to protecting battered women. Shirley had taken matters into her own hands. "I'm interested. I wonder how big the problem is, that's all."

"Personally—a dozen women over the years. When the children were older it would have been too hard to explain, so I helped the group in other ways: organizing transportation, donating money, that kind of thing. But since the girls got married and Asher was in New York, there've been a half dozen or so."

Ruth thought about Asher and his promise to tell his parents about Ruth's dream. How he'd put off telling them, and Ruth had questioned his sincerity when it came to supporting her career with regard to his parents. Did he never suspect they were involved with helping abused women too?

"Leon knows about this society?" Ruth asked.

"Yes. Can you hand me the meat knife?"

Ruth pulled the knife from its drawer and handed it to her mother-in-law, who began trimming the meat.

"Does he know everything? All of it? And he supports it?"

"It was his idea to renovate the attic."

Her father-in-law was a mensch, no doubt about it. Hopefully, his son was too.

Ruth suddenly pictured the lovely unclaimed *tchotchkes* on her dresser. They must have been left behind by girls the Appelbaums had helped. She paused as an unwelcome thought occurred to her. "Are there girls with nowhere to go now—with me and Asher staying in the attic?"

"No, I found an alternate nearby, don't worry. We haven't needed it yet. Not all the girls come through Philadelphia."

"Your daughters? Alice and Abigail don't know? They're not curious?"

"They're busy with their own lives, and the women don't stay long. A week, maybe two, and then they move on. It will be different for Carrie because she's expecting, but we'll find the right place, or someone will."

"Do you worry Eli will search for the baby?"

"I do, but one thing at a time. There's always a way. We just haven't figured it out yet."

If anyone could solve this problem, Shirley would. She wasn't just a polite housewife and prickly mother-in-law. She was a doer. A trailblazer, even. Was she someone who would understand Ruth's goals and dreams?

Maybe. Maybe not. But Ruth wished Asher knew this side of his mother. She couldn't help but think he would respect it.

Guilt seized Ruth. She lived in Shirley's house, loved her son, strove to please her. Ruth had made assumptions about this woman and had kept things from her, things that affected Shirley's son, her eventual grandchildren.

"You can bring me the meat rub from the pantry. It's the one in the green jar."

"Could you stop for a minute? Please," Ruth said.

Shirley paused and turned to her. "What's wrong? We need to start dinner."

"I want to say I'm sorry," Ruth said.

"Nothing to be sorry about. You did a good job today, in a difficult situation."

"No, I mean about marrying Asher. I'm sorry we eloped. You didn't deserve that. He said you wouldn't care."

"Well, he was wrong, but I daresay you two were doing what you thought was best."

Ruth knew Shirley was hurt about the elopement, but now she seemed hurt by what her son thought he knew about her. Ruth wanted to smooth things over. "I'm going to try even harder to understand where you're coming from. I made too many false assumptions about you. Now that I see how much you care about strangers, I know how much your son must mean to you. I'll do better at discussing things with you. I promise."

"Thank you." Shirley's voice hitched as she spoke, and Ruth wondered if it was because she was touched by this sentiment or if she was simply exhausted from everything that had gone on today.

"I really do love him and want him to be happy," Ruth said.

"I know."

"He wants me to be happy too."

"Of course he does."

Ruth paused and gathered her thoughts. Shirley had opened up to Ruth today, sharing a very private part of herself, of her mission in life. Shouldn't Ruth open up a bit in return? Cement their relationship a little more? "I'm going to get a job."

"Is that so?"

Ruth's defensiveness bubbled up because she knew she'd made a mistake. She should have waited for Asher. "I'll explain later."

Shirley put the knife on the counter, her eyes boring into Ruth's. "You're not normally at a loss for words, Ruth. Speak up."

Ruth couldn't quite tell if Shirley was encouraging her—or baiting her. Ruth debated what to say and held her breath. One. Two. Three.

"I'm studying to take the bar exam." Ruth blurted it out faster than she'd wanted and stared at Shirley.

"We thought you went to Barnard." Shirley smiled.

"I did, as an undergrad, before Columbia. The law's the way I think I can help girls like Carrie. By changing the system. Asher thought you wouldn't understand." The words raced out. Ruth exhaled her secret in one big breath, and the confession lightened her. She'd manage the fallout. Shirley deserved honesty. Especially after today. Even if it meant Ruth was no longer seen as a promising daughter-in-law.

"Why did it take you so long to tell me?" Shirley's voice was flat, not accusing, more inquisitive.

"I guess we were scared to disappoint you. That I wasn't what you wanted for Asher."

Shirley said nothing for a moment, then, "Don't let anyone silence your voice, Ruth. Not even me." Her voice was gentle, like she was speaking to a baby.

Ruth blinked. Was her mother-in-law giving her permission to live life the way she wanted? Permission to stop following society's rules?

Shirley opened her mouth as if to say something else, and shut it. "I should take my own advice," she mumbled, then cleared her throat. "I have a confession too, Ruth. Leon and I knew about Columbia."

"How?" Unless Asher had told his mother. But she could trust him, couldn't she?

"I wasn't about to let a stranger move into my house. I did some digging. Jewish geography, you know. It wasn't that hard. And do you know what we found?"

"I wouldn't try to guess." Even though Ruth had no other secrets, she still worried what her in-laws had found out.

"We discovered a nice Jewish girl who had just finished Columbia Law School. I figured you were only there to find a husband. You found one, of course, but as I started to get to know you, I realized that wasn't the reason you were studying law. I imagine you must want to use your education. It isn't something I would've done, but times are changing. Who knows what things will be like when you have children."

Ruth blushed. Yes, there was so much she didn't know about this family.

"You gave up your home and put your dreams on hold for our son. You have nothing to prove. The etiquette lessons, the hair, the fashions—they're not important."

Ruth doubted this and twisted her mouth. "I don't believe you."

Shirley laughed. "Fine, I do think they're important, but not the *most* important. Love and loyalty rank higher. And honesty, under the right circumstances."

"I agree." Ruth could not believe she agreed with her mother-in-law. Times really were changing.

Shirley nodded. Ruth brought the spices for the rub and they worked side by side in companionable quiet. In silence there was a new comfort for Ruth. She hoped Shirley felt the same way.

Shirley broke it. "You know, if you don't take that exam soon, I'll have your father to answer to."

"What does he have to do with this?"

"His only daughter was moving into my house a hundred miles away. You don't think he gave me and Leon the third degree? When the dust settled, and we realized we all had the same interests at heart, your father confirmed what we'd already discovered about your career aspirations."

"Oh no."

"He's a real mensch, Ruth. Asher was taking you away, but he saw the love between you. Of course, he had an advantage. He actually knew Asher." Shirley covered her mouth with her hand and then lowered it. "I'm sorry. My mouth talks sometimes before my brain can stop it."

"I know the feeling."

Shirley laughed. "It was hard for your father to let you go so far away, but he really loves you. He asked us to promise two things. To treat you like our own daughter and encourage you to always follow your dreams. So you wouldn't lose who you are, who he raised you to be. You don't want us in trouble with your father, do you?"

Verklempt, Ruth swallowed and shook her head. She smiled. "Of course not."

"You'll understand when you're a parent too." Shirley walked over to Ruth and squeezed her hands, transmitting affection and conveying pride—or trying to. "I may not have had a great experience with lawyers, but I do believe you will be one of the good ones."

Ruth smiled. She might even have been blushing. She might not know what it was like to have a mother, but the warmth she felt from having this mother-in-law, this woman, her new family, here to support her, was something she wanted to keep.

Chapter 27

LILLIAN

When Lillian returned home from Shirley's without the coffee can with its dollars and coins, she should have felt lighter, but she didn't. Weighed down by everything she'd learned that day, she might as well have been carrying bricks.

Anna, Shirley, Carrie—so many women had lived with brutal secrets. Including her blameless mother. It was so unfair. And the effects went out like ripples on the water—women injured, children without parents. Her mother must have had strength of her own to survive. And to make sure that Lillian never got hurt by her father. The least she could do was honor that by being strong herself.

She entered the kitchen to find Pammie and Penny dunking Oreos into milk. She noticed the crumbs on the table, the milk mustache on Penny's lip, and felt so grateful she had these girls. Grateful that they could live a life with her, with their father. But she would make sure they understood that their good fortune wasn't everyone's. That women suffered in some marriages. She would make sure that her girls didn't wind up in those kinds of marriages, that they spoke for themselves, that they were independent.

She gave them a quick hello and dashed toward the basement.

"Mother, do you want some Oreos?" Penny called. Lillian had to admit she was a sweet girl, if a little indulged by her circumstances.

"Thank you. Maybe later." Lillian closed the basement door behind her and began sorting through the clothes that she hoped would suit and fit Carrie, now and after the baby, as well as some of her old forgotten maternity dresses she'd hidden away in a steamer trunk. She piled everything into a rickety laundry cart that would also accommodate the baby clothes and maternity wear Irene would drop off soon.

Lillian claimed a used coffee tin from the storage shelves. She'd always kept a few in case they came in handy for something. Peter used to tease her about it. Taking it upstairs, she dropped in a few coins, and instead of the echo evoking a feeling of emptiness, her heart raced at the promise of saving her change and extra money to help a girl in need. She'd give all the money she had—the money Peter gave her—if she thought it would help someone like her mother.

A stifled sob caught in Lillian's throat. She couldn't get the photo that she'd been shown at Friends Hospital—the photo of Anna's scar—out of her mind. She ran to the rec room and pulled out more photo albums. Open. Open. This one. The next one. Pulled the photos from the pages where they had been glued so many years before. Searching.

She didn't find any more hidden photos, but she couldn't believe what she saw. Why had she never noticed before?

Within minutes, she had photos strewn over half the floor—picture after picture of her mother in long sleeves, stockings, and scarves at the same time everyone else wore sleeveless shirts, shorts, even bathing suits. How had she not noticed this discrepancy in all the times she'd viewed these pictures?

Would she even have believed it if she had?

Lillian didn't fight back her sobs now. She let them rip.

"Mother?" Penny and Pammie walked into the room, Penny holding a plate of Oreos. Pammie carrying a glass of milk. They almost looked too scared to come closer. Lillian sniffled and rubbed her tears off her eyes, hoping her mascara wasn't too smeared. Her daughters weren't used to seeing her cry, and she didn't want to frighten them more than they already were right now, watching their mother break down.

Lillian knew all too well how challenging it was to watch one's mother break.

"We brought you cookies and milk," Pammie said.

Lillian managed to smile. A child's comforting gesture. Pammie could be sweet when she wanted to be too.

"What's wrong?" Penny asked, and Lillian knew her concern was genuine.

"I need to tell you about your grandmother—my mother," Lillian said.

"We know. She lives at the hospital," Penny said.

"Well, there's more."

"It's a mental hospital. We know," Pammie said.

Lillian found herself choking up again and blew her nose in an effort to stem her tears so she could explain things to her girls. They deserved to know the truth.

"It's okay if she's crazy," Penny said, her voice reassuring.

Crazy? No. Their grandmother wasn't crazy. She was abused. At the thought of her mother and the reason she was in Friends Hospital, Lillian found herself sobbing again, soaking her tissue. Penny began to cry too, burying her head on her sister's shoulder. Pammie had always been the strong one, and even she gasped for breath.

Lillian was pretty sure her daughters didn't know exactly why they were crying, perhaps in sympathy with their mother, but it was clear they were sad too.

"I need to tell you something. Your grandmother wasn't . . . wasn't crazy. Not at first," Lillian said. "She was hurt by my father. Do you understand?"

They nodded, though Lillian wasn't sure they did. They'd been protected from society's hidden dark side until now. "And when he died, his parents had her committed to a mental hospital so no one would find out what he'd done to her."

"Did he hurt you too?" Pammie said, opening her eyes wide.

Penny ran to her and put her arms around her mother. "Was he mean to you?"

Lillian shook her head, and she sensed relief as her daughters exhaled. This was something Lillian struggled to make sense of. Her father, she remembered, had been a strict disciplinarian but not violent—never toward her. He required As in all her classes at school. She had to make her bed each morning, take her dishes to the sink as soon as dinner was finished, and help with household and yard chores. But weren't all fathers like that?

And he'd also built sandcastles, unwrapped ice-cream bars, and jumped her over waves. She believed the photographs, the notes, and what her mother could no longer tell her, because there was something in her heart that she knew was true: her mother had been fine one day and the next was taken away from her.

It was like she and her mother had known and lived with two different men.

"I don't understand," Penny said. "Why did she have to go away if he was the bad one?"

Lillian closed her eyes and sighed. "I don't know exactly what happened; I was younger than you. But it was wrong. I don't think anyone believed her, and in those days . . ." She hesitated. What she was about to say was still true. She let out a breath. "In those days people thought that the men knew what was best for the women, so if he hurt her, she must have deserved it."

"What did your grandparents say?" Pammie asked.

"They were the ones who sent her there. Either because they didn't believe her, or so no one would find out the truth about their son. I don't think we'll ever know, now that they're gone."

"That's really sad," Penny said.

"Yes, it is sad."

"Can we go see her? Take her flowers, or candy?" This suggestion from Pammie surprised Lillian. Maybe she hadn't failed her older daughter as much as she'd thought.

"See who?" Peter was in the doorway, looking at the three of them—and the mess of photographs around them—with a face full of confusion.

Lillian wiped her hands over her tears and then on her skirt, getting black streaks on the fabric. She hoped she didn't look as bad as she felt. No husband should come home to three crying females.

"Are you okay?"

"Of course. The girls and I were just talking about something sad." She stood and looked hard at Peter. She wasn't going to discuss this now. "So—what are you doing home so early?"

Peter still looked puzzled, but he followed her lead. "The electricity went out at the office. In the whole area. It won't be fixed for hours. We sent everyone home."

Lillian nodded.

"We want to see our grandmother," Pammie said to him.

"Was that what you were talking about? I don't think that's a good idea," Peter said, and frowned at Lillian.

"But we never met her, and we want to," Penny said.

Lillian swelled with pride at the compassion and kindness of her daughters. Maybe she didn't have that much work to do after all.

"Go upstairs and finish your homework. Your mother and I will discuss it."

The girls rolled their eyes and slipped past Peter. When the sound of their footsteps proved they were on the next floor, Peter gave Lillian a sigh.

"It was their idea. They caught me crying, so I told them why," she said.

"They shouldn't go. It's too difficult. Too frightening for them."

"They're stronger than you think. And they should know their grandmother."

"It's a bad idea. You know how heartbreaking that place is. How . . . disturbing . . . your mother can be. Just look at how upset you are. So no. No visits for the girls."

During dinner, no one mentioned Anna. Lillian, Peter, Pammie, and Penny ate roasted chicken, baby peas, and Rice-A-Roni. They talked about their days as if Lillian and the girls hadn't cried over their abused mother and grandmother. Hadn't asked Peter if they could visit.

Lillian made sure to keep smiling at Peter, at the girls, keeping the dinner conversation light and pleasant. But in her heart, she made a vow. She would be a coward in a cardigan no more.

And she would do things her way.

The next morning, life went on as normal, centered around breakfast and coffee—and Peter's expectations. Everything needed to look ordinary so that Lillian could help Carrie without arousing suspicion.

"Lillian, did you hear me? I'm going to invite the Bookbinders for dinner after the holidays. Don't you want to write it down on your calendar or something?"

Lillian topped off Peter's coffee and poured herself a second cup. She nodded.

"What do you remember about Art Bookbinder?" Peter said.

"Nothing, why?" Lillian went back to the flapjacks.

"He's coming in today and I want to schmooze."

"I'm sure you'll do fine."

"What's his wife's name again?"

"I don't know."

"How many kids do they have?"

"No idea."

Peter gritted his teeth and his voice rose. "Well, when did he open the upholstery shop?"

Lillian popped a piece of rye bread into the toaster and pressed the lever. "I can't remember."

"What's wrong, Lillian? You always know these things." She could hear the exasperation in his voice.

"I'm sorry, dear, I'm preoccupied."

She wanted to say that he should probably know these things about his own clients anyway, but instead she said, "Shirley, the girls, and I are working on a special project, so I'm going to be busy with that until the holidays." Lillian paused.

"Does this have anything to do with your mother?" Peter said.

She remained silent and waited until, without a word, the girls put their plates in the sink and slid out of the kitchen.

"I don't want to talk about it."

"Be careful, Lil."

He couldn't possibly know about Carrie. "What do you mean?"

"You know we can't take our daughters there, so don't press it. Your mother is senile. I don't think we know exactly what she will do, will say, in front of the girls."

Back to that topic, then. Relatively safe. "She wasn't always like this. I want to understand her, Peter. I want to be more empathetic and less judgmental. I think she can help us."

"Us?"

"Yes, all of us. You, me, Pammie, and Penny. Who better to teach us empathy than my own impaired mother?"

"You think our daughters need to learn empathy?"

"I do. There are people in the world who need us to care about them. And . . . I want our girls to know that no matter what happens, they can use their voices and we will listen to them."

"They know that."

"I don't think they do. We haven't given them a very good example."

"Are you saying I don't listen to you?"

"I'm saying I don't always speak up."

Peter looked at Lillian. "Did I do something?"

She registered the uncertainty on his face and in his voice. "I don't blame you. Not completely."

Peter stopped buttering his toast. "What's that supposed to mean?"

"It's just that if a man says something, people believe him. When a woman says something difficult, she's hormonal, pregnant, or hysterical. She might even get sent away, so no one has to deal with her. If our girls are ever in trouble, I want them to be believed when they speak their truth."

Peter reached for her hand. "It's hard to accept. I understand. If your mother had spoken up . . ."

He'd missed the point. This was about the girls and their future happiness. "We don't know that she didn't."

"Right. But if she did, no one was listening." Peter looked in Lillian's eyes the way he did when he wanted to kiss her, but he drew no closer. "I promise that will never happen to our girls or to you."

"It won't, if we teach our daughters that they must find the courage to stand up for themselves, even when things are hard, and even when no one believes them. We can't assume they'll just know that. What better way to make the point than to show them their own grandmother?" She glanced at him. "They asked to go, you know."

Peter gave her a loving smile. "Lillian Diamond, you are something."

"I want them to be empathetic. Like their father."

He shook his head, and leaned in for a kiss. "I've always trusted your instincts before. If you feel that strongly about it, we'll take them."

She laughed and kissed him tenderly. When their lips parted, she said, "Margaret."

"What?"

"Art's wife is named Margaret."

They laughed. She was grateful that he trusted her instincts, that he was willing to go along with this smaller request. Because this would give him practice. He'd need to work up to the even bigger issue that was coming. The one he couldn't possibly be expecting.

Chapter 28

RUTH

Ruth was freshening up before dinner. She had put on a clean wool dress and pink lipstick and was brushing her hair. Thirty-one. Thirty-two. Thirty-three. She would need fifty strokes to keep the oils distributed and the shine in her locks. Thirty-four. She now found she wanted to look her best, even on a day like this. Like Shirley said, times were changing.

Asher burst into the attic, carrying a plate of Shirley's homemade rugelach.

"What's wrong?" he said.

"Nothing."

"Why does my mother think I need to bring you cookies? Why wouldn't she tell me anything about what you're doing up here?"

Ruth wanted to laugh, but she felt like playing this out a bit. Having a little fun with Asher before she broke the news. "I'm freshening up for dinner. I think your mother meant that rugelach for you. She probably thought that you'd need them more than I would."

"What's going on?"

"She knows, Asher. About law school. About the bar exam. About me wanting a career. Both your parents do."

"You and my mother got into it?" He sat on the bed, his face pale, the plate cockeyed in his hands. When the cookies started to slide off the plate, he set it on the bed. "I'm sorry. I never meant for you to face them alone."

Ruth could tell by his face that he meant it. Still, why not tease him a little? "All alone," Ruth said, feigning as much of a somber tone as she could manage.

"Honey, I'll go talk to them. Tell them I'm behind you one hundred percent. That . . . if they don't accept your career . . . we'll move out."

Ruth realized she might have gone too far with Asher, but she was touched at how he stood up for her. How lucky she was that her husband was such a fine man, raised by such fine parents, lucky that Asher had a father who showed him how to respect, appreciate, and stand by his wife.

She felt so close to him at that moment. Closer than she'd ever felt. Any doubts she had disappeared.

"How did it come out?" Asher said.

Ruth's heart sank. She should have expected that question. Prepared an answer. She'd been on such a roller coaster today—Carrie, Shirley's confession, telling Shirley about law school and finding out she already knew—Asher had been the last thing on Ruth's mind.

Now he wanted details.

And she couldn't say. Couldn't tell her best friend.

Couldn't tell him about Carrie, about Shirley, about the Esthers, about teaming up with his mother to help Carrie escape. Asher was her husband, yet she had to keep these secrets. Carrie's life, the lives of other women, depended on it. And Shirley couldn't tell him either.

"We were making brisket together, and it just seemed like the right time." Ruth turned her face so he wouldn't see her lie splayed all over it.

"She never lets anyone help her with the brisket," Asher said. "Perhaps that's why it smells extra tasty this evening." He smiled at Ruth. "What did she say?"

"That they already knew."

"What?"

Ruth smiled at the idea that she knew more about Shirley than Asher did. She was honored that her mother-in-law trusted her with her deepest secrets.

But these secrets were Shirley's to tell, not Ruth's.

Dinner was livelier than Ruth expected, and it was a nice change from the heaviness of the day. As they ate the meal of perfectly cooked brisket, brussels sprouts, and potato kugel, Ruth felt a rush of belonging. Leon asked about the bar exam and what she felt her most challenging classes were in law school.

"Ruth volunteered at Legal Aid in New York," Asher said. "She helped abused women and their children."

The table got quiet for a moment. Ruth wondered exactly how much Asher knew about his mother's history and his father's involvement. She suspected it wasn't much, if anything at all, but Ruth knew she must never ask him. He would have to volunteer the information himself.

"That's admirable," Shirley said.

"Someone needs to stick up for those who need help," Leon said.

"You're right," Ruth said, giving him a conspiratorial look. "Thanks."

The next day, after Leon and Asher had left for work, Ruth barreled into the kitchen and slapped a paper down on the counter in front of Shirley.

"It's a list of names and phone numbers. My father and two of my brothers want to help."

Shirley raised an eyebrow.

"What? I didn't tell them anything I shouldn't have."

Shirley seemed to be waiting for more.

"Okay, when I spoke to them last night, they wanted to be sure I was happy. Quizzed me about Asher, about you and Leon, about how you were treating me."

Shirley looked taken aback. "Really?"

"Relax. I told them it was for my friends at Legal Aid in New York. They knew I volunteered there. They don't think anything of it now. They want to help. It makes them feel closer to me to do something together, even though I'm a hundred miles away."

"In that case, great. I have a list as well." Shirley looked pleased as she set a cup of coffee in front of Ruth. "Just saccharin, right?"

Ruth nodded at the kindness.

By ten o'clock, Ruth, Shirley, Lillian, and Irene were sitting around the map-draped dining room table drinking coffee and eating Shirley's apricot *schnecken*. Shirley and Lillian were writing lists of names and addresses alphabetically and geographically, marking the map with Xs. Ruth and Irene rose and began folding baby clothes, diapers, and blankets, smoothing out maternity dresses, ready to pack in a donated steamer trunk, together with bath essentials, books, and a few tchotchkes to personalize a strange place—a miniature Liberty Bell, a C-shaped brass paperweight, and the silver tray from Ruth and Asher's dresser. The trunk would be sent ahead to wherever Carrie was going to be living.

"Why do men get away with bad behavior just because they're men?" Ruth said as she folded cloth diapers into squares. "We should have been able to call the police for Carrie and know she'd be safe."

"It doesn't work that way," Shirley said.

"It should," Ruth said. "It could." Someone needed to change that.

"I agree," Lillian said. "I'm embarrassed to say I've been part of the problem."

Ruth looked over at her.

"I didn't believe what you said, until I saw Carrie. I should have known better. I should have believed you, Ruth. I'm sorry for how I treated you."

Ruth nodded. Somehow her vindication wasn't as sweet as she'd expected, knowing there were few people who believed beaten women at all, and few laws that would protect them.

"I, of all people, should have listened," Lillian said, and paused before seeming to come to a decision. "Apparently . . . my father burned my mother with a cigar. And who knows what else he did."

A collective gasp seemed to pull all the air from the room.

"You never said. I guess we all have family secrets," Ruth said.

Of all the people, Lillian.

"I only just found out. From my mother," Lillian said.

"You have a mother?" Irene's absurd question refilled the room with normalcy and titters of inappropriate laughter. Even Lillian's. Abashed, Irene clarified. "I meant living."

Shirley stood behind Lillian and patted her shoulder. "I'm so sorry."

"I was a child. I didn't know."

"How did you find out?" Shirley asked, moving around to face Lillian and grasping her hands.

"Admittance records."

"Admittance?" Ruth asked.

Lillian sighed. "For the last twenty-four years my mother has been in a hospital." She looked at the floor. "A mental hospital."

"Oh, how awful for you," Irene said.

Yes, Ruth thought. Her own mother had died. How must it feel to have a mother who was alive, yet unavailable? To have your mother be a living, breathing woman you couldn't have over for dinner or talk to about your problems? Ruth suddenly felt a new kinship toward Lillian and was reminded that she was more than an etiquette maven.

Lillian looked up. "Well, I won't be embarrassed or ashamed anymore. She's at Friends. They treat her very well and take good care of her."

Ruth's previous anger at Lillian for not listening when she told her about Carrie was replaced by deep compassion. How the sight of Carrie's injuries must have pained her—at a different level than it did Ruth and Irene. All the shame surrounding mental institutions, the horror of having a brutal father. And Ruth knew all too well what it was like to live without a mother.

"And your husband knows?" Irene asked.

"Of course Peter knows," Shirley said. "Right?"

"It's not like keeping a secret is below our moral benchmark," Ruth said. The girls chuckled.

"Not only does Peter know, but he got her moved from where she was to Friends sixteen years ago—and he pays the bills."

"Now that's a good man. That's love and devotion," Shirley said. "And I should know."

The doorbell rang, and Shirley hurried to answer it.

A few moments later, she ushered Carrie into the dining room. Her bruises were fading somewhat, and she'd covered them with thick makeup, so they were hardly visible, unless you knew. If she didn't know better, Ruth would have said she looked almost cheerful.

Ruth felt proud of her friend. It was a huge sacrifice for Carrie to leave Eli, leave her home here, but Ruth knew, unequivocally, that it was the right thing.

Carrie set a box from Liss's bakery in the center of the map, covering Kansas, which was void of any X.

"How delicious. You shouldn't have," Shirley said.

"I'm glad you did." Irene untied the string on the box and leaned across the western US to peek inside.

"I wanted to thank you for being so kind," Carrie said. "And to say I want us to get back to our etiquette lessons."

"What do you mean?" Intuition raced through Ruth, leaving shivers in its wake, as though one of her brothers had smacked her in the face with a snowball.

"We're staying in Wynnefield," Carrie said as if she hadn't a care in the world.

"What?" As the word left Ruth's mouth, she realized it was more confrontational than she'd have liked.

"We who?" Irene asked.

"Oh dear," Shirley said.

"This is good news, don't you see?" Carrie went on. "Eli said if it was that important to me, we'd stay in Wynnefield. I love him, girls, and this is my chance at real happiness. While I'm so grateful you wanted to help me, I don't need help. We are going to be fine." She held out her skirt as if to curtsey and swiveled. "He's being so sweet and attentive."

Ruth became nauseated. How could Carrie trust Eli after what he'd done?

"You didn't tell him anything about what we planned, did you?" Shirley's face betrayed her agitation.

"No, I think it would hurt his feelings that I hadn't trusted him."

"Men like that can't be trusted," Shirley said. "I hope Harriet kept this to herself too."

Ruth understood the danger immediately. They and their future work would all be at risk if Eli discovered the rest of them had been planning to help his wife escape.

"No. Harriet wouldn't do that," Carrie said.

Carrie was too trusting. Did she still not understand? "Don't be so sure."

"Harriet's on my side. She just wants me to be happy."

"Happy with a husband who hurts you?" Ruth asked.

"He's different now, I promise. He understands I won't live like that anymore."

That's what Ruth was afraid of.

The women only nibbled at the butter cookies Carrie had brought. Their appetites seemed to have disappeared. No point in carrying on with their activities now.

Carrie watched them as Shirley stored away the map, paper, and pencils. Ruth removed the leaves from the table and stacked dessert plates at its center. She boiled water for tea and Sanka. All of them except Carrie packed up and stored the collected goods on basement shelves and in the closet.

No one spoke about it, but it was clear how wrong they felt Carrie's decision was—how dangerous for her and the baby.

"I'm sorry you did all this work for nothing." Carrie's cheerfulness had dimmed now. No one contradicted her.

Ruth knew, like the rest of them, that Carrie's life would likely be lived on a knife-edge, at best. But Shirley had told them yesterday that the Secret Esther Society didn't coerce or cajole. Ruth wished they did.

But she had memorized the locations while she feigned ease with Carrie's decision to stay with Eli—just in case. Carrie chatted away about the upcoming holy days, about her plans for the nursery, about the roast chicken she would make for dinner, as if everything was perfectly normal. Safe.

As if the others were no longer terrified for her.

Finally, she stood, saying she had to make dinner preparations before Eli got home. As the women walked her to the door, Shirley rested her hand on Carrie's back. "You know you can call or come here any time of the day or night, for any reason."

Carrie nodded and, after a pause, she kissed Shirley's cheek. "I'll be fine."

Irene took Carrie's arm. "I'll make sure she gets home safely."

Ruth waved. What a loaded statement.

Lillian looked like she wanted to say something too, then stepped back and folded her hands. After they'd left, the rest of them took a collective breath.

Ruth broke the silence. "Carrie wasn't the first, and she won't be the last to stay with a man who beat her."

"I don't understand. How *can* she stay?" Lillian asked.

Shirley didn't mince her words. "Hope and shame are a potent cocktail, leaving girls drunk with tolerance."

"Isn't there something else we can do?" Ruth said.

Lillian shook her head. "There's a communal denial about their problem—and a legal system that favors these barbaric men."

"Even while in hospital beds, bandaged and in casts, many girls believe they've 'asked for it,'" Shirley said. "And if they don't at first, the fact no one believes them makes them question their own sanity, their own part in the problem."

Ruth couldn't, wouldn't, let it go. "We've got to do something before it's too late."

Shirley put a hand on her daughter-in-law's shoulder. "I understand how you feel, believe me. Nonetheless, no one has ever strong-armed or guilted women into accepting help."

Ruth couldn't believe it. She agreed with her mother-in-law again.

Chapter 29

LILLIAN

At nine o'clock on Saturday morning, Lillian sat on the patio's wicker rocker, a steaming cup of coffee in hand to warm and wake her as she breathed in the cool fall air.

Fall. The season of change.

Lillian still hadn't accepted Carrie's decision to stay with Eli, but she had resigned herself to that fact. All she could do was hope that it would all work out, that maybe Carrie would be the one person whose husband would change.

Today wasn't going to be errand day. This was the day Lillian would introduce her daughters to their grandmother, so she'd chosen elegance over function and worn her tan gabardine suit.

In her make-believe memory, her mother had sported a similar outfit. It would have matched her light-brown hair, which now looked many shades lighter due to the gray. Her mother rarely wore a suit—she had been partial to skirts and blouses, and seemed to be, still. An unintentional preference from the past? A favorite of hers?

Either way, the choices were a hint of the woman Lillian had known, and that comforted her, made her hope that the mother she knew would somehow reveal herself to the next generation.

Anna would have had a Gimbels discount, but her clothes had never been showy or posh—or even good. But she had been beautiful, with a round face, big blue eyes, and petite nose and mouth, all pleasantly positioned and proportioned. *Lovely* had been a word associated with Anna not only for her looks but also for her disposition.

The same was said about Penny.

Pearls lost their luster, and flowers lost their vibrancy—and so had Anna lost much of her own shine and bloom. But *she* was not the one who needed to change; it was Lillian. And the world that Lillian's children inhabited. Today was the first step toward that.

As she walked into the house to refresh her cup of coffee, Pammie and Penny raced down the stairs.

They passed their father in the foyer and galloped into the kitchen, where they'd soon delight in the cinnamon buns Lillian had set out on the table.

Peter twiddled his fingers as he paced the foyer. Lillian knew why he was worried. They were adults and even they had trouble visiting the mental institution. How would their girls react?

Lillian channeled the sane part of her mother and offered Anna's solution for anxiety. "Come have some cinnamon buns. You'll feel better."

In the kitchen, Pammie gulped her milk. "What should I call her? I don't want to call her *Grandma*, since I never met her before."

Peter looked at Lillian for guidance. "That's fine," she said. "It might confuse her, anyway. Just call her Anna."

"Can we ask to see her scar?" Pammie rubbed her arm.

"No." Penny shook her head.

"Then how do we know it happened?"

"It's important to believe our friends and family," Lillian said. "Even if it's hard to do. It's our job to be open-minded. Do you know what that means?"

Pammie nodded. "It means trusting someone even if you don't want to?"

Peter smiled. "Not exactly. Being open-minded means seeing things in new ways. Or seeing people in new ways, even if it's hard."

Lillian grabbed Pammie's hand. "If you ever told me someone hurt you, I would believe you—even though it would make me sad and angry that it happened."

"Don't worry about me, I wouldn't allow it. I would kick him in the—"

Lillian stomped her foot. "Pamela Rachel, don't be fresh!"

"Well, I would."

Peter cleared his throat, flustered at the bluntness. "That's no way for a lady to talk."

But it was exactly how Lillian wanted her daughters, and all girls, to think. She cleared the table. "How about this? If a boy or a man is unkind to you, or makes you uncomfortable in any way, tell me and Daddy. We promise to believe you and help you."

"What if you really like him?" Penny asked.

Lillian's father's smile popped to mind. A memory of sweet cigar aromas filled her nose. What would she have done? Would she have turned on the father she loved? Then she thought about Anna, being taken to the institution, being robbed of her freedom, of her family. "Yes, you tell us—especially if we like him. You're more important."

Peter's eyes filled. "Always."

Yes, Lillian understood, Peter was on her side, on their side. It wouldn't always be easy. Perhaps it wasn't supposed to be. It would be difficult when she got the courage to tell him how she wanted to change her life—their lives.

"Why didn't your mother tell her mom and dad?" Penny asked.

"Her father had died a long time before that. And maybe she was too ashamed or embarrassed to say anything to her mother."

"Why didn't she tell someone else?"

This question should have plagued Lillian, but she knew the answer. "She may have. We don't know." Lillian cringed at the thought that Anna probably *did* tell someone—just like Ruth had told Lillian. "It's possible no one believed her. Back then, they didn't treat injured women the way they should. That's why it's important to tell someone if you're in trouble—to stand up for yourself. Make sure you're heard."

The family stepped outside to the sidewalk, and Lillian hurried back to the kitchen. She returned to the car with a Tupperware container. "I almost forgot my mother's cookies," she said.

Peter opened the car door for her but paused before he let her in. "I know I don't say it, but you're a good daughter." He stepped aside for Lillian to enter. "And a good mother."

As they piled into the Lincoln, Lillian flooded with gratitude.

Forty-five minutes later, the Diamonds arrived at Friends Hospital. Autumn leaves camouflaged the buildings, but Lillian saw through the gold and red and orange. Even gold sparkles couldn't make this place what it wasn't. It wasn't a temporary healing place or a stopover for Anna; it was her home. It had been, for many years. Years in which Lillian now admitted she had been ashamed to admit her mother was hospitalized. Now she believed that dying was likely the best thing her father could have done for them. It hadn't been her husband's death but his cruelty that had caused Anna's nervous breakdown and her commitment to that first asylum. Lillian was sure of it. Anna's early senility was unrelated, the doctor had said. Lillian didn't believe that one bit.

But if her father had lived, her mother would have lived in danger. Lillian might have been in danger as well.

As she had learned firsthand from Carrie, domestic violence was rarely an isolated instance.

Peter parked the car, and the girls eyed the building in front of them. Penny was the first to speak. "It looks kinda nice, like a school or something."

As they left the car and walked toward the building, Lillian had to acknowledge that her mother was better off committed than married to her father. When Peter opened the door for them, she pushed aside thoughts of how her mother might have coped if she'd received kindness from Lillian's grandparents.

Her grandparents—her grandmother in particular. Lillian had so far ignored the feelings—the anger—she had toward them. Gran had given her a home after her mother was taken away, but she should have done something to help long before. And yet, Lillian didn't have all the facts. There was so much for her to learn about what really happened.

As the family neared Anna's room, the reality of the hospital settled back around Lillian. Today was about her daughters' grandmother, not Lillian's mother, and she would focus on that. She would search out her cousins on her mother's side when the dust settled. Rekindle those lost relationships. See what they knew.

Everything in due time. She'd ease into the knowledge, the pain, of what had been done to her mother, to her. She'd had enough shocks lately and needed to go easy on herself too.

Inside the double doors of the common room, Lillian draped her arms over her daughters' shoulders in a reassuring hug. "She may not understand you're my children, but don't let that bother you."

Lillian, Pammie, and Penny left Peter standing against the wall as if he was propping it up. They walked to a small table where Anna sat alone with a deck of cards. Slight and lonely, but pretty, with long gray hair and a yellow dress.

"Hi, Anna, do you remember me?"

Anna smiled at Lillian, which did not answer the question. "Are these your children?"

"They are." Lillian nudged the girls forward. "This is Pammie—"

"And I'm Penny." She reached out her hand and Anna clasped it.

Anna looked at Lillian. "Can they stay?"

Words tangled into a knot and lodged in Lillian's throat. She nodded and the girls sat with Anna, who indicated the pack of cards. "Do you want to play go fish?"

"Okay," Pammie said. "But I should warn you, I always win."

Lillian opened her mouth to admonish her older daughter, but Anna hooted. The capricious laughter stung and hugged Lillian's heart. It had been so long since she'd heard it.

"This one's a firecracker," Anna said. The word, once used to describe Lillian, made her feel happy and sad at the same time.

"We brought cookies," Penny said. "We know you like them. Right, Mom?"

Lillian placed the container on the middle of the table and Penny peeled back the lid. "Don't worry," Lillian said. "No raisins."

The visit ended when Anna nodded off at the table, in the middle of a game of war, chin to her chest. Lillian had been surprised at her own reaction to this encounter. Instead of feeling ashamed that her mother was a patient, Lillian was delighted that Anna and her girls had found a way to enjoy each other's company. Penny and Pammie had engaged her mother—their grandmother—for almost an hour. The longer Lillian had watched the three of them, the more normal Anna seemed.

Troubled, yes; simple, yes—but almost normal.

If an hour of cards could produce conversation and laughter, how would Anna be now if Lillian had been more mindful for the past sixteen or more years? If she'd visited more frequently? Lillian wished she could go back, but she could only change the future, not the past.

As the Diamonds walked to the car, Pammie and Penny gathered a few red and gold leaves from the ground.

"Is she allowed out?" Penny asked, without maliciousness.

"Who, Anna?" The idea seemed so foreign to Lillian.

"Yes. I think she would like our back patio."

"She said she likes flowers," Pammie said.

"When did she say that?" Lillian asked.

"During go fish," Pammie said. "You were standing by the wall with Daddy. She likes grape soda, too, but she doesn't have it often. I think we should take her some next time."

Lillian reached out to the girls and drew them into a hug.

"What was that for?" Pammie asked.

"For being kind," Lillian *kvelled*.

"So can she come to our house? She's family, right? She should be able to visit," Penny said.

Lillian looked at Peter and shrugged. She knew she'd pressed things by wanting the girls to meet Anna and she didn't want to push too far too fast.

"We'll ask," Peter said.

Lillian gasped. "We will?"

"How else will we know?" he said. "Anna's never left in all these years. Maybe it's unconventional, but that doesn't mean it's bad."

"Your dad is right." Lillian turned to her daughters, grateful for her family. "We'll ask."

Later that day, Lillian sat in the basement on an old metal folding chair, sorting and refolding the stowed-away-for-Carrie baby clothes. Pink. Blue. White. Yellow and green. She still hadn't reconciled Carrie's decision to stay with Eli, and the peaceful and repetitive chore helped to soothe the commotion in her heart.

Pammie and Penny had exceeded Lillian's expectations and filled her with a mother's joy—and a daughter's joy. They weren't clairvoyant, yet somehow her husband and daughters had given Lillian what she longed for—what she'd asked for. A family that had each other's backs.

Fold, stack.

Fold, stack.

Fold, stack.

She heard someone open the squeaky basement door and start down the stairs. "Lil?"

"Down here."

Peter walked down the steps. He looked around the basement. "Where are the girls?"

"Penny is at Linda's and Pammie is at Margot's. They know we're going out. They'll be home at five."

Peter sat on a chair. "What's going on down here?"

"Just thinking about my mother."

"Anything else?"

Yes, she wanted to say. She wanted to tell him all about Carrie, about the Esthers, about Shirley's abuse. About how she'd come to realize that not everything was as it appeared in people's marriages. About how she wanted to help women who suffered at the hands of their husbands. But she'd promised to remain silent. And she wasn't quite certain that he'd agree with her plans. "No, nothing."

"Don't you think I have the right to know?"

"The right to know what?" There was no way for him to know about Carrie, Lillian told herself.

He pointed to each stack of baby clothes. "That we're having another baby. All the clothes. The secret project. Wanting *more* meant more children."

Lillian almost laughed out loud in relief. Peter thought she was pregnant. She was thirty-five, and she was done having babies after Penny. Had he forgotten?

"It most certainly did not. We are not having a baby." She glanced at her stomach. She had changed out of her suit into evergreen cuffed ankle slacks and an amber merino sweater—a fitted ensemble. "Do I look like I'm having a baby?"

"No, but I figure it's early." His face was unreadable.

"Peter, the last thing I want is another child. I gathered these clothes for someone who *is* expecting—it made me feel good to help someone who really needed it without getting anything in return."

"Oh." Peter sounded disappointed. He'd always wanted a son, but had never insisted on another child. She walked over and hugged him, resting her face against his chest. "Wanting more isn't about wanting more children, it's about feeling like I'm doing something worthwhile in the world—something besides helping you win contracts."

He leaned away and looked down at her. "I thought you liked helping me."

Lillian took a step back. This wasn't going the way she'd hoped. "I do. This isn't against *you*, Peter, it's *for* me. There's a difference. I want to *make* a difference. I want to be sure our daughters are aware of women like my mother. So they're not just learning how to be pretty and proper. So they don't become complacent."

Peter looked like he had no idea what she was talking about. Well, he couldn't read her mind. She'd have to tell him what she was thinking. "I'm going to help women who are in situations like my mother was with my father. It happens much more than you know. I can help ensure someone listens to them. That there are places where hurt women can go for help before they end up in a hospital, or worse."

Lillian didn't have the words to define exactly who these women were or what was happening to them, but she knew from Shirley that this kind of cruel behavior went overlooked throughout their community and others. Peter would have to listen and trust her.

"Places?"

Lillian had no idea if there was such a thing or not, but she aimed to find out. "Yes."

"You've given this a lot of thought."

"I have." Even though she had no idea how she could help or what she would do.

"So this is what you meant? You want to help women whose husbands beat them?"

"As of now, yes."

"That might be dangerous."

"It's important to do this. For them and for me. It's one way to make it up to my mother—to do what I can to ensure her suffering wasn't for nothing."

"You'll be careful?" Peter's eyes were troubled, but Lillian sensed that something had changed. "When you believe in yourself, other people will believe in you too," she'd heard her grandfather say, without understanding what he meant. Now she did.

"I will."

"You come to me if you need anything, you hear me?"

"Loud and clear."

"So, no baby?"

Lillian smiled. "No baby, Peter."

Peter picked up one of the blue baby outfits. "I was hoping for a boy."

Lillian chuckled, stood, and brushed Peter's hair off his forehead. "We could get a boy—dog."

Peter laughed, and Lillian recognized the sound of yes. "You know, Lil, your mother isn't the only one who wants you to be happy."

Inconvenient tears pooled in Lillian's eyes and rendered everything blurry. She reached for Peter's hand, lifted it to her lips, and kissed his palm three times. She looked up at him and held his gaze.

He stepped toward her and leaned close, his mouth to her ear. "It's two o'clock in the afternoon," he whispered.

"Uh-huh." Sparklers flickered inside Lillian's head. "The girls won't be home until five."

Chapter 30

RUTH

Ruth came back inside from her late-morning studying on the patio when it started to drizzle. She had work to do, helping Shirley. She positioned the leaves in the dining room table and set six places for lunch. Shirley's Lenox china and crystal sparkled. The silver shined. The crisp linen tablecloth gleamed from starch. Fan-folded napkins adorned each plate. The delicious, herbaceous aroma of roasted chicken wafted in from the kitchen and filled the air.

Shirley stepped into the dining room, untying her apron.

"How does it look?" Ruth asked.

She'd set an elegant table but purposely sought her mother-in-law's praise. Ruth understood now that doing so was a sign of respect and gratitude, not one of debasement. Shirley smiled when Ruth asked. The consideration pleased them both—Ruth to give it and Shirley to receive it. Ruth had mistakenly seen Shirley as difficult to please, but her mother-in-law was a cinch now that Ruth understood her.

"It looks lovely." Shirley walked to the front window and pushed aside the sheer curtains. "Set out the umbrella stand, please. They're bound to need it."

Ruth reached into the coat closet, pulled out a Chinese-inspired, painted porcelain umbrella stand, and placed it next to the front door.

From there, she saw Shirley walking around the dining room table, inspecting it all, arms crossed. Ruth braced for criticism or correction or for Shirley to move a glass, or a spoon, or a chair. Instead, Shirley added a short vase of mums. The finishing touch.

"Thank you for doing this," Ruth said. "It means a lot for me to be able to host my friends." Ruth wanted to take advantage of the time she had with the girls. Soon she would have to focus on the bar exam and then her job as a lawyer.

"I hear that Harriet is coming back, as well as Carrie, and I'm glad." Shirley smiled at her. "I want Carrie to feel comfortable here, no matter what. What better way to express that than with a little lunch?"

Over the past week, Ruth had seen Carrie once and spoken to her daily. Her friend was happy—or seemed to be. Maybe she really was. Ruth was hoping to be made wrong on this count.

As the rain fell, the house filled with arriving friends. Irene. Lillian. Harriet. They gathered in the living room, umbrellas and boots and rain bonnets stored in the hall closet. Irene and Shirley wrapped themselves in afghans, citing a chill. Irene dried her wet face with a tea towel, apologizing when she saw she'd transferred some of her makeup to it. "Not exactly good etiquette," she said ruefully. She opened her compact and reapplied her spice-colored lipstick, more subdued than some of her previous shades.

Ruth checked her own face in the mirror by the door. Fine and dandy. She glanced up at the sky outside; the rain looked like it was letting up, but Carrie might be drenched when she arrived. She'd probably walked, unless Eli drove her.

Shirley, Ruth, and Lillian had privately agreed to leave out any discussion about Carrie's domestic situation—doubly so since Harriet would be there. Today would be about mending fences and cementing friendships, not stoking old wounds and disagreements.

While she and Ruth were making lunch earlier, Shirley had suggested that the more comfortable Carrie felt about being with them, the more likely she might be to reach out if Eli attacked her again. As for Harriet, well, they had to be sure she didn't dish to anyone about the plan for Carrie's escape. Best to keep her happy so she stayed quiet. Hopefully, she'd think the plan had been abandoned and wouldn't make trouble.

As the women relaxed and waited for Carrie to show up, the house filled with laughter and conversation. Important, life-changing topics were discussed, like the Diamonds' dislike of raisins, Heidi's toddler escapades, Shirley's schnecken recipe, Ruth's bar exam studies.

The telephone rang and Ruth skittered to the kitchen. "I'll get it." She lifted the receiver. "Hello?"

"Ruth? It's me."

"Carrie?"

"Yes. I've changed my mind. I want to leave Eli." Ruth heard rustling on Carrie's end of the line, suggesting Carrie was prepping to be on the move. "I'm packing a few things; I'll be there soon."

Ruth was terrified and relieved at the same time. Her head filled with questions about what had changed since yesterday, when Carrie had sounded fine. The fact Carrie was calling was a good sign, though. If she were badly hurt, she might not have been able to talk. Yet something serious must have happened if she wanted to leave her husband. Twenty-four hours ago, Carrie had been certain her life was on track. "What happened?"

"I'll explain when I get there."

Goose bumps crawled up Ruth's arm, but right now it didn't matter what had happened. Time couldn't be wasted. Carrie should leave, but she had to be careful. Eli must not discover she planned to go. "Carrie, don't stop to pack, just—"

Rumbles and a crash reverberated through the receiver. Ruth's heart sank. She had to remain calm for her friend, had to assess the situation. "Carrie? Are you okay?"

Click.

The dial tone buzzed in her ear. Ruth tapped the chrome cradle several times. "Carrie?" she yelled into the receiver, and then hung up. She turned around. The group had congregated in the kitchen. "We have to go!" she said in a fear-soaked whisper. "Carrie's in trouble!"

"What happened?" Shirley remained calm and went after the facts. "Is she hurt? Does she need an ambulance?"

"I don't know. She didn't say. Just that she wants to leave Eli." Ruth hurried to the coat closet but shook with fear and was unable to grip the knob. "We have to go!" Her timbre and tenor had returned, but not her grasp. Shirley stepped up beside her and, with her hand atop Ruth's, opened the door.

"The line went dead." Ruth fought back tears, had no other words.

Lillian put a hand on Ruth's shoulder. It comforted her, reminding her she wasn't alone. "I'll drive." Lillian herded the group out the door and into the rain, now heavier than ever.

Shirley stopped at the door. "I'll be right there. I have to make a quick telephone call."

Riding in Lillian's passenger seat, Ruth anticipated every stop and turn on the way to Carrie's. A more direct route would have been the foot-path that cut through the breezeways between the smaller houses. But they needed to take the car for speed, and in case Carrie needed to be driven away.

Ruth shuddered as all the reasons that Carrie might have called ran through her mind.

Hurry, hurry, she thought. What was the point of this fancy vehicle with its dials and buttons and knobs if it couldn't help them get to Carrie in time? In time for what, Ruth didn't know.

Couldn't Lillian drive any faster?

Ruth leaned forward as if to add some momentum, as if she had the power to speed up their journey. Rain rushed past on the windshield and side windows, making visibility a challenge. She gritted her teeth to stop them from chattering.

The car stopped and Ruth fixed her gaze on Carrie's front door. She had to help her friend, but fear of what she might find, or what danger she herself might face, made her hesitate momentarily. At Legal Aid, she'd seen the wicked things men could do to women. Yet this was different from working with strangers in New York.

Carrie was her friend.

It shouldn't have made a difference, yet it overwhelmed her.

This wasn't researching laws. This was being in the heat of the moment with a man who was cruel, unlike the kind father and brothers she had, the sweet husband she'd married.

Eli was the type of man who could kill a woman, and there were few laws to protect women from the Elis of the world.

Ruth stared ahead through the rain and shivered. What if they were too late to help Carrie? She squeezed her eyes closed. The women at Legal Aid were safely in front of Ruth when she saw them. But now she was at Carrie's house. What if it was too late to save her friend's life?

The passenger door swung open. Shirley was standing on the other side. "Come on. We can't just sit here. Let's go." Her words snapped above the rain's whoosh and patter.

As Shirley's hand tugged Ruth's arm, chilly rain landed on Ruth's leg.

She broke out of her trance. She stepped out and under Shirley's umbrella. Two car doors slammed. Ruth wasn't alone. *Right.* Besides Shirley, she had Lillian, Irene, and Harriet there. If Eli was on a rampage, it would be five against one. Relief flooded her veins.

Together, they could do this.

Huddled next to Shirley, Ruth looped her arm into her mother-in-law's, and she was grateful she'd made peace with her and had her strength beside her. She'd had support through life from her father and brothers. Now she had it from a . . . well, a mother-in-law.

Shirley patted her. "Follow me." She detached herself from Ruth and marched ahead up the path. Ruth followed, shifting between a run and a walk, while the rain slowed to a drizzle. Behind her, she heard three sets of feet splashing their way up the path. She and Shirley reached the front steps, and Ruth took them two at a time. She looked back at Shirley. "Tell me what to do."

Lillian, Irene, and Harriet joined them on the steps, forming a solid wall of women.

"We're ready when you are." Irene kept her voice low.

"But this wasn't the plan," Harriet said. Everyone turned to her. "I'm just worried that we don't know what we're doing."

"Nothing matters right now except Carrie and her safety," Shirley said, looking at Harriet, who nodded. She shifted her gaze to Lillian. "Not what anyone thought." She looked back at Harriet. "Or what was planned. There was a troubling telephone call, and we're here to make sure Carrie is okay."

"She's not okay. We're wasting time," Ruth said.

Shirley knocked on the door. "Let me do the talking."

Ruth stepped down one step, now behind Shirley and next to Lillian, who, though she had dismissed Eli's cruelty at one time, looked to be totally on board to assist now.

Shirley rang the doorbell. No answer.

"Carrie?" She yelled at the door as if it were an intercom.

Ruth held her breath as they listened. That's how it felt—like all airflow had stopped. In her, and around her.

"Carrie?" Shirley yelled again into an imaginary microphone. "You said you were coming over for lunch. You didn't show up, and we missed you. We're just making sure you're okay."

No reply, not a sound from inside the house.

Ruth's heart hammered so loud she was surprised Carrie's neighbors weren't staring out the window at the racket. Had the neighbors heard Shirley too?

Shirley tried the doorknob, turned to the girls, and shrugged.

"It's unlocked," she said. "I'm going in."

Harriet grabbed her arm. "Should you?"

"Someone has to," Shirley said. "You can wait out here."

"I'm coming with you," Ruth said.

"Me too," echoed Lillian and Irene.

Shirley turned the knob and pushed open the door. They stepped inside and crowded into the foyer. The gray day rendered the small space dark, and then, as her eyes adjusted, Ruth's sight line was clear. Carrie was lying on her back on a green sofa.

Next to her, kneeling on the floor, his back to the group, his head hanging down—was Eli.

The brute. Ruth's fear evaporated, replaced by anger. She growled. Shirley reached out to hold Ruth back, but she pushed her away. There was a house full of witnesses—what could Eli do? They could all tell the police. Someone would have to listen.

Ruth ran around him, closer to Carrie's head than her feet. Carrie moaned and Eli looked up, mouth open.

"Who are you?" Eli said. He turned and saw the others.

Another moan from Carrie, this time even weaker.

"Oh, honey." Eli laid his cheek on Carrie's hand. She drew the hand away, but he grabbed it anyway, patted it. "You fell," he said. Carrie glanced at Ruth with bloodshot eyes. Ruth hoped they were only red from crying.

Eli looked up at Ruth. "You know she's expecting."

"Yes, we know about the baby." Shirley walked over and stood next to Ruth. "We're going to take her to the doctor."

"No!" Eli rose to his feet.

He was a small man, short and thin, with combed-back hair and black-framed glasses. He looked . . . safe. Harmless. This was a man who had golfed with Asher. Maybe even had lunch or drinks with him when the game was over. He was the last guy anyone would expect to get violent.

Eli noticed the women glowering at him and lowered his voice. "I mean, I'll take her. I'm her husband."

Carrie's eyes fluttered wide open. "What's going on? Why are you all here?"

"You tell us," Ruth said. "You didn't show up for lunch, so we came to check on you." Ruth knew it was best to not mention they knew about the abuse, lest Eli suspect Carrie wanted to escape.

Carrie glanced at Eli, looking confused.

"I must've fallen." Carrie stared at Ruth. "You know how clumsy I am."

Ruth knew her friend was far from clumsy. This was Carrie's furtive, conspiratorial cry for help. Ruth wouldn't let her down. She nodded but said nothing.

"Thank you for checking in, ladies," Eli said, his voice urbane, self-assured. The perfect vice-principal. By that time, Lillian was holding Carrie's hand, and Irene was stroking her forehead. "But I'll take care of my wife," Eli said. "This is none of your business."

"You're wrong!" Harriet said.

A glint of light appeared above Eli and whipped across the air like a shooting star.

Thud.

Someone or something had made contact, but it had happened so fast, and the room was so dim, Ruth wasn't entirely sure what had happened.

She looked at Eli. He wobbled slightly. He rubbed his shoulder and swung around, revealing Harriet with a metal bucket in one hand.

Harriet? Had Harriet just hit Eli? She'd been the most skeptical about the abuse Carrie had suffered. Perhaps seeing it for herself had touched something in her. Some strong sense of injustice. Or some sense that her denial had contributed to yet another injury to her friend.

"What the hell?" Eli yelled.

"Leave her alone," Harriet said, her face pale, but calm and determined.

Ruth wondered if this was how someone looked when they were in shock.

"She's my wife." Eli spat out the words. "That's my baby." This was not a man to step aside from a brawl.

Shirley straightened, her words offered in a calming tone. "Exactly. So let us help your baby's mother." She looked at Carrie. "Can you stand?"

Carrie nodded, though it was difficult for her to rise from the sofa. Lillian pulled her up, and Carrie leaned against her.

"See?" Shirley said. "I'm sure she's fine, but you want the baby to be checked out. Any good father would, as I'm sure you are." She was calm, unthreatening, believable.

With her arm around Carrie, Ruth inched past Eli toward the front door, held open by Lillian. They needed to get Carrie in the car, and she'd be safe.

Eli's blank stare might have been resignation, maybe even compliance, a wide-eyed expression that could have been mistaken for fear, had Ruth not known better. She watched his every move as she babystepped, Carrie by her hip. Eli's gaze landed on Carrie, and his face shifted into a smile—no, more of a smirk, with the power to chill Ruth like it was a freezer.

He poked the air in front of Ruth. "I know what you're doing!" His breath was hot and oniony. Ruth wanted to turn her face away, but she froze, not sure if there were more words coming. Not sure what stoked his anger, what pacified it.

She'd seen herself as educated and experienced, yet her time at Legal Aid had not prepared her for this in-person wrestling match.

Shirley stepped forward. "That's enough!"

Eli raised his arms and roared, more like a bear than a human.

All Ruth knew was that they had to get out of there—fast.

"I saw the suitcase!" he bellowed.

"No, Eli. It's not what you think." Carrie wriggled away from Ruth, groaning with each painful movement. "I'm not going anywhere! I was just packing up some things I thought Harriet might want to borrow for her honeymoon."

Eli hesitated, then he lunged at his wife. "Liar!"

Shirley stepped forward, blocking his path to Carrie and raising her hand like she was stopping traffic. "I said, that's enough."

Eli made a fist and swung his arm back to let Shirley have it. She didn't move, stood strong, about to be slammed. Just before Eli could make contact, Carrie reached around, and with two hands, pushed him as if moving a boulder.

Eli lost his balance, flailed his arms, and kicked his legs, but wasn't able to right himself.

As if he was a falling tree, he crashed to the ground hip first, his head smashing against a brass end table with a sickening crack, and he bounced to the floor.

As much as the women wanted him disabled, they couldn't help but cringe at the violence—except for Carrie. Her vengeance seemed to have burst its floodgates and made her forget her injuries. She made a move toward him, but Ruth and Lillian held her back. The women backed up as they saw the carpet around Eli's head fill with blood. A red, viscous mess oozed out from a large gash, forming a puddle.

The gruesome sight seemed to snap Carrie back to herself. "No!" she screamed. "Call an ambulance, he's bleeding."

Blood was the only thing that moved on Eli.

Shirley knelt to feel his pulse and shook her head. Harriet and Irene stepped away. Lillian held on to Carrie to keep her steady.

"I think it's too late," Ruth said. Yet she didn't know how something like this could have happened. A man who had spoken to them moments ago was lying dead in front of them. The life snuffed out of him. Ruth had wanted Carrie to get away, and she found Eli's behavior reprehensible . . . but death . . . was never part of the plan.

She looked at the others. All were showing shades of shock, levels of unforeseen grief at the loss of life in front of them. Ruth wasn't sure which one of them had squeaked, which one of them whimpered, which one of them gasped.

One minute Eli was a threat, and then he wasn't. Ruth was both relieved and shocked that she didn't regret the loss of his life. She would keep those thoughts to herself and support Carrie however she needed.

"We have to call the police," Carrie said.

Police would learn that Carrie had committed murder. Manslaughter, to be accurate, but Carrie had caused her husband's death while trying to protect Shirley.

The irony was ugly—no one would call the police on Eli for hurting Carrie. She wouldn't let them. Yet she was willing to call them on herself. She believed she was the one who should be punished.

Carrie's mind had been so skewed from all the trauma. Ruth didn't know which abuse was sadder.

Lillian covered her eyes. Irene wrapped an arm around Harriet, who gave little gasps of disbelief. Sadness enveloped the room, nipping little pieces of their souls out of them.

"It was an accident. That's for sure," Ruth said. "You didn't mean it, Carrie. We all saw. He was going to hit you, hit Shirley, and you stopped him." The women nodded, huddling closer to Carrie.

Shirley walked around Eli, leaving a wide berth, and grasped Carrie's hands. "But we have to get our story straight."

Yes, Ruth thought. *To protect Carrie. To protect these women.*

Carrie reached out for Ruth and sank to the floor, taking Ruth with her. She sobbed, soaking Ruth's shoulder. Was Carrie sad, or relieved, or some indescribable combination?

It didn't matter. Carrie had been defending herself. Protecting her baby. There was no premeditation. She needed to escape to save her unborn child from more beatings. She only tried to leave. It should be an easy legal matter. Carrie was covered in red welts, nearly unconscious when the women arrived. They were witnesses to Eli's brutality. He'd nearly socked Shirley.

And yet.

Ruth knew the law was rarely on a woman's side. It would stay that way until people like her fought to change it.

"Shh," Ruth said as she eased Carrie to the sofa. "It will be okay." She wished she believed that for a minute. She had a law degree and still had no idea what to do under the circumstances. She looked at her mother-in-law, who nodded at her.

"What happened before we got here?" Ruth asked Carrie.

"We fought this morning. It was stupid. We argued over baby names and he pushed me. I hit my head on the cabinet. That's when I realized I had to protect my baby, I had to go. He was mad and left— that's when I called you—but he must've come home to apologize. He saw the suitcase and yanked it away. Pushed me. I fell and blacked out. Eli must have helped me to the sofa. But what if something happened to me after the baby came? There would be no one protecting her." Carrie stared into her lap. "I didn't mean to hurt him. I would never . . . never . . . kill him." She began to cry. Silent tears rolled down her face.

Ruth knew she couldn't understand what Carrie was going through, but she also didn't comprehend the compassion. She shivered with the knowledge that if Eli wasn't on the floor, then it would be Carrie instead. Carrie had to think about herself, and her baby. She had to let them take care of the rest.

Shirley walked over and smoothed Carrie's hair back from her face. "Carrie, dear. I know this is a very difficult time, but there is one immediate alternative. Do you still want the Esther Society to send you away? I can make some calls and you could leave tonight."

Ruth gave her mother-in-law a quizzical look. The lawyer in her knew how this would look to police. An open-and-shut case. Carrie killed him and ran—that's all they'd see. Her guilt would be assumed. And Ruth had no idea what the neighbors might have seen or heard. What they might tell the police.

Carrie, her face scared and unsure, looked from Shirley to Ruth and back again. She could barely get the words out. "I . . . I don't know."

Ruth wanted Carrie to be safe and knew that the Esthers provided a logical option, but it filled her with sorrow. If the Esther Society hid Carrie, Ruth might never see her friend again.

Lillian came up and stood beside Shirley. "We can also help you arrange a funeral and go back to your parents or find a new place in Philly," Lillian said.

Ruth was oddly comforted not just by Lillian's presence now but also by Lillian having these protocols and rules to create order out of chaos.

"Your choice," Shirley said to Carrie. "We are here to stand by you, to keep you safe and to keep your secrets, no matter what."

"I need time . . . this is too much."

Shirley nodded but looked worried as she checked her watch.

Ruth snapped into action. She pointed to Lillian. "In the meantime, can you unpack Carrie's suitcase and put everything away as best you can? We don't want it to look like she was leaving."

Ruth turned to Harriet. "That bucket has to go back wherever you found it. It was raining, so if you poured water out, add some back in."

Lillian nodded at Ruth.

Shirley said, "Irene, can you make a pot of coffee and pour cups for each of us? Ladies, you'll need to drink from your own cup, and be sure to leave lipstick prints on them. We want to make it look like we were sitting around the kitchen table, crumbs and all."

Ruth was grateful to have Shirley—and her wisdom—in her corner. The details were so important. The girls rushed to their assignments, and Shirley crouched by Carrie and Ruth. They had things to discuss, yet Carrie was in desperate need of soothing.

When Lillian, Irene, and Harriet returned to the living room some minutes later, Ruth looked up. Shirley sat next to Carrie, holding her hand.

"I will call the police and report a terrible accident," Ruth said.

The others looked at her, wondering, confused. Ruth continued, "When asked, we will say we were in the kitchen having coffee and chatting when we heard a crash."

"A crash?" Carrie asked. She still seemed dazed by it all.

"Eli must have stopped home to get something—you weren't expecting him—and he tripped," Ruth clarified.

Shirley chimed in as if she and Ruth were a tag team. "It was just a terrible accident. No one's at fault. You all understand?"

"Shouldn't we call for an ambulance too?" Carrie asked.

"It's too late to help him, but you're right," Ruth said. "It supports our story."

Carrie covered her face with her hands. "He can't hurt me anymore?" Her words were spoken through disbelieving sobs. "He can't hurt the baby?"

Ruth hugged her. "That's right."

Shirley, Ruth, Lillian, Irene, and Harriet grasped hands in a protective semicircle around Carrie.

"But I pushed him," she whispered.

The girls looked at Ruth. "Shh," Ruth said. "No, you didn't. He tripped."

Ruth knew that Carrie had no chance unless they all stood by this story.

Lillian took Carrie's chin in her hand and lifted it so that Carrie had to look directly into her eyes. "Listen, Carrie. You were in the kitchen having coffee with your friends. Eli fell and hit his head before any of us even knew he was home. Remember?"

Carrie looked like she didn't know what to say.

"Do you hear me, Carrie?" Lillian's tone was even and unwavering. The etiquette maven was setting new rules, a new world order. For their little world, anyway.

Carrie hesitated, then nodded slightly. Lillian cocked her head. Carrie's nod got stronger, definite.

Ruth lifted the receiver and dialed emergency services, crossing her fingers behind her back so the others couldn't see. She prayed for strength for them all. They'd need all the help they could get.

There were different kinds of justice, she realized.

Chapter 31

LILLIAN

Lillian had no experience with the police, so she sat in Carrie's living room, wringing her hands, waiting her turn to be questioned and hoping her distress would be enough to convince the police of their story. Until they took her into the kitchen for official questioning, Lillian would keep quiet.

The irony of elective silence wasn't lost on her.

She'd strived to speak up to Peter and the girls. She worked to express herself regarding her parents. Now Lillian had chosen to keep quiet about what happened to Carrie and then Eli.

Maybe that was the difference. Choice.

Lillian used to believe she'd chosen the role of strong, silent housewife. In truth, she hadn't looked for anything else, for other ways to be. It had seemed ideal.

She'd found patterns easy to follow, until she lived her life by rote and found herself overlooked and undervalued.

It wasn't all Peter's fault. She'd allowed it. She gave up her choices because she'd never stopped to realize she had them. Carrie had surrendered her choices to a man who turned out to be brutal. The same had happened to Anna. Those women never suspected the men they loved would hurt them.

But Lillian had more choice than she gave herself credit for *because* of who she'd married. Now she had to trust herself, and Peter's love for her, and become the woman she wanted to be—and the mother she wanted to be.

As she sat in the living room, she watched the firemen moving in an orderly way around the house. They'd done this sort of thing before. They had a protocol to follow. Lillian and her friends had no such rules to guide them through a situation like this. But at least they had each other.

Real women were not a chain of cutout paper dolls, as some would have people believe. Each one was different, special, unique—whether they were in trouble or, like Lillian, just finding their way. There needed to be a way to protect the Carries and Annas of the world, to protect their children, like Lillian and Carrie's unborn baby.

Firemen carried Eli's body past gawking neighbors out on the street. At least the rain had stopped.

As soon as the firemen removed Eli's body, Lillian heaved a sigh of relief. Thank goodness he was gone. She felt compelled to open a window, letting the damp air's melancholy chill cleanse the room. For a moment, the truth of all that brutality was whisked away on a sheer breeze. Consequences, and perhaps nightmares, would come later, but for now they needed air to breathe.

The police led the women, one by one, into the kitchen to be questioned. So far, everyone had been released from the interrogation spot back into the front yard, including Carrie. No one had been arrested, so Lillian hoped that meant everyone had stuck to Ruth's plan and that it was working. Unless the police had additional inquiries up their sleeves.

"Lillian Diamond?" the officer asked, even though she was the only one left.

The detective indicated a kitchen chair and Lillian sat down. She knew she was strong, that she could toe the line when needed, but she'd never been challenged in quite this way. Never when a murder was involved.

She was expert in the truth—in hiding it, telling it, using half-truths—whichever would further what she needed. Right now, she faced the ultimate test of her grace. She prayed she wouldn't turn into Humpty-Dumpty. Wouldn't slip and break by speaking the wrong truth. In Carrie's case, the *whole* truth put them all at risk. Details of Eli's death would remain secret—unless Lillian cracked.

The weight of what happened, and the question of what would happen next, sat squarely on her chest.

The policeman got right to the point. "Mrs. Diamond, when did you become aware that Mr. Blum was home?"

As Lillian took in a breath, she was certain of one thing: Carrie was better off without Eli. Holding the scales of justice in her hands, Lillian wouldn't risk Carrie's future—any of their futures—by telling the truth. She owed it to her mother.

When Lillian was released, she went outside to the yard and found the Diamond Girls whispering in one corner. She walked over to Shirley and nodded toward Carrie.

"What happens now?" she whispered. "She can't stay here."

Shirley glanced toward Carrie and then back at Lillian. "Actually, we'll help Carrie go wherever she wants. Our job is to get her somewhere safe, and technically, we've done that."

"We can't leave her to fend for herself!" Lillian swooped in with unexpected maternal verve, and she could tell by the look on Shirley's face that her friend was surprised by it.

Lillian didn't care. "We need to switch gears and get Carrie to whatever is next for her." She would do it herself if she had to. Carrie might be physically safe from Eli, but the mental and emotional repercussions of what had happened were evident in her red-rimmed stare.

"Let's find out what she wants," Lillian said. "I venture no one has asked her that in a long time."

Shirley smiled.

By late afternoon, the rain had completely stopped, and the September sun was poking out from behind a few high clouds. Lillian ignored the lure of the radio dial and opted for quiet in the car as they drove Carrie to the bus station downtown. Lillian looked at Carrie in the passenger seat, head turned, staring out the window. Thank God she was safe. Lillian wasn't surprised that Carrie was despondent—she'd just lost her husband. But Ruth, Irene, and Harriet in the back seat were unusually quiet too.

Lillian understood why Carrie wanted to go home to Atlantic City, but it made no sense that she didn't want to telephone her family to let them know she was coming.

"I'll tell them in person," Carrie said before they'd left Wynnefield. "It's going to be hard for them to hear Eli is gone, let alone anything else."

"But you're going to tell them what he was really like?" Ruth asked.

Carrie shrugged. "They might want to know why I'm not planning the funeral. I'll tell them his sister is doing it because I'm too upset." She shrugged again.

Lillian recognized uncertainty in Carrie's downcast eyes and could surmise what she was probably thinking. She feared being blamed, or not believed, the way Lillian's grandparents had blamed or doubted her mother.

Lillian shook her head to dispel the memory. She was sorry Carrie had been in danger, but at the same time, she was glad the women had stepped in to help her. For the first time in a long while, she'd felt a part of something important, something bigger than herself. Without saying much, Lillian had used her voice and made it clear to herself and to others what was critical—the safety and happiness of her friends.

Happiness had taken on a new meaning. It had more facets than a few hard-and-fast rules in a book.

When they reached the bus depot, Lillian pulled up to the curb. Ruth, Irene, and Harriet slid out of the back seat and lifted Carrie's two suitcases out of the car. When Lillian started to leave the car to see Carrie off, Carrie stayed in her seat and turned to her.

"Thank you for everything," Carrie said.

"It was all of us," Lillian said. "And you're welcome."

"I mean for the etiquette lessons. Without them, I would never have met you all. Would have had no one to turn to. So thank you for having me, for teaching me."

"It was nothing," Lillian said.

Carrie touched her hand. "Oh, you're wrong. You taught me to trust my friends and reminded me what it was like to have fun."

Fun? "I don't think—"

"Oh, I know that wasn't the point," Carrie said.

Yet why not? Lillian thought. *Isn't that the reason to have etiquette? To be graceful and kind—to enjoy life and each other?* "It should have been the only point," Lillian said, feeling suddenly humbled.

"It was one of the first things you told us—that we'd learn who our friends are. And I did. You kept your promise." Carrie squeezed Lillian's hand.

Lillian swallowed a sob and squeezed back, and Carrie stepped out of the car into the circled embrace of her friends. Lillian had done something good with those etiquette lessons—maybe without realizing it. She'd connected these girls to each other, to her, and to Shirley. They were the right people at the right time, and her lessons, meant for propriety and social grace, had taught them compassion and chutzpah.

In many ways, she had Ruth to thank for that too. Ruth's brazen questioning had turned them all into more courageous women.

There were tears on every face as she watched Carrie leave with her bags. Tears of sadness, and tears of hope for a better life for their friend.

When they got back into the car, it surprised Lillian that it was Harriet who slid into the passenger seat. Of all the girls, perhaps she should be most proud of the change in Harriet. Not because of who she was or how she'd acted, but because of how much she'd had to change and how, when the time came, she stood up for what was right.

Lillian listened to the girls' banter about keeping their relationship going with Carrie. Grand plans for letter writing, visiting the baby, beach antics. This reminded Lillian of how young the girls were—there was nary a mention of Carrie's loss. No one talked of what it would be like for Carrie to be a young widow, to raise her child alone. To try to support her family on one income while paying for childcare.

Losing Eli meant different challenges for Carrie than living with him, but her life would be challenging all the same. Reminders of living in Wynnefield would likely be unwelcome. It would be enough that she'd be reminded of Eli whenever she looked at her little boy or girl. Reminded of how he died. Of how he hurt her. Of how he might have hurt their child.

Carrie would need to move on. To heal. It wouldn't be easy. Reminders of this place could hold her back.

In truth, it was unlikely these girls would ever see Carrie again. But that was not Lillian's lesson to teach. She would let time handle that one.

When Lillian pulled up in front of the Appelbaums' with the girls, Shirley was waiting on the patio. It was almost dinnertime, so Lillian needed to get home. Some things didn't change and, to be honest, she didn't want them to.

Sharing mealtime with Peter and their daughters was the way Lillian wanted to end her day from now on. She'd continue to work with Peter on the social dynamics and division of labor in their home. Speaking up? Well, that would take practice, and she was sure listening would take practice as well.

That was okay. They were her family.

When the Diamond Girls scooted out of Lillian's car, Shirley gathered them into a huddle and waved Lillian over.

Carrie had been right. Lillian knew who her friends were. She felt pride swell when she acknowledged her part in creating the friendships.

"I know you all have to get home," Shirley said. "I just wanted to thank you for making Carrie and the baby safe."

"Not exactly what the Esther Society had in mind," Ruth said, which was just what Lillian had been thinking. Even though she was sorry for Carrie's pain, Lillian was glad she knew where Carrie would be living and could picture her at the beach, on Steel Pier, pushing a baby carriage on the boardwalk.

"I think the point is her safety," Irene said.

"Just because this hasn't happened before doesn't mean we should've done anything different," Lillian said. She still had to put everyone at ease. It was an ingrained part of her.

"Who said this has never happened before?" Shirley asked.

Lillian gaped at Shirley. When she looked at the others, she realized they were doing the same.

"Irene is right. The important thing is that our friend is out of danger," Harriet said.

Harriet. Lillian wouldn't have expected that response from her. Yes, she'd really grown. "You won't tell anyone what happened?" Lillian asked.

Harriet shook her head and adopted an innocent expression. "Tell anyone what?"

Once in the car, Lillian rolled down her car window. Shirley and Ruth were still outside, heading into the Appelbaums' house. "Shirley," Lillian called.

The women didn't seem to hear her. Lillian could hear them, though.

"Mom," Ruth said to Shirley, "do you think we could have apple pie for dessert?"

Lillian couldn't see Shirley's face, but she was pretty sure there was a big smile on it.

Chapter 32

RUTH

Ruth walked in the door ahead of Shirley. For maybe the first time, the younger Mrs. Appelbaum felt hugged by her house, her home. She finally believed Shirley found her worthy of everything that the house and the family—her family—had to offer.

"I'll help you make dinner." Ruth turned to Shirley. Ruth would stay up in the night to study. But for now she needed to be the good daughter-in-law Shirley expected.

"You'll do no such thing," Shirley said.

Ruth turned and stared at Shirley.

"Don't give me this look," Shirley said. "I want you to go upstairs and study."

Ruth kissed Shirley on the cheek and popped up the first two stairs and ran the rest, then turned around on the landing, waving at Shirley when she remembered her mother-in-law didn't like Ruth running around the house.

"Go!" Shirley waved back at Ruth, giving her permission to run.

Ruth would use this gift of time; she'd cuddle up on the window seat with one of her books.

Then she pushed open the attic door, and there sat Asher on the floor.

Asher looked up. "Oh, drat."

"Not quite the greeting I would have expected," Ruth said.

"I wanted it to be a surprise," Asher said. He shifted his gaze to the corner of the room, and Ruth's followed; there stood a wooden desk with curved legs and carved swirly details.

It was perfect.

She glanced at her husband. Of course it was. Just like Ruth and Asher.

She walked to the desk and slid her fingers across the top as if checking for dust, which she most certainly was not.

"How did you do this?"

"My mother wanted it delivered when your friends were here. But she called me a few hours ago to tell me you wouldn't be home. So Dad brought me here early to accept the delivery."

She pulled open the center drawer and saw a stack of legal pads and at least a dozen sharpened yellow pencils. She closed the drawer.

Ruth's throat clogged with prickles just like those pencil points.

This man knew her and deserved her trust.

Ruth walked to the edge of their bed and sat atop a quilt Shirley had placed there. Ruth patted the space next to her.

Asher seemed to glide over to her. He sat.

"I want to tell you what's been going on," Ruth said.

Asher kissed the top of her head, pulled back, and looked into her eyes.

His face was all Ruth could see.

"Now and always," Asher said. "I'm listening."

EPILOGUE

RUTH

Montgomery County, Pennsylvania
Orphans' Court
April 2005

"All rise. This court is now in session. Judge Ruth Cohen-Appelbaum presiding."

The sound of the bailiff's voice was Ruth's cue to enter her courtroom. After twenty-two years on the bench, the words still humbled her—but never so much as today, when her granddaughter's civics class composed most of the gallery. Ruth glanced at the tips of her black shoes, raised the sides of her robe to keep from tripping on the stairs, and stepped up to the bench.

After she sat, she waited for the collective sound of everyone else doing the same thing to subside, and then called the court to order.

Every day, when the courtroom full of people rose and sat based on her presence, Ruth had the same thought: *If only I'd had this much sway with my four children when they were growing up.*

She nodded at the occupants seated at the plaintiff's table, then scanned the courtroom for her granddaughter Jenna. Ruth found her sitting next to Ruth's nearly ninety-year-old mother-in-law, Shirley, who had insisted on chaperoning her great-granddaughter's field trip—further proving her theory that the Appelbaum women were forces of nature.

There was something about Jenna's big blue eyes solemnly staring at Ruth that struck her. Those eyes had looked at Ruth for seventeen years, yet today's expression evoked a new gravitas.

Her grandmother was the judge.

The dichotomy pulled at Ruth as well.

She'd been both a *bubbe* and a judge since Jenna was born, but never at the same time in front of this girl.

Ruth cleared her throat and looked down at her case files. Allocations of inheritances, one guardianship petition, one adoption. A few other things but, all in all, an easy docket. Ruth was relieved. She'd heard the scuttlebutt that she was called Hardass Appelbaum behind her back. But today she would give them no reason to whisper that in the halls, where her great-granddaughter might overhear, might feel bad about her grandmother being called names.

Truth was, Ruth never minded the nickname and secretly considered it a badge of honor after all she'd seen and done.

Though Ruth never saw Carrie Blum again, and rarely thought about her, she knew her time with that long-ago friend had burrowed under her skin, had become a breathing part of her and driven her actions of the last four decades. Memories of Carrie had slowly faded in Ruth's mind, replaced with kids and work and years, but Carrie was always there, residing in the empty space where the little piece of her soul had been pinched out that day. Like an ache she learned to live with and ignore.

The field-trip morning passed without incident. Jenna smiled at every ruling:

Money for tutors.

Money for summer camp.

Guardianship granted.

A foster son welcomed into a forever family.

Sometimes Ruth missed the grittier work of her young-lawyer life. She'd helped establish Philadelphia Legal Assistance—a band of non-lawyer volunteers who helped people with family court cases wade through their custody forms, mental health assessments, and the gathering of information about crimes against children. Irene volunteered for the group until she divorced Stephen and moved to Cherry Hill. The last Ruth heard, Irene had married a doctor and had another baby.

Jenna and her classmates were so young, had so much of their lives ahead of them. She had picketed against the war in Iraq and marched on Washington with her mother. And she had wanted to be a lawyer since she understood that the same bubbe who crocheted ponchos for her dolls also made rules for other people—total strangers—to follow.

"And they have to follow everything Bubbe says?" Jenna had asked her mother a month ago, thinking Ruth had fibbed to her.

"They'll go to jail if they don't," Ruth's daughter, Trudy, replied.

Ruth chuckled inwardly, remembering that her daughter had said that. Having a mother for a judge hadn't impressed a teenage Trudy, who wanted nothing to do with law—or with her father's accounting business. Ruth was okay with Trudy's choices because they were hers—besides, a dentist daughter was no slouch.

When court recessed for lunch, the class came to Ruth's chambers so they could see what a judge's chambers were like. The moment they entered, hands waggled in the air.

"We have some questions, Your Honor," the teacher said. "If that's okay."

"Of course." Ruth pointed to a plain-looking girl in the back, standing apart from Jenna and her perky friends.

"What year did you become a lawyer?" she asked.

Ruth smiled. *Facts.* She liked facts. "I passed the bar in 1963." She winked at Shirley, who had been quiet in the corner, but had an unmistakable glow of familial pride emanating from her.

"According to the internet, you focused your career on helping families."

They'd researched Ruth on the internet. She must remember to ask one of her grandchildren what they'd found. Ruth's facts were hardly secrets, but she never checked them herself. "That's true."

"Why?" the girl asked. "Why become that kind of lawyer?"

Jenna turned to her and snapped, "Because she wanted to help people, of course." Ruth's granddaughter huffed and rolled her eyes as if it were absurd to question a judge's motives. Asher had always said Jenna had Ruth's chutzpah, her determination. She also had Ruth's stubbornness.

"That's true," Ruth said. "And it was more acceptable for women lawyers back in the day." This was another fact, although what she had learned about Shirley and Carrie had led Ruth definitively down the path of family law. She decided not to share the specifics. Not yet. Her lifetime of doing good for others could never possibly compensate for the women and children that society had failed to protect, and some days, she just didn't want to think of that.

Jenna and her class were about to head back to school, yet something still nagged at Ruth. She wondered how many of her granddaughter's classmates had already experienced some form of abuse in their own families. She wondered if they knew there were people who would listen to them.

If they knew the abuse was not their fault.

Ruth wondered if things had really changed enough, if all women and children felt safe enough to expose the secrets in their family when those secrets jeopardized their health. Their future.

She looked at the children in front of her. Was there anyone in that class who needed to know they could reach out and get help? She would ask Jenna later if their teacher gave the class a list of resources for children in danger.

After the students cleared out, Ruth still had an hour before court resumed. Enough time to run a small errand. She bought a bouquet of flowers at the corner market and walked two blocks to The Peabody, the poshest condos in the area.

Ruth pushed the black button outside the door. Buzz.

"Hello?"

"It's Ruth." A second buzz allowed her to open the door, sign in at the front desk, then head to the elevator. When it opened on the top floor, Ruth patted her hair, exhaled, and stepped into Lillian's foyer.

Ruth often wondered whether Lillian missed the big house and yard she once had, but with Sunny passed away, her daughter Pammie living with her own family, and Penny living with her girlfriend in New York, it had been a good while since Lillian had decided that a luxury condo was a more manageable way to retire—especially now that Peter was undergoing chemotherapy.

"To what do we owe this honor, Your Honor?" Ruth was surprised to hear Harriet's voice and to see that she was visiting too, decked out in pink-and-green golf gear. If it hadn't been a workday for Ruth, Harriet would have probably handed her a screwdriver and put her to work.

But Ruth didn't mind that Harriet only gave her a hug today; there were never enough of those to go around.

"Had a spare hour and thought I'd come by to see our girl," Ruth said as they made their way to the kitchen, where Lillian was already pouring Ruth a cup of coffee. Ruth held out the flowers.

"They're lovely, Ruth, thank you." Lillian was as freshly pressed as ever, though Ruth could see the toll Peter's prostate cancer had taken, etched in the lines on her face. Harriet took the flowers from Ruth and grabbed a vase.

"Didn't you have Jenna's class visiting today? How did it go?" Lillian asked.

"Fine. Mom came with them, and I'm pretty sure Jenna got a history lesson on women's rights on the way home." Ruth waved her hand as if shooing a mosquito. "Well, fine, until one of the girls asked why I'd decided on family law. I've been thinking about it ever since. About telling the truth, the whole truth, and nothing but the truth."

"What did you say?" Lillian asked.

"What I always say—that it was easier back then for a woman to practice family law, if she could get a job in law at all."

"It's not a lie," Harriet said.

"A part of me feels like I owe Jenna the whole story. So younger women know what's at stake. So others know they're not alone and that it's safe to reach out for help. That they don't deserve to be shamed or blamed."

"You don't owe anyone anything." Lillian arranged the flowers in a vase. "And the Esther Society is well known for its women's shelters nowadays. But Jenna may be interested to hear about when it was different. She'll love you more for everything you did."

"Everything *we* did," Ruth said. "Still, there's Carrie to consider."

Lillian said, "If it bothers you, leave Carrie out of it, or change people's names to protect the innocent. Isn't that how it works?"

"I think it might feel good to finally tell the whole story," Ruth said.

"Then go ahead," Harriet said. "You can still be the smart one. But make me the pretty one."

"Just make sure I'm the one with the best manners," Lillian said.

Ruth laughed. "Deal."

DOMESTIC VIOLENCE RESOURCES

The following resources are available if you or someone you know is a victim of domestic violence:

Crucial Networks

The National Network to End Domestic Violence

https://nnedv.org/

The National Coalition Against Domestic Violence

https://ncadv.org/

NCADV's network of state coalitions

https://ncadv.org/state-coalitions

National Domestic Violence Hotline

https://www.thehotline.org/

Noteworthy Experts

Lundy Bancroft

https://lundybancroft.com/

Shahida Arabi

https://selfcarehaven.wpcomstaging.com/

Dr. Ramani

http://doctor-ramani.com/

Important Books

Why Does He Do That? Inside the Minds of Angry and Controlling Men and *Should I Stay or Should I Go? A Guide to Knowing If Your Relationship Can—and Should—Be Saved*

by Lundy Bancroft

Unmasking Narcissism: A Guide to Understanding the Narcissist in Your Life

by Mark Ettensohn

A Cry for Justice: How the Evil of Domestic Abuse Hides in Your Church

by Jeff Crippen and Anna Wood

No Visible Bruises: What We Don't Know About Domestic Violence Can Kill Us

by Rachel Louise Snyder

Complex PTSD: From Surviving to Thriving: A Guide and Map for Recovering from Childhood Trauma

by Pete Walker

Resources compiled by writer and advocate Janna Leadbetter, who founded Breaking the Silence for Women. The platform of education and empowerment for survivors of domestic abuse can be found on Facebook.

ACKNOWLEDGMENTS AND AUTHOR'S NOTE

I often listened to James Taylor's greatest hits while I wrote this book, even though in the world of my characters it would be years until his music would be released and become popular. I felt as if I had a crystal ball and was privy to the soundtrack of my characters' futures.

I felt that way while writing much of this book, which takes place before the publication of *The Feminine Mystique* by Betty Friedan, before women's lib or the second wave of feminism, and long before #MeToo. I had to refrain from giving the women in the book too much hope or insight. At times it was difficult to ignore what I knew would happen to change their lives—the assassinations of John F. Kennedy, Martin Luther King, Jr., and Robert Kennedy, the civil rights movement, Woodstock, miniskirts, the moon landing. I strove to stay entrenched in the characters' 1962 world, where my twenty-first-century opinions and knowledge were irrelevant. It was not great for my ego, but while I was writing, *I* ceased to matter.

Writing Ruth was a respite. She was my sometimes-reluctant rebel, my always forward thinker, loosely inspired in part by the early life of Justice Ruth Bader Ginsburg. May her memory be a blessing.

I sometimes felt sorry for Lillian and wanted to shake her sensibilities into another decade. Shirley came to life for me as the protective, bold, sometimes misguided matriarchal figure who still clung to her weekly beauty parlor appointments.

What wasn't difficult about writing this book was picturing Wynnefield, a real West Philadelphia neighborhood that filled my paternal grandmother's, Mildred Nathan's, collection of photo albums and reels of home movies, now stored in the cloud. My dad's family all lived in Wynnefield, on Peach Street and Columbia Avenue, where my grandparents lived until I was five, not far from where readers first meet Lillian and the Diamond Girls, but in a small row house. My parents drove me up and down (it's quite hilly) and around Wynnefield, recounting memories and pointing out what used to be. My aunt Linda also shared her memories and answered my questions. The setting wouldn't have been so vivid to me without their help.

Fun facts: My dad went to Overbrook High School at the same time as Wilt Chamberlain but before Will Smith. Wynnefield is the West Philadelphia neighborhood Smith rapped about in the nineties.

The story and structure in this book were greatly influenced by the insights of Danielle Egan-Miller, Jodi Warshaw, Danielle Marshall, and Tiffany Yates Martin—the stars in my writing and publishing universe. I would not be here without them.

And then there's my proverbial village. A socially distanced high five for Sherrie Agre, Julie Artz, Sheila Athens, Kim Brock, Susan Brownmiller, Mark Cameron, Emily Carpenter, Gabriella Dumpit, Carole and Ray Farley, Joan Fernandez, Mary Beth Gale, Susan Gloss, Kelly Harms, Kelly Hartog, Ashley Hasty, Fern Katz, Janna Leadbetter, Miriam Lichtenberg, Kathryn Mariani, Carolyn McGill, Dr. Pamela Nadell, Renée Rosen, Ellie Roth, Renee San Giacomo, Judith Soslowsky, Pamela Toler, and Nancy Yaeger. Much respect and thanks to Priya Gill for being my spreadsheet fairy godmother.

Manny Katz, I missed your input.

An extra big germless hug to the dream team—Michele Montgomery, Priya Gill, and Gabi Coatsworth for crossing my t's and dotting my i's when I was under the weather.

Much love and a special thank-you to my brother, David Nathan, for helping with just about everything else so I could write this book.

To my fascinating friends Natasha, Oksana, and Katarina: thank you for the daily support, the weekly chats, and most of all, for the keys to our magical writing bungalow. And I'm grateful for the thousands of accountability emails I've exchanged with Pamela Toler and for our long-standing and special friendship.

A shout-out to my Early Bird writing family—the two Pamelas, Virginia, Nancy, Joan, Catherine, Stephanie, Della, Priya, Heather, and Sheila; and to the WFWA Zoom Writing Date writers—you know who you are—you transformed the pandemic into something bearable for me—especially you, Michele Montgomery.

Curmudgeon Book Club, thank you for reminding me I am also a reader.

To Tall Poppy Writers, WFWA Historical Fiction Group, and Lake Union Authors, your support is unparalleled.

To my readers, thank you all for your emails, reviews, kind words, encouragement, and social media support. I keep you all in my heart when I write. Lucky for me, it's getting kind of crowded in there.

In addition to gathering oral histories, I read and/or referenced the following books while writing this story. Each one added to my understanding of the era. I used what I learned but employed my imagination to best serve the story. *Amy Vanderbilt's New Complete Book of Etiquette*; *Etiquette* by Emily Post; *The Luella Cuming Studio Course in Social Awareness, Poise, and Gracious Living* by Luella Cuming; *McCall's Book of Everyday Etiquette*; *Not to People Like Us: Hidden Abuse in Upscale Marriages* by Susan Weitzman; *Philadelphia Jewish Life 1940–1985*, edited by Murray Friedman; *The Astronaut Wives Club* by Lily Koppel; *Amy Vanderbilt's Complete Book of Etiquette: A Guide to Gracious Living*;

The Feminine Mystique by Betty Friedan; *The Jewish Community of West Philadelphia* by Allen Meyers; *The Persian Pickle Club* by Sandra Dallas.

I especially thank my kids, Zachary, Chloe, and Taylor, who, as adults, allow me to parent them. I'm grateful they sometimes flip the roles because they are much smarter than I am.

Last but not least, after thirty years of raising fabulous dogs, I'm #catmom to a handsome gray rescue named Riggins. He's the ideal writing and pandemic companion, star of my Instagram, and paws-down winner of the Most Mellow Cat Award.

You can find me (and Riggins) online just about everywhere: @ AmySueNathan. You can email me at AmySueNathan@gmail.com, and you can sign up for my short but delightful monthly newsletter at www. amysuenathan.com.

If you'd like to supply chocolate as I write my next novel, let me know.

ABOUT THE AUTHOR

Amy Sue Nathan is the author of five novels, including *The Last Bathing Beauty* and *Left to Chance*, and the founder of the award-winning *Women's Fiction Writers* blog, named a Best Website for Writers by *Writer's Digest*. Her stories and essays have appeared in such publications as the *Chicago Tribune*, *Chicago Parent*, *Writer's Digest*, and *HuffPost*, and online in the *New York Times*, among others. She is also a lover of gray cats, hot coffee, and bold lipsticks, and she has raised two extraordinary humans—her proudest accomplishment. Amy graduated from Temple University and lives and writes near Philadelphia. For more information, visit www.amysuenathan.com.